DEMON'S CONSORT

"I don't trust you," T'uupieh said. "I trust only myself. And, of course, I did not come alone."

Picking up the rag pouch at her side, she calmly separated the folds of cloth that held her secret companion.

"It is true," Chwiul trilled softly. "They call you Demon's Consort. . . ."

She turned the amber lens of the demon's precious eye and settled its gaze on Chwiul. He drew back slightly. "A demon has a thousand eyes, and a thousand thousand torments for those who offend it." She quoted from the Book of Ngoss, whose rituals she had used to bind the demon to her.

Chwiul stretched nervously, as if he wanted to fly away. But he only said, "Then I think we understand each other. . . . I want you to kill someone for me. . . ."

—from *Eyes of Amber*

Science Fiction from SIGNET

☐ **OUTCASTS OF HEAVEN BELT** by Joan D. Vinge.
(#E8407—$1.75)*

☐ **WHO CAN REPLACE A MAN?** by Brian Aldiss.
(#Y7083—$1.50)†

☐ **GALAXIES LIKE GRAINS OF SAND** by Brian Aldiss.
(#Y7044—$1.25)

☐ **GREYBEARD** by Brian Aldiss (#Y6929—$1.25)†

☐ **THE LONG AFTERNOON OF EARTH** by Brian Aldiss.
(#E8575—$1.75)

☐ **THE DARK LIGHT YEARS** by Brian Aldiss.
(#W8582—$1.50)

☐ **CASE AND THE DREAMER** by Theodore Sturgeon.
(#W7933—$1.50)

☐ **THE CITY AND THE STARS** by Arthur C. Clarke.
(#W7990—$1.50)

☐ **TALES OF TEN WORLDS** by Arthur C. Clarke.
(#W8328—$1.50)

☐ **2001: A SPACE ODYSSEY** by Arthur C. Clarke.
(#J7765—$1.95)

☐ **THE LOST WORLDS OF 2001** by Arthur C. Clarke.
(#E7865—$1.75)

☐ **A FALL OF MOONDUST** by Arthur C. Clarke.
(#E8320—$1.75)

☐ **PILLARS OF SALT** by Barbara Paul. (#E8619—$1.75)*

☐ **SURVIVOR** by Octavia Butler. (#E8673—$1.75)*

☐ **A CAT OF SILVERY HUE (HORSE CLANS IV)** by Robert Adams.
(#E8836—$1.75)*

* Price slightly higher in Canada
† Not available in Canada

EYES OF AMBER
and other stories

by Joan D. Vinge

WITH AN INTRODUCTION BY
Ben Bova

A SIGNET BOOK
NEW AMERICAN LIBRARY
TIMES MIRROR

ACKNOWLEDGMENTS AND PERMISSIONS

The poem "Night Journey to the Spherical Man" is by Russell Grattan;
copyright © 1969, The Vorpal Galleries, San Francisco. Reprinted
by permission of the author.

"Eyes of Amber," copyright © 1977 by The Condé Nast Publications
Inc., first appeared in the June, 1977, issue of *ANALOG Science
Fiction-Science Fact.*

"To Bell the Cat," copyright © 1977 by Davis Publications, Inc., first
apeared in the Summer, 1977, issue of *Isaac Asimov's Science
Fiction Magazine.*

"View from a Height," copyright © 1978 by The Condé Nast Publications Inc., first appeared in the June, 1978, issue of *ANALOG
Science Fiction-Science Fact.*

"Media Man," copyright © 1976 by The Condé Nast Publications Inc.,
first appeared in the October, 1976, issue of *ANALOG Science
Fiction-Science Fact.*

"The Crystal Ship," copyright © 1976 by Joan Vinge, first appeared in
the story collection entitled *The Crystal Ship* edited by Robert
Silverberg.

"Tin Soldier," copyright © 1974 by Damon Knight, first appeared in the
story collection entitled *Orbit 14* edited by Damon Knight.

SIGNET, SIGNET CLASSICS, MENTOR, PLUME AND MERIDIAN BOOKS
are published by The New American Library, Inc.,
1301 Avenue of the Americas, New York, New York 10019

First Signet Printing, September, 1979

1 2 3 4 5 6 7 8 9

PRINTED IN THE UNITED STATES OF AMERICA

TO VERNON, *SINE QUO NON*

Contents

Introduction by Ben Bova   1

Eyes of Amber   7

To Bell the Cat   45

View from a Height   74

Media Man   90

The Crystal Ship   140

Tin Soldier   202

Introduction

Joan Vinge: The Turing Criterion

Is science fiction prophetic?

Do science fiction stories truly reveal what the future will be? Do science fiction writers have a special insight into tomorrow?

Well . . . yes and no.

Frederik Pohl once said that the predictive powers of science fiction writers are akin to the accuracy of a broken clock. That is, a broken clock is correct twice a day (unless it's a 24-hour digital). And if you put together enough science fiction stories, some of the events described in the stories will come true, eventually.

But science fiction writers are not so much trying to predict the precise unfolding of the future as they are trying to describe future events that *could happen*—given certain trends and assumptions.

Yet, in a way they never intended and probably don't consciously realize even today, science fiction writers do indeed give us a type of predictive power to see into the future. Not by what they write so much as by what they *are*.

Back in the 1920s and early 1930s, science fiction cocooned itself, in the United States, into a publishing ghetto of pulp magazines. The writers who contributed to these early pulps, with their lurid covers and sterile interiors, came mainly from three sources: professional writers who earned their living by grinding out story after story for coolie wages; retired men, usually with a technical or scientific background, who could afford to write as a hobby; and eager-eyed youngsters, many of them bent on careers in science or engineering, who had the energy and devotion to put their dreams on paper.

No women. Or, at best, very few. And for the most part, when an editor accepted a story by a woman back in those days, he changed the author's name either to a masculine gender or to an epicene set of initials. (Back in those days!

In the late sixties, *Playboy* published Ursula K. LeGuin's fine "Nine Lives" under the byline of "U. K. LeGuin.")

In the late thirties and the war-torn forties, more and more science fiction stories were written by working scientists and engineers. The youngsters of the previous decade had grown up and started their professional careers. Often they disguised their names or used noms-de-plume, because their colleagues and bosses would frown on the idea of their contributing to science fiction magazines—which every right-thinking person "knew" were nothing but trashy pulp junk.

The writers, by their very way of living, were predicting the uptight fifties.

A few women began appearing regularly in the science fiction magazines in the forties and fifties. Under their own names, even. But very few. And for the most part they wrote stories that were easily identifiable as "women's stories."

In the explosive sixties it became clear that most of the new writers joining the science fiction field were not coming from the research labs and drafting tables, but from the classrooms and libraries of the liberal arts side of the campus. Science fiction was being kissed by the New Wave—an influx of writers who demanded style, characterization, and all those other fancies they teach you in literature courses. Among the New Wave writers were many women.

If you examined the people who were producing science fiction stories in the sixties, and the style and tone of their stories, you could easily have predicted the fractionation of American (and world) societies that has happened during the seventies. Blessed with modern communications and mobility, every self-styled minority group in society is demanding more-than-equal rights for itself. It's a dizzying, frightening whirl.

Unless you take a look at the science fiction writers of the seventies, and at their stories.

Which brings us to Joan Vinge.

The first time I noticed Joan Vinge's name was in a co-by-line with Vernor Vinge, on a very good, highly original science fiction story. A husband-wife team, obviously. More than one writer had discovered, by the early seventies, the tax advantages of putting his wife's name alongside his own.

I was the editor of *Analog* magazine then, a bastion of "hard core" science fiction, stories in which believable science and technology formed a sturdy backbone to each plot. I was seeking stories in which human characterization and true human emotions could be given equal play with the hardware and scientific ideas.

In came a story by Joan Vinge—alone—called "Media Man." Solid scientific background, fascinatingly detailed planetary system that formed the stage on which her actors performed, and an equally fascinating set of characters: real people, with human problems and emotions.

If an editor has any socially-useful function at all, it is the ability to recognize new talent. I made a mental note to pay special attention to anything written by Joan Vinge.

In the meantime, we were having a bit of fun with *Analog*'s readers. Since the magazine's founding, back in 1930 under the title of *Astounding Stories of Super Science*, the readers of the magazine had been predominantly male. Even in the early seventies, it was assumed that *Analog*'s readership was overwhelmingly male.

Yet more and more story manuscripts arriving at my desk had female bylines on them. More and more letters to the editor were from women—many of them decrying the jut-jawed chauvinism implicit in most science fiction stories. And whenever I lectured to a science fiction audience, I saw a strong and continuously growing share of women in the audiences.

So we published a Special Women's Issue of *Analog* in June 1977. And the lead story for that issue, the story that was illustrated on the cover, was "Eyes of Amber" by Joan D. Vinge.

The issue was a smashing success and made the point that we were trying to make: that science fiction in general, and *Analog* in particular, were no longer the exclusive domain of men. The field, and the magazine, were open to the entire human race, not just to one half of it.

Oh, we got loud complaints. A few hyperactive women wrote in to heap scorn on us because we didn't proclaim an All-Male Issue whenever there were no women represented in the magazine. Some of the more frightened males predicted the end of the world because we had "given in" to the Women's Movement.

But I chuckled all the way to the circulation manager's office.

One of the reasons I chuckled was the choice of Joan Vinge's story as the lead fiction for that issue. Social movements aside, each issue of a commercial magazine must sell enough copies to make a profit for the publisher, and I knew that Joan Vinge's novelette would help us to do that. Moreover, if there had been no byline on the story, and no hoopla about the Special Women's Issue, I doubt that most readers could have told whether "Eyes of Amber" had been written by a man or a woman.

Which brings us to the Turing Criterion, and the hope that I see for the future.

The Turing Criterion is a simple test, first suggested in 1950 by A. M. Turing, the English mathematician and logician, to answer a science-fictional type of question: How can you tell if a computer is intelligent? That is, as intelligent as a human being, or perhaps even more so.

Turing devised a simple test. You sit at a keyboard in a room. The keyboard is connected to a person, or perhaps to a computer, in another room beyond your sight. You converse with this other entity, typing out your half of the conversation and reading the other half coming out of the typewriter. If you cannot tell whether or not you are talking to a machine or a human being, then the machine (assuming you were talking to a machine all along) is intelligent.

If you took the bylines off most science fiction stories, you could still tell the gender of the author fairly easily. But I don't think that applies to stories written by Joan D. Vinge. This is not a perjorative statement, nor is it a particular form of praise. It is a statement of fact, a fact that offers real hope for the future.

Joan Vinge writes good fiction. Period. She blends believable science with believable characters: no easy task. She does not write "women's stories" any more than she writes "men's stories." She does not champion any cause except the cause of good literature and solid entertainment.

When all the demonstrations are over, when all the minority groups have exhausted themselves and finally learned that they are parts of a society and they must help to make that society work, not pull it apart, the verities of human behavior will remain. *That* is what Joan Vinge writes about—the verities of human behavior, no matter where in the universe her characters happen to be.

Joan is a symbol of the coming age of social integration and progress. The hope she represents is that men and women of talent and intelligence can work together and solve the problems that blaze in today's headlines.

Her stories can be read as adventures, as entertainment, as fascinating glimpses of exotic futures. But you can also see in her stories the unmistakable fact that a young female author has integrated the diverse disciplines of science and literature, and brought out of them some of the best work being created in the science fiction field today.

I realize that I've gone through roughly 1,500 words of prose without telling you anything at all about Joan D. Vinge herself—about her background in archaeology, her degree in anthropology, her struggle to write, her personal lifestyle and visions of the future.

None of that is really important. Her *stories* are what count, and you hold in your hand a collection of her best. You'll learn more about Joan D. Vinge from reading these entertaining, exciting, fascinating stories than you will ever learn from reading any biography.

So read and enjoy.

—BEN BOVA

Manhattan
February 1979

Eyes of Amber

The beggar woman shuffled up the silent evening street to the rear of Lord Chwiul's town house. She hesitated, peering up at the softly glowing towers, then clawed at the watchman's arm. "A word with you, master—"

"Don't touch me, hag!" The guard raised his spear butt in disgust.

A deft foot kicked free of the rags and snagged him off balance. He found himself sprawled on his back in the spring melt, the spear tip dropping toward his belly, guided by a new set of hands. He gaped, speechless.

The beggar tossed an amulet onto his chest. "Look at it, fool! I have business with your lord."

The beggar woman stepped back; the spear tip tapped him impatiently.

The guard squirmed in the filth and wet, holding the amulet up close to his face in the poor light. "You . . . you are the one? You may pass."

"Indeed!" Muffled laughter. "Indeed I may pass—for many things, in many places. The Wheel of Change carries us all." She lifted the spear. "Get up, fool . . . and no need to escort me. I'm expected."

The guard climbed to his feet, dripping and sullen, and stood back while she freed her wing membranes from the folds of cloth. He watched them glisten and spread as she gathered herself to leap effortlessly to the tower's entrance, twice his height above. He waited until she had vanished inside before he even dared to curse her.

"Lord Chwiul?"

"T'uupieh, I presume." Lord Chwiul leaned forward on the couch of fragrant mosses, peering into the shadows of the hall.

"*Lady* T'uupieh." T'uupieh strode forward into the light, letting the ragged hood slide back from her face. She took a fierce pleasure in making no show of obeisance, in coming

7

forward directly as nobility to nobility. The sensuous ripple of a hundred tiny *miih* hides underfoot made her callused feet tingle. *After so long, it comes back too easily. . . .*

She chose the couch across the low waterstone table from him, stretching languidly in her beggar's rags. She extended a finger claw and picked a juicy *kelet* berry from the bowl in the table's scroll-carven surface; let it slide into her mouth and down her throat, as she had done so often, so long ago. And then, at last, she glanced up, to measure his outrage.

"You dare to come to me in this manner—"

Satisfactory. *Yes, very . . .* "I did not come to you. You came to me . . . you sought my services." Her eyes wandered the room with affected casualness, taking in the elaborate frescoes that surfaced the waterstone walls even in this small private room. Particularly in this room? she wondered. How many midnight meetings, for what varied intrigues, were held in this room? Chwiul was not the wealthiest of his family or clan; and appearances of wealth and power counted in this city, in this world—for wealth and power were everything.

"I sought the services of T'uupieh the Assassin. I'm surprised to find that the Lady T'uupieh dared to accompany her here." Chwiul had regained his composure; she watched his breath frost, and her own, as he spoke.

"Where one goes, the other follows. We are inseparable. You should know that better than most, my lord." She watched his long pale arm extend to spear several berries at once. Even though the nights were chill, he wore only a body-wrapping tunic, which let him display the intricate scaling of jewels that danced and spiraled over his wing surfaces.

He smiled; she saw the sharp fangs protrude slightly. "Because my brother made the one into the other, when he seized your lands? I'm surprised you would come at all—how did you know you could trust me?" His movements were ungraceful; she remembered how the jewels dragged down fragile, translucent wing membranes and slender arms, until flight was impossible. Like every noble, Chwiul was normally surrounded by servants who answered his every whim. Incompetence, feigned or real, was one more trapping of power, one more indulgence that only the rich could afford. She was pleased that the jewels were not of high quality.

"I don't trust you," she said. "I trust only myself. But I have friends who told me you were sincere enough—in this case. And of course, I did not come alone."

"Your outlaws?" Disbelief. "That would be no protection."

Picking up the rag pouch at her side, she calmly separated the folds of cloth that held her secret companion.

"It is true." Chwiul trilled softly. "They call you Demon's Consort. . . ."

She turned the amber lens of the demon's precious eye so that it could see the room, as she had seen it, and then settled its gaze on Chwiul. He drew back slightly, fingering moss. " 'A demon has a thousand eyes, and a thousand thousand torments for those who offend it.' " She quoted from the Book of Ngoss, whose rituals she had used to bind the demon to her.

Chwiul stretched nervously, as if he wanted to fly away. But he only said, "Then I think we understand each other. And I think I have made a good choice: I know how well you have served the Overlord, and other court members. . . . I want you to kill someone for me."

"Obviously."

"I want you to kill Klovhiri."

T'uupieh started, very slightly. "You surprise me in return, Lord Chwiul. Your own brother?" *And the usurper of my lands. How I have ached to kill him slowly, so slowly, with my own hands . . . but always he is too well guarded.*

"And your sister, too—my lady." Faint overtones of mockery. "I want his whole family eliminated; his mate, his children . . ."

Klovhiri . . . and Ahtseet. Ahtseet, her own younger sister, who had been her closest companion since childhood, her only family since their parents had died. Ahtseet, whom she had cherished and protected; dear, conniving, traitorous little Ahtseet, who could forsake pride and decency and family honor to mate willingly with the man who had robbed them of everything. Anything to keep the family lands, Ahtseet had shrilled; anything to keep her position. But that was not the way! Not by surrendering, but by striking back. . . . T'uupieh became aware that Chwiul was watching her reaction with unpleasant interest. She fingered the dagger at her belt.

"Why?" She laughed, wanting to ask, *"How?"*

"That should be obvious. I'm tired of coming second. I want what he has—your lands and all the rest. I want him out of my way, and I don't want anyone else left with a better claim to his inheritance than I have."

"Why not do it yourself? Poison them, perhaps . . . it's been done before."

"No. Klovhiri has too many friends, too many loyal clansmen, too much influence with the Overlord. It has to be an 'accidental' murder. And no one would be better suited than you, my lady, to do it for me."

T'uupieh nodded vaguely, assessing. No one could be better chosen for a desire to succeed than she . . . and also, for a position from which to strike. All she had lacked until now was the opportunity. From the time she had been dispossessed, through the fading days of autumn and the endless winter—for nearly a third of her life, now—she had haunted the wild swamp and fenland of her estate. She had gathered a few faithful servants, a few malcontents, a few cutthroats, to harry and murder Klovhiri's retainers, ruin his phib nets, steal from his snares and poach her own game. And for survival, she had taken to robbing whatever travelers took the roads that passed through her lands.

Because she was still nobility, the Overlord had at first tolerated and then secretly encouraged her banditry. Many wealthy foreigners traveled the routes that crossed her estate, and for a certain commission, he allowed her to attack them with impunity. It was a sop, she knew, thrown to her because he had let his favorite, Klovhiri, have her lands. But she used it to curry what favor she could, and after a time the Overlord had begun to bring her more discreet and profitable business—the elimination of certain enemies. And so she had become an assassin as well—and found that the calling was not so very different from that of noble: both required nerve, and cunning, and an utter lack of compunction. And because she was T'uupieh, she had succeeded admirably. But because of her vendetta, the rewards had been small—until now.

"You do not answer," Chwiul was saying. "Does that mean your nerve fails you, in kith-murder, where mine does not?"

She laughed sharply. "That you say it proves twice that your judgment is poorer than mine. . . . No, my nerve does not fail me. Indeed, my blood burns with desire! But I hadn't thought to lay Klovhiri under the ice just to give my lands to his brother. Why should I do that favor for you?"

"Because obviously you cannot do it alone. Klovhiri hasn't managed to have you killed in all the time you've plagued him, which is a testament to your skill. But you've made him too wary—you can't get near him when he keeps himself so well protected. You need the cooperation of someone who has his trust—someone like myself. I can make him yours."

"And what will be my reward if I accept? Revenge is sweet, but revenge is not enough."

"I will pay what you ask."

"My estate." She smiled.

"Even you are not so naïve—"

"No." She stretched a wing toward nothing in the air. "I am not so naïve. I know its value. . . ." The memory of a golden-clouded summer's day caught her—of soaring, soaring on the warm updrafts above the steaming lake . . . seeing the fragile rose-red of the manor towers spearing light far off above the windswept tide of the trees . . . the saffron and crimson and aquamarine of ammonia pools, bright with dissolved metals, that lay in the gleaming melt-surface of her family's land, the land that stretched forever, like the summer. . . . "I know its value." Her voice hardened. "And that Klovhiri is still the Overlord's pet. As you say, Klovhiri has many powerful friends, and they will become your friends when he dies. I need more strength, more wealth, before I can buy enough influence to hold what is mine again. The odds are not in my favor—now."

"You are carved from ice, T'uupieh. I like that." Chwiul leaned forward. His amorphous red eyes moved along her outstretched body, trying to guess what lay concealed beneath the rags in the shadowy foxfire-light of the room. His eyes came back to her face.

She showed him neither annoyance nor amusement. "I like no man who likes that in me."

"Not even if it meant regaining your estate?"

"As a mate of yours?" Her voice snapped like a frozen branch. "My lord, I have just about decided to kill my sister for doing as much. I would sooner kill myself."

He shrugged, lying back on the couch. "As you wish." He waved a hand in dismissal. "Then, what will it take to be rid of my brother—and of you as well?"

"Ah." She nodded, understanding more. "You wish to buy my services, and to buy me off, too. That may not be so easy to do. But . . ." *But I will make the pretense, for now.* She speared berries from the bowl in the tabletop, watched the silky sheet of emerald-tinted ammonia water that curtained one wall. It dropped from heights within the tower into a tiny plunge basin, with a music that would blur conversation for anyone who tried to listen outside. Discretion, and beauty. . . .

The musky fragrance of the mossy couch brought back her childhood suddenly, disconcertingly: the memory of lying in a soft bed, on a soft spring night. . . . "But as the seasons change, change moves me in new directions. Back into the city, perhaps. I like your tower, Lord Chwiul. It combines discretion and beauty."

"Thank you."

"Give it to me, and I'll do what you ask."

Chwiul sat up, frowning. "My town house!" Recovering: "Is that all you want?"

She spread her fingers, studied the vestigial webbing between them. "I realize it is rather modest." She closed her hand. "But considering what satisfaction will come from earning it, it will suffice. And you will not need it, once I succeed."

"No . . ." He relaxed somewhat. "I suppose not. I will scarcely miss it, after I have your lands."

She let it pass. "Well then, we are agreed. Now, tell me, where is the key to Klovhiri's lock? What is your plan for delivering him—and his family—into my hands?"

"You are aware that your sister and the children are visiting here, in my house, tonight? And that Klovhiri will return before the new day?"

"I am aware." She nodded with more casualness than she felt, seeing that Chwiul was properly, if silently, impressed at her nerve in coming here. She drew her dagger from its sheath beside the demon's amber eye and stroked the serrated blade of waterstone-impregnated wood. "You wish me to slit their throats while they sleep under your very roof?" She managed the right blend of incredulity.

"No!" Chwiul frowned again. "What sort of fool do you—" He broke off. "With the new day, they will be returning to the estate by the usual route. I have promised to escort them, to ensure their safety along the way. There will also be a guide, to lead us through the bogs. But the guide will make a mistake—"

"And I will be waiting." T'uupieh's eyes brightened. During the winter the wealthy used sledges for travel on long journeys, preferring to be borne over the frozen melt by membranous sails or dragged by slaves where the surface of the ground was rough and crumpled. But as spring came and the surface of the ground began to dissolve, treacherous sinks and pools opened like blossoms to swallow the unwary. Only an experienced guide could read the surfaces, tell sound waterstone from changeable ammonia-water melt. "Good," she said softly. "Yes, very good. . . . Your guide will see them safely foundered in some slush hole, and then I will snare them like changeling phibs."

"Exactly. But I want to be there when you do; I want to watch. I'll make some excuse to leave the group, and meet you in the swamp. The guide will mislead them only if he hears my signal."

"As you wish. You've paid well for the privilege. But come alone. My followers need no help, and no interference." She sat up, let her long webbed feet down to rest again on the sensuous hides of the rug.

"And if you think that I'm a fool, and playing into your hands myself, consider this: you will be the obvious suspect when Klovhiri is murdered. I'll be the only witness who can swear to the Overlord that your outlaws weren't the attackers. Keep that in mind."

She nodded. "I will."

"How will I find you, then?"

"You will not. My thousand eyes will find you." She rewrapped the demon's eye in its pouch of rags.

Chwiul looked vaguely disconcerted. "Will—*it* take part in the attack?"

"It may, or it may not; as it chooses. Demons are not bound to the Wheel of Change like you and me. But you will surely meet it face to face—although it has no face—if you come." She brushed the pouch at her side. "Yes—do keep in mind that I have my safeguards too, in this agreement. A demon never forgets."

She stood up at last, gazing once more around the room. "I shall be comfortable here." She glanced back at Chwiul. "I will look for you, come the new day."

"Come the new day." He rose, his jeweled wings catching light.

"No need to escort me. I shall be discreet." She bowed, as an equal, and started toward the shadowed hall. "I shall definitely get rid of your watchman. He doesn't know a lady from a beggar."

"The Wheel turns once more for me, my demon. My life in the swamps will end with Klovhiri's life. I shall move into town . . . and I shall be lady of my manor again, when the fishes sit in the trees!"

T'uupieh's alien face glowed with malevolent joy as she

turned away, on the display screen above the computer terminal. Shannon Wyler leaned back in his seat, finished typing his translation, and pulled off the wire headset. He smoothed his long blond slicked-back hair, the habitual gesture helping him reorient to his surroundings. When T'uupieh spoke he could never maintain the objectivity he needed to help him remember he was still on Earth, and not really on Titan, orbiting Saturn, some billion and a half kilometers away. *T'uupieh, whenever I think I love you, you decide to cut somebody's throat....*

He nodded vaguely at the congratulatory murmurs of the staff and technicians, who literally hung on his every word waiting for new information. They began to thin out behind him as the computer reproduced copies of the transcript. Hard to believe he'd been doing this for over a year now. He looked up at his concert posters on the wall, with nostalgia but with no regret.

Someone was phoning Marcus Reed; he sighed, resigned.

" 'Vhen the fishes sit in the trees'? Are you being sarcastic?"

He looked over his shoulder at Dr. Garda Bach's massive form. "Hi, Garda. Didn't hear you come in."

She glanced up from a copy of the translation, tapped him lightly on the shoulder with her forked walking stick. "I know, dear boy. You never hear anything vhen T'uupieh speaks. . . . But what do you mean by this?"

"On Titan that's summer—when the triphibians metamorphose for the third time. So she means maybe five years from now, our time."

"Ah! Of course. The old brain is not what it vas. . . ." She shooked her gray-white head; her black cloak swirled out melodramatically.

He grinned, knowing she didn't mean a word of it. "Maybe learning Titanese on top of fifty other languages is the straw that breaks the camel's back."

"*Ja, ja,* maybe it is. . . ." She sank heavily into the next seat over, already lost in the transcript. He had never, he thought, expected to like the old broad so well. He had become aware of her Presence while he studied linguistics at Berkeley—she was the *grande dame* of linguistic studies, dating back to the days when there had still been unrecorded languages here on Earth. But her skill at getting her name in print and her face on television, as an expert on what everybody "really meant" had convinced him that her true talent lay in merchandising. Meeting her at last, in person, hadn't changed his mind about that, but it had convinced him forever that she knew her stuff about cultural linguistics. And that, in turn, had convinced him her accent was a total fraud. But despite the flamboyance, or maybe even because of it, he found that her now archaic views on linguistics were much closer to his own feelings about communication than the views of either one of his parents.

Garda sighed. "Remarkable, Shannon! You are simply re-markable—your feel for a wholly alien language amazes me. Whatever vould ve have done if you had not come to us?"

"Done without, I expect." He savored the special pleasure that came of being admired by someone he respected. He looked down again at the computer console, at the two shin-ing green-lit plates of plastic thirty centimeters on a side, which together gave him the versatility of a virtuoso violinist and a typist with a hundred thousand keys—his link to T'uupieh, his voice: the new IBM synthesizer, whose touch-sensitive control plates could be manipulated to re-create the impossible complexities of her language. God's gift to the world of linguistics . . . except that it required the sensitivity and inspiration of a musician to fully use its range.

He glanced up again and out the window, at the now familiar fog-shrouded skyline of Coos Bay. Since very few linguists were musicians, their resistance to the synthesizer had been like a brick wall. The old guard of the aging New Wave—which included His Father the Professor and His Mother the Communications Engineer—still clung to a fruit-less belief in mathematical computer translation. They still struggled with ungainly programs weighed down by endless morpheme lists, that supposedly would someday generate any message in a given language. But even after years of refine-ment, computer-generated translations were still uselessly crude and sloppy.

At graduate school there had been no new languages to seek out, and no permission for him to use the synthesizer to explore the old ones. And so—after a final bitter family argu-ment—he had quit graduate school. He had taken his belief in the synthesizer into the world of his second love, music; into a field where, he hoped, real communication still had some value. Now, at twenty-four, he was Shann the Music Man, the musician's musician, and a hero to an immense gen-eration of aging fans, and a fresh new one that had inherited their love for the ever-changing music called "rock." And neither of his parents had willingly spoken to him in years.

"No false modesty," Garda was chiding. "Vhat could ve have done vithout you? You yourself have complained enough about your mother's methods. You know ve vould not have a tenth of the information about Titan ve have gained from T'uupieh if she had gone on using that damned computer translation."

Shannon frowned faintly, at the sting of secret guilt. "Look, I know I've made some cracks—and I meant most of them—but I'd never have gotten off the ground if she hadn't done all the preliminary analysis before I even came." His mother had already been on the mission staff, having worked for years at NASA on the esoterics of computer communication with satellites and space probes, and because of her linguistic background, she had been made head of the newly pulled-together staff of communications specialists by Marcus Reed, the Titan project director. She had been in charge of the initial phonic analysis: using the computer to compress the alien voice range into one audible to humans, then breaking up the complex sounds into more, and simpler, human phones, she had identified phonemes, separated morphemes, fitted them into a grammatical framework, and assigned English sound equivalents to it all. Shannon had watched her on the early TV interviews, looking unhappy and ill at ease while Reed held court for the spellbound press. But what Dr. Wyler the Communications Engineer had had to say, at last, had held him on the edge of his seat; unable to resist, he had taken the next plane to Coos Bay.

"Vell, I meant no offense," Garda said. "Your mother is obviously a skilled engineer. But she needs a little more . . . flexibility."

"You're telling me." He nodded ruefully. "She'd still love to see the synthesizer drop through the floor. She's been out of joint ever since I got here. At least Reed appreciates my 'value.' " Reed had welcomed him like a long-lost son when he first arrived at the institute: Wasn't he a skilled linguist as well as an inspired musician, didn't he have some time between gigs, wouldn't he like to extend his visit, and get an insider's view of his mother's work? He had agreed, modestly, to all three—and then the television cameras and reporters had sprung up as if on cue, and he understood clearly enough that they were there to record the visit not of Dr. Wyler's kid, but of Shann the Music Man.

But he had gotten his first session with a voice from another world. And with one hearing he had become an addict . . . because their speech was music. Every phoneme was formed of two or three superposed sounds, and every morpheme was a blend of phonemes, flowing together like water. They spoke in chords, and the result was a choir, crystal bells ringing, the shattering of glass chandeliers.

And so he had stayed on and on, at first only able to watch his mother and her assistants with agonized frustration. His mother's computer-analysis methods had worked well in the initial transphonemicizing of T'uupieh's speech, and they had learned enough very quickly to send back clumsy responses, using the probe's echo-locating device, to keep T'uupieh's interest from wandering. But typing input at a keyboard, and expecting even the most sophisticated programming to transform it into another language, still would not work even for known human languages. And he knew, with an almost religious fervor, that the synthesizer had been designed for just this miracle of communication, and that he alone could use it to capture directly the nuances and subtleties a machine translation could never supply. He had tried to approach his mother about letting him use it, but she had turned him down flat: "This is a research center, not a recording studio."

And so he had gone over her head to Reed, who had been delighted. And when at last he felt his hands moving across the warm, faintly tingling plates of light, tentatively recreating the speech of another world, he had known that he had been right all along. He had let his music commitments go to hell, without a regret, almost with relief, as he slid back into the field that had always come first.

Shannon watched the display, where T'uupieh had settled back with comfortable familiarity against the probe's curving side, half obscuring his view of the camp. Fortunately both she and her followers treated the probe with obsessive care, even when they dragged it from place to place as they constantly moved camp. He wondered what would have happened if they had inadvertently set off its automatic defense system, which had been designed to protect it from aggressive animals; it delivered an electric shock that varied from merely painful to fatal. And he wondered what would have happened if the probe and its "eyes" hadn't fit so neatly into T'uupieh's beliefs about demons. The idea that he might never have known her, or heard her voice . . .

More than a year had passed already since he, and the rest

of the world, had heard the remarkable news that intelligent life existed on Saturn's major moon. He had no memory at all of the first two fly-bys of Titan, back in '79 and '81—although he could clearly remember the 1990 orbiter that had caught fleeting glimpses of the surface through Titan's swaddling of opaque golden clouds. But the handful of miniprobes it had dropped had proved that Titan profited from the same "greenhouse effect" that made Venus a boiling hell. And even though the seasonal temperatures never rose above two hundred degrees Kelvin, the few photographs had shown, unquestionably, that life existed there. The discovery of life, after so many disappointments throughout the rest of the solar system, had been enough to initiate another probe mission, one designed to actually send back data from Titan's surface.

That probe had discovered a life form with human intelligence, or rather, the life form had discovered the probe. And T'uupieh's discovery had turned a potentially ruined mission into a success: the probe had been designed with a main, immobile data-processing unit and ten "eyes" or subsidiary units, that were to be scattered over Titan's surface to relay information. The release of the subsidiary probes during landing had failed, however, and all of the "eyes" had come down within a few square kilometers of its own landing in the uninhabited marsh. But T'uupieh's self-interested fascination and willingness to appease her "demon" had made up for everything. . . .

Shannon looked up at the flat wall screen again, at T'uupieh's incredible, inhuman face—a face that was as familiar now as his own in the mirror. She sat waiting with her boundless patience for a reply from her "demon": she would have been waiting for over an hour by the time her transmission reached him across the gap between their worlds; and she would have to wait as long again while they discussed a response and he created the new translation. She spent more time now with the probe than she did with her own people. *The loneliness of command.* He smiled. The almost flat profile of her moon-white face turned slightly toward him—toward the camera lens; her own fragile mouth smiled gently, not quite revealing her long, sharp teeth. He could see one red pupilless eye, and the crescent nose-slit that half-ringed it; her frosty cyanide breath shone blue-white, illuminated by the ghostly haloes of St. Elmo's fire that wreathed the probe all through Titan's interminable eight-day nights. He could see balls of light hanging like Japanese lanterns on the drooping snarl of icebound branches in a distant thicket.

It was unbelievable . . . or perfectly logical, depending on which biological expert was talking . . . that the nitrogen- and ammonia-based life on Titan should have so many analogues with oxygen- and water-based life on Earth. But T'uupieh was not human, and the music of her words time and again brought him messages that made a mockery of any ideals he tried to harbor about her, and their relationship. So far in the past year she had assassinated eleven people, and with her outlaws had murdered God knew how many more, in the process of robbing them. The only reason she cooperated with the probe, she had as much as said, was that only a demon had a more bloody reputation; only a demon could command her respect. And yet, from what little she had been able to show them and tell them about the world she lived in, she was no better or no worse than anyone else—only more competent. Was she a prisoner of an age, a culture, where blood was something to be spilled instead of shared? Or was it something biologically innate that let her philosophize brutality, and brutalize philosophy?

Beyond T'uupieh, around the nitrogen campfire, some of her outlaws had begun to sing—the alien folk melodies that in translation were no more than simple, repetitious verse. But heard in their pure, untranslated form, they layered harmonic complexity on complexity: musical speech in a greater pattern of song. Shannon reached out and picked up the headset again, forgetting everything else. He had had a dream, once, where he had been able to sing in chords. . . .

Using the long periods of waiting between their communications, he had managed, some months back, to record a series of the alien songs himself, using the synthesizer. They had been spare and uncomplicated versions compared to the originals, because even now his skill with the language couldn't match that of the singers, but he couldn't help wanting to make them his own. Singing was a part of religious ritual, T'uupieh had told him. "But they don't sing because they're religious; they sing because they like to sing." Once, privately, he had played one of his own human compositions for her on the synthesizer and transmitted it. She had stared at him (or into the probe's golden eye) with stony, if tolerant, silence. She never sang herself, although he had sometimes heard her softly harmonizing. He wondered what she would say if he told her that her outlaws' songs had already earned him his first Platinum Record. Nothing, probably—but knowing her, if he could make the concepts clear, she would probably be heartily in favor of the exploitation.

He had agreed to donate the profits of the record to NASA (and although he had intended that all along, it had annoyed him to be asked by Reed), with the understanding that the gesture would be kept quiet. But somehow, at the next press conference, some reporter had known just what question to ask, and Reed had spilled it all. And his mother, when asked about her son's sacrifice, had murmured, "Saturn is becoming a three-ring circus," and left him wondering whether to laugh or swear.

Shannon pulled a crumpled pack of cigarettes out of the pocket of his caftan and lit one. Garda glanced up, sniffing, and shook her head. She didn't smoke, or anything else (although he suspected she ran around with men), and she had given him a long wasted lecture about it, ending with, "Vell, at least they're not tobacco." He shook his head back at her.

"What do you think about T'uupieh's latest victims, then?" Garda flourished the transcript, pulling his thoughts back. "Vill she kill her own sister?"

He exhaled slowly around the words "Tune in tomorrow, for our next exciting episode! I think Reed will love it; that's what I think." He pointed at the newspaper lying on the floor beside his chair. "Did you notice we've slipped to page three?" T'uupieh had fed the probe's hopper some artifacts made of metal—a thing she had said was only known to the "Old Ones"—and the scientific speculation about the existence of a former technological culture had boosted interest in the probe to front-page status again. But even news of that discovery couldn't last forever. "Gotta keep those ratings up, folks. Keep those grants and donations rolling in."

Garda clucked. "Are you angry at Reed or at T'uupieh?"

He shrugged dispiritedly. "Both of 'em. I don't see why she won't kill her own sister—" He broke off as the subdued noise of the room's numerous project workers suddenly intensified, and concentrated. Marcus Reed was making an entrance, simultaneously solving everyone else's problems, as always. Shannon marveled at Reed's energy, even while he felt something like disgust at the way he spent it. Reed exploited everyone and everything with charming cynicism, in the ultimate hype for Science—and watching him at work had gradually drained away whatever respect and good will

Shannon had brought with him to the project. He knew that his mother's reaction to Reed was close to his own, even though she had never said anything to him about it; it surprised him that there was something they could still agree on.

"Dr. Reed—"

"Excuse me, Dr. Reed, but—"

His mother was with Reed now as they all came down the room; she looked tight-lipped and resigned, her lab coat buttoned up as if she was trying to avoid contamination. Reed was straight out of *Manstyle* magazine, as usual. Shannon glanced down at his own loose gray caftan and jeans, which had led Garda to remark, "Are you planning to enter a monastery?"

"We'd really like to—"

"Senator Foyle wants you to call him back—"

" . . . yes, all right; and tell Dinocci he can go ahead and have the probe run another sample. Yes, Max, I'll get to that. . . ." Reed gestured for quiet as Shannon and Garda turned in their seats to face him. "Well, I've just heard the news about our 'Robin Hood's' latest hard contract."

Shannon grimaced quietly. He was the first one to have facetiously called T'uupieh "Robin Hood." Reed had snapped it up and dubbed her ammonia swamps "Sherwood Forest" for the press. After the truth about her bloodthirsty body counts began to come out, and it even began to look as if she was collaborating with "the Sheriff of Nottingham," some reporter had pointed out that T'uupieh bore no more resemblance to Robin Hood than she did to Rima the Bird-Girl. Reed had said, laughing, "Well, after all, the only reason Robin Hood stole from the rich was that the poor didn't have any money!" That, Shannon thought, had been the real beginning of the end of his tolerance.

" . . . this could be used as an opportunity to show the world graphically the harsh realities of life on Titan—"

"Ein Moment," Garda said. "You're telling us you vant to let the public vatch this atrocity, Marcus?" Up until now they had never released to the media the graphic tapes of actual murders; even Reed had not been able to argue that that would have served any real scientific purpose.

"No, he's not, Garda." Shannon glanced up as his mother began to speak. "Because we all agreed that we would *not* release any tapes just for purposes of sensationalism."

"Carly, you know that the press has been after me to release those other tapes, and that I haven't, because we all voted against it. But I feel this situation is different—a demonstration of a unique, alien sociocultural condition. What do you think, Shann?"

Shannon shrugged, irritated and not covering it up. "I don't know what's so damn unique about it: a snuff flick is a snuff flick, wherever you film it. I think the idea stinks." Once, at a party while he was still in college, he had watched a film of an unsuspecting victim being hacked to death. The film, and what all films like it said about the human race, had made him sick to his stomach.

"*Ach*—there's more truth than poetry in that!" Garda said.

Reed frowned, and Shannon saw his mother raise her eyebrows.

"I have a better idea." He stubbed out his cigarette in the ashtray under the panel. "Why don't you let me try to talk her out of it?" As he said it he realized how much he wanted to try, and how much success could mean to his belief in communication—to his image of T'uupieh's people, and maybe his own.

They both showed surprise this time. "How?" Reed said.

"Well . . . I don't know yet. Just let me talk to her, try to really communicate with her, find out how she thinks and what she feels—without all the technical garbage getting in the way for a while."

His mother's mouth thinned; he saw the familiar worry-crease form between her brows. "Our job here is to collect that 'garbage.' Not to begin imposing moral values on the universe. We have too much to do as it is."

"What's 'imposing' about trying to stop a murder?" A certain light came into Garda's faded blue eyes. "Now, that has real . . . social implications. Think about it, Marcus."

Reed nodded, glancing at the patiently attentive faces that still ringed him. "Yes—it does. A great deal of human interest." Answering nods and murmurs. "All right, Shann. There are about three days left before morning comes again in 'Sherwood Forest.' You can have them to yourself, to work with T'uupieh. The press will want reports on your progress. . . ." He glanced at his watch and nodded toward the door, already turning away. Shannon looked away from his mother's face as she moved past him.

"Good luck, Shann." Reed threw it back at him absently. "I wouldn't count on reforming 'Robin Hood,' but you can still give it a good try."

Shannon hunched down in his chair, frowning, and turned

back to the panel. "In your next incarnation may you come back as a toilet."

T'uupieh was confused. She sat on the hummock of clammy waterstone beside the captive demon, waiting for it to make a reply. In the time that had passed since she'd found it in the swamp, she had been surprised again and again by how little its behavior resembled all the demon-lore she knew. And tonight—

She jerked, startled, as its grotesque, clawed arm came to life suddenly and groped among the icy-silver spring shoots pushing up through the melt at the hummock's foot. The demon did many incomprehensible things (which was fitting) and it demanded offerings of meat and vegetation and even stone—even, sometimes, some part of the loot she had taken from passersby. She had given it those things gladly, hoping to win its favor and its aid; she had even, somewhat grudgingly, given it precious metal ornaments of the Old Ones that she had stripped from a whining foreign lord. The demon had praised her effusively for that; all demons hoarded metal, and she supposed that it must need metals to sustain its strength; its domed carapace, gleaming now with the witchfire that always shrouded it at night, was an immense metal jewel the color of blood. And yet she had always heard that demons preferred the flesh of men and women. But when she had tried to stuff the wing of the foreign lord into its maw, it spit him out with a few dripping scratches and told her to let him go. Astonished, she had obeyed, and let the fool run screaming off to be lost in the swamp.

And then tonight . . . "You are going to kill your sister, T'uupieh," it had said to her tonight, "and two innocent children. How do you feel about that?" She had spoken what had come first, and truthfully, into her mind: "That the new day cannot come soon enough for me! I have waited so long—too long—to take my revenge on Klovhiri! My sister and her brats are a part of his foulness, better slain before they multiply." She had drawn her dagger and driven it into the mushy melt, as she would drive it into their rotten hearts.

The demon had been silent again, for a long time, as it always was. (The lore said that demons were immortal, and so she had always supposed that it had no reason to make a quick response; she had wished, sometimes, that it would show more consideration for her own mortality.) Then at last it had said, in its deep voice filled with alien shadows, "But

the children have harmed no one. And Ahtseet is your only
sister, she and the children are your only blood kin. She has
shared your life. You say that once you"—the demon paused,
searching its limited store of words—"cherished her, for that.
Doesn't what she once meant to you mean anything now?
Isn't there any love left, to slow your hand as you raise it
against her?"

"Love!" she had said, incredulous. "What speech is that, oh
Soulless One? You mock me—" Sudden anger had bared her
teeth. "Love is a toy, my demon, and I have put my toys behind me. And so has Ahtseet . . . she is no kin of mine. Betrayer, betrayer!" The word hissed like the dying embers of
the campfire; she had left the demon in disgust, to rake in the
firepit's insulating layer of sulfury ash and lay on a few more
soggy branches. Y'lirr, her second in command, had smiled
at her from where he lay in his cloak on the ground, telling
her that she should sleep. But she had ignored him and gone
back to her vigil on the hill.

Even though this night was chill enough to recrystallize the
slowly thawing limbs of the *safilil* trees, the equinox was long
past, and now the fine mist of golden polymer rain presaged
the golden days of the approaching summer. T'uupieh had
wrapped herself more closely in her own cloak and pulled up
the hood, to keep the clinging, sticky mist from fouling her
wings and ear membranes, and she had remembered last summer, her first summer, which she would always remember. . . . Ahtseet had been a clumsy, flapping infant as that
first summer began, and T'uupieh the child had thought her
new sister was silly and useless. But summer slowly transformed the land and filled her wondering eyes with miracles,
and her sister was transformed too, into a playful, easily led
companion who could follow her into adventure. Together
they learned to use their wings and to use the warm updrafts
to explore the boundaries and the freedoms of their heritage.

And now, as spring moved into summer once again,
T'uupieh clung fiercely to the vision, not wanting to lose it, or
to remember that childhood's sweet, unreasoning summer
would never come again, even though the seasons returned,
for the Wheel of Change swept on, and there was never a
turning back. No turning back . . . she had become an adult
by the summer's end, and she would never soar with a child's
light-winged freedom again. And Ahtseet would never do
anything again. Little Ahtseet, always just behind her, like

her own fair shadow. *No! She would not regret it! She would be glad—*

"Did you ever think, T'uupieh," the demon had said suddenly, "that it is wrong to kill anyone? You don't want to die, no one wants to die too soon. Why should they have to? Have you ever wondered what it would be like if you could change the world into one where you—where you treated everyone else as you wanted them to treat you, and they treated you the same? If everyone could . . . live and let live." Its voice slipped into blurred overtones that she couldn't make out.

She had waited, but it said no more, as if it were waiting for her to consider what she'd already heard. But there was no need to think about what was obvious: "Only the dead 'live and let live.' I treat everyone as I expect them to treat me, or I would quickly join the peaceful dead! Death is a part of life. We die when fate wills it, and when fate wills it, we kill.

"You are immortal, you have the power to twist the Wheel, to turn destiny as you want. You may toy with idle fantasies, even make them real, and never suffer the consequences. We have no place for such things in our small lives. No matter how much I might try to be like you, in the end I die like all the rest. We can change nothing, our lives are preordained. That is the way among mortals." And she had fallen silent again, filled with unease at this strange wandering of the demon's mind. But she must not let it prey on her nerves. Day would come very soon, she must not be nervous; she must be totally in control when she led this attack on Klovhiri. No emotion must interfere, no matter how much she yearned to feel Klovhiri's blood spill bluely over her hands, and her sister's, and the children's. . . . Ahtseet's brats would never feel the warm wind lift them into the sky, or plunge, as she had, into the depths of her rainbow-petaled pools, or see her towers spearing light far off among the trees. *Never! Never—*

She had caught her breath sharply then, as a fiery pinwheel burst through the wall of tangled brush behind her, tumbling past her head into the clearing of the camp. She watched it circle the fire—spitting sparks, hissing furiously in the quiet air—three and a half times before it spun on into the darkness. No sleeper wakened, and only two stirred. She clutched one of the demon's hard angular legs, shaken, knowing that the circling of the fire had been a portent—but not knowing what it meant. The burning silence it left behind oppressed her; she stirred restlessly, stretching her wings.

And utterly unmoved, the demon had begun to drone its strange, dark thoughts once more: "Not all you have heard about demons is true. We can suffer"—it groped for words again—"the . . . the consequences of our acts; among ourselves we fight and die. We *are* vicious, and brutal, and pitiless, but we don't like to be that way. We want to change into something better, more merciful, more forgiving. We fail more than we win, but we believe we *can* change. And you are more like us than you realize. You can draw a line between—trust and betrayal, right and wrong, good and evil; you can choose never to cross that line."

"How, then?" She had twisted to face the amber eye as large as her own head, daring to interrupt the demon's speech. "How can one droplet change the tide of the sea? It's impossible! The world melts and flows, it rises into mist, it returns again to ice, only to melt and flow once more. A wheel has no beginning, and no end; no starting place. There is no 'good,' no 'evil'—no line between them. Only acceptance. If you were a mortal, I would think you were mad!"

She had turned away again, her claws digging shallow runnels in the polymer-coated stone as she struggled for self-control. *Madness* . . . was it possible? she wondered suddenly. Could her demon have gone mad? How else could she explain the thoughts it had put into her mind? Insane thoughts, bizarre, suicidal—but thoughts that would haunt her.

Or could there be a method in its madness? She knew that treachery lay at the heart of every demon. It could simply be lying to her when it spoke of trust and forgiveness—knowing she must be ready for tomorrow, hoping to make her doubt herself, make her fail. Yes, that was much more reasonable. But then, why was it so hard to believe that this demon would try to ruin her most cherished goals? After all, she held it prisoner, and though her spells kept it from tearing her apart, perhaps it still sought to tear apart her mind, to drive her mad instead. Why shouldn't it hate her, and delight in her torment, and hope for her destruction?

How could it be so ungrateful! She had almost laughed aloud at her own resentment, even as it formed the thought. As if a demon ever knew gratitude! But ever since the day she had netted it in spells in the swamp, she had given it nothing but the best treatment. She had fetched and carried, and made her fearful followers do the same. She had given it the best of everything—anything it desired. At its command she had sent out searchers to look for its scattered eyes, and it had allowed, even encouraged, her to use the eyes as her own, as watchers and protectors. She had even taught it to understand her speech (for it was as ignorant as a baby about the world of mortals) when she realized that it wanted to communicate with her. She had done all those things to win its favor because she knew that it had come into her hands for a reason, and if she could gain its cooperation, there would be no one who would dare to cross her.

She had spent every spare hour in keeping it company, feeding its curiosity, and her own, as she fed its jeweled maw; until gradually those conversations with the demon had become an end in themselves, a treasure worth the sacrifice of even precious metals. Even the constant waiting for its alien mind to ponder her questions and answers had never tired her; she had come to enjoy sharing even the simple pleasures of its silences, and resting in the warm amber light of its gaze.

T'uupieh looked down at the finely woven fiber belt which passed through the narrow slits between her side and wing, and held her tunic to her. She fingered the heavy, richly amber beads which decorated it—metal-dyed melt trapped in polished waterstone by the jewelsmith's secret arts—and which reminded her always of her demon's thousand eyes. *Her* demon . . .

She looked away again, toward the fire, toward the cloak-wrapped forms of her outlaws. Since the demon had come to her she had felt both the physical and the emotional space that she had always kept between herself as leader and her band of followers gradually widening. She was still completely their leader, perhaps more firmly so because she had tamed the demon, and their bond of shared danger and mutual respect had never weakened. But there were other needs, which her people might fill for each other, but never for her.

She watched them sleeping like the dead—as she should be sleeping now—preparing themselves for tomorrow. They took their sleep sporadically, when they could, as all commoners did—as she did now, too, instead of hibernating the night through like proper nobility. Many of them slept in pairs, man and woman, even though they mated with a commoner's chaotic lack of discrimination whenever a woman felt the season come upon her. T'uupieh wondered what they must imagine when they saw her sitting here with the demon far into the night. She knew what they believed, what she encouraged all to believe: that she had chosen it for a consort, or that it had chosen her. Y'lirr, she saw, still slept alone. She trusted and liked him as well as she did anyone; he was quick and ruthless, and she knew that he worshipped her. But he was a commoner, and more important, he did not challenge her. Nowhere, even among the nobility, had she found anyone who offered the sort of companionship she craved . . . until now, until the demon had come to her. No, she would not believe that all its words had been lies—

"T'uupieh!" The demon called her name buzzingly in the misty darkness. "Maybe you can't change the pattern of fate, but you can change your mind. You've already defied fate by turning outlaw and by defying Klovhiri. Your sister was the one who accepted"—unintelligible words—"only let the Wheel take her. Can you really kill her for that? You must understand why she did it, how she *could* do it. You don't have to kill her for that—you don't have to kill any of them. You have the strength, the courage, to put vengeance aside, and find another way to your goals. You can choose to be merciful—you can choose your own path through life, even if the ultimate destination of all life is the same."

She stood up resentfully, matching the demon's height, and drew her cloak tightly around her. "Even if I wished to change my mind, it is too late. The Wheel is already in motion, and I must get my sleep if I am to be ready for it." She started away toward the fire, stopped, looking back. "There is nothing I can do now, my demon. I cannot change tomorrow. Only you can do that. Only you."

She heard it, later, calling her name softly as she lay sleepless on the cold ground. But she turned her back toward the sound and lay still, and at last sleep came.

Shannon slumped back into the embrace of the padded chair, rubbing his aching head. His eyelids were sandpaper, his body was a weight. He stared at the display screen, at T'uupieh's back turned stubbornly toward him as she slept beside the nitrogen campfire. "Okay, that's it. I give up. She won't even listen. Call Reed and tell him I quit."

"That you've quit trying to convince T'uupieh?" Garda said. "Are you sure? She may yet come back. Use a little more emphasis on—spiritual matters. Ve must be certain ve have done all ve can to . . . change her mind."

To save her soul, he thought sourly. Garda had gotten her

early training at an institute dedicated to translating the Bible; he had discovered in the past few hours that she still had a hidden desire to proselytize. *What soul?* "We're wasting our time. It's been six hours since she walked out on me. She's not coming back. . . . And I mean quit everything. I don't want to be around for the main event. I've had it."

"You don't mean that," Garda said. "You're tired, you need the rest too. Vhen T'uupieh vakes, you can talk to her again."

He shook his head, pushing back his hair. "Forget it. Just call Reed." He looked out the window, at dawn separating the mist-wrapped silhouette of seaside condominiums from the sky.

Garda shrugged, disappointed, and turned to the phone.

He studied the synthesizer's touchboards again, still bright and waiting, still calling his leaden, weary hands to try one more time. At least when he made this final announcement it wouldn't have to be direct to the eyes and ears of a waiting world; he doubted that any reporter was dedicated enough to still be up in the glass-walled observation room at this hour. Their questions had been endless earlier tonight, probing his feelings and his purpose and his motives and his plans, asking about "Robin Hood's" morality, or lack of it, and his own, about a hundred and one other things that were nobody's business but his own.

The music world had tried to do the same thing to him once, but then there had been buffers—agents, publicity staffs—to protect him. Now, when he'd had so much at stake, there had been no protection, only Reed at the microphone eloquently turning the room into a sideshow, with Shann the Man as chief freak, until Shannon had begun to feel like a man staked out on an ant hill and smeared with honey. The reporters gazed down from on high, critiquing T'uupieh's responses and criticizing his own, and filled the time gaps when he needed quiet to think with infuriating interruptions. Reed's success had been total in wringing every drop of pathos and human interest out of his struggle to prevent T'uupieh's vengeance against the Innocents . . . and by that, had managed to make him fail.

No. He sat up straighter, trying to ease his back. No, he couldn't lay it on Reed. By the time what he'd had to say had really counted, the reporters had given up on him. The failure belonged to him, only him: his skill hadn't been great enough, his message hadn't been convincing enough—he was the one who hadn't been able to see through T'uupieh's eyes clearly enough to make her see through his own. He had had his chance to really communicate, for once in his life—to communicate something important. And he'd sunk it.

A hand reached past him to set a cup of steaming coffee on the shelf below the terminal. "One thing about this computer," a voice said quietly, "it's programmed for a good cup of coffee."

Startled, he laughed without expecting to and glanced up. His mother's face looked drawn and tired; she held another cup of coffee in her hand. "Thanks." He picked up the cup and took a sip, felt the hot liquid slide down his throat into his empty stomach. Not looking up again, he said, "Well, you got what you wanted. And so did Reed. He got his pathos, and he gets his murders, too."

She shook her head. "This isn't what I wanted. I don't want to see you give up everything you've done here just because you don't like what Reed is doing with part of it. It isn't worth that. Your work means too much to this project, and it means too much to you."

He looked up.

"*Ja*, she is right, Shannon. You can't quit now—we need you too much. And T'uupieh needs you."

He laughed again, not meaning it. "Like a cement yo-yo. What are you trying to do, Garda, use my own moralizing against me?"

"She's telling you what any blind man could see tonight, if he hadn't seen it months ago." His mother's voice was strangely distant. "That this project would never have had this degree of success without you. That you were right about the synthesizer. And that losing you now might—"

She broke off, turning away to watch as Reed came through the doors at the end of the long room. He was alone this time, for once, and looking rumpled. Shannon guessed that he had been asleep when the phone call came, and was irrationally pleased at having awakened him.

Reed was not so pleased. Shannon watched the frown that might be worry or displeasure, or both, forming on his face as he came down the echoing hall toward them. "What did she mean, you want to quit? Just because you can't change an alien mind?" He entered the cubicle and glanced down at the terminal—to be sure that the remote microphones were all switched off, Shannon guessed. "You knew it was a long shot, probably hopeless. You have to accept that she doesn't want to reform, accept that the values of an alien culture are going to be different from your own."

Shannon leaned back, feeling a muscle begin to twitch with fatigue along the inside of his elbow. "I can accept that. What I can't accept is that you want to make us into a bunch of damn panderers. Christ, you don't even have a good reason! I didn't come here to play sound track for a snuff flick. If you go ahead and feed the world those murders, I'm laying it down. I don't want to give all this up, but I'm not staying for a kill-porn carnival."

Reed's frown deepened; he glanced away. "Well? What about the rest of you? Are you still privately branding me an accessory to murder too? Carly?"

"No, Marcus—not really." She shook her head. "But we all feel that we shouldn't cheapen and weaken our research by making a public spectacle of it. After all, the people of Titan have as much right to privacy and respect as any culture on Earth."

"*Ja*, Marcus, I think ve all agree about that."

"And just how much privacy does anybody on Earth have today? Good God—remember the Tasaday? And that was thirty years ago. There isn't a single mountaintop or desert island left that the all-seeing eye of the camera hasn't broadcast all over the world. And what do you call the public crime surveillance laws—our own lives are one big peep show."

Shannon shook his head. "That doesn't mean we have to—"

Reed turned cold eyes on him. "And I've had a little too much of your smartass piety, Wyler. Just what do you owe your success as a musician to, if not publicity?" He gestured at the posters on the walls. "There's more hard sell in your kind of music than any other field I can name."

"I have to put up with some publicity push or I couldn't reach the people. I couldn't do the thing that's really important to me—communicate. That doesn't mean I like it."

"You think I enjoy this?"

"Don't you?"

Reed hesitated. "I happen to be good at it, which is all that really matters. Because you may not believe it, but I'm still a scientist, and what I care about most of all is seeing that research gets its fair slice of the pie. You say I don't have a good reason for pushing our findings. Do you realize that NASA lost all the data from our Neptune probe just because somebody in effect got tired of waiting for it to get to Neptune and cut off our funds? The real problem on these long outer-planet missions isn't instrumental reliability, it's financial reliability. The public will pay out millions for one of your concerts, but not one cent for something they don't understand."

"I don't make—"

"People want to forget their troubles, be entertained . . . and who can blame them? So in order to compete with movies, and sports, and people like you—not to mention ten thousand other worthy government and private causes—we have to give the public what it wants. It's my responsibility to deliver that, so that the 'real scientists' can sit in their neat bright institutes with half a billion dollar's worth of equipment around them, and talk about 'respect for research.' "

He paused; Shannon kept his gaze stubbornly. "Think it over. And when you can tell me how what you did as a musician is morally superior to or more valuable than what you're doing now, you can come to my office and tell me who the real hypocrite is. But think it over, first—all of you." Reed turned and left the cubicle.

They watched in silence until the double doors at the end of the room hung still. "Vell . . ." Garda glanced at her walking stick, and down at her cloak. "He does have a point."

Shannon leaned forward, tracing the complex beauty of the synthesizer terminal, feeling the combination of chagrin and caffeine pushing down his fatigue. "I know he does, but that isn't the point I was trying to get at! I didn't want to change T'uupieh's mind, or quit either, just because I objected to selling this project. It's the way it's being sold, like some kind of kill-porn show perversion, that I can't take." When he was a child, he remembered, rock concerts had had a kind of notoriety, but they were as respectable as a symphony orchestra now, compared to the "thrill shows" that had eclipsed them as he was growing up: where "experts" gambled their lives against a million-dollar pot, in front of a crowd who came to see them lose; where masochists made a living by self-mutilation; where they ran *cinéma vérité* films of butchery and death.

"I mean, is that what everybody really wants? Does it really make everybody feel good to watch somebody else bleed? Or are they going to get some kind of moral-superiority thing out of watching it happen on Titan instead of here?" He looked up at the display, at T'uupieh, who still lay sleeping, unmoving and unmoved. "If I could have changed T'uupieh's mind, or changed what happens here, then maybe I could have felt good about something. At least about myself. But who am I kidding?" T'uupieh had been right all along, and now he had to admit it to himself: that there had never been any way he could change either one. "T'uupieh's just like the rest of them, she'd rather cut off your hand than shake it . . . and doing it vicariously means we're no better. And none of us ever will be." The words to a song older than he was slipped into his mind, with sudden irony: " 'One man's hands can't build' "—he began to switch off the terminal—" 'anything.' "

"You need to sleep . . . ve all need to sleep." Garda rose stiffly from her chair.

" ' . . . but if one and one and fifty make a million . . .' " his mother matched his quote softly.

Shannon turned back to look at her, saw her shake her head; she felt him looking at her, glanced up. "After all, if T'uupieh could have accepted that everything she did was morally evil, what would have become of her? She knew: it would have destroyed her—we would have destroyed her. She would have been swept away and drowned in the tide of violence." His mother looked away at Garda, back at him. "T'uupieh is a realist, whatever else she is."

He felt his mouth tighten against the resentment that sublimated a deeper, more painful emotion; he heard Garda's grunt of indignation.

"But that doesn't mean that you were wrong, or that you failed—"

"That's big of you." He stood up, nodding at Garda, and toward the exit. "Come on."

"Shannon."

He stopped, still facing away.

"I don't think you failed. I think you did reach T'uupieh. The last thing she said was 'Only you can change tomorrow.' I think she was challenging the demon to go ahead, to do what she didn't have the power to do herself. I think she was asking you to help her."

He turned, slowly. "You really believe that?"

"Yes, I do." She bent her head, freed her hair from the collar of her sweater.

He moved back to his seat; his hands brushed the dark, unresponsive touchplates on the panel. "But it wouldn't do any good to talk to her again. Somehow the demon has to stop the attack itself. If I could use the 'voice' to warn them . . . Damn the time lag!" By the time his voice reached them, the attack would have been over for hours. How could he change anything tomorrow if he was always two hours behind?

"I know how to get around the time-lag problem."

"How?" Garda sat down again, mixed emotions showing on her broad, seamed face. "He can't send a varning ahead of time; no one knows when Klovhiri will pass. It vould come too soon, or too late."

Shannon straightened up. "Better to ask, 'Why?' Why are you changing your mind?"

"I never changed my mind," his mother said mildly. "I never liked this either. . . . When I was a girl, we used to believe that our actions *could* change the world; maybe I've never stopped wanting to believe that."

"But Marcus is not going to like us meddling behind his back, anyway." Garda waved her staff. "And what about the point that perhaps ve do need this publicity?"

Shannon glanced back irritably. "I thought you were on the side of the angels, not the devil's advocate."

"I am!" Garda's mouth puckered. "But—"

"Then what's such bad news about the probe making a last-minute rescue? It'll be a sensation."

He saw his mother smile, for the first time in months. "Sensational . . . if T'uupieh doesn't leave us stranded in the swamp for our betrayal."

He sobered. "Not if you really think she wants our help. And I know she wants it—I *feel* it. But how do we beat the time lag?"

"I'm the engineer, remember? I'll need a recorded message from you, and some time to play with that." His mother pointed at the computer terminal.

He switched on the terminal and moved aside. She sat down and started a program documentation on the display; he read, REMOTE OPERATIONS MANUAL. "Let's see . . . I'll need feedback on the approach of Klovhiri's party . . ."

He cleared his throat. "Did you really mean what you said, before Reed came in?"

She glanced up; he watched one response form on her face and then fade into another smile. "Garda, have you met My Son the Linguist?"

"And when did you ever pick up on that Pete Seeger song?"

"And My Son the Musician . . ." The smile came back to him. "I've listened to a few records in my day." The smile turned inward, toward a memory. "I don't suppose I ever told you that I fell in love with your father because he reminded me of Elton John?"

T'uupieh stood silently, gazing into the demon's unwavering eye. A new day was turning the clouds from bronze to gold; the brightness seeped down through the glistening, snarled hair of the treetops, glanced from the green translucent cliff-faces and sweating slopes, to burnish the demon's carapace with light. She gnawed the last shreds of flesh from a bone, forcing herself to eat, scarcely aware that she did. She had already sent out watchers in the direction of the town, to keep watch for Chwiul . . . and Klovhiri's party. Behind her the rest of her band made ready now, testing weapons and reflexes or feeding their bellies.

And still the demon had not spoken to her. There had been many times when it had chosen not to speak for hours on end, but after its mad ravings of last night, the thought obsessed her that it might never speak again. Her concern grew, lighting the fuse of her anger, which this morning was already short enough; until at last she strode recklessly forward and struck it with her open hand. "Speak to me, *mala'ingga!*"

But as her blow landed, a pain like the touch of fire shot up the muscles of her arm. She leaped back with a curse of surprise, shaking her hand. The demon had never lashed out at her before, never hurt her in any way. But she had never dared to strike it before; she had always treated it with calculated respect. . . . *Fool!* She looked down at her hand, half afraid to see it covered with burns that would make her a cripple in the attack today. But the skin was still smooth and unblistered, only bright with the smarting shock.

"T'uupieh! Are you all right?"

She turned, to see Y'lirr, who had come up behind her looking half frightened, half grim. "Yes." She nodded, controlling a sharper reply at the sight of his concern. "It was nothing." He carried her double-arched bow and quiver; she put out her smarting hand and took them from him casually, slung them at her back. "Come, Y'lirr, we must—"

"T'uupieh." This time it was the demon's eerie voice that called her name. "T'uupieh, if you believe in my power to

twist fate as I like, then you must come back and listen to me
again."

She turned back, felt Y'lirr hesitate behind her. "I believe
truly in all your powers, my demon!" She rubbed her hand.

The amber depths of its eye absorbed her expression and
read her sincerity, or so she hoped. "T'uupieh, I know I did
not make you believe what I said. But I want you to"—its
words blurred unintelligibly—"in me. I want you to know my
name. T'uupieh, my name is—"

She heard a horrified yowl from Y'lirr behind her. She
glanced around—seeing him cover his ears—and back, paralyzed by disbelief.

"—Shang'ang."

The word struck her like the demon's fiery lash, but the
blow this time struck only in her mind. She cried out, in desperate protest, but the name had already passed into her
knowledge, *too late!*

A long moment passed; she drew a breath and shook her
head. Disbelief still held her motionless as she let her eyes
sweep the brightening camp, as she listened to the sounds of
the wakening forest and breathed in the spicy acridness of the
spring growth. And then she began to laugh. She had heard a
demon speak its name, and she still lived—and was not blind,
not deaf, not mad. The demon had chosen her, joined with
her, surrendered to her at last!

Dazed with exaltation, she almost did not realize that the
demon had gone on speaking to her. She broke off the song
of triumph that rose in her, listening:

" . . . then I command you to take me with you when you
go today. I must see what happens, and watch Klovhiri pass."

"Yes! Yes, my—Shang'ang. It will be done as you wish.
Your whim is my desire." She turned away down the slope,
stopped again as she found Y'lirr still prone where he had
thrown himself down when the demon spoke its name.
"Y'lirr?" She nudged him with her foot. Relieved, she saw
him lift his head, watched her own disbelief echoing in his
face as he looked up at her.

"My lady . . . it did not—?"

"No, Y'lirr," she said softly; then more roughly, "Of course
it did not! I am truly the Demon's Consort now; nothing shall
stand in my way." She pushed him again with her foot,
harder. "Get up. What do I have, a pack of sniveling cowards
to ruin the morning of my success?"

Y'lirr scrambled to his feet, brushing himself off. "Never

that, T'uupieh! We're ready for any command . . . ready to deliver your revenge." His hand tightened on his knife hilt.

"And my demon will join us in seeking it out!" The pride she felt rang in her voice. "Get help to fetch a sledge here, and prepare it. And tell them to move it *gently*."

He nodded, and for a moment as he glanced at the demon she saw both fear and envy in his eyes. "Good news." He moved off then with his usual brusqueness, without glancing back at her.

She heard a small clamor in the camp and looked past him, thinking that word of the demon had spread already. But then she saw Lord Chwiul, come as he had promised, being led into the clearing by her escorts. She lifted her head slightly, in surprise—he had indeed come alone, but he was riding a *bliell*. They were rare and expensive mounts, being the only beast she knew of large enough to carry so much weight, and being vicious and difficult to train as well. She watched this one snapping at the air, its fangs protruding past slack, dribbling lips, and grimaced faintly. She saw that the escort kept well clear of its stumplike webbed feet, and kept their spears ready to prod. It was an amphibian, being too heavy ever to make use of wings, but buoyant and agile when it swam. T'uupieh glanced fleetingly at her own webbed fingers and toes, at the wing membranes along her sides that could only lift her body now for bare seconds at a time. She wondered, as she had so many times, what strange turns of fate had formed, or transformed, them all.

She saw Y'lirr speak to Chwiul, pointing her out, saw his insolent grin and the trace of apprehension that Chwiul showed looking up at her; she thought that Y'lirr had said, "She knows its name."

Chwiul rode forward to meet her, with his face under control as he endured the demon's scrutiny. T'uupieh put out a hand to casually—gently—stroke its sensuous, jewel-facet side. Her eyes left Chwiul briefly, drawn by some instinct to the sky directly above him, and for half a moment she saw the clouds break open. . . .

She blinked, to see more clearly, and when she looked again it was gone. No one else, not even Chwiul, had seen the gibbous disc of greenish gold, cut across by a line of silver and a band of shadow-black: the Wheel of Change. She kept her face expressionless, but her heart raced. The Wheel appeared only when someone's life was about to be changed profoundly—and usually the change meant death.

Chwiul's mount lunged at her suddenly as he stopped before her. She held her place at the demon's side, but some of the *bliell's* bluish spittle landed on her cloak as Chwiul jerked at its heavy head. "Chwiul!" She let her emotion out as anger. "Keep that slobbering filth under control, or I will have it struck dead!" Her hand fisted on the demon's slick hide.

Chwiul's near-smile faded abruptly, and he pulled his mount back, staring uncomfortably at the demon's glaring eye.

T'uupieh took a deep breath and produced a smile of her own. "So you did not quite dare to come to my camp alone, my lord."

He bowed slightly, from the saddle. "I was merely hesitant to wander in the swamp on foot, alone, until your people found me."

"I see." She kept the smile. "Well then, I assume that things went as you planned this morning. Are Klovhiri and his party all well on their way into our trap?"

"They are. And their guide is waiting for my sign, to lead them off safe ground into whatever mire you choose."

"Good. I have a spot in mind that is well ringed by heights." She admired Chwiul's self-control in the demon's presence, although she sensed that he was not as easy as he wanted her to believe. She saw some of her people coming toward them with a sledge to carry the demon on their trek. "My demon will accompany us, by its own desire. A sure sign of our success today, don't you agree?"

Chwiul frowned as if he wanted to question that but didn't quite dare. "If it serves you loyally, then yes, my lady. A great honor and a good omen."

"It serves me with true devotion." She smiled again, insinuatingly. She stood back as the sledge came up onto the hummock, watched as the demon was settled onto it, to be sure her people used the proper care. The fresh reverence with which her outlaws treated it, and their leader, was not lost on either Chwiul or herself.

She called her people together then, and they set out for their destination, picking their way over the steaming surface of the marsh and through the slimy slate-blue tentacles of the fragile, thawing underbrush. She was glad that they covered this ground often, because the pungent spring growth and the ground's mushy unpredictability changed the pattern of their passage from day to day. She wished that she could have separated Chwiul from his ugly mount, but she doubted that he would cooperate, and she was afraid that he might not be able to keep up on foot. The demon was lashed securely onto its sledge, and its sweating bearers pulled it with no hint of complaint.

At last they reached the heights overlooking the main road—though it could hardly be called one now—that led past her family's manor. She had the demon positioned where it could look back along the overgrown trail in the direction of Klovhiri's approach, and sent some of her followers to secrete its eyes farther down the track. She stood then gazing down at the spot below where the path seemed to fork, but did not: the false fork followed the rippling yellow bands of the cliff face below her, directly into a sink caused by ammonia-water melt seeping down and through the porous sulfide compounds of the rock. There they would all wallow while she and her band picked them off like swatting *ngips*—she thoughtfully swatted a *ngip* that had settled on her hand—unless her demon . . . unless her demon chose to create some other outcome.

"Any sign?" Chwiul rode up beside her.

She moved back slightly from the cliff's crumbly edge, watching him with more than casual interest. "Not yet. But soon." She had outlaws posted on the lower slope across the track as well, but not even her demon's eye could pierce too deeply into the foliage along the road. It had not spoken since Chwiul's arrival, and she did not expect it to reveal its secrets now. "What livery does your escort wear, and how many of them do you want killed for effect?" She unslung her bow and began to test its pull.

Chwiul shrugged. "The dead carry no tales; kill them all. I shall have Klovhiri's soon. Kill the guide, too—a man who can be bought once, can be bought twice."

"Ah—" She nodded, grinning. "A man with your foresight and discretion will go far in the world, my lord." She nocked an arrow in the bowstring before she turned away, to search the road again. Still empty. She looked away restlessly, at the spiny silver-blue-green of the distant fog-clad mountains; at the hollow fingers of upthrust ice, once taller than she was, stubby and diminishing now along the edge of the nearer lake. The lake where last summer she had soared—

A flicker of movement, a small unnatural noise, pulled her eyes back to the road. Tension tightened the fluid ease of her movement as she made the trilling call that would send her band to their places along the cliff's edge. *At last.* Leaning forward eagerly for the first glimpse of Klovhiri, she spotted the guide, and then the sledge that bore her sister and the children. She counted the numbers of the escort, saw them all emerge into her unbroken view on the track. But Klovhiri . . . where was Klovhiri? She turned back to Chwiul; her whisper struck out at him, "Where is he? Where is Klovhiri?"

Chwiul's expression lay somewhere between guilt and guile. "Delayed. He stayed behind, he said there were still matters at court—"

"Why didn't you tell me that?"

He jerked sharply on the *bliell*'s rein. "It changes nothing! We can still eradicate his family. That will leave me first in line to the inheritance, and Klovhiri can always be brought down later."

"But it's Klovhiri I want, for myself." T'uupieh raised her bow, the arrow tracked toward his heart.

"They'll know who to blame if I die!" He spread a wing defensively. "The Overlord will turn against you for good; Klovhiri will see to that. Avenge yourself on your sister, T'uupieh—and I will still reward you well if you keep the bargain!"

"This is not the bargain we agreed to!" The sounds of the approaching party reached her clearly now from down below; she heard a child's high notes of laughter. Her outlaws crouched, waiting for her signal, and she saw Chwiul prepare for his own signal call to his guide. She looked back at the demon, its amber eye fixed on the travelers below. She started toward it. It could still twist fate for her. *Or had it already?*

"Go back, go back!" The demon's voice burst over her, down across the silent forest, like an avalanche. "Ambush . . . trap . . . you have been betrayed!"

"—betrayal!"

She barely heard Chwiul's voice below the roaring; she looked back in time to see the *bliell* leap forward, to intersect her own course toward the demon. Chwiul drew his sword; she saw the look of white fury on his face, not knowing whether it was for her or the demon itself. She ran toward the demon's sledge, trying to draw her bow, but the *bliell* covered the space between them in two great bounds. Its head swung toward her, jaws gaping. Her foot skidded on the slippery melt and she went down; the dripping jaws snapped futilely shut above her face. But one flailing leg struck her heavily and knocked her sliding through the melt to the demon's foot.

The demon. She gasped for the air that would not fill her lungs, trying to call its name; saw with incredible clarity the beauty of its form, and the ululating horror of the *bliell* bearing down on them to destroy them both. She saw it rear above her, above the demon; saw Chwiul, either leaping or thrown, sail out into the air—and at last her voice came back to her and she screamed the name, a warning and a plea, "Shang'ang!"

And as the *bliell* came down, lightning lashed out from the demon's carapace and wrapped the *bliell* in fire. The beast's ululations rose off the scale; T'uupieh covered her ears against the piercing pain of its cry. But not her eyes: the demon's lash ceased with the suddenness of lightning, and the *bliell* toppled back and away, rebounding lightly as it crashed to the ground, stone dead. T'uupieh sank back against the demon's foot, supported gratefully as she filled her aching lungs, and looked away—

To see Chwiul, trapped in the updrafts at the cliff's edge, gliding, gliding . . . and she saw the three arrows that protruded from his back, before the currents let his body go and it disappeared below the rim. She smiled and closed her eyes.

"T'uupieh! T'uupieh!"

She blinked them open again, resignedly, as she felt her people cluster around her. Y'lirr's hand drew back from the motion of touching her face as she opened her eyes. She smiled again at him, at them all, but not with the smile she had had for Chwiul. "Y'lirr . . ." She gave him her hand and let him help her up. Aches and bruises prodded her with every small movement, but she was certain, reassured, that the only real damage was an oozing tear in her wing. She kept her arm close to her side.

"T'uupieh—"

"My lady—"

"What happened? The demon—"

"The demon saved my life." She waved them silent. "And—for its own reasons—it foiled Chwiul's plot." The realization, and the implications, were only now becoming real in her mind. She turned, and for a long moment gazed into the demon's unreadable eye. Then she moved away, going stiffly to the edge of the cliff to look down.

"But the contract—" Y'lirr said.

"Chwiul broke the contract! He did not give me Klovhiri." No one made a protest. She peered through the brush, guessing without much difficulty the places where Ahtseet and

her party had gone to earth below. She could hear a child's
whimpered crying now. Chwiul's body lay sprawled on the
flat, in plain view of them all, and she thought she saw more
arrows bristling from his corpse. Had Ahtseet's guard riddled
him too, taking him for an attacker? The thought pleased her.
And a small voice inside her dared to whisper that Ahtseet's
escape pleased her much more. . . . She frowned suddenly at
the thought.

But Ahtseet had escaped, and so had Klovhiri—and so she
might as well make use of that fact, to salvage what she
could. She paused, collecting her still-shaken thoughts. "Ahtseet!" Her voice was not the voice of the demon, but it
echoed satisfactorily. "It's T'uupieh! See the traitor's corpse
that lies before you—your own mate's brother, Chwiul! He
hired murderers to kill you in the swamp—seize your guide,
make him tell you all. It is only by my demon's warning that
you still live."

"Why?" Ahtseet's voice wavered faintly on the wind.

T'uupieh laughed bitterly. "Why, to keep the roads clear of
ruffians. To make the Overlord love his loyal servant more,
and reward her better, dear sister! And to make Klovhiri hate
me. May it eat his guts out that he owes your lives to me!
Pass freely through my lands, Ahtseet; I give you leave—this
once."

She drew back from the ledge and moved wearily away,
not caring whether Ahtseet would believe her. Her people
stood waiting, gathered silently around the corpse of the
bliell.

"What now?" Y'lirr asked, looking at the demon, asking
for them all.

And she answered, but made her answer directly to the
demon's silent amber eye. "It seems I spoke the truth to
Chwiul after all, my demon. I told him he would not be needing his town house after today. . . . Perhaps the Overlord will
call it a fair trade. Perhaps it can be arranged. The Wheel of
Change carries us all, but not with equal ease. Is that not so,
my beautiful Shang'ang?"

She stroked its day-warmed carapace tenderly, and settled
down on the softening ground to wait for its reply.

Afterword

"Eyes of Amber" is a Cinderella story—figuratively, if not literally. Ben Bova wrote to ask me if I would do a lead story for the June 1977 "women's issue" of *Analog* magazine, and the deadline he gave me was about a month away. I was delighted, but at the same time frantic because I write very slowly, and there was no story sitting on the back burner in my mind at the time, just itching to be written. I had to pull something essentially out of a hat—or out of my idea box, in this case.

An idea box is an extremely useful tool for a writer. I find a 3x5 card box works to keep my collection straight. Often a single idea isn't enough to support a whole story, so it pays to collect ideas and keep them somewhere together. In times of need they can be taken out and spread around, combined and recombined until they create interesting resonances that begin to build a story. That's essentially what I did to create "Eyes of Amber."

I began by taking the idea of an emotionally (but not physically) intimate relationship between human and alien, from a book I'd read about an Indian man and a wolf, and I added to that the details of a dream I'd had about a female assassin in a medieval setting. I also took the suggestion of my husband, Vernor, that I set the story on Titan, a moon of Saturn, one of the few bodies left in the solar system that scientists feel have the potential for developing some form of life. Because I'm frequently inspired by music, I also wove in elements of a Buffy St. Marie song about a benign "demon lover." By fusing all these elements together, I created the basic fabric of the story. Once I had the basics, I sat down and wrote and wrote, sometimes ten or twelve hours a day. My basic rate of word production is very slow and very constant. In order to write faster I have to write longer hours, and the process of writing is a kind of extended daydreaming, almost meditation. My body gets very twitchy when forced to sit motionless for long periods; the discipline of a close dead-line proved to me that I could raise my basic level of endur-ance.

But after the story was written I felt a certain alienation from it, perhaps because it had been "forced out" and hadn't been allowed to develop at its own natural rate. In the process of writing a story at my "normal" speed, I have more of an opportunity to feel comfortable with its personality than I did with this one. When I received a letter telling me that it had been nominated for a Hugo I was stunned. I de-cided at that point that this story was determined to make me like it. I swore that if it actually won the Hugo, like a wicked stepmother I would have to beg its forgiveness for my lack of faith. . . . It did, and I hope I've made amends by making it the title story of this anthology.

Although "Eyes of Amber" was basically written as an ad-venture, one of the underlying themes of the story (and, I hope, one of the reasons it was nominated for the Hugo) is the importance of communication: communicating with alien beings (who may simply be other human beings); the idea that behind real communication lies understanding, and that with understanding we can perhaps work to overcome our fears. It also questions the right of any being or society to in-terfere with the value structures of another culture—can we really be sure that the values we impose on them are superior to the ones they already have? Do we have the right to prose-lytize? Life is made up of shades of gray, rather than the pure absolutes of right and wrong. There are no easy an-swers, for the characters, for the writer, for the reader.

To Bell the Cat

Another squeal of animal pain reached them from the bubble tent twenty meters away. Juah-u Corouda jerked involuntarily as he tossed the carved gaming pieces from the cup, spoiling his throw. "Hell, a triad. . . . Damn that noise; it's like fingernails on metal."

"Orr doesn't know the meaning of 'surrender.'" Albe Hyacin-Soong caught up the cup. "It must be driving him crazy that he can't figure out how those scaly little rats survive all that radioactivity. How they ever evolved in the first place—"

"He doesn't know the meaning of the word 'mercy.'" Xena Soong-Hyacin frowned at her husband, her hands clasping her elbows. "Why doesn't he anesthetize them?"

"Come on, Xena," Corouda said. "They're just animals. They don't feel pain like we do."

"And what are any of us, Juah-u, but animals trying to play God?"

"I just want to play squamish," Albe muttered.

Corouda smiled faintly, looking away from Xena toward the edge of the camp. A few complaints, hers among them, had forced Orr to move his lab tent away from the rest. Corouda was just as glad. The noises annoyed him, but he didn't take them personally. Research was necessary; Xena—any scientist—should be able to accept that. *But the bleeding hearts are always with us.* No matter how comfortable a society became, no matter how fair, no matter how nearly perfect, there was always someone who wanted flaws to pick at. Some people were never satisfied; he was glad he wasn't one of them. And glad he wasn't married to one of them. But then, Albe always liked a good argument.

"Next you'll be telling me that *he* doesn't feel anything either!" Xena pointed.

"Keep your voice down, Xena. He'll hear you. He's right over there. And don't pull down straw men; he's got nothing to do with this. He's Piper Alvarian Jary; he's supposed to suffer."

"He's been brainwiped. That's like punishing an amnesiac; he's not the same man—"

"I don't want to get into that again," Albe said, unconvincingly.

Corouda shook his head, pushed the blond curls back under his peaked cap and moved further into the shade. They sat cross-legged on the soft, gray-brown earth with the studied primitivism all wardens affected. He turned his head slightly to look at Piper Alvarian Jary, sitting on a rock in the sun; alone as usual, and as usual within summoning range of Hoban Orr, his master. Piper Alvarian Jary, who for six years—six years! Was it only six?—had been serving a sentence at Simeu Biomedical Research Institute, being punished in kind for the greatness of his sin.

Not that he looked like a monster now, as he sat toying endlessly with a pile of stones. He wore a plain, pale coverall sealed shut to the neck in spite of the heat; dark hair fell forward into his eyes above a nondescript sunburned face. He could have been anyone's menial assistant, ill at ease in this group of ecological experts on an unexplored world. He could have been anyone—

Corouda looked away, remembering the scars that the sealed suit probably covered. But he *was* Piper Alvarian Jary, who had supported the dictator Naron—who had bloodied his hands in one of the most brutal regimes in mankind's long history of inhumanity to man. It had surprised Corouda that Jary was still young. But a lifetime spent as a Catspaw for Simeu Institute would age a man fast. *Maybe that's why he's sitting in the sun; maybe he wants to fry his brains out.*

"—that's why I wanted to become a warden, Albe!" Xena's insistent voice pulled his attention back. "So that we wouldn't have to be a part of things like this . . . so that I wouldn't have to sit here beating my head against a stone wall about the injustice and the indifference of this society—"

Albe reached out distractingly and tucked a strand of her bound-up hair behind her ear. "But you've got to admit this is a remarkable discovery we've made here. After all, a natural reactor—a concentration of uranium ore so rich that it's fissioning. The only comparable thing we know of happened on Terra a billion years before anybody was around to care." He waved his hand at the cave mouth 200 meters away. "And right in that soggy cave over there is a live one, and animals survive in it! To find out how they could have adapted to that much radiation—isn't it important for us to find that out?"

"Of course it is." Xena looked pained. "Don't patronize me, Albe. I know that as well as you do. And you know that's not what I'm talking about."

"Yes, I know it isn't. . . ." He sighed in surrender. "This whole expedition will be clearing out soon; they've got most of the data they want already. And then the six of us can get down to work and forget we ever saw any of them; we'll have a whole new world all to ourselves."

"Until they start shipping in the damned tourists—"

"Hey, come on," Corouda said, too loudly. "Come on. What're we sitting here for? Roll them bones."

Albe laughed, and shook the cup. He scattered the carved shapes and let them group in the dirt. "Hah, Two-square."

Corouda grunted. "I know you cheat; if I could just figure out how. Xena—"

She turned back from gazing at Piper Alvarian Jary, her face tight.

"Xena, if it makes you feel any better, Jary doesn't feel anything. Only in his hands, maybe his face a little."

She looked at him blankly. "What?"

"Jary told me himself; Orr killed his sense of feeling when he first got him, so that he wouldn't have to suffer needlessly from the experiments."

Her mouth came open.

"Is that right?" Albe pushed the sweatband back on his tanned, balding forehead. "Remember last week, he backed into the campfire. . . . I didn't know you'd talked to him, Juah-u. What's he like?"

"I don't know. Who knows what somebody like that is really like? A while back he came and offered to check a collection of potentially edible flora for me. . . ." And Jary had returned the next day with the samples, looking tired and a little shaky, to tell him exactly what was and wasn't edible, and to what degree. It was only later, after he'd had time to run tests of his own, that he had understood how Jary had managed to get the answers so fast, and so accurately. "He ate them, to see if they poisoned *him*. Don't ask me why he did it; maybe he enjoys being punished."

Xena withered him with a look.

"I didn't know he was going to eat them." Corouda slapped at a bug, annoyed. "Besides, he'd have to drink strychnine by the liter to kill himself. They made Jary into a walking biological lab—his body manufactures an immunity to anything, almost on the spot; they use him to make vaccines. You can cut off anything but his head and it'll grow back—"

"Oh, for God's sake." Xena stood up, her brown face flushed. She dropped the cup between them like something unclean, and strode away into the trees.

Corouda watched her go; the wine-red crown of the forest gave her shelter from his insensitivity. In the distance through the trees he could see the stunted vegetation at the mouth of the reactor cave. Radiation had eaten out an entire hillside, and the cave's heart was still a festering radioactive sink hot enough to boil water. Yet some tiny alien creatures had chosen to live in it . . . which meant that this expedition would have to go on stewing in the sun until Orr made a breakthrough, or made up his mind to quit. Corouda sighed and looked back at Hyacin-Soong. "Sorry, Albe. I even disgusted myself this time."

Albe's expression eased. "She'll cool down in a while. . . . Tell her that, when she comes back."

"I will." Corouda rolled his shirtsleeves up another turn, feeling uncomfortably hot. "Well, we need three if we're going to keep playing." He gestured at Piper Alvarian Jary, still sitting in the sun. "You wanted to know what he's like—why don't we ask him?"

"Him?" Incredulity faded to curiosity on Albe's face. "Why not? Go ahead and ask him."

"Hey, Jary!" Corouda watched the sunburned face lift, startled, to look at him. "Want to play some squamish?" He could barely see the expression on Jary's face, barely see it change. He thought it became fear, decided he must be wrong. But then Jary squinted at him, shielding his eyes against the sun, and the dark head bobbed. Jary came toward them, watching the ground, with the unsure, shuffling gait of a man who couldn't find his footing.

He sat down between them awkwardly, an expressionless smile frozen on his mouth, and pulled his feet into position.

Corouda found himself at a loss for words, wondering why in hell he'd done this. He held out the cup, shook it. "Uh—you know how to play squamish?"

Jary took the cup and shook his head. "I don't g-get much chance to play anything, W-warden." The smile turned rueful, but there was nothing in his voice. "I don't get asked."

Corouda remembered again that Piper Alvarian Jary stuttered, and felt an undesired twinge of sympathy. But hadn't he heard, from somebody, that Jary had always stuttered? Jary had finally loosened the neck of his coveralls; Corouda could see the beginning of a scar between his collarbones, running down his chest. Jary caught him staring; a hand rose instinctively to close the seal.

Corouda cleared his throat. "Nothing to it, it's mostly luck. You throw the pieces, and it depends on the—"

Another mindless squall came from the tent behind them. Jary glanced toward it.

"—the distribution, the way the pieces cluster. . . . Does that bother you?" The bald question was out before he realized it, and left him feeling like a rude child.

Jary looked back at him as though it hadn't surprised him at all. "No. They're just animals. B-better them than me."

Corouda felt his anger rise, remembering what Jary was . . . until he remembered that he had said the same thing.

"Piper! Come here, I need you."

Corouda recognized Hoban Orr's voice. Jary recognized it too, climbed to his feet, stumbling with haste. "I'm sorry, the Doctor wants me." He backed away; they watched him turn and shuffle off toward Orr's tent. His voice had not changed. Corouda suddenly tried not to wonder why he was needed. . . . *Catspaw: person used by another to do something dangerous or unpleasant.*

Corouda stood up, brushing at his pants. Jary spent his time outside while Orr was dissecting: Piper Alvarian Jary, who had served a man who made Attila the Hun, Hitler, and Kahless look like nice guys. Corouda wondered if it were possible that he really didn't like to watch.

Albe stood with him and stretched. "What did you think of that? That's the real Piper Alvarian Jary, all right. 'Better them than me . . . just a bunch of animals.' He probably thinks we're all a bunch of animals."

Corouda watched Jary disappear into the tent. "Wouldn't surprise me at all."

Piper Alvarian Jary picked his way cautiously over the rough, slagged surface of the narrow cave ledge, setting down one foot and then the other like a puppeteer. Below him, some five meters down the solid rock surface here, lay the shallow liquid surface of the radioactive mud. He rarely

looked down at it, too concerned with lighting a path for his
own feet. Their geological tests had shown that a seven-meter
layer forty meters down in the boiling mud held a freakish
concentration of fissile ores, hot enough once to have eaten
out this strange, contorted subterranean world. He risked a
glance out into the pitch blackness, his headlamp spotlighting
grotesque formations cast from molten rock; silvery metallic
stalactites and stalagmites, reborn from vaporized ores. Over
millennia the water-saturated mass of mud and uranium had
become exothermic and then cooled, sporadically, in one spot
and then another. Like some immense witches' caldron, the
whole underground had simmered and sputtered for nearly
half a million years.

Fumes rising in Jary's line of sight shrouded his vision of
the tormented underworld; he wondered vaguely whether the
smell would be unpleasant, if he could remove the helmet of
his radiation suit. Someone else might have thought of Hell,
but that image did not occur to him.

He stumbled, coming up hard against a jagged outcrop-
ping. Orr's suited form turned back to look at him, glittered
in the dancing light of his own headlamp. "Watch out for
that case!"

He felt for the bulky container slung against his hip, reassuring his nerveless body that its contents were still secure.
Huddled inside it, creeping over one another aimlessly, were
the half dozen sluggish, rat-sized troglodytes they had captured this trip. He turned his light on them, but they did not
respond, gazing stupidly at him and through him from the
observation window. "It's all right, D-doctor."

Orr nodded, starting on. Jary ducked a gleaming stalactite,
moved forward quickly before the safety line between them
jerked taut. He was grateful for the line, even though he had
heard the warden named Hyacin-Soong call it his leash. Hyacin-Soong followed behind him now with the other warden,
Corouda, who had asked him to play squamish this morning.
He didn't expect them to ask him again; he knew that he had
antagonized Hyacin-Soong somehow—maybe just by existing.
Corouda still treated him with benign indifference.

Jary glanced again at the trogs, wishing suddenly that Orr
would give up on them and take him home. He wanted the
safety of the Simeu Institute, the security of the known. He
was afraid of his clumsiness in these alien surroundings,
afraid of the strangers, afraid of displeasing Orr. . . . He let
the air out of his constricted lungs in a long sigh. Of course

he was afraid; he had good reason to be. He was Piper Alvarian Jary.

But Orr would never give up on the trogs, until he either broke the secret code of their alien genes or ran out of specimens to work with. Orr wanted above all to discover how they had adapted to the cave in the geologically short span of time the reactor had been stable—everyone in the expedition wanted to know that. But even the trogs' basic biology confounded him: what the functions were of the four variant kinds he had observed; how they reproduced, when they appeared to be sexless, at least by human standards; what ecological niches they filled, with such hopelessly rudimentary brains. And particularly, how their existence was thermodynamically possible. Orr believed that they seined nutrients directly from the radioactive mud, but even he couldn't accept the possibility that their food chain ended in nuclear fission. The trogs themselves were faintly radioactive; they were carbon-based, could withstand high pressures, and perceived stimuli far into the short end of the EM spectrum. And that was all that Orr was certain of, so far.

Jary clung with his gloved hands to the rough wall above the ledge as it narrowed, and remembered touching the trogs. Once, when he was alone, he had taken off his protective gloves and held one of them in his bare hands. Its scaled, purplish-gray body had not been cold and slippery as he had imagined, but warm, sinuous, and comforting. He had held onto it for as long as he dared, craving the sensual, sensory pleasure of its motion and the alien texture of its skin. He had caressed its small unresponsive body, while it repeated over and over the same groping motions unperturbed, like an untended machine. And his hands had trembled with the same confusion of shame and desire that he always knew when he handled the experimental animals. . . .

There had been a time when he had played innocently with the soft, supple, pink-eyed mice and rabbits, the quick, curious monkeys, and the iridescent fletters. But then Orr had begun training him as an assistant; and observation of the progress of induced diseases, the clearing away of entrails and blood, the disposal of small, ruined bodies in the incinerator chute had taught him their place, and his own. Animals had no rights and no feelings. But when he held the head of a squirming mouse between his fingers and looked down into the red, amorphous eyes, when he caught its tail for the jerk that would snap its spine, his hands trembled. . . .

The ground trembled with the strain of pent-up pressures; Jary fell to his knees, not feeling the bruising impact. Behind him he heard the curses of the wardens and saw Orr struggle to keep his own balance up ahead. When his hands told him the tremor had passed, he began to crawl toward Orr, using his hands to feel his way, his palms cold with sweat. He could not compensate for unexpected motion; it was easier to crawl.

"Piper!" Orr jerked on the safety line. "Get up, you're dragging the specimen box."

Jary felt the wardens come up behind him, and heard one of them laugh. The goad of sudden sharp memory got him to his feet; he started on, not looking back at them. He had crawled after the first operation, the one that had killed his sense of touch—using his still-sensitive hands to lead his deadened body. The lab workers had laughed; and he had laughed too, until the fog of his repersonalization treatment began to lift, until he began to realize that they were laughing at him. Then he had taught himself, finally, to walk upright like a human being; to at least look like a human being.

Up ahead he saw Orr stop again, and realized that they must have reached the Split already. "Give me some more light up here."

He moved forward to slacken the line between them and shined his lamp on the almost meter-wide crevice that opened across their path. The wardens joined him; Orr gathered himself in the pool of their light and made the jump easily. Jary moved to the lip of the cleft and threw the light of his headlamp down, down; saw its reflection on the oily, gleaming water surface ten meters below. He swayed.

"Don't stand so close to the edge!"

"Just back up, and make the jump."

"Don't think about it—"

"Come on, Jary; we don't have all day!"

Hyacin-Soong struck at his shoulder just as he started forward. With a choked cry of protest he lost his footing, and fell.

The safety line jerked taut, battering him against the tight walls of the cleft. Stunned and giddy, he dangled inside a kaleidoscope of spinning light and blackness. And then, incredulous, he felt the safety line begin to give. . . . Abruptly it let go, somewhere up above him, and he dropped six meters more to the bottom.

"Jary! Jary—?"

"Can you hear us?"

Jary opened his eyes, dimly surprised that he could still see—that his headlamp still functioned, and the speakers in his suit, and his brain. . . .

"Are you all right, Piper?"

Orr's voice registered, and then the meaning of the words. A brief, astonished smile stretched Jary's mouth. "Yes, Doctor, f-fine!" His voice was shaking. The absurdity of his answer hit him, and he began to laugh.

"Get ahold of yourself; you're going into shock. What about the specimens?"

Jary breathed deeply, obediently, and looked down. He found himself up to his waist in steaming water. His legs would not respond when he tried to move them; for a moment he wondered if he'd broken his back. But his groping hands found thick mud thirty centimeters below the water's surface, and he realized that he was only trapped, not paralyzed. The specimen case drifted half-submerged, almost out of his reach. He lunged, caught the strap and pulled it back, floundering. The trogs inside had been shaken out of their torpor; their frantic scrabbling startled him.

"Well? What happened?"

Jary noticed that his lunge for the box had driven him deeper into the mud; the water was up to his chest now. "I've g-got it. But I'm st-st-stuck in the mud; I'm sinking." He glanced up at the external radiation meters inside his helmet. "Every dosimeter's in the red; my suit's going to overload f-fast." He leaned back, trying to see Orr's face past the convex curve of the cleft wall. He saw only a triple star, three headlamp beams far above him, shafting down between the verticle walls of the slit.

"Keep your head up so we can see you; we'll throw you down a line." He recognized Corouda's voice, saw the rope come spiraling down into his piece of light. "Tie it around your waist."

The end of the rope hung twisting half a meter above his head. He struggled upward, clinging to the wall, but his muddy gloves could not hold the slick fibers and he dropped back, sinking deeper. "It's too short. I c-can't do it."

"Then tie on the specimen case, at least."

"I can't reach it!" He struck at the rock wall with his fist. "I'm sinking deeper, I'll fry. G-get me out!"

"Don't thrash," Corouda said evenly, "you'll sink faster. You'll be all right for at least fifteen minutes in that suit.

Find a handhold on the wall and keep it. We'll be back soon with more equipment. You'll be all right."

"B-but—"

"Don't let go of that case."

"Yes, Doctor . . ." The triple star disappeared from his view, and he lost track of the cleft's rim. He could touch both walls without stretching his arms; he found a low ledge protruding, got the specimen case and one elbow up onto it. Steam clouded his faceplate and he wiped it away, smearing the glass with water and mud instead. The trogs had grown quiet on the ledge, as if they were waiting with him. There was no sound but his own quick breathing; the trap of rock cut him off utterly from even the reassurance of another human voice. He was suddenly glad to have the trogs for company.

The minutes stretched. Huddled in his cup of light, he began to imagine what would happen if another earth tremor closed this tiny fracture of the rock . . . what would happen if his suit failed. . . . Sweat trickled down his face like tears; he shook his head, not knowing whether he was sweating with the heat of the mud or the strain of waiting. His suit could have torn when he fell; the radioactive mud could be seeping in, and he would never know it. He had been exposed to radiation in some of Orr's experiments; it had made him sick to his stomach, and once all his hair had fallen out. But he had never had to see the flesh rot off of his bones, his body disintegrating in front of his eyes. . . .

His numb hand slipped from the ledge, and he dropped back into the mud. He hauled himself out again, panting, sobered. He had too much imagination; that was what Orr had always told him. And Orr had taught him ways to control his panic during experimentation, as he had taught him to control his body's biological functions. He should know enough by now not to lose his head. But there were still times when even everything he knew was not enough. And it was then that he came the closest to understanding what Piper Alvarian Jary had done, and why he deserved his punishment.

He relaxed his breathing, concentrating on what was tangible and real: the glaring moon-landscape of the mottled wall before his face, the bright flares of pain as he flexed the hand he had bruised against the stone. He savored the vivid sensory stimulation that was pain, that proved he was alive, with a guilty hunger heightened by fear. The gibbous, mirrorlike eyes of the trogs pooled at the view window of the box, reflecting light, still staring intently through him as if they saw into another world. He remembered that they could, and turned his head slightly, uneasily. He froze, as the small, beslimed face of another trog broke the water beside his chest; then two, and three . . . suddenly half a dozen.

Moving with a sense of purpose that he had never seen them show, they began to leap and struggle up the face of the wall—and up his own suit, as though he was nothing more than an extension of the stone. He stayed motionless, not able to do anything but stare as stupidly as his own captives. His captives . . . a trog dropped from his shoulder onto the ledge; they were all trying to reach the box. Had the captive ones called them here? But how? They were stupid, primitive; creatures with rudimentary brains. How could they work together?

But they *were* working together, clustered now around the box, some probing with long webbed fingers, the larger ones pushing and prying. They searched its surface with their bodies, oblivious to the light of his headlamp, as though the only way they could discover its nature was through their sense of touch. He remembered that they were blind to the segment of the EM spectrum that to him was visible light. He *was* only a part of the rock, in their darkness. And here in the darkness of the cave they were reasoning, intelligent creatures—when outside in the camp they had never shown any kind of intelligence or group activity; never anything at all. Why? Did they leave their brains behind them in the mud when they surfaced?

Jary wondered suddenly if he had lost his own mind. No, it was really happening. If his mind was ever going to snap, it would have happened long ago. And there was no doubt in his mind that these animals had come here for one reason— to free the captives from their cage. These animals . . .

He watched their tireless, desperate struggle to open the cage, knowing that it was futile, that they could only fail in the end. The captive trogs were doomed, because only a human being could open the lock to set them free. Only a human being—

His hand rose crookedly, dripping mud, and reached out toward the case; the trogs seemed to recoil, as if somehow they sensed him coming. He unsealed the lock, and pulled up the lid. The trogs inside shrank down in confusion as the ones on the outside scrambled over the ledge. "C-come on!" He pulled the box to him angrily and shook it upside down, watched their ungainly bodies spill out into the steaming water.

He set the case back on the ledge and clung there, his mind strangely light and empty. And then he saw the second circle of brightness that lapped his own on the wall, illuminating the empty cage. He looked up, to see Corouda suspended silently from a line above his head, feet braced against the shadowed rock. He could see Corouda's dark eyes clearly, and the odd intentness of his face. "Need some help, Jary?"

He looked back at the empty box, his hand still holding onto the strap. "Yes."

Corouda nodded, and tossed him a rope.

Isthp: But we must contact these creatures. We have seen at last that they *are* beings, alien, but like ourselves; not some unknown force. They have mobiles with forms which can be known.

(Warm heavy currents billow upward)
  (Mobiles rise together)
    (Sussuration of thermal neutron clouds)

Mng: They have souls which can be reached. The shining mobile that released our captives, when all we did could not—we must contact that one's sessile, and make our problem known. These aliens must have space flight too; they are not native here. They can help us.

(My tendrils flatten)
  (Golden-green carbonaceous webs)
    (Bright gamma deepens to red as we rise)

Ahm: Our only problem is that these aliens wish to destroy us! That being did not truly shine with life—it was a cold creature of darkness, dripping warm mud.

(Silty currents, growing colder as this one rises)
    (Soft darkness above, we rise toward darkness)

Mng: But its sessile realized our distress. It released your mobiles. It showed good will. We did not know of the aliens' true nature; perhaps they only begin to grasp our own.

(Silent absence of neutron flux)

Ahm: But how do we know they would leave us in peace, even then? We have sent our mobiles into the upper darkness

to begin the ritual three times already. And three times they
have attacked us viciously. We have only six months left. Our
mobiles must complete the ritual in the soft upper reaches, or
there will be no new sessiles. We are growing old; it takes
time to focus the diffision, the obliqueness of a new young
mind. We cannot wait until the next Calling.

   (It grows softer, colder)
     (The bright world dims around us)
      (Grayed, delayed radiation)
       (Only whispers from the neutron clouds)

Isthp: That is true. But surely we can make them understand. . . . We must take the risk, in order to gain anything
worthwhile.
   (Cool sandy crosscurrents)

Scwa: And what is there worth risking our wholeness and
sanity for that we do not already have? We set out to colo-
nize a new world—and we have done so.
   (Darkness; dimming, whispering darkness)
     (Soft atmospheric spaces, hard basalt)

Isthp: But we have not! We are trapped in this pocket of
light, with barely room to exercise our mobiles, on a dark
and hostile world. Every century our lifespace grows less. The
ore concentration is only a fluke, undependable. This is not
the world you wanted, one like our own that generates perpe-
tual light. There is no future here.
   (Crackling gusts of prompt neutrons)
     (Swept upward, swept upward)
      (Hold back, Swift One, wait for the rest)

Ahm: What do you propose, then? That we return to *our*
world, where there is no room for us? That we should depend
on these alien monsters to take us there?
   (Darkness, blind darkness on all sides)
     (Dim warm radiance of mud)

Mng: There are not monsters! They might help us find a better world!
(*****************)

Kle: We are content here. We are colonists, not explorers; we
ask only to be able to breed our mobiles together . . . *such*

pride, to feel the quickness of body, or the grace of supple
fingers; to know that I have chosen the best to breed with
. . . and to meditate in peace.
   (Mud-pools pulse with dim ruby radiance)
     (Smooth basalt . . . and the rarefied atmosphere of the
       upper reaches)
     (I perceive that I shine in all my parts)

Mng: What is the point of breeding the finest mobiles, if they
have no purpose? They build nothing for you, they contribute
nothing—you are not a whole being; you are a debased
breeder of pets. *To breed mobiles that can gaze upon the*
starry universe, that is truly beautiful. If it were possible to
breed mobiles like ours which ran the ship, which could perhaps see the true nature of the aliens from the upper
darkness—that would be worthy. But we have no way to
create anything worthy here.
   (Crackling gusts grow dim and gentle)
     (Push this mobile; currents slip)
       (Bright depths below us now . . . they halo the mo-
        biles of my radiant friend *Isthp*, Gamma-shine-
        through-Molten-Feldspar)

Ahm: Worthy—breeding artificial mobiles and building artificial machines? Machines that fail, like all ephemeral, material
objects.

Bllr, Rhm, Tfod: Technician *Mng*!

Mng: After five hundred years, still you have not reconciled
an accident. You are well named, *Ahm*, who is Darkness-Ab-
sence-of-Radiation.
   (Begin first alignment)
     (How they shine . . . how I shine)
       (Shine against darkness)
        (Shine)

Ahm: It was spaceflight that brought true Darkness into our
lives. It is the purpose of the body's sessile to remain fixed, to
seek the perfection of mind and mobile, not to tumble like a
grain of silt through the nothingness between worlds.
   (Cluster)
     (Form first pattern)
       (Gray-ruby gleaming mudpools)

Isthp: *The "nothingness" of space is full of light, if one has mobiles to perceive it. Strange radiation, that trembles in my memory still.* Technology frees the sessile as meditation frees the soul. So do sessiles become the mobiles of God.
  (All gather, to form the patterns)
    (Heaviness of solid rock density)
      (Beautiful to behold)

Ahm: Heresy. Heresy! Blasphemer.
  (All gather, my mobiles)
    (True breeding. Fine breeding.)

Mng: *Ahm*, you make me lose control—!
  (*****************)

Isthp: Peace, my beloved *Mng*, Cloud-Music. I am not offended. As our Nimbles differ from our Swifts, so do our very souls differ, one being's from another's. We were never meant to steep quietly in the depths, you and I.
  (Gently, my Strong One, move with control)
    (Vibration ripples lap the shore; mudpools settle)
      (Pass under, pass through)

Mng: *Ahm*, you must think of the future generations—why do our mobiles answer the Calling now, but to create new sessiles, who will soon be breeding new mobiles of their own? Our space here will shrink as our numbers increase, and soon it will become like the homeworld . . . and then, much worse. We do not have the resources, or the equipment, or the time, to restructure our lifespace here. You are selfish—
  (Stray whisper of the neutron breeze)
    (Pressure shifts the rock)
      (Tendrils brushing)

Zhek: *You* are selfish! You only wish to return to space, to inflict more danger and discomfort on us all, for the sake of your perverted mechanical-mobile machines.
  (Subtle flow of color on radiant forms)
    (First movement of receptiveness)

Scwa: *I remember dim blackness and killing cold . . . anguish in all my mobiles, as they bore my sessile container over the pathless world-crust.* We have suffered too much already, from the failure of the ship; we few barely reached

here alive. I for one am not ready for more trials. *Mind the mobiles! Enter a new phase of the pattern* . . .
  (All circle together)
    (Weave nets of life-shine)
      (The patterns multiply)

Rhm, Tfod, Zhek, Kle: Agreed, agreed.

Isthp, Mng: We must contact the shining creature!

Jary lay back on the examining table while Orr checked his body for broken bones and scanned him with a radiation counter. Out of the corner of his eye he could see the empty specimen box, still lying on the floor where Orr had dumped it when he entered the tent. Orr had kept him waiting while he talked with Corouda outside—but so far he hadn't said anything more about the loss of the trogs. Jary wondered how much Corouda had really seen—or whether he had seen anything. No one had ever looked at him the way Corouda had, at the bottom of the cleft . . . and so he couldn't be sure what it really meant.

"There's nothing wrong with you that's worth treating." Orr gestured him up. "Hairline fractures on a couple of your ribs."

Jary sat up on the table's edge, mildly relieved, pressing his bruised hand down against the cold metal surface. Orr was angry; he knew the way every line settled on that unexpressive face. But Orr might only be angry because he'd lost the specimens.

"Something else bothering you?"

"Yes—" he answered the graying back of Orr's head, because Orr had already turned away to the storage chests. "You l-let me fall. Didn't you?" He had found the muddy safety line intact, and the unfastened latch at the end.

Orr turned around, surprised, and looked at him. "Yes, I did. I had to release the rope or you might have dragged me into the crevice with you."

Jary laughed sharply.

Orr nodded, as though he had found an answer, "Is that why you did it?"

"What?"

"Turned the specimens loose. Because I let you fall—is that it?"

"No." Jary glanced unwillingly at the case on the floor. "I m-mean, it just c-c-came open; I told you. When it f-fell." The stutter was worse when he got nervous.

"Why didn't you tell me that immediately?"

"I didn't know!" His hands tightened on the metal; he slid down from the table.

"Stay there." Orr set a tray of instruments and specimen plates on the table beside him. "Those locks don't just 'come open.' You opened it, Piper, and let them go—out of personal spite."

"No." He shook his head, enduring Orr's pale scrutiny.

"Don't lie to me." Orr's expression changed slightly, as Jary's face stayed stubborn. "Warden Corouda told me he saw you do it."

No—The word died this time before it reached his mouth. His gaze broke. He looked down at his feet, traced a scar with his eyes.

"So." The satisfied nod, again. Orr reached out and caught his wrist. "You know how important those animals are. And you know how much trouble and risk is involved in bringing them back." Orr forced Jary's hand down onto the shining tabletop, with the strength that was always a surprise to him. Orr picked up a scalpel.

Jary's fingers tightened convulsively. "They'll g-g-grow back!"

Orr didn't look at him. "I need some fresh tissue samples; you'll supply them. Open your fist."

"Please. Please don't hurt my h-hands."

Orr used the scalpel. And Jary screamed.

"What are you doing in here, Orr?"

A sharp and angry woman's voice filled the tent space. Jary blinked his vision clear, and saw Warden Soong-Hyacin standing inside the entrance, her eyes hard with indignation. She looked at the scalpel Orr still held, at the blood pooling in Jary's hand. She called to someone outside the tent; Corouda appeared beside her in the opening. "Witness this for me."

Corouda followed her gaze, and he grimaced. "What's going on?"

"Nothing that concerns you, Wardens." Orr frowned, more in annoyance than embarrassment.

"Anything that happens on our world concerns us," Soong-Hyacin said. "And that includes your torture—"

"Xena." Corouda nudged her. "What's he doing to you, Jary?"

Jary gulped, speechless, and shrugged; not looking at Corouda, not wanting to see his face.

"I was taking some tissue samples. As you can see." Orr picked up a specimen plate, set it down. "My job, and his function. Nothing to do with 'your world,' as you put it."

"Why from his hands?"

"He understands the reason, Warden. . . . Go outside and wait, Piper. I'll call you when I want you."

Jary moved around the table, pressing his mouth shut against nausea as he looked down at the instrument tray; he slipped past the wardens and escaped, gratefully, into the fresh air.

Corouda watched Jary shuffle away in the evening sunlight, pulled his attention back into the tent.

"If you don't stop interfering with my work, Warden Soong-Hyacin, I'm going to complain to Doctor Etchamendy."

Xena lifted her head. "Fine. That's your privilege. But don't be surprised when she supports us. You know the laws of domain. Thank you, Juah-u . . ." She turned to go, looked back at him questioningly.

Corouda nodded. "In a minute." He watched Orr treat the specimen plates and begin to clear away the equipment. "What did you mean when you said 'he understands the reason'?"

Orr pushed the empty carrying case with his foot. "I questioned him about the troglodytes, and he told me that he let them loose, out of spite."

"Spite?" Corouda remembered the expression behind Jary's mud-spattered faceplate, at the bottom of the crevice. And Jary had told Orr that the lock had broken, after they had pulled him up. . . . "Is that how you got him to admit it?" He pointed at the table.

"Of course not"—irritation. Orr wiped the table clean, and wiped off his hands. "I told him that you'd seen him do it."

"I told you I didn't see anything!"

Orr smiled sourly. "Whether you told me the truth or not is of no concern. I simply wanted the truth from him. And I got it."

"You let him think—"

"Does that matter to you?" Orr leaned on the table and studied him with clinical curiosity. "Frankly, I don't see why any of this should matter to you, Warden. After all, you, and Soong-Hyacin, and the other fifteen billion citizens of the Union were the ones who passed judgment on Piper Alvarian Jary. You're the ones who believe his crimes are so heinous that he deserves to be punished without mercy. You sanctioned his becoming my Catspaw—my property, to use as I see fit. Are you telling me now that you think you were wrong?"

Corouda turned and left the tent, and left the question unanswered.

Piper Alvarian Jary sat alone on his rock, as he always did. The evening light threw his shadow at Corouda like an accusing finger; but he did not look up, even when Corouda stood in front of him. Corouda saw that his eyes were shut.

"Jary?"

Jary opened his eyes, looked up, and then down at his hands. Corouda kept his own gaze on Jary's pinched face. "I told Orr that I didn't see what happened. That's all I said. He lied to you."

Jary jerked slightly, and then sighed.

"Do you believe me?"

"Why would you b-bother to lie about it?" Jary raised his head finally. "But why should you b-bother to tell me the truth. . . ." He shrugged. "It doesn't matter."

"It matters to me."

Something that was almost envy crossed Jary's face. He leaned forward absently to pick up a stone from the pile between his feet. Corouda saw it was a piece of obsidian: night-black volcanic glass with the smoothness of silk or water, spotted with ashy, snowflake impurities. Jary cupped it for a moment in his lacerated palms, then dropped it like a hot coal, wincing. It fell back into the pile, into a chain reaction, cascading a rainbow of colors and textures. Two quick drops of red from Jary's hand fell into the colors; he shut his eyes again with his hands palm-up on his knees, meditating. This time Corouda watched, forcing himself, and saw the bleeding stop. He wondered with a kind of morbid fascination how many other strange abilities Jary had.

Jary opened his eyes again; seemed surprised to find Corouda still in front of him. He laughed suddenly, uncomfortably. "You're welcome to play with my rocks, Warden, since you let me play squamish. B-but I won't join you." He pushed a rock forward carefully with his foot.

Corouda leaned over to pick it up: a lavender cobble

flecked with clear quartz, worn smooth by eons rolled in the rivers of some other world. He smiled at the even coolness and the solidness of it; the smile stopped when he realized how much more that must mean to Jary.

"Orr lets me have rocks," Jary was saying. "I started collecting when they sent me to the Institute. If I held still and did what I was told, sometimes somebody would let me go out and walk around the grounds. . . . I like rocks: They don't d-d-die," his voice cracked unexpectedly. "What did you really see, there in the cave, W-warden?"

"Enough." Corouda sat down on the ground and tossed the rock back into the pile. "Why did you do it, Jary?"

Jary's eyes moved aimlessly, searching the woods for the cave mouth. "I d-don't know."

"I mean—what you did to the people on Angsith. And on Ikeba. Why? How could anyone—"

Jary's eyes came back to his face, blurred with the desperate pain of a man being forced to stare at the sun. "I don't remember. I don't remember. . . ." He might have laughed.

Corouda had a sudden, sickening double vision of the strutting, uniformed Jary who had helped to turn worlds into charnel houses . . . and Jary the Catspaw, who collected stones.

Jary's hands tightened into fists. "But *I* did it. I *am* P-piper Alvarian Jary! I am guilty." He stretched his fingers again with a small gasp; his palms oozed bright blood like a revelation. "Fifteen b-billion people can't be wrong . . . and I've been lucky."

"Lucky?" Corouda said, inadequately.

Jary nodded at his feet. "Lucky they gave me to Orr. Some of the others . . . I've heard stories . . . they didn't care who they gave them to." Then, as if he sensed Corouda's unspoken question, "Orr only punishes me when I do something wrong. He's not cruel to me . . . he didn't have to make sure I wouldn't feel p-pain. He doesn't care what I did; I'm just something he uses. At least I'm useful." His voice rose slightly: "I'm really very grateful that I'm so well off. That I only spend half my time cut up like a f-flatworm, or flat on my back with fever and diarrhea, or vomiting or fed through a tube or cleaning up the guts of d-dead animals—" Jary's hands stopped short of his face. He wiped his face roughly with the sleeve of his coveralls and stood up, scattering rocks.

"Jary—wait a minute." Corouda rose to his knees. "Sit down."

Jary's face was under control again; Corouda couldn't tell whether he turned back gladly or only obediently. He sat down hard, without hands to guide him.

"You know, if you wanted to be—useful . . ." Corouda struggled with the half-formed idea. "The thing you did for me, testing those plants; the way you can synthesize antidotes and vaccines. You could be very useful, working on a new world—like this one."

Jary gaped at him. "What do you m-m—" he bit his lips —"mean?"

"Is there any way Orr would be willing to let you work for some other group?"

Jary sat silently while his disbelief faded through suspicion into nothing. His mouth formed the imitation of a smile that Corouda had seen before. "It cost too much to make me a b-biochemical miracle, Warden. You couldn't afford me . . . unless Orr disowned me. Then I'd be nobody's—or anybody's."

"You mean, he could just let you go? And you'd be free?"

"Free." Jary's mouth twitched. "If I m-made him mad enough, I guess he would."

"My God, then why haven't you made him mad enough?"

Jary pulled his hands up impassively to his chest. "Some people like to l-look at my scars, Warden. If I didn't belong to a research institute, they could do more than just look. They could do anything they wanted to. . . ."

Corouda searched for words, and picked a burr from the dark-brown sleeve of his shirt.

Jary shifted on the rock, shifted again. "Simeu Institute protects me. And Orr n-needs me. I'd have to make him angrier than he ever has been before he'd throw me out." He met Corouda's eyes again, strangely resentful.

"Piper!"

Jary stood up in sudden reflex at the sound of Orr's voice. Corouda saw that he looked relieved, and realized that relief was the main emotion in his own mind. Hell, even if Orr would sell Jary, or loan him, or disown him—how did he know the other wardens would accept it? Xena might, if she was willing to act on her rhetoric. But Albe wasn't even apologetic about causing Jary to fall. . . .

Jary had gone past him without a word, starting back toward Orr's lab.

"Jary!" Corouda called after him suddenly. "I still think

Piper Alvarian Jary deserved to be punished. But I think they're punishing the wrong man."

Jary stopped and turned back to look at him. And Corouda realized that the expression on his face was not gratitude, but something closer to hatred.

"All right, you're safely across. I'll wait here for you."

Jary stood alone in the darkness on the far side of the Split, pinned in the beam of Orr's headlamp. He nodded, breathing hard, unsure of his voice.

"You know your way from here, and what to do. Go and do it." Orr's voice was cutting; Orr was angry again, because Etchamendy had supported Soong-Hyacin's complaint.

Jary reached down for the carrying case at his feet. He shut his eyes as he used his hand, twitched the strap hurriedly up onto his shoulder. He turned his back on Orr without answering and started on into the cave.

"Don't come back without them!"

Jary bit down on the taste of unaccustomed fury and kept walking. Orr was sending him into the cave totally alone to bring back more trogs, to complete his penance. As if his stiffened, bandaged hands weren't enough to convince him how much of a fool he'd been. He had lost half his supper on the ground because his hands could barely hold a spoon . . . he would catch hell for his clumsy lab work tomorrow . . . he couldn't even have the comfort of touching his stones. Orr didn't give a damn if he broke both his legs, and had to crawl all the way to the cave's heart and back . . . Orr didn't care if he broke his neck, or drowned in radioactive mud—

Jary stopped suddenly in the blackness. What was wrong with him; why did he feel like this—? He looked back, falling against the wall as the crazy dance of his headlamp made him dizzy. There was no echoing beam of light; Orr was already beyond sight. Deliberately he tightened his hands, startling himself back into reason with a curse. Orr wouldn't have made him do this if he thought it would get him killed; Orr hated waste.

Jary pushed himself away from the wall, looking down at the patches of dried mud that still caked his suit. Most of it had fallen off as he walked; his dosimeters barely registered what was left. He started on, moving more slowly, picking his way across the rubble where the ledge narrowed. After all, he wasn't in any hurry to bring back more trogs; to let Orr prove all over again how futile it had been to turn them loose . . . how futile his own suffering had been; how futile everything was—

And all at once he understood. It was Corouda. "Corouda—!" He threw the word like a challenge into the blackness. That damned Corouda was doing this to him. Corouda, who had done the real act of torture . . . that bastard Corouda, who had pretended interest to draw him out, and then used false pity like a scalpel on his sanity: telling him that just because he couldn't remember his crimes, he was guiltless; that he was being punished for no reason. Trying to make him believe that he had suffered years of hatred and abuse for nothing. No, he was guilty, guilty! And Corouda had done it to him because Corouda was like all the rest. The whole universe hated him; except for Orr. Orr was all he had. And Orr had told him to bring the trogs, or else— He slipped unexpectedly and fell down, going to his elbows to save his hands. Orr was all he had. . . .

Isthp: We must make the shining mobile understand us. How shall we do it, *Mng*? They do not sense our communication.
   (Thin darkness)

Mng: But they see us. We must show them an artifact . . . a pressure suit, perhaps; to reveal our level of technology, and our plight, together.
   (Mudpools vibrate with escaping gases)
    (Patterns of light)

Isthp: Exactly! I will rouse my second Nimble; it is my smallest, perhaps it can still wear a suit . . . *I summon* . . .
   (Find the suit, and bear it upward)
    (Weave the circle together)

Ahm: We will not allow you to do this. We are the majority; we forbid contact with the alien's mobile. We will stop you if you try it.
   (Cold fluid lapping basalt)

Isthp: But its sessile is a creature of good will; even you must admit that, *Ahm*—it set your mobiles free.
   (My patterns are subtle)
    (Pulse softly and glow)

Ahm: *I saw great shining fingers reaching toward me . . . fear, hope . . . to set my mobiles free . . .* But the thing we must communicate is that we wish to be left alone! Let us use the shining mobile as a warning, if the aliens return again. It can make the invisible aliens visible, and let us flee in time.
   (Draw in the circle)
      (Draw in)
         (Strange radiance)

Mng: No, we must ask more! Show it that we are an intelligent life form, however alien. We must seek its help to rescue us from this forsaken place!
   (Close the net)
      (Mobiles draw in)
         (A light in the darkness)

Ahm, Scwa, Tfod, Zhek: No. No.
   (Radiance, strange light)

Isthp: Yes, beloved friend Mng—we will have our freedom, and the stars: Look, look with all your mobiles; it shows itself! It shines—
   (Strange radiance)
      (Light flickering like gamma through galena)
         (Hurry! Bear the suit upward)

Ahm: The shining one returns! Take care, take care—
   (Patches of radiance flowing closer)

Blir: Break the pattern, prepare to flee. Make its light our warning.
   (It shines)
      (Prepare for flight)
         (Prepare)

Mng: Make it our hope!
   (Patches of radiance)
      (It shines)

Echoes of his fall came back to Jary from a sudden distance; he guessed that he must be close to the main chamber already. He climbed to his feet, unable to crawl, and eased past the slick patch of metallic ore. It flashed silver in his light as he looked down, making him squint. The red path-markers fell away beyond it; he fumbled his way down the rough incline, half sliding, feeling the ceiling arch and the walls withdraw around him.

Here in the main chamber a firm, ore-veined surface of basalt flowed to meet the water surface of the radioactive depths; here they had found the trogs. He passed a slender pillar bristling with spines of rose quartz, touched one with the back of his hand as he passed. In the distance he saw the glimmer of the water's edge, rising tendrils of steam. His stomach tightened, but he was barely aware of it: in the nearer distance the filigree of ore-veins netted light—and a cluster of trogs lay together on the shore. He swept the surface with his headlamp, saw another cluster, and another, and another, their blind, helpless forms moving sedately in a bizzare mimickry of ritual dance.

He had never had the chance to stand and watch them; and so he did, now. And the frightening conviction began to fill his mind that he was seeing something that went beyond instinct; something beyond his comprehension. But they were just animals! Even if they cared about what happened to their fellow creatures; even though they had risked death to perform a rescue . . . it was only instinct.

He began to move toward them, trying to flex his bandaged fingers, trying not to imagine the pain when he tried to keep his hold on a squirming trog body. . . . He stopped again, frowning, as the trogs' rhythmic dance suddenly broke apart. The small clumps of bodies aligned, turning almost as one to face him, as if they could see him. But that was impossible, he knew they couldn't see a human—

A dozen trogs skittered back and disappeared into the pool; the rest milled, uncertain. He stopped, still five meters up the bank. They were staring at him, he was sure of it, except that they seemed to be staring at his knees, as if he were only half there. He risked one step, and then another—and all but two clumps of trogs fled into the pool. He stood still, in the beginnings of desperation, and waited.

His numb body had begun to twitch impatiently before another trog moved. But this time it moved forward. The rest began to creep toward him then, slowly, purposefully. They ringed his feet, staring up at his knees with the moon-eyed reverence of worshipers. He went down carefully onto one knee, and then the other; the trogs slithered back. They came forward again as he made no further motion, their rudderlike hindquarters dripping mud. They came on until they reached his knees, and began to pluck at his muddy suit legs. He held himself like a statue, trying to imagine their purpose with a mind that had gone uselessly blank. Long, webbed fingers grasped his suit, and two of the trogs began to climb up him, smearing the suit with fresh mud. He did not use his hands to pull them off, even though his body shuddered with his awareness of their clinging forms. The dials inside his helmet began to flicker and climb.

He shut his eyes—"L-leave me alone!"—opened them again, after a long moment.

Almost as if they had heard him, the trogs had let go and dropped away. They all squatted again in front of him, gazing now at his mud-slimed chest. He realized finally that it must be the radioactive mud they saw—that made his suit shine with a light they could see. Were they trying, in some clumsy way, to discover what he was? He laughed softly, raggedly. "I'm P-piper Alvarian Jary!"

And it didn't matter. The name meant nothing to them. The trogs went on watching him, unmoved. Jary looked away at last as another trog emerged from the pool. He stared as the mud slid from its skin; its skin was like nothing he had ever seen on a trog, luminous silver reflecting his light. The skin bagged and pulled taut in awkward, afunctional ways as it moved, and it moved with difficulty. All the trogs were staring at it now; and as he tried to get to his feet and move closer, they slithered ahead of him to surround the silver one themselves. Then abruptly more trogs swarmed at the edge of the pool; he watched in confusion as the mass of them attacked the silver trog, forcing it back into the mudpool, sweeping the few who resisted with it.

Jary stood waiting in the darkness while seconds became minutes, but the trogs did not return. Bubbles of escaping gas formed ripple-rings to shatter along the empty shore, but nothing else moved the water surface. He crouched down, staring at the tracks of wet mud where the trogs had been, staring down at his own muddy suit.

They weren't coming back; he was sure of that now. But why not? What was the silver trog, and why hadn't he seen one before? Why had the others attacked it? Or had they only been protecting it, from him?

Maybe they had suddenly realized what he was: not Piper Alvarian Jary, but one of the invisible monsters who attacked them without warning.

And he had let them get away. Why, when they had climbed his suit, begging to be plucked off and dropped into his box——? But they had come to him in trust; they had put themselves into his hands, not knowing him for what he was.

Not knowing him . . .

And from that moment he knew that he would never tell Orr about the rescue, or the dance, or the silver trog—or the way the trogs had gathered, gazing up at him. Their secret life would be safe with him . . . all their lives would be safe with him. He touched his muddy suit. Inadvertently they had shown him the way to make sure they could be warned whenever he came again with Orr. Maybe, if he was lucky, Orr would never see another trog. . . . Jary closed his hands, hardening his resolution. Damn Orr! It would serve him right.

But what if Orr found out what he'd done? Orr might even disown him, for that: abandon him here. . . . But somehow the thought did not frighten him, now. Nothing they could do to him really mattered, now—because his decision had nothing to do with his life among men, where he lived only to pay and pay on a debt that he could never repay. No matter how much he suffered, in the universe of men he carried the mark of Cain, and he would never stop being Piper Alvarian Jary.

But here in this alien universe his crime did not exist. He could prove what he could never prove in his own world, that he was as free to make the right choice as the wrong one. Whatever happened to him from now on, it could never take away the knowledge that somewhere he had been a savior, and not a devil: a light in the darkness. . . .

Jary got to his feet and started back up the slope, carrying an empty cage.

Afterword

"To Bell the Cat" is one of those stories that mutate as they develop. In the beginning I was intrigued by the old anecdote in which mice try to bell a cat so that it can't creep up on them unawares. The story usually involves a certain mouse who is delegated to do the deed, and how that "Jack the Giant-Killer" mouse does it without becoming the cat's dinner. My original premise was about tiny aliens attempting to protect themselves from the huge humans who were in essence the "cats" of the story. But somewhere along the way I realized that in order to bell the cat you really need to enlist the cat's cooperation. The mutant seed was sown, and at that point the character of Jary, the Catspaw, the tool of other human beings (as a cat is a tool), began to grow—a cat who for his own reasons might choose to side with the mice. As I worked with Jary's character, he began to take over the story; some characters are "born" with innately strong personalities that affect the story they're in in unpredictable ways. In this case Jary's relationships with the aliens and the other humans became more important than the direct interface between the humans and the aliens. As a result the story turned downbeat, and became a more serious exploration of the ambiguities of right and wrong, the nature of justice and punishment, guilt and redemption. In the end Jary must make his own separate peace . . . because ultimately we are all our own Higher Authority.

"To Bell the Cat," apart from being Jary's story, is still a story of alien contact, however. And as such it is really one of my most illusive stories. I have yet to meet anyone who fully understood the concept of how the aliens functioned—a fact which has been very disappointing to me. Writers and fans often get into discussions about truly alien behavior, the complaint usually being that many so-called aliens in the literature are really no more than human beings wearing funny suits—in effect, they behave exactly like human beings, not in a truly alien way. But in attempting to create beings who *are* really alien, a writer runs the risk of simply making them incomprehensible to the reader. That may have been the case with these aliens . . . and so a few words of explanation are probably called for:

The aliens in "To Bell the Cat" are masterpieces of genetic specialization. There are countless examples of specialization on Earth. Spider monkeys have no thumbs; their thumbs atrophied and disappeared because the digit only got in the way when they were swinging through the trees. Giraffes evolved long necks for getting at foliage that other animals couldn't reach. Carnivores and herbivores, hooves and fingernails and claws, all are examples of nature's genetic engineering. The aliens in this story have carried the trend toward specialization to an extreme—they have adapted to a highly radioactive environment; and their "sessiles" are essentially their brains, which remain stable and protected while their various "mobiles" or body parts (which have different basic functions, depending on their general body design) are totally independent. Free to range far afield, guided by autonomous but very primitive brains, the mobiles are in continuous "radio" contact with the sessiles, sending and receiving data constantly. The sessiles have levels of concentration that would boggle a human mind, allowing them to communicate with one another while at the same time controlling their various mobiles. Breeding new body parts is a relatively simple process and a rather esoteric pastime for the aliens; but actually recreating themselves—creating a new consciousness—is a much more complex process, and it was this ritual which the humans were inadvertently disrupting.

"To Bell the Cat" is also one of my most obscure stories in another sense—I know of people who have gotten into arguments because most of them had never seen it, and swore that I'd never written a story by that name. I'm pleased to have it more widely available at last.

View from a Height

SATURDAY, THE 7TH
I want to know why those pages were missing! How am I supposed to keep up with my research if they leave out pages—?

(Long sighing noise.)

Listen to yourself, Emmylou: You're listening to the sound of fear. It was an oversight, you know that. Nobody did it to you on purpose. Relax, you're getting Fortnight Fever. Tomorrow you'll get the pages, and an apology too, if Harvey Weems knows what's good for him.

But still, five whole pages; and the table of contents. How could you miss *five* pages? And the table of contents.

How do I know there hasn't been a coup? The Northwest's finally taken over completely, and they're censoring the media—and like the Man without a Country, everything they send me from now on is going to have holes cut in it.

In *Science?*

Or maybe Weems has decided to drive me insane—?

Oh, my God . . . it would be a short trip. Look at me. I don't have any fingernails left.

("Arrwk. Hello, beautiful. Hello? Hello?")

("Ozymandias! Get out of my hair, you devil." Laughter. "Polly want a cracker? Here . . . gently! That's a boy.")

It's beautiful when he flies. I never get tired of watching him, or looking at him, even after twenty years. Twenty years . . . What did the Psittacidae do, to win the right to wear a rainbow as their plumage? Although the way we've hunted them for it, you could say it was a mixed blessing. Like some other things.

Twenty years. How strange it sounds to hear those words, and know they're true. There are gray hairs when I look in the mirror. Wrinkles starting. And Weems is bald! Bald as an egg, and all squinty behind his spectacles. How did we get

74

that way, without noticing it? Time is both longer and shorter than you think, and usually all at once.

Twelve days is a long time to wait for somebody to return your call. Twenty years is a long time gone. But I feel somehow as though it was only last week that I left home. I keep the circuits clean, going over them and over them, showing those mental home movies until I could almost step across, sometimes, into that other reality. But then I always look down, and there's that tremendous abyss full of space and time, and I realize I can't, again. You can't go home again.

Especially when you're almost one thousand astronomical units out in space. Almost there, the first rung of the ladder. Next Thursday is the day. Oh, that bottle of champagne that's been waiting for so long. Oh, the parallax view! I have the equal of the best astronomical equipment in all of near-Earth space at my command, and a view of the universe that no one has ever had before; and using them has made me the only astrophysicist ever to win a Ph.D. in deep space. Talk about your field work.

Strange to think that if the Forward Observatory had massed less than its thousand-plus tons, I would have been replaced by a machine. But because the installation is so large, I in my infinite human flexibility, even with my infinite human appetite, become the most efficient legal tender. And the farther out I get the more important my own ability to judge what happens, and respond to it, becomes. The first—and maybe the last—manned interstellar probe, on a one-way journey into infinity . . . into a universe unobscured by our own system's gases and dust . . . equipped with eyes that see everything from gamma to ultra-long wavelengths, and ears that listen to the music of the spheres.

And Emmylou Stewart, the captive audience. Adrift on a star . . . if you hold with the idea that all the bits of inert junk drifting through space, no matter how small, have star potential. Dark stars, with brilliance in their secret hearts, only kept back from letting it shine by Fate, which denied them the critical mass to reach their kindling point.

Speak of kindling: the laser beam just arrived to give me my daily boost, moving me a little faster, so I'll reach a little deeper into the universe. Blue sky at bedtime; I always was a night person. I'm sure they didn't design the solar sail to filter light like the sky . . . but I'm glad it happened to work out that way. Sky-blue was always my passion—the color, texture, fluid purity of it. This color isn't exactly right; but it doesn't matter, because I can't remember how any more. This sky is a sun-catcher. A big blue parasol. But so was the original, from where I used to stand. The sky is a blue parasol . . . did anyone ever say that before, I wonder? If anyone knows, speak up—

Is anyone even listening? Will anyone ever be?

("Who cares, anyway? Come on, Ozzie—climb aboard. Let's drop down to the observation porch while I do my meditation, and try to remember what days were like.")

Weems, damn it, I want satisfaction!

SUNDAY, THE 8TH

That idiot. That intolerable moron—how could he do that to me? After all this time, wouldn't you think he'd know me better than that? To keep me waiting for twelve days, wondering and afraid: twelve days of all the possible stupid paranoias I could weave with my idle hands and mind, making myself miserable, asking for trouble—

And then giving it to me. God, he must be some kind of sadist. If I could only reach him, and hurt him the way I've hurt these past hours—

Except that I know the news wasn't his fault, and that he didn't mean to hurt me . . . and so I can't even ease my pain by projecting it onto him.

I don't know what I would have done if his image hadn't been six days stale when it got here. What would I have done, if he'd been in earshot when I was listening; what would I have said? Maybe no more than I did say.

What can you say, when you realize you've thrown your whole life away?

He sat there behind his faded blotter, twiddling his pen, picking up his souvenir moon rocks and laying them down— looking for all the world like a man with a time bomb in his desk drawer—and said, "Now don't worry, Emmylou. There's no problem . . ." Went on saying it, one way or another, for five minutes; until I was shouting, "What's *wrong*, damn it?"

"I thought you'd never even notice the few pages . . ." with that sidling smile of his.

And while I'm muttering, "I may have been in solitary confinement for twenty years, Harvey, but it hasn't turned my brain to mush," he said, "So maybe I'd better explain, first—" and the look on his face; oh, the look on his face. "There's been a biomed breakthrough. If you were here on Earth, you . . . well, your body's immune responses could be

. . . made normal . . ." And then he looked down, as though he could really see the look on my own face.

Made normal. Made normal. It's all I can hear. I was born with no natural immunities. No defense against disease. No help for it. No. *No, no, no,* that's all I ever heard, all my life on Earth. Through the plastic walls of my sealed room; through the helmet of my sealed suit. . . . And now it's all changed. They could cure me. But I can't go home. I knew this could happen; I knew it had to happen someday. But I chose to ignore that fact, and now it's too late to do anything about it.

Then why can't I forget that I could have been f-free. . . .

. . . I didn't answer Weems today. Screw Weems. There's nothing to say. Nothing at all.

I'm so tired.

MONDAY, THE 9TH

Couldn't sleep. It kept playing over and over in my mind. . . . Finally took some pills. Slept all day, feel like hell. Stupid. And it didn't go away. It was waiting for me, still waiting, when I woke up.

It isn't fair—!

I don't feel like talking about it.

TUESDAY, THE 10TH

Tuesday, already. I haven't done a thing for two days. I haven't even started to check out the relay beacon, and that damn thing has to be dropped off this week. I don't have any strength; I can't seem to move, I just sit. But I have to get back to work. Have to . . .

Instead I read the printout of the article today. Hoping I'd find a flaw! If that isn't the greatest irony of my entire life. For two decades I prayed that somebody would find a cure for me. And for two more decades I didn't care. Am I going to spend the next two decades hating it, now that it's been found?

No . . . hating myself. I could have been free, they could have cured me; if only I'd stayed on Earth. If only I'd been patient. But now it's too late . . . by twenty *years*.

I want to go home. I want to go home. . . . But you can't go home again. Did I really say that, so blithely, so recently? *You* can't: You, Emmylou Stewart. You are in prison, just as you have always been in prison.

It's all come back to me so strongly. Why me? Why must I

be the ultimate victim? In all my life I've never smelled the sea wind, or plucked berries from a bush and eaten them, right there! Or felt my parents' kisses against my skin, or a man's body. . . . Because to me they were all deadly things.

I remember when I was a little girl, and we still lived in Victoria—I was just three or four, just at the brink of understanding that I was the only prisoner in my world. I remember watching my father sit polishing his shoes in the morning, before he left for the museum. And me smiling, so deviously, "Daddy . . . I'll help you do that, if you let me come out—"

And he came to the wall of my bubble and put his arms into the hugging gloves, and said, so gently, "No." And then he began to cry. And I began to cry too, because I didn't know why I'd made him unhappy. . . .

And all the children at school, with their "spaceman" jokes, pointing at the freak; all the years of insensitive people asking the same stupid questions every time I tried to go out anywhere . . . worst of all, the ones who weren't stupid, or insensitive. Like Jeffrey . . . no, I will not think about Jeffrey! I couldn't let myself think about him then. I could never afford to get close to a man, because I'd never be able to touch him. . . .

And now it's too late. Was I controlling my fate, when I volunteered for this one-way trip? Or was I just running away from a life where I was always helpless; helpless to escape the things I hated, helpless to embrace the things I loved?

I pretended this was different, and important . . . but was that really what I believed? No! I just wanted to crawl into a hole I couldn't get out of, because I was so afraid.

So afraid that one day I would unseal my plastic walls, or take off my helmet and my suit; walk out freely to breathe the air, or wade in a stream, or touch flesh against flesh . . . and die of it.

So now I've walled myself into this hermetically sealed tomb for a living death. A perfectly sterile environment, in which my body will not even decay when I die. Never having really lived, I shall never really die, dust to dust. A perfectly sterile environment; in every sense of the word.

I often stand looking at my body in the mirror after I take a shower. Hazel eyes, brown hair in thick waves with hardly any gray . . . and a good figure; not exactly stacked, but not unattractive. And no one has ever seen it that way but me. Last night I had the Dream again . . . I haven't had it for such a long time . . . this time I was sitting on a carved wooden beast in the park beside the Provincial Museum in Victoria; but not as a child in my suit. As a college girl, in white shorts and a bright cotton shirt, feeling the sun on my shoulders, and—Jeffrey's arms around my waist. . . . We stroll along the bayside hand in hand, under the Victorian lamp posts with their bright hanging flower-baskets, and everything I do is fresh and spontaneous and full of the moment. But always, always, just when he holds me in his arms at last, just as I'm about to . . . I wake up.

When we die, do we wake out of reality at last, and all our dreams come true? When I die . . . I will be carried on and on into the timeless depths of uncharted space in this computerized tomb, unmourned and unremembered. In time all the atmosphere will seep away; and my fair corpse, lying like Snow White's in inviolate sleep, will be sucked dry of moisture, until it is nothing but a mummified parchment of shriveled leather and bulging bones. . . .

("Hello? Hello, baby? Good night. Yes, no, maybe. . . . Awk. Food time!")

("Oh, Ozymandias! Yes, yes, I know . . . I haven't fed you, I'm sorry. I know, I know . . .")

(Clinks and rattles.)

Why am I so selfish? Just because I can't eat, I expect him to fast, too. . . . No. I just forgot.

He doesn't understand, but he knows something's wrong; he climbs the lamp pole like some tripodal bem, using both feet and his beak, and stares at me with that glass-beady bird's eye, stares and stares and mumbles things. Like a lunatic! Until I can hardly stand not to shut him in a cupboard, or something. But then he sidles along my shoulder and kisses me—such a tender caress against my cheek, with that hooked prehensile beak that could crush a walnut like a grape—to let me know that he's worried, and he cares. And I stroke his feathers to thank him, and tell him that it's all right . . . but it's not. And he knows it.

Does he ever resent his life? Would he, if he could? Stolen away from his own kind, raised in a sterile bubble to be a caged bird for a caged human. . . .

I'm only a bird in a gilded cage. I want to go home.

WEDNESDAY, THE 11TH

Why am I keeping this journal? Do I really believe that sometime some alien being will find this, or some starship from Earth's glorious future will catch up to me . . . glorious future, hell. Stupid, selfish, short-sighted fools. They ripped the guts out of the space program after they sent me away, no one will ever follow me now. I'll be lucky if they don't declare me dead and forget about me.

As if anyone would care what a woman all alone on a lumbering space probe thought about day after day for decades, anyway. What monstrous conceit.

I did lubricate the bearings on the big scope today. I did that much. I did it so that I could turn it back toward Earth . . . toward the sun . . . toward the whole damn system. Because I can't even see it. All the planets out to Saturn, all the planets the ancients saw, are crammed into the space of two moon diameters; and too dim and small and faraway below me for my naked eyes, anyway. Even the sun is no more than a gaudy star that doesn't even make me squint. So I looked for them with the scope. . . .

Isn't it funny how when you're a child you see all those drawings and models of the solar system with big, lumpy planets and golden wakes streaming around the sun. Somehow you never get over expecting it to look that way in person. And here I am, one thousand astronomical units north of the solar pole, gazing down from a great height . . . and it doesn't look that way at all. It doesn't look like anything; even through the scope. One great blot of light, and all the pale tiny diamond chips of planets and moons around it, barely distinguishable from half a hundred undistinguished stars trapped in the same arc of blackness. So meaningless, so insignificant . . . so disappointing.

Five hours I spent, today, listening to my journal, looking back and trying to find—something, I don't know, something I suddenly don't have anymore.

I had it at the start. I was disgusting; Pollyanna Grad-student skipping and singing through the rooms of my very own observatory. It seemed like heaven, and a lifetime spent in it couldn't possibly be long enough for all that I was going to accomplish, and discover. I'd never be bored, no, not me. . . .

And there was so much to learn about the potential of this place, before I got out to where it supposedly would matter, and there would be new things to turn my wonderful extended senses toward . . . while I could still communicate easily with my dear mentor Dr. Weems, and the world. (Who'd ever have thought, when the lecherous old goat was my thesis adviser at Harvard, and making jokes to his other grad students about "the lengths some women will go to protect their virginity," that we would have to spend a lifetime together.)

There was Ozymandias' first word . . . and my first birthday in space, and my first anniversary . . . and my doctoral degree at last, printed out by the computer with scrolls made of little x's and taped up on the wall. . . .

Then day and night and day and night, beating me black and blue with blue and black . . . my fifth anniversary, my eighth, my decade. I crossed the magnetopause, to become truly the first voyager in interstellar space . . . but by then there was no one left to *talk* to anymore, to really share the experience with. Even the radio and television broadcasts drifting out from Earth were diffuse and rare; there were fewer and fewer contacts with the reality outside. The plodding routines, the stupifying boredom—until sometimes I stood screaming down the halls just for something new; listening to the echoes that no one else would ever hear, and pretending they'd come to call; trying so hard to believe there was something to hear that wasn't *my* voice, *my* echo, or Ozymandias making a mockery of it.

("*Hello, beautiful. That's a crock. Hello, hello?*")

("Ozymandias, get *away* from me—")

But always I had that underlying belief in my mission: that I was here for a purpose, for more than my own selfish reasons, or NASA's (or whatever the hell they call it now), but for Humanity, and Science. Through meditation I learned the real value of inner silence, and thought that by creating an inner peace I had reached equilibrium with the outer silences. I thought that meditation had disciplined me, I was in touch with myself and with the soul of the cosmos. . . . But I haven't been able to meditate since—it happened. The inner silence fills up with my own anger screaming at me, until I can't remember what peace sounds like.

And what have I really discovered, so far? Almost nothing. Nothing worth wasting my analysis or all my fine theories—or my freedom—on. Space is even emptier than anyone dreamed, you could count on both hands the bits of cold dust or worldlet I've passed in all this time, lost souls falling helplessly through near-perfect vacuum . . . all of us together. With my absurdly long astronomical tapemeasure I have fixed precisely the distance to NGC 2419 and a few other features, and from that made new estimates about a few more distant ones. But I have not detected a miniature black hole insatiably vacuuming up the vacuum; I have not pierced the invisible clouds that shroud the ultra-long wavelengths like fog; I have not discovered that life exists beyond the Earth in even the most tentative way. Looking back at the solar system I see nothing to show definitively that we even exist, anymore. All I hear anymore when I scan is electromagnetic noise, no coherent thought. Only Weems every twelfth night, like the last man alive. . . . Christ, I still haven't answered him.

Why bother? Let him sweat. Why bother with any of it? Why waste my precious time?

Oh, my precious time. . . . Half a lifetime left that could have been mine, on Earth.

Twenty years—I came through them all all right. I thought I was safe. And after twenty years, my facade of discipline and self-control falls apart at a touch. What a self-deluded hypocrite I've been. Do you know that I said the sky was like a blue parasol eighteen years ago? And probably said it again fifteen years ago, and ten, and five—

Tomorrow I pass 1000 AUs.

THURSDAY, THE 12TH

I burned out the scope. I burned out the scope. I left it pointing toward the Earth, and when the laser came on for the night it shone right down the scope's throat and burned it out. I'm so ashamed. . . . Did I do it on purpose, subconsciously?

(*"Good night starlight. Arrk. Good night. Good . . ."*)

("Damn it, I want to hear another human voice—!")

(*Echoing, "voice, voice, voice, voice, voice . . ."*)

When I found out what I'd done I ran away. I ran and ran through the halls. . . . But I only ran in a circle: This observatory, my prison, myself . . . I can't escape. I'll always come back in the end, to this green-walled room with its desk and its terminals, its cupboards crammed with a hundred thousand dozens of everything, toilet paper and magnetic tape and oxygen tanks. . . . And I can tell you exactly how many steps it is to my bedroom or how long it took me to crochet the afghan on the bed . . . how long I've sat in the dark and silence, setting up an exposure program or listening for the feeble pulse of a radio galaxy two billion light-years away. There will never be anything different, or anything more.

When I finally came back here, there was a message waiting. Weems, grinning out at me half-bombed from the screen—"Congratulations," he cried, "on this historic occasion! Emmylou, we're having a little celebration here at the lab; mind if we join you in yours, one thousand astronomical units from home—?" I've never seen him drunk. They really must have meant to do something nice for me, planning it all six days ahead. . . .

To celebrate I shouted obscenities I didn't even know I knew at him, until my voice was broken and my throat was raw.

Then I sat at my desk for a long time with my jackknife lying open in my hand. Not wanting to die—I've always been too afraid of death for that—but wanting to hurt myself. I wanted to make a fresh hurt, to take my attention off the terrible thing that is sucking me into my self like an imploding star. Or maybe just to punish myself, I don't know. But I considered the possibility of actually cutting myself quite calmly; while some separate part of me looked on in horror. I even pressed the knife against my flesh . . . and then I stopped and put it away. It hurts too much.

I can't go on like this. I have duties, obligations, and I can't face them. What would I do without the emergency automechs? . . . But it's the rest of my life, and they can't go on doing my job for me forever—

Later.

I just had a visitor. Strange as that sounds. Stranger yet—it was Donald Duck. I picked up half of a children's cartoon show today, the first coherent piece of nondirectional, unbeamed television broadcast I've recorded in months. And I don't think I've ever been happier to see anyone in my life. What a nice surprise, so glad you could drop by. . . . Ozymandias loves him; he hangs upside down from his swing under the cabinet with a cracker in one foot, cackling away and saying, "Give us a kiss, *smack-smack-smack*". . . . We watched it three times. I even smiled, for a while; until I remembered myself. It helps. Maybe I'll watch it again until bedtime.

FRIDAY, THE 13TH

Friday the Thirteenth. Amusing. Poor Friday the Thirteenth, what did it ever do to deserve its reputation? Even if it had any power to make my life miserable, it couldn't hold a candle to the rest of this week. It seems like an eternity since last weekend.

I repaired the scope today; replaced the burned-out parts.

Had to suit up and go outside for part of the work . . . I haven't done any outside maintenance for quite a while. Odd how both exhilarating and terrifying it always is when I first step out of the airlock, utterly alone, into space. You're entirely on your own, so far away from any possibility of help, so far away from anything at all. And at that moment you doubt yourself, suddenly, terribly . . . just for a moment.

But then you drag your umbilical out behind you and clank along the hull in your magnetized boots that feel so reassuringly like lead ballast. You turn on the lights and look for the trouble, find it and get to work; it doesn't bother you anymore. . . . When your life seems to have torn loose and be drifting free, it creates a kind of sea anchor to work with your hands; whether it's doing some mindless routine chore or the most intricate of repairs.

There was a moment of panic, when I actually saw charred wires and melted metal, when I imagined the damage was so bad that I couldn't repair it again. It looked so final, so— masterful. I clung there by my feet and whimpered and clenched my hands inside my gloves, like a great shining baby, for a while. But then I pulled myself down and began to pry here and unscrew there and twist a component free . . . and little by little I replaced everything. One step at a time; the way we get through life.

By the time I'd finished I felt quite calm, for the first time in days; the thing that's been trying to choke me to death this past week seemed to falter a little at my demonstration of competence. I've been breathing easier since then; but I still don't have much strength. I used up all I had just overcoming my own inertia.

But I shut off the lights and hiked around the hull for a while, afterward—I couldn't face going back inside just then: looking at the black convex dish of the solar sail I'm embedded in, up at the radio antenna's smaller dish occluding stars as the observatory's cylinder wheels endlessly at the hub of the spinning parasol. . . .

That made me dizzy, and so I looked out into the starfields that lie on every side. Even with my own poor, unaugmented senses there's so much more to see out here, unimpeded by atmosphere or dust, undominated by any sun's glare. The brilliance of the Milky Way, the depths of star and nebula and farthest galaxy breathlessly suspended . . . as I am. The realization that I'm lost for eternity in an uncharted sea.

Strangely, although that thought aroused a very powerful

emotion when it struck me, it wasn't a negative one at all: It was from another scale of values entirely; like the universe itself. It was as if the universe itself stretched out its finger to touch me. And in touching me, singling me out, it only heightened my awareness of my own insignificance.

That was somehow very comforting. When you confront the absolute indifference of magnitudes and vistas so overwhelming, the swollen ego of your self-important suffering is diminished. . . .

And I remembered one of the things that was always so important to me about space—that here *any*one has to put on a spacesuit before they step outside. We're all aliens, no one better equipped to survive than another. I am as normal as anyone else, out here.

I must hold onto that thought.

SATURDAY, THE 14TH

There is a reason for my being here. There is a reason.

I was able to meditate earlier today. Not in the old way, the usual way, by emptying my mind. Rather by letting the questions fill up the space, not fighting them; letting them merge with my memories of all that's gone before. I put on music, that great mnemonic stimulator; letting the images that each tape evoked free-associate and interact.

And in the end I could believe again that my being here was the result of a free choice. No one forced me into this. My motives for volunteering were entirely my own. And I was given this position because NASA believed that I was more likely to be successful in it than anyone else they could have chosen.

It doesn't matter that some of my motives happened to be unresolved fear or wanting to escape from things I couldn't cope with. It really doesn't matter. Sometimes retreat is the only alternative to destruction, and only a madman can't recognize the truth of that. Only a madman . . . Is there anyone "sane" on Earth who isn't secretly a fugitive from something unbearable somewhere in their life? And yet they function normally.

If they ran, they ran toward something, too, not just away. And so did I. I had already chosen a career as an astrophysicist before I ever dreamed of being a part of this project. I could have become a medical researcher instead, worked on my own to find a cure for my condition. I could have grown up hating the whole idea of space and "spacemen," stumbling through life in my damned ugly sterile suit. . . .

But I remember when I was six years old, the first time I saw a film of suited astronauts at work in space . . . they looked just like me! And no one was laughing. How could I help but love space, then?

(And how could I help but love Jeffrey, with his night-black hair, and his blue flightsuit with the starry patch on the shoulder. Poor Jeffrey, poor Jeffrey, who never even realized his own dream of space before they cut the program out from under him. . . . I will not talk about Jeffrey. I will not.)

Yes, I could have stayed on Earth, and waited for a cure! I knew even then there would have to be one, someday. It was both easier and harder to choose space, instead of staying.

And I think the thing that really decided me was that those people had faith enough in me and my abilities to believe that I could run this observatory and my own life smoothly for as long as I lived. Billions of dollars and a thousand tons of equipment resting on me; like Atlas holding up his world.

Even Atlas tried to get rid of his burden; because no matter how vital his function was, the responsibility was still a burden to him. But he took his burden back again too, didn't he; for better or worse. . . .

I worked today. I worked my butt off getting caught up on a week's worth of data processing and maintenance, and I'm still not finished. Discovered while I was at it that Ozymandias had used those missing five pages just like the daily news: crapped all over them. My sentiments exactly! I laughed and laughed.

I think I may live.

SUNDAY, THE 15TH

The clouds have parted.

That's not rhetorical—among my fresh processed data is a series of photo reconstructions in the ultra-long wavelengths. And there's a gap in the obscuring gas up ahead of me, a break in the clouds that extends thirty or forty light-years. Maybe fifty! Fantastic. What a view. What a view I have from here of everything, with my infinitely extended vision: of the way ahead, of the passing scene—or looking back toward Earth.

Looking back. I'll never stop looking back, and wishing it could have been different. That at least there could have been two of me, one to be here, one who could have been normal, back on Earth; so I wouldn't have to be forever torn in two by regrets—

(*"Hello. What's up, doc? Avast!"*)

("Hey, watch it! If you drink, don't fly.")

Damn bird. . . . If I'm getting maudlin, it's because I had a party today. Drank a whole bottle of champagne. Yes; I had *the* party . . . we did. Ozymandias and I. Our private 1000 AU celebration. Better late than never, I guess. At least we did have something concrete to celebrate—the photos. And if the celebration wasn't quite as merry as it could have been, still I guess it will probably seem like it was when I look back on it from the next one, at 2000 AUs. They'll be coming faster now, the celebrations. I may even live to celebrate 8000. What the hell, I'll shoot for 10,000. . . .

After we finished the champagne . . . Ozymandias thinks '98 was a great year, thank God he can't drink as fast as I can . . . I put on my Strauss waltzes, and the *Barcarolle*: Oh, the Berliner Philharmonic; their touch is what a lover's kiss must be. I threw the view outside onto the big screen, a ballroom of stars, and danced with my shadow. And part of the time I wasn't dancing above the abyss in a jumpsuit and headphones, but waltzing in yards of satin and lace across a ballroom floor in nineteenth-century Vienna. What I wouldn't give to be *there* for a moment out of time. Not for a lifetime, or even a year, but just for an evening; just for one waltz.

Another thing I shall never do. There are so many things we can't do, any of us, for whatever the reasons—time, talent, life's callous whims. We're all on a one-way trip into infinity. If we're lucky we're given some life's work we care about, or some person. Or both, if we're very lucky.

And I do have Weems. Sometimes I see us like an old married couple, who have grown to a tolerant understanding over the years. We've never been soul mates, God knows, but we're comfortable with each others' silences. . . .

I guess it's about time I answered him.

Afterword

"View from a Height" came very neatly out of one paragraph in an *Analog* article. The article, written by Dr. Robert L. Forward, was about a manned astronomical observatory traveling on a one-way trip out of the solar system into space. In the article, Dr. Forward speculated briefly on what sort of person would choose to dedicate a lifetime to such a journey. This story was an attempt to answer that question.

Many writers can't talk about a new idea before the story is written because talking about the idea takes away the need to express it, and then the story itself never gets put on paper. I belong to the group of writers who actually *need* to talk about an idea—I find that the give-and-take of sharing it reveals possibilities I hadn't considered before; the feedback stimulates my creative processes. I talked about this story with Vernor—who has served as technical adviser and general editor on all of these stories, to one extent or another—and the basic idea of a woman with no immune responses came out of our discussions. (The parrot came about because I wanted her to have some form of companionship, and I wanted it to be lasting companionship. Since parrots are very long-lived, she had a good chance of having Ozymandias for life.) I'm fond of this story for a number of reasons, but particularly because I think there is a universality to Emmylou's crisis and her resolution of it. We are all on a one-way trip—there is really no going back for any of us. The only choice we really have is to make the best of whatever options the choices we've made already have left to us.

"View from a Height" is the first really successful short story I've written. My natural length seems to be longer—a "short" story for me tends to run somewhere between 15,000 and 25,000 words. An actual short story (of under 7,500 words) is probably the most difficult type of prose writing to do effectively; it requires a great deal of discipline and a lot of work to create characters and develop a setting so quickly. (That may be why I've shied away from it.) But on the other hand, story ideas do have natural lengths built into them—in order for a story to succeed, the basic idea has to be given its head to some extent, and not forced into a preset mold. A short story that has been overinflated into a novella is usually tedious, just as a novella squeezed into short-story length is disappointing, like a too-small helping of dessert. As I write I've begun to develop a sense of how long a story needs to be before I begin it. I felt that this idea was meant to be a short story, and the actual writing of it didn't resist that feeling. The end product was something I felt comfortable and right about, and relieved. (The writer's sixth sense is not always fail-safe, however. I just finished a "normal" 60,000-word novel—which in the end has come out closer to 200,000 words. Writing is nothing if not a learning experience.)

Media Man

The sound of silence filled the black and silver vacuum of the Mecca docking field, echoed from the winking distillery towers, the phosphorescently glowing storage sacks of gases, the insectoid forms of the looming cargo freighters. But it only filled the helmet of Chaim Dartagnan's suit by an effort of will, as his mind blocked the invidious clamor from the helmet's speakers:

"Demarch Siamang, Demarch Siamang—!"

"—true that you're going to—"

"What will you be bringing back?"

"—rescue the stranded—?"

"Hey, Dartagnan, c'mon, Red, give your ol' buddies a break!"

Dartagnan smiled, released the mooring rope to casually readjust his camera strap against his shoulder. *Eat your hearts out, bastards. Any one of you'd break my neck to be here instead of me.* He glanced back across the glaring, pitted gravel of the field. At the very front of the crowd of curious beyond the gate he saw the elbowing desperation of his fellow mediamen, cameras draped across the barrier; the security guard shoved them back with what looked like relish. Independents all, crawling all over each other to get at the big story, or the unique pitch, that would win the attention of a corporate head, and earn them a place in the ranks of a corporation's promotional crew. *There but for the grace of Siamang and Sons go I* . . . He had won, by flattering the hell out of Old Man Siamang; won the chance to prove his reporting and image-hyping skills as the only mediaman along on this (he saw it in rhetoric) History-Making Journey, a Daring Rescue by a Siamang Scion, a Philanthrophic Family's Mission of Mercy . . . *My ass*, Dartagnan thought. He saw the two corporate cameramen filming his passage, the colored armbands that made them Siamang's men; his stomach constricted over an unexpected pang of hope.

He glanced up, at the purity of blackness unmarred by atmosphere, at the stars. Somewhere below his feet, through kilometers of nearly solid rock, was the tiny, pale spinel of the sun Heaven. He would be seeing it again, soon enough—he focused on the looming grotesqueness tethered at the end of the mooring cable, bifurcated by the abrupt edge of the asteroid's horizon: the converted volatile freighter that would take them across the Main Belt, and on in, to Heaven's second planet, to pick up one man . . . and a treasure. The three jutting booms that kept its nuclear electric rockets suspended away from the living quarters clutched rigid cylinders instead of the usual flimsy volatiles sack; it carried a liquid-fuel rocket for their descent to the planet's surface.

The rest of the party was clustering now beneath the ship. He pulled himself along the final length of cable, unslung his camera and checked its pressure seal, plugged the recording jack into his suit's radio. He began to film, identifying one figure from another by the intricately colored geometric patternings on their suits. There was Old Man Siamang, praising the nobility of a single human life; no effort should be too great to save this man—and a salvage find that could benefit all the people of the Demarchy. . . . Dartagnan shook his head, behind his shielding faceplate. The Demarchy was an absolute democracy, and its philosophy was every man for himself, unless he got in the way of too many others . . . or he happened to have something too many others wanted.

Chaim knew, because it was his business to know, that a prospector had gotten himself stranded on Planet Two when his landing craft broke down. The prospector's radioed distress calls had been monitored; and knowing, like everyone else, that no one would come after him unless it was worth his while, he had revealed that he had found a considerable cache of prewar salvage items, including computer software that could streamline any distillery's volatile processing.

The distilleries were among the few of the small, independent corporations of the Demarchy to have the resources to send a ship in after him, and his discovery provided them with the motivation. Siamang and Sons had as much motivation as anyone, but they also had one crucial additional asset: they alone had the rocket engines available for a landing craft. And so Siamang and Sons would be in the first to reach Planet Two, making them most likely to get the rights to the prize as well.

Old Man Siamang had finished his speech, and the handful

of representatives of other distilleries responded with all the sincerity their silent applause implied. Sabu Siamang, the old man's son and heir, added a few words, equally insincere. *But great copy.* Siamang was sending his own son on a journey into the unknown, a landing on a world with not only a substantial gravity well, but also the unpredictability of an atmosphere. Maybe there was no one else Old Siamang would trust; but Dartagnan had heard it rumored that there were other reasons why the old man might want the future corporate head to face a little reality, and responsibility. Young Siamang said goodbye to his father—any resentment well disguised under a gracious respectfulness—and to his wife. Dartagnan felt surprise that a woman of her position had come out onto the surface, even for this short a time. Her voice was calm, self-assured, like her husband's. Chaim wondered whether she did it for appearance, or if she'd wanted to come; he felt another sharp, sudden emotion, ignored it, unsure even of what it was.

He filmed the ritual of cordial bowing, the leavetaking, the others going back across the field; filming and being filmed, he followed Sabu Siamang up into the waiting ship.

Dartagnan kicked free of his suit in the cramped alcove, with the unconscious grace of a man who had spent his whole life on planetoids where gravity was almost nonexistant. He pulled himself through the doorway into the control room, took in the instrument panels: Siamang leaned lightly against one, probing carelessly among the rows of dark buttons.

"Don't touch those! . . . please, Demarch Siamang." The soft, almost girlish voice had a cutting edge of irritation that dulled abruptly with remembered deference.

Dartagnan looked past Siamang in the dim half-light; saw the pilot, the third and final member of their expedition. *Just a kid,* he thought, startled: a slim boy in a dark, formless jumpsuit, with short sky-black hair; average height, his own height, maybe two meters. Epicanthic folds almost hooded the bad temper in the boy's dark, upturning eyes.

Siamang looked around, startled at the tone; an expression of not-quite-apology formed on his face. "Oh, sorry." A broad expanse of smile showed against his dark skin, darker hair. Dartagnan irrelevantly remembered animal faces frescoed on an antique table. (He had never seen any real animal larger than an insect; they were extreme rarities since the

Civil War.) Chaim was never sure of the color of Siamang's eyes, but only that they struck with the blinding intensity of a spotlight. He saw the pilot falter and look down. Siamang looked back at Dartagnan, relaxing. Chaim faced the blinding gaze easily, used to not-seeing a face. Siamang was in his mid-thirties, perhaps ten years older than Dartagnan himself, and the rich embroidery of his loose jacket, the precise tailoring of his tight breeches, the shine on his boots, were blinding in their own right. *The well-dressed demarch . . .* "You haven't met our pilot, have you? Mythili Fukinuki . . . Our token mediaman, Mythili—"

Something in Siamang's voice made the pilot's surname into a double double-entendre. Dartagnan looked back at the pilot, stared, as suspicion became realization. *My God, a woman—?* He didn't say it aloud; was grateful, as her eyes snapped up, burning with hostility. He had never seen a female pilot; they were as much of a rarity as a living animal. He realized belatedly that Siamang had not introduced him, apparently wasn't planning to. He wondered if Siamang had already forgotten his name. "Uh—my name's Chaim Dartagnan. My friends call me Red." He raised a hand, gestured at the auburn friz of his hair, above his own faded-brown skin.

The pilot categorized him with a look he had grown used to.

Siamang's easy laughter filled the uneasy space between them. "I didn't think mediamen had any friends."

Dartagnan matched the laughter, added a careful note of self-deprecation. "I guess I should've said 'acquaintances.'"

"Red, here, is up from the media ranks, Mythili. If he does a good job Dad's going to hire him permanently. So be nice to him; you may have to be seeing a lot more of him." He winked, and the pilot's expression changed slightly; Chaim estimated that the temperature in the room dropped ten degrees. "How does it feel, Red, to be up here now, instead of down there with the rest of the coprophage corps?"

Dartagnan laughed again, meaning it. "Real good, Boss. Just fine. I plan to make a habit of it."

"We're scheduled for departure in one kilosecond, Demarch Siamang," the pilot said. "Maybe you ought to check your cabin to make sure all your belongings are aboard. Just down the passageway—" She pointed at the hole in the middle of the floor, ringed by an aluminum guardrail.

"Good idea." Siamang pushed himself away from the

panel, moving by her as he half-drifted toward the well. "Good to be aboard, Fukinuki. . . ." His hand slid down over her buttocks in passing.

If looks could kill, we'd be dead men. Dartagnan studied the floor, waiting to be turned to stone.

"Well?"

He glanced up, not focusing.

"You have the crew's dormitory all to yourself. Do you want to check out your belongings or not?" She pointed again. She had moved out of range of the exit well.

He waved at his camera and sack of gear, at his own threadbare, unembellished jacket. "This's it; I travel light." He grinned ingratiatingly at nothing, got no response. "You know . . . uh . . . I have the same problem. Everybody's always asking me, 'Where's the Three Musketeers?' " It was a subject of morbid fascination to him that the most stupid and illiterate of men seemed somehow to have heard of that obscure Old World novel.

"I don't know what you're talking about." She drifted to the control panel, caught hold of a stabilizing strap, began to check readings.

"What's—"

"And before you ask, 'What's a nice girl like me doing in a job like this,' I'll tell you. It's because I want to be here. And yes, no, no, and no. Yes, I am sterile. No, I wasn't born that way. No, I'm not sorry I did it. And no, I did not get the job by agreeing to put out for my passengers—I got it because I'm a damn good pilot! . . . Any more questions, mediaman?"

"No . . . I guess that about covers them all." He raised his hands, palms out in surrender. "But actually," he lied, "I was only planning to ask if you'd mind my filming our departure on your screen."

"I do mind. The control room's a restricted area as far as the passengers are concerned."

"It's my job—"

"It's *my* job. Keep your lens out of it."

He shrugged, and bowed, and stepped into the well.

Supplies and equipment had been stored in the crew's quarters, filling most of the space from ceiling to floor, wall to wall. Dartagnan found the one remaining bunk halfway up a wall and strapped himself onto it, comforted by the feeling of closeness, used to it. *My God, is it really happening? . . .*

He shut his eyes, hands under his head, relaxed his body abruptly, thoroughly, like switching off a machine. Memories from the time when he had piloted his father's ship showed him the images he would have seen on this ship's viewscreen, as they rose almost silently, almost without sensation of movement, from Mecca's surface. His imagination expanded, for a vision of the entire Heaven system, circling in a sea of darkness.

The Heaven system consisted of a G-class star orbited by four planets. The two inner worlds, nameless, were essentially uninhabitable, one too hot, one too cold, with nearly nonexistent atmospheres. The two outer worlds were gas giants: Discus, a carnelian scarab set within twenty separate bands of sun-silvered dust and frozen gases; Sevin, dim green, and unreachable since the Civil War. Both of these worlds were also uninhabited.

But between Planet Two and Discus lay an asteroid belt, the Heaven Belt, that once had held a thriving human colony richer even than its parent Earth. But the Civil War had destroyed Heaven Belt, bringing death to nearly one hundred million people, most of its population; and now the Belt was for the most part a vast ruin, where the still-living preyed on the artifacts of the dead in order to keep on living. Among the small isolated pockets of humanity that still continued, the Demarchy had survived almost intact, due to its location. The Demarchy lay in the trojan asteroids, a 140,000-kilometer teardrop of planetoids trapped forever sixty degrees ahead of Discus in its orbital path. The Demarchy had been able to continue trade within itself, and with another surviving subculture, the inhabitants of the icebound debris that circled just beyond the rings of Discus proper. The Ringers supplied the volatiles—oxygen, hydrogen—and hydrocarbons necessary to life, as they had once supplied them to the whole of Heaven Belt. In return, the Demarchy provided the Rings with the pure minerals and refined ores that it had in plenty.

Even before the war the corporations that dominated the Demarchy's economy and its trade had been primarily small and fragmented. The self-interested nature of the Demarchy's town-meeting style of government discouraged monopolies, and so the inherent competitiveness of capitalism had gone to an extreme. The same sophisticated communications network that kept the Demarchy's radical democracy functioning also provided a medium for the expression of corporate competition, and as a result the citizens of the Demarchy were dunned by a constant flow of news disguised by promotion, promotions disguised as news. The need for an ever slicker, more compelling distortion of the truth had created a new ecological niche in Demarchy society, one that had been filled by the pen-for-hire, the mediaman, willing to say anything, sell anything, without question, for the highest bidder. Willing to do anything at all to impress a corporate head—

Dartagnan grew rigid unconsciously; pain knifed him in the stomach. He pressed his hands down over the pain, sighed, remembering the bribes, the lies, the haunting of offices and corridors, the long, long megaseconds it had taken to catch Old Man Siamang's ear at last, in a public washroom . . . the obsequious flattery it had taken to win an interview, and in his office, the careful camera angles, the fulsome praise. Sabu Siamang had been there too, easy, gracious, charming, the complete gentleman. Dartagnan had used the same fawning approach on him, with mixed results. Sabu had asked his name, bemused, and asked, "What happened to the Three Musketeers?" Dartagnan had laughed too loudly.

Dartagnan winced mentally, opened his eyes, staring at the wall. . . . But Old Siamang had liked his work, had offered him this bizarre journey as a reward; ten megaseconds away from civilization, putting him out of touch with everything he needed to know. But if he did his job well, that wouldn't matter; when he returned to Mecca city he would be Siamang's man, and his life would be secure at last.

He thought about Mythili Fukinuki, Goody Two-Shoes, I-don't-put-out-for-the-passengers, wondered how the hell she'd ever won the old man's alleged heart. A woman pilot, for God's sake—one of those women who put selfish interests and personal ambition above their own biological role as women, as childbearers, as the preservation of mankind's future.

Before the Civil War there had been no reason why women could not work or travel in space; but the war had changed many things, even for the Demarchy. The Demarchy still had the resources to preserve sperm, but not ova; because of the high shipboard radiation levels men were exposed to—both from solar storms and from the dirty atomic fission batteries of their own ships—they were usually sterilized, and a supply of undamaged sperm was put aside for the time when they were ready to raise a family. Sound, fertile women had no similar recourse, and so they were encouraged, even forced, to remain in the relative safety of the cities, protected by walls of stone, supported by their men. But with the comparatively high background radiation from the dirty postwar power sources, even in the "protected" cities the percentage of defective births was on the rise. Women who could produce a healthy child were considered to be one of the Demarchy's prime assets. But to some of them, that still wasn't enough. . . . *She had contacts. That's the only way anybody ever gets anything.*

He heard someone moving, in the commons on the next level; he got up, taking his camera with him. Mythili Fukinuki was heating containers of food in the pantry. He drifted up behind her, looked over her shoulder.

"Lunchtime?"

She twisted to face him, startled; light danced along the tines of the fork in her hand.

Chaim jerked back, awkwardly, through half a somersault. He righted himself, hands raised. "Hey, all I want is lunch!"

Her face eased into a mocking smile; he wondered who was being mocked. "There are the bins—pick out what you want. Remember to close the lids tightly. This is an infrared heater, there's the trash. Eat when you want to, clean up after yourself." She turned back, fixed her containers with a *clack* onto the magnetized tray, moved away to the table.

He joined her with his own tray, half sitting on air in the near-normal gravity of the ship's constant acceleration. She frowned faintly, went on eating, in silence. Uncomfortable, he began. "I'm impressed. This is a hell of a nice ship. I—"

"Well, it looks like the two of you are getting along even better than I imagined." Siamang drifted down through the ceiling well. "Put in a good word for me, Red; if you get any further."

Dartagnan looked up, feeling the edge of Siamang's voice. He offered a grin. "I sure will, Boss . . . if I get any further."

The pilot picked up her tray wordlessly, made a wide circuit upward to the entry well, and disappeared. Chaim heard the door of her cabin slam to, and in the silence, the click of a lock. This time it was Siamang who laughed too loudly. Siamang glanced at the pantry, the empty table, the fork spearing a sticky lump of vegetable-in-sauce halfway to Dartagnan's mouth. Siamang raised his eyebrows, used his eyes.

Dartagnan lowered the fork, noticed something new and peculiar about the eyes. "I just started, Boss, if you want to take mine. I can heat up some more." He offered with his hands, pushed himself away from the table.

"You're sure you don't mind; thanks, Red." Siamang moved complacently in toward the table as Chaim moved away. His voice slurred, barely noticeable. "One thing you must have that I don't is a way with women . . . if you could call that one a woman. Must come from all the lies you tell." He picked up the fork. "You impress me, Red. How can you mediamen tell so many lies, so convincingly? Are you born that way?"

Chaim focused on Siamang's eyes for half a second, trying to be certain of what he saw. Siamang's eyes probed the private darknesses of his mind like a spotlight; he looked away, unfocused. *An aggressor* . . . The disjointed word burned on his eyelids like an afterimage. But the eyes were too bright, glassy, the pupils dilated until he couldn't see an iris. Siamang was high on something; Dartagnan didn't know what, didn't want to know. He smiled inanely. "No, Boss, nobody's born that way. It takes practice; a hell of a lot of practice." He flipped the cover casually down over his camera lens, drifted toward the pantry. He had the sudden unhappy thought that there wouldn't be many scenes worth recording during their transit to Planet Two. He said a quick, silent prayer, to no one in particular, that Siamang would give him some decent footage when they got there.

"Tell me something else, Red . . ." Siamang's voice went on, teasing, vaguely condescending.

Dartagnan grinned, not seeing Siamang, or the room, or even the ship, but only the starry void beyond. *It's going to be a long trip. It better be worth it.*

After the first few hundred kiloseconds Dartagnan stopped carrying his camera, stopped doing almost everything that brought him into contact with the others. Siamang stayed closed in his room, passing the time in a world that Chaim was not interested in visiting; he came out only for meals, for an occasional, teasing attack on Dartagnan's scruples, or a casual pass at the pilot. The pilot stayed locked in her own cabin, doing what, Dartagnan didn't know, didn't care; she came out only to eat and check readings in the control room, avoiding them both.

But he used the opportunity of her absence, eventually, to ignore her arbitrary restrictions and get into the control room himself. He filmed the view of stars that showed on the screen; stayed, watching the screen in the comfortable, clicking silence, escaping from the blank-walled boredom of his cluttered quarters below.

His eyes began to drift from the central viewscreen, studying the projected strings of numbers, the intricate geometric filigrees that showed on the peripheral screens. He frowned absently at the angle of the sun, the position of the lightweight screen beyond the ship's hull that kept sunlight from striking directly on the landing module. He reached out at last, typed an inquiry into the computer, watched as the string of figures changed on one screen, began to flash, on and off.

"What do you think you're doing?"

He jerked guiltily, caught hold of the panel as he turned, saw the pilot rise up into the room. "I think one of the propellant tanks on the landing module is heating up; you might want to adjust the sunshade—"

"Get away from there. I told you the control room was off limits! What have you done . . ." She pushed off from the rungs that circled the well's perimeter, came up to the panel. "Of all the stupid—" Her eyes went to the flashing figures on the screen, back down to the panel. Her hand queried, got the same answer. "You're right." She looked up at him again as if she'd never seen him before. "How could you know that?"

"Mediamen know everything." He saw her expression begin to change back. "Well—actually, I'm a qualified pilot."

"*You?*" She blinked. "I didn't think—"

"Funny. I think the same things about women."

She turned back to the panel; he watched her reposition the sunshade. She said, very softly, defensively, "I don't usually make those mistakes. But I haven't been coming up here as much as I should . . . I shouldn't let him get to me!"

"Siamang?"

She nodded, not looking at him, the soft, shadowed curve of her mouth drawing tight.

"Yeah." He shrugged. "Not exactly what you'd call easy to love, is he?" *But believe me, I've known worse. . . .*

"He's a sadist!" Her voice shook.

Dartagnan felt his throat close, swallowed. "What do you mean? You mean he—"

"No. No, he's too 'civilized' for that. He's a psychological sadist. When he's with his father, with the other corporation men, he's fine, charming, *normal*. But when it's someone he doesn't—respect—he . . ." she broke off, searching for the word, ". . . he . . ."

"He 'teases.' " Chaim nodded. "I'll show you my scars, if you'll show me yours." He hesitated. "Why do you put up with it?"

"I like my job! He—doesn't travel much."

He heard a noise below; his slow smile widened with insincerity as he looked toward the well. "Heads up."

Siamang appeared, pinned them against the panel with his gaze as he pushed upward past the rim of the well. "So here you are"—too congenially. He held a drink bulb in his hand, sucked at the straw.

"Hello, Boss." Dartagnan bowed. "We were just talking about what a pleasure it is to work for Siamang and Sons."

Siamang laughed in disbelief. "I thought we were supposed to confine our socializing to the lower levels."

"I was just getting a little footage of the stars, a little arty effect; with the pilot's supervision. . . ." He raised his hands apologetically.

"He was just leaving," Mythili said, her voice brittle.

"Good. Don't want to break the rules, do we, Red?" Siamang tossed his drink bulb out into the air. Chaim watched it arc slowly downward toward the cold metal of the floor. "Time for a refill." He sank, like the bulb, disappeared below floor level. His door opened, closed.

"You're always surrendering, aren't you, Dartagnan? Always lying."

Dartagnan looked back at the pilot's rigid face, feeling her distaste, and down at his hands, still palm-out in the air. He pulled them in against his sides, unexpectedly ashamed, covered the twinge of his stomach. "Yeah." He wiped his hands on his jacket. "Always lying flat on my back, while the whole damned universe screws my integrity." He stepped into the well.

Mythili Fukinuki caught at the ceiling, stopped herself from drifting on down into the dormitory. Dartagnan looked up, almost surprised.

"Do you mind?"

"Not if you don't." He pushed aside his camera on the bunk. "Make yourself at home. I'm harmless."

She floated down; her knees bent slightly as she reached the floor, stabilizing. Her short, shining hair moved softly across her forehead; her skin was the color of antique gold in the strong light. Chaim glanced away uneasily.

Her own dark eyes searched the emptiness, avoiding him. "Why do you do it, if it—"

" 'What's a nice boy like me doing in a job like this?' " He grinned, peering down at her, like the Cheshire Cat. She flushed. The grin disappeared, leaving him behind. "Somebody has to do it."

"But *you* don't." She brushed back her hair. "Not if you really hate it so much."

"The voice of experience?" He baited her, smarting with the things she didn't say. "Goody Two-Shoes, female pilot, tell our viewers how you got where you are. And don't tell me it was clean living. It was connections."

Her mouth tightened. "That's right, it was. My uncle was a freighter pilot; my father got him to use his influence. But they did it because it was what *I* wanted."

"Well, good for them; good for you. We should all have it so good. If we did, maybe I'd be where you are, instead of where I am."

"There are other jobs. You don't need influence—"

"—to dump fertilizer into a hydroponics tank for the rest of my life? To break up rocks in a refinery? Sure. All the dead-end jobs in the universe, back home on Delhi. . . . Being a mediaman, at least I've got a chance, at money, at making contacts . . . at maybe getting free, getting a ship of my own again, someday. If this's what I have to do to get it—whatever I have to do—I will."

She settled slowly onto a box. "Oh. . . . What happened to your ship? What kind of ship was it?"

"It wasn't my ship . . . my father's. He taught me all I know; like they say." He laughed oddly. "He was a prospector, it was a flyin' piece of junk. I never saw it till I was eighteen. I hardly ever saw him. My mother was a contract mother."

"Oh"—almost sorrow.

He nodded. "When I was eighteen my father dropped in out of the black like a meteor, and told me I was going prospecting. I spent fifty megasecs learning to pilot a ship, scouting artifacts on rocks with names I'd never even heard of, hardly ever seeing anybody but him . . . and a lot of corpses." He laughed again, not hearing it. "I thought I'd go crazy. Finally he gave up and let me go home, instead. The next thing we heard from him, he claimed he'd made the strike of his life . . . and the next thing we heard, he was dead. He'd smashed up the ship, and smashed himself up, in a lousy docking accident. Some corporation picked up his salvage find; we never got a thing. I had to start doing something then, to support my mother . . . and here I am. I thought I'd enjoy being a mediaman, after fifty megaseconds of prospecting. . . . Now, even solitary confinement sounds good."

"Why did your mother let you do it? Doesn't she know—?" Sympathy softened the clear, straight lines of her face.

"What was she supposed to do? Dump fertilizer instead of me?" He shrugged. "She's nice-looking, she got married, maybe a hundred megasecs ago. I don't hear from her much, now; her husband doesn't appreciate me, for obvious reasons. . . . While my father was alive, she never even contracted to have anybody else's children. Funny—he stayed with us maybe seven times in six hundred megaseconds, never gave her a thing, except me; but she loved him, I think she always hoped he'd marry her someday." He grunted. "Wouldn't that make a great human-interest filler. . . . Sorry, I haven't been filling my quota of compulsive conversation for the last megasecond." And watching her, all at once he was overwhelmingly aware of another need that had not been fulfilled for too long. The fact that she made no effort at all at sensuality made her suddenly, unbearably sensual. He unbuttoned the high collar of his loose, gray-green jacket, shifted uncomfortably above the edge of the bunk, almost losing his balance.

"My father," she said, looking down, unaware, "wanted a son. But he couldn't have one . . . genetic damage. That's why he let me become a pilot; it was like having a son, for him. But there's nothing wrong with that." Her voice rose slightly. "Because piloting is what I always wanted to do."

"Was it? Or was it really just that you wanted to please your father?" He wondered what had made him say that.

She looked up sharply. "It was what I wanted. If a mediaman isn't satisfied to stay in his 'place,' why should I have to be?"

Something in her look cracked the barrier of his invulnerable public face. He nodded, "It's not easy, is it? They never make it easy. . . ."

She smiled, very faintly. "No, Dartagnan . . . they never do. But maybe you've helped, a little."

"Call me Chaim?"

"I thought your friends called you 'Red'?"

"I don't have any friends."

She shook her head, still smiling; pushed up from the box, rose toward the entrywell. "Yes, you do."

Alone, he meditated on stars until his desire subsided, leaving a warmth in his mind that had nothing to do with sex. He savored it, as he listened to her heating food in the commons above his head; heard something else, Siamang's voice:

"How about heating something up for me, Mythili?"

"I'm a pilot, not a cook, Demarch Siamang. You'll have to do it yourself."

"That's not what I meant."

Dartagnan heard a magnetized tray clatter on the counter, a choked noise of indignation. "Do that for yourself, too!"

More faintly, a door slammed shut. Chaim let her image back into his mind, grinned at it, rueful. *Well, your friendship is better than nothing, poor Goody Two-Shoes* . . .

But he saw little more of her, as a friend or in any other way, for the next four and a half megaseconds; their mutual dislike of Siamang, and fear of provoking him, still came between them, an impassable barrier.

Until finally Planet Two filled the viewscreen: alien, immense, a painter's palette in sterile grays—gray-blue, gray-green, gray-brown. A castaway's grateful voice filled the speaker static; tracing his radio fix, Mythili put them into a polar orbit, breaking the hypnotic flow of grays with the blinding whiteness of ice caps. For the first time, Chaim saw clouds—pale, wispy streamers of frozen water vapor trapped high in the planet's atmospheric layer. He recorded it all, and was filled with a rare wonder at being one of the few human beings in Heaven system ever to have seen it firsthand. It occurred to him that the clouds seemed more common than he remembered from pictures; he managed to make intelligent conversation about it, standing at Mythili's side. And as they made final preparations to enter the ungainly craft that would take them down out of orbit, she asked him quietly to assist her in the landing.

He sat strapped into the heavily padded seat beside her own, in the cabin that seemed cramped even to him. Siamang sat behind them, apparently sober, surprisingly silent. Chaim studied Mythili's movements, saw his own nervousness reflected on her face, but making her movements sharper, more certain, as though it only augmented her skill. She freed them from the grasp of the parent ship, executed the first rocket burn that broke them out of their orbit . . . and began the descent maneuver that neither she nor any living pilot in Heaven system had ever done, with the exception of the man stranded below.

They entered the upper atmosphere; she began the second burn. She would have to maintain a crucial balance: too swift a rate of descent would result in their destruction . . . but too slow a one would exhaust the ship's fuel resources while they were still high above the surface. No ships had been constructed for over two billion seconds in the Heaven system that were capable of using a planet's atmosphere to slow their descent—because since the war there had never been a need for such a ship, until now. No nuclear electric rocket could produce the acceleration necessary for a planetary landing. And so this ship, that could provide the necessary thrust to slow their descent, had been constructed of makeshift parts, and with makeshift technology, in scarcely two megaseconds' time.

Chaim read off their altitude and rate of descent from instruments that had never been calibrated for second-to-second precision at six hundred meters per second; clutched the instrument panel with sweating hands, fighting against his own sudden, unaccustomed weight. Mythili dropped them down toward the signal of the radio beacon, the viewscreen virtually useless, blocked by the intermittent glare of their rockets, and the angle of their descent. She bit off a gasp, or a curse, each time they were buffeted or swept from the line of their trajectory by the terrifying force of the unseen atmospheric turbulence.

And at one thousand meters, she began the final burn. Chaim raised his voice, as the sound of the rockets reached them, growing: ". . . six hundred meters, twenty meters per second, five hundred meters"—he felt thrust increase—"four hundred meters, eighteen meters per second . . . three hundred meters . . . two hundred . . . one hundred meters, ten meters per second . . ." She cut thrust again, their rate of descent stabilized. ". . . fifty meters, ten meters per second . . . forty meters . . . thirty . . . twenty meters . . . Mythili, we're—" She increased thrust to full; ten meters per second squared crushed him down into his seat. The viewscreen was blind with dust; the ship lurched, noise drowned his words, vibration rattled his teeth. "—too fast!"

Impact jarred through him, almost an anticlimax. Mythili

cut power; seconds passed before the silence registered. He blinked at the screen, still swirling gray, and pushed up in his seat against gravity's unfamiliar hand. "Congratulations," he laughed, finding himself breathless, "it's a planet. . . . And I didn't get a single damned shot of the whole descent!"

She drooped, triumphant, laughing with him. "If you'd been filming instead of being my co-pilot, I don't think we'd be here to worry about it."

He bobbed his head, "Too kind"—touched her with his eyes. She held his gaze, smiling.

"Is it my imagination, or is it getting cold in here?" Dartagnan watched his breath frost as he spoke. He struggled with his spacesuit, feeling leaden and clumsy. He heard Siamang swear in irritation in the cramped space behind him.

"It's not your imagination—the atmosphere acts like water, it's conducting all our heat away right through the hull." Mythili massaged her arms as she studied the viewscreen. "Siamang's engineers predicted something like this."

Chaim saw the dome of the abandoned experimental station, nearly a kilometer away across the flat, subpolar plain; and closer in, the ungainly bulk of the prospector's ship. *Both of us made a better landing than we had a right to. . . .* Beyond them both, along the incredibly distant horizon, he thought he saw a dusting of pale snow pocked with broad, shallow craters: the south-polar icecap of Planet Two. He imagined the incredible volatile resources this world represented; remembered abruptly that they were all at the bottom of a gravity well.

"Come on, Red. Get your camera and let's get going. This is what we came for!" Siamang's voice was good-natured, eager. Chaim felt a surge of relief, hoping Siamang's professional business dealings would be easier to record than his private life.

"Coming, Boss. . . . Aren't you coming?" He looked back at Mythili. "Walking on a planet isn't something everybody's done."

She nodded. "I know. But I have to stay with the ship, it's not very well designed to deal with the effects of an atmosphere. I have to keep the cabin warm enough so that the instruments don't freeze, and enough fuel has to be bled from the tanks so that they don't rupture. And besides"—she lowered her voice—"I stay out of corporate business dealings."

"I see. Well, I'll show you my home movies, when I get

back." He settled his helmet onto his head, latched it, picked up his camera. He staggered, stunned by its weight. The surface gravity of Planet Two was over a hundred times normal; he suddenly wished he'd accepted the corporation's offer of a lightweight prewar camera, instead of insisting on his own.

"Come *on*, Red!"

He followed Siamang through the lock and down the precarious rungs of the ladder. The atmospheric pressure kept his suit from ballooning; it clutched him as he moved, with hands of ice.

"Damn it!" Siamang stumbled sideways, struck by an invisible blow: wind, Dartagnan realized, as it shoved him roughly back against the side of the ship. His helmet rang on metal. The surface air had been calm when they set down, but the wind was rising now, swirling the blue-gray dust into translucent curtains. Between the gusts he caught sight of a tiny figure starting toward them from the dome.

They struggled out across the shallow, flame-fused dish of the ship's landing area, went on across the fine, loose surface of the dust. "We're real dirt-siders now, Boss," he said cheerfully, more cheerfully than he felt. Dust sandblasted his faceplate; he shut his eyes against it, beginning to sweat, already shivering. Siamang didn't answer, struggled to keep his footing; his face was grim, barely visible behind his helmet glass. Dartagnan looked up at the sky, the spinel sun grown large against an alien ultramarine blue. He thought of sapphire, the only thing he could remember that possessed the same purity of color. *They should have named it Blue instead of Two . . . Blue Hell.* He looked down again, across the blue-gray plain at the dome, hardly larger, and at the suited figure closing with them now, proof that they were actually making headway. He let his camera slip off of his stiffening shoulder, wrapped the strap around a numb, gloved hand.

"If you aren't a sight for sore eyes!" A stranger's voice burst from his helmet speakers; the prospector, castaway, welcoming committee of one. The man held out his hands as he reached them, shook each of theirs, bowing, all at once. He moved almost easily, Chaim noticed, envious.

"That's not all that's sore," Siamang said, his congeniality sounding strained. "Let's get in out of this damned atmosphere."

"Sure, of course. Let me take that for you, I'm used to this." The man reached for Dartagnan's camera.

Chaim waved him off, recalling his duty. "No, thanks, I'm

with the media . . . let me get a shot of this . . ." He moved
out, hefting the camera, plugged in, focused, pressed the trigger, tripping over his own feet. *Historic Moment, Historic
Rescue, Historic Setting . . . Cameraman Busts His Ass. . . .*
They were passing the prospector's stranded ship. Siamang's
voice reached him: "Get a shot of that, Red."

"Right, Boss." He did a closeup of the name painted on
the hull, and the silhouette of an insect. "The *Esso Bee?*" He
laughed incredulously, heard the others laugh, in amusement,
and in startled recognition. He looked back toward the prospector's shadowed face. "Kwaime Sekka-Olefin, I presume?"
He remembered the details of the original news broadcast.
Their stranded man was an heir to a distillery fortune, but
the actual corporation had been destroyed during the Civil
War: Sekka-Olefin Volatiles, Esso for short, and this "secret"
experimental station had been run by them before the war.

"That's right; and damned glad to meet you!" The man
laughed again. "My God—it's wonderful!"

"Our pleasure," Siamang said easily, "our pleasure to be of
service, to one man or all mankind."

They reached the low dome at last. Dartagnan recorded it
for posterity, set in the desolation of wind and dust and
snow, tried to keep his chattering teeth from recording on the
soundtrack. Breathing hard, he trudged ahead to film their arrival, found the dark, welcoming entrance of the shelter. A
passageway led steeply down, he noticed, as they passed
through the airlock; he realized the main part of the installation must be underground, to help maintain an even interior temperature. He noticed that one wall of the passage
was oddly serrated. He backed slowly toward it, filming, as
the others entered the hall; stared, through the lens, as
Sekka-Olefin suddenly lunged toward him. "Look out—!"
Olefin's voice rattled in his helmet. Olefin's glove caught at
his arm, missed, as Dartagnan stepped out onto the air.

The air let him down, and with a yelp of surprise he fell
backward down the stairs. The camera landed on his stomach. He lay dazed and battered, gasping for breath, seeing
stars without trying. The others reached him, somehow man-
aging not to land on top of him. They lifted the camera off
of him, hauled him to his feet.

"You all right, Red?"

"Say, didn't you see the steps there—?"

"Steps?" he mumbled. "What do you mean—uh!" His right
ankle buckled under a fraction of his mass, pain shot up his

leg, on up his spine like an electric shock. "My leg . . ." He pressed back against the corridor wall, balancing on one foot. "Hurts like hell."

"Hell's what this place is," Siamang muttered, disgusted. "How about your camera?" He dropped it into Dartagnan's arms.

Dartagnan lost his balance, Olefin reached out and caught him. He shook the sealed case, probed it, turned it over and peered through the lens. His chest hurt. He replugged the recording jack. "Looks okay. . . . Ought to be a great shot of the ceiling as I went over backward." He tasted blood from his split lip. "I think the damned thing landed on top of me on purpose."

"Good thing it's tougher than you are," Siamang said, "or you might be out of a job, Red."

Dartagnan laughed, weakly. He looked back up the passageway: the purpose of the serrated wall was appallingly obvious to him, in hindsight; steps, a series of plateaus for breaking downward momentum under high gravity. *That's adding insult to injury.* . . . He grimaced.

The prospector offered him a shoulder to lean on, and they went on along the hall.

"How about a drink, to celebrate the occasion? To celebrate my not having to drink alone." Olefin picked a bottle up off the floor, in the littered cubicle that had been his home for the past ten megaseconds. Dartagnan noticed a pile of other bottles, mostly empty.

"Sounds good. I could use some antifreeze; this place is instant death. How cold does it get here, anyway? It must be zero degrees Kelvin. . . ." Siamang rubbed circulation back into his fingers. They had taken off their suits, at Olefin's urging; the air would have been uncomfortably cool under other circumstances.

"No . . . no, it only gets down to about two hundred thirty degrees Kelvin after the sun sets. Of course, that's not counting the chill factor." Olefin grinned.

Dartagnan sat on the bare cot, his leg up, his ankle swelling inside his boot. Olefin glanced back at him, questioning. Chaim noticed that the eyes were green, freckled with brown, under the heavy brows, brow ridges. Olefin was in his fifties, and well preserved for a man who had spent most of his life in space. His unkempt, uncut hair was receding, silvering at the temples, a startling brightness against his brown skin. *Dis-*

tinguished Scion of Old Money . . . didn't know any of 'em were real people. Dartagnan shook his head. "No, thanks . . . I'm a teetotaler."

Siamang looked surprised.

"Medicinal purposes?" Olefin asked, gestured with the bottle.

"That's why I don't." He shook his head again, sincerely remorseful. "I can't drink. Got an ulcer." He wiped his bloody lip.

Siamang's surprise burst out in laughter. "An ulcer? What've *you* got to worry about, Red?"

"I worry about having to refuse a free drink. I could sure use one."

Olefin poured vodka into hemispherical cups; the clear liquid stayed level and didn't ooze back up the sides as he poured. Afraid to start feeling sorry for himself, Dartagnan reached for his camera. "Would you say you were lucky in finding so much intact here, Demarch Sekka-Olefin? It looks like all the life-support systems are still functional. Did that save your life? What happened to the researchers stationed here, after the war?" It almost felt good to him, after seven megaseconds of enforced silence.

Olefin leaned forward on his stool, sharing the eagerness for the sound of his own voice. "Yes, I sure as hell was lucky. Would've been damned fatal on board the *Esso Bee.* But nothing actually happened to damage this station during the Civil War; nobody knew it was here except Esso. After the war nobody was in a position to come here at all. . . . From the looks of things, the crew must have starved to death."

Dartagnan swallowed. *God, the public will love this. . . .* "But . . . uh, the valuable salvage finds you made will mean that they didn't die in vain? Their discoveries will go to help the living—?"

"Yes . . . yes! In ways I never expected." Olefin's voice took on a vaguely fanatical note. "Did you know that—"

Siamang shifted impatiently, set down his cup. "Demarch Sekka-Olefin; Red. If I'm not imposing"—there was no trace of sarcasm—"I'd like to ask that the interviewing be postponed until we've had the chance to discuss more important matters."

"Oh. Certainly. . . ." Olefin broke off, seemed suddenly almost glad of the interruption. "Anything I can do, considering what you've done for me."

Siamang composed his face as Dartagnan turned the camera on him. "Of course, the most important matter, the basic reason I've come four hundred million kilometers, is—"

—*more money*, Dartagnan thought.

"—to see that you get safely off of this miserable hell-world of a planet." He produced something packaged in foam from his thin folder. "This is the replacement unit, complete with the instructions, for the component that was damaged when your ship landed here on Planet Two."

Olefin beamed like a child with a birthday present; but Chaim noted the dark flash of another sort of humor that moved behind the hazel eyes. " 'For want of a chip, the ship was lost!' To think of all the time and money I put in, perfecting the *Esso Bee* and a nuke electric that could drag home half a planet; the best design possible—to have it all go for nothing, because one single piece of electronics was put on the outside, when it should have been on the inside. . . . Thank you—I literally can't thank you enough, Demarch Siamang; but I'll do my best." He stood, reached out to shake Siamang's hand heartily. Seated again, he poured himself another drink, raised it in salute, drank it down.

"Well, you can repay us, in a sense . . ." Siamang paused, poised, disarmingly reticent. ". . . by giving Siamang and Sons the opportunity to be the first corporation to make an offer on the computer software that you reported finding."

Olefin gave a quick nod, barely visible, that was not meant to be agreement.

Siamang went on, oblivious. "As you obviously know, it would be vital in streamlining our distilling processes—"

"And in streamlining the processing of a lot of other distilleries," Olefin interrupted with unexpected smoothness. "What I had in mind, Demarch Siamang, was to call a public auction on the media for all the salvage, when I return to the Demarchy. I planned to offer to you, or whoever came after me, a substantial percentage of the take as a reward—"

Siamang's expression tightened imperceptibly. "What we had in mind, Demarch Sekka-Olefin, was more on the order of a flat fee offer on the software. We're not interested in any of the rest; you could bargain however you wanted on that. But it's very important to us—naturally—that Siamang and Sons is the firm to get those programs."

And a general auction wouldn't guarantee you did. Dartagnan hid a smile behind his camera. He realized suddenly why Siamang and Sons had wanted an edited tape, and not live transmission, on this rescue mission: business transactions were never meant to be public affairs.

"I understand your feelings, Siamang; come from a distillery family myself. But I feel a covert agreement with one firm is too monopolistic, not in keeping with the Demarchy's traditions of free enterprise. . . . And besides, to be blunt, I've got important plans for the profit I'll be making on this salvage, and I want to get as good a deal on it as possible. That software is by far the most valuable part of it."

"I see." Siamang's eyes flickered to the replacement part safely settled on Olefin's knees. Chaim guessed, without trying, what wish he made. "Well, then, if you don't mind, I'll make that pleasant trek to our ship one more time, and radio the home company about your position on the matter." His smile was sunlight on the cold edge of his voice. "They may give me a little more flexibility in making an offer. . . ." He bowed.

Chaim stood up, goaded by an indefinable unease; he sat down again abruptly.

Siamang glanced back, pulling on his suit. "You stay here, Red. Finish your interview. You'd just slow me up. I don't intend to spend any more time out in that open air than I have to." He bowed again courteously to Sekka-Olefin, and left the room.

Dartagnan listened to the odd shuffling of unaccustomed footsteps recede, and swore under his breath, with pain and frustration. He lifted the camera again, compulsively, protective coloring. Through the lens he saw Olefin shake his head, hand up, and reach to pour himself another drink. Chaim let the camera drop, irritated, but relieved to see that the prospector wasn't drinking this one down like the others. There was plenty of time for an interview; with the communications time lag Siamang wouldn't be back for at least three thousand seconds.

Olefin grinned. "A little loosens tongues, and makes life easier; a lot loosens brains, and makes it hell. I try to draw the line. . . . Fall was worse than you care to admit, wasn't it? Where does it hurt? . . . Maybe I ought to have a look at that ankle." He stood up.

Dartagnan leaned back against the cold wall, laughed once. "Ask me where it doesn't hurt! Black and blue and green all over. . . . Thanks; but you'd have to cut off my boot, by now, and it's the only one I've got. Doesn't matter, we'll be back in normal gee soon and it won't give me any trouble. I just have to get the job done now—" He winced as Olefin's fingers probed along his ankle.

"Job comes before everything, even you, huh? So you're a corporate flak. . . ." Olefin's fist rapped the sole of his boot, "Siamang's man?"

"I'm—hoping to be!" through clenched teeth. "So when he tells me to jump, I don't ask why, or how . . . I just ask, 'Is this high enough?' "

"You won't be doing much jumping for a while, for anybody. Got a sprain, maybe a fracture." The green/brown eyes studied him, amused; he wondered exactly what was funny. Olefin went back to pick his drink off of a dusty shelf. "Don't think I could stand to work for anybody else. Comes from being raised among the idle rich, I suppose. . . ."

"You don't have to be rich, believe me." Dartagnan settled on an elbow, and the cot creaked.

Olefin looked at him, the rough brows rose.

He smiled automatically. "My father was a prospector. Rock poor, to the day he died . . . just when he'd finally found something big, or so he claimed." Establish a rapport with the subject, get a better interview. . . .

"That right? What was his name?" An encouraging interest showed on Olefin's face.

"Dartagnan—Gamal Dartagnan."

"Yeah, I knew him." Olefin nodded at his drink. "Didn't know he had a son. Only talked to him four or five times."

"You and me both. He took me out with him, though. Just before the last trip he made."

"That's right . . . heard about his accident. Very sorry to hear it."

Chaim shifted his weight. "They called it an accident."

Olefin sat down, said carefully, "Are you saying you don't think it was?"

He shrugged. "My father'd been prospecting for a long time; he knew enough not to make a mistake that big. And it seemed a little coincidental to me that a corporation just happened to be right there to pick up his find."

"Somebody had to get there first." Sekka-Olefin shook his head. "I suppose in your line of work you don't see the best side of corporate policy. But not many stoop to that kind of thing; that would be suicide, if it ever got out. Maybe his instruments went out. Accidents happen, people make mistakes . . . space doesn't give you a second chance."

Dartagnan nodded, looking down. "Maybe so. Maybe that

is what happened. I suppose you'd know the truth if anybody would—you play both sides of the game. . . . He held that damned junk-heap together with frozen spit. . . ."

Olefin sipped his drink, expressionless. "What made you decide to quit prospecting to become a mediaman?"

Dartagnan wondered suddenly who was interviewing whom. "Prospecting. Maybe I didn't know when I was well off."

"But now it's too late."

He wasn't sure whether it was a question or a moral judgment. "Not if I make good in this job. . . ."

Olefin nodded, at something. "How'd you like another long-term job instead?"

Chaim sat up, not hiding his eagerness. "Doing what—prospecting?"

"Conducting a media campaign."

Dartagnan slumped forward, oddly disappointed. "That's —a hell of a compliment, from a total stranger. Are you sure you mean it? And what kind of a campaign—what are you planning to sell?"

"Planet Two."

Dartagnan sat up straight again, "What?"

"The colonizing of Planet Two from the Demarchy."

God almighty; a job offer from a maniac. A rich maniac. . . . He reached for his camera. *At least this won't be dull—*

"Let's forget about that thing for a while." Olefin shook his head. "I'll talk to it all you want, if you accept the job. But hear me out, before you type me as a crank."

Chaim grinned sheepishly. "Whatever you say." He toyed with the lens, aiming it where it lay; he jammed the trigger ON. A sound pierced his left eardrum, barely audible even to him, at the extreme upper end of the register. He gambled that Olefin's hearing wasn't good enough to pick it up. *More than one way to get a good interview . . . a job in the hand's worth two in the offing.* "Okay, then, would you care to expand on your reasons for wanting to establish a colony on a hellhole like Planet Two?" He settled back, hands massaging his injured leg.

Olefin laughed, sobered. "How many megaseconds would you estimate Heaven Belt has left?"

Dartagnan looked at him blankly. "Before what?"

"Before civilization collapses entirely; before we all join the hundred million people who died right after the Civil War."

Dartagnan remembered Mecca city, a man-made geode in the heart of the rock, towers like crystal growths in every imaginable shading of jewel color. He tried to imagine it as a place of death, and failed. "I don't know about the scavengers back in the Main Belt, but I don't see any reason why the Demarchy can't go on forever, just as it always has."

"Don't you? . . . No, I suppose you don't. Nobody does; I suppose they don't want to face the inevitability of death. And who am I to blame them?"

"We all have to die someday."

"But who really believes that? Maybe the fact that Esso was wiped out by the war, the fact that I was squandering literally the last of the family fortune, made me see it so clearly: that humanity's existence here has a finite end; and that end's in sight. Speaking of making mistakes, we made a hell of a big one—the Civil War—and one mistake in Heaven and you're damned forever. Damned dead. . . .

"Existing in an asteroid belt depends entirely on an artificial ecosystem; everything that's vital for life, we have to process or make ourselves—air, water, food; everything. But like any other ecosystem—more than most—you destroy enough of it, and nothing that's left can survive for long. It has to retreat, or die. Back in the Solar Belt they had Earth to retreat to, if they need it, where everything necessary for life happened naturally. But at the time Heaven was colonized, this hadn't happened to them, so they didn't foresee the need. When the old Belters colonized this system, they figured that the raw elements—the ores and the minerals, the frozen gases around Discus—were all they had to have. Never occurred to anyone that sometime they wouldn't be able to process them.

"But that's what's happened. Most of the capital industry in Heaven was destroyed during the war. What we've got left is barely adequate, and there's no way we can expand or even replace it. Hell, the Ringers are hardly surviving now, and if they go under I don't know how our own distilleries are going to make it. . . . How good are you at holding your breath?"

Dartagnan laughed uneasily. "But—" He groped for a rebuttal, found his mind empty . . . like his sudden vision of the future. "But—all right. So maybe you're right, we are sliding downhill to the end. . . . If there's nothing we can do to save ourselves, why worry about it? Just make the best of what we've got, while we've still got it."

"But that's the point! There is something we can do—starting now, we can establish a colony here on Planet Two, against the time when technology fails and the Demarchy can't support us anymore."

"I don't see the point." Dartagnan shook his head. "It's even harder to stay alive here than out in space. Even in a suit, you'd freeze to death! The atmosphere sucks the warmth out of you, even now, when the sun's up. And the gravity—"

"Gravity here's only one quarter what the human body was built to withstand. As for the cold—our equipment wasn't designed to deal with it, but it'd be easy enough to adapt; all we need is better insulation. This's no worse than parts of old Earth. Antarctica, for instance. No warmer than this, and snow up to here; but they didn't mind. The greatest thing human beings have going for them is adaptability! If those dirtsiders could do it, a Belter can do it." Olefin's hands leaped with emphasis, his eyes gleaming like agate, lit by an inner vision. "In fact, part of my idea for a media campaign would be to rename this planet Antarctica: 'Return to nature, cast off the artificial environment; live the way man was meant to live—'"

"I don't know. . . ." Dartagnan's head moved again in negation. "You sure this place is no colder than Earth? Besides, the atmosphere's still unbreathable."

"But it's not! That's one of the most crucial points the public has to be made aware of. One of the experimental projects here was a study of the atmospheric conditions—and it proved conclusively that the atmosphere of this world is denser than it was when we first came into the system. The way the various periodicities of its orbit add up right now is causing the polar caps to melt, freeing the gases. The atmosphere's thin and dry compared to what we're used to, but it's breathable. I know; I've tried it."

"For how long?" Dartagnan felt a sudden constricted panic, at the thought of trying to breathe an alien atmosphere; his hand rose to his throat. "How's that possible? How could there be enough free oxygen?"

"Don't know. But there is; I've been out two, three kilosecs at a time."

Dartagnan looked down, polishing the polish on the worn vinyl of his boot. "You'd have to live underground, I suppose; help to conserve heat. But we do that anyhow. And solar power—it's a lot closer in to the sun. . . ."

"There, you see!" Olefin nodded eagerly. "You're starting

to see the possibilities. It's the answer; we had to find an answer, and this is it. This can make your career! With the money I make off of this salvage sale, we can launch a media campaign that'll convert the entire Demarchy. What do you say, Dartagnan?"

Chaim stopped polishing, kept his face averted. "I want a chance to think over what you told me first, Demarch Sekka-Olefin. I still can't really see this place as the Garden of Allah. . . . I'll give you my answer before we lift off, all right?" He realized that the real question he needed an answer to was whether this was what he wanted to do with the rest of his life . . . or whether he really had any choice. But a kind of excitement rose in him like desire, to fill the void Olefin's future had created with the knowledge that if he sold himself to Sekka-Olefin, he might not be selling out at all.

"Fair enough," Olefin was saying, smiling as though he already had his answer. "Expect my numerous bloodsucking relations are going to be prostrate with grief when they hear about my plans for this salvage money. They didn't appreciate my spending what was left of the family inheritance on this project. I didn't name that ship out there; they named it, after me . . ." He laughed at his own joke.

Dartagnan began a grin, heard footsteps in the hall and felt his face lose all expression again. He drew his aching leg off of the cot, positioned it gingerly on the floor. He stood up, and was suddenly afraid to move.

Olefin leaned past him, pulled a long T-barred pole from under the cot, and held it out. Chaim saw that the ends were wrapped in rags. "Here," Olefin said, "use my crutch. I fell down the goddam steps in the dark when I first got here."

Chaim finished the grin this time, as Siamang arrived in the doorway, helmet under his arm. Dartagnan's eyes moved from Olefin's face to Siamang's. He realized suddenly that he had made his decision. He bowed.

Siamang bowed to them in return, his gaze shielded by propriety. "I trust I haven't inconvenienced you, Demarch Sekka-Olefin. I'm sure you want to make your repairs and get off of this miserable planet as soon as possible." He chafed his arms through his suit. "My pilot tells me we'll have to lift off before sunset, ourselves; our storage batteries are getting low from trying to maintain temperatures in the ship. But I've got good news—permission to do whatever's necessary to reach an agreement with you about that software." A gleam like a splinter of ice escaped his eyes. Dartagnan tried to see whether his pupils were dilated, couldn't.

"Good, then." Olefin nodded. "Maybe we can discuss business matters further, after all."

"My hope as well. But first—if you don't mind—I would like to take a look at what we're going to be bargaining for."

Olefin looked vaguely surprised; Dartagnan wondered what Siamang thought he could tell simply by looking at program spools. Olefin shrugged. "If *you* don't mind going back out into the 'weather,' Demarch Siamang. I've got them aboard the *Esso Bee.*"

Siamang grimaced. "That's what I was afraid of. But yes, I'd still like to see them."

They made their way across the shifting, slatey dust to the base of Olefin's landing craft. Dartagnan stopped, staring at the ladder that climbed the mass of the solid-fuel module between jutting pod-feet. His muscles twitched with fatigue, his ankle screamed abuse along the corridors of his nerves.

Siamang looked at his upturned faceplate. "You'll never make it up there, Red." Siamang's voice inside his helmet was oddly unperturbed, and slurred, very slightly. "Don't worry about it, you've got plenty of film footage. Just record the audio . . . and worry about how you'll get back on board our own ship." Siamang's glove closed lightly on his shoulder, good-humoredly, unexpectedly. Startled, he watched them climb the ladder and disappear through the lock.

Dartagnan settled on a rung of the ladder, grateful that for now at least the atmosphere was at rest, and kept its own invisible hands off of him. The sun was dropping down from its zenith in the ultramarine shell of the sky; he noticed tiny flecks of gauzy white sticking to the flawless, sapphire purity of blue, very high up. He realized he was seeing clouds from below. He began to shiver, wondered when the others would finish their business, and whether it would be before he froze to death. Their cautious haggling droned on, filling his ears; he began to feel sleepy under the anesthetic of cold. . . .

He shook his head abruptly, stood up, waking himself with pain. He realized then that the ghost-conversation inside his helmet was no longer either droning or polite, heard Siamang threatening. "This's my last offer, Olefin. I advise you to take it, or I'll have to—"

"Put it away, Siamang. Threats don't work with me. I've been around too long—"

Dartagnan heard vague, disassociated noises, a cry, a *thud*. And finally, Siamang's voice: "Olefin. Olefin?" Numbed with another kind of coldness, Chaim focused his camera on the hatchway, and waited.

Siamang appeared, dragging Olefin's limp, suited form. He gave it a push; Dartagnan stumbled back as it dropped like a projectile to the dust in front of him, to lie twisted, unmoving. Dumbfounded, he went on filming: the corpse; Siamang's descent of the ladder; the Death of a Dream.

Siamang came toward him across the fire-fused dust, took the camera out of his nerveless hands. He pried the thumb-sized film cassette loose and threw it away. Dartagnan saw it arc downward, disappear somewhere out on the endless blue-gray silt of the plain: his own future, mankind's future, Sekka-Olefin's last will and testament, lost to his heirs—lost to mankind, forever. "That wouldn't have made very good copy, now, would it?" Siamang dropped the camera, stepped on the fragile lens aperture with his booted foot. He picked it up again, handed it back. "Too bad your camera broke when you took that fall. But we don't hold bad luck against a man, as long as he cooperates. I'm sure I can depend on you to cooperate, in return for the proper incentive?"

Dartagnan struggled to reach his voice. "He—he's really dead?" *No corporation would stoop to murder, Olefin had said. . . .*

Siamang nodded; his hand moved slightly. Dartagnan saw the dark sheen of metal. Siamang was armed. A dart gun; untraceable poison. "I *can* depend on you, can't I, Red? I'd like to keep this simple."

Dartagnan whispered mindlessly, "I'm your man, Boss . . . body and soul." Thinking, *I'll see you in hell for this; if it's the last thing I ever do.*

"That's what I figured. . . . It was an accident, he fell; he was too damned fragile, he'd been in space too long. I never intended to kill him. But that doesn't make much difference, under the circumstances. So I think we'll just say he was alive when we left him. His body'll freeze out here, nobody can prove he didn't fall after we left—if anybody ever even bothers to investigate. Anybody could see he drank too much."

"Yeah . . . anybody." The wind was rising, butting against Dartagnan's body; the dust shifted under his feet, eroding his stability.

"I'm sure you can construct a moving account of our mission, even without film—a portrait in words of the grateful old man, the successful conclusion of our business transaction. . . ." Siamang brushed the metal container fixed at the waist of his suit. "Do a good, convincing job, and I'll make it more than worth your while." Dartagnan felt more than saw the aggressor's eyes assess him, behind Siamang's helmet glass. "What's your fondest wish, Red? Head of our media staff? Company pilot? Maybe a ship of your own? . . . Name it, it's yours."

"A ship," he mumbled, startled. "I want a ship," thinking wildly, *The smart businessman knows his client. . . .*

"Done." Siamang bowed formally, offered a gloved hand. Chaim took the hand, shook it.

Siamang's heavy boot kicked the bottom of his crutch, and it flew free; Dartagnan landed flat on his back in the dirt.

"Just remember your place, Red; and don't get any foolish ideas." Siamang turned away, started back toward their ship across the lifeless plain.

Dartagnan belly-flopped into the airlock, lay gasping for long seconds, before he pulled himself to his feet and started it cycling. He removed his helmet, picked up his crutch, started after Siamang into the control room. The vision of Mythili Fukinuki formed like a fragile blossom in the empty desolation of his mind; he forced his face into obedient blankness, hoped it would hold, as the image in his mind became reality.

She stood at the panel, arms folded, listening noncommittally to Siamang's easy lies. Chaim entered the cramped cabin. She glanced at him as Siamang said, "Isn't that about all, Red?"

"I guess so, Boss." He nodded, not sure what he had agreed to. He stopped, balancing precariously, as her eyes struck him like a slap.

"I'm afraid that's not all, Demarch Siamang." Mythili pushed away from the panel, set her gaze of loathing hatred against Siamang's own impenetrable stare. A small knife glittered suddenly in her hand. "There's the matter of a murder." She gained the satisfaction of seeing Siamang's self-confidence suddenly crack. "I didn't like what I heard when you talked to your father, and so I monitored your suit radio. I heard everything. . . ." She looked again at Dartagnan, and away. "And I intend to tell everything, when we get back to the Demarchy. You won't get away with it."

" 'Never underestimate the power of a woman.' " Siamang

smiled sourly, flexing his hands. "I don't suppose it would do any good to point out that if you turn me in you'll be out of a job; whereas if you were willing to play along, you could have any job you wanted?"

"No," she said, "it wouldn't. Not everybody has a price."

"I didn't expect you would, in any case. But I expect you're getting a great deal of pleasure out of doing this to me, Fukinuki. . . . Unfortunately, there's another old saying, 'Never underestimate your enemy.' I'm terminating your services, Mythili. You're not going to get the chance to talk." Siamang produced the gun, raised it.

She stiffened, lifted her head defiantly. "You won't kill me. I'm your pilot; you need me to get you home."

"That's where you're wrong. As you pointed out to me, Red here is a qualified pilot. So I don't really need you anymore. You've made yourself expendable. Drop the knife, Mythili." His hand tightened. "Drop it or I'll kill you right now."

Slowly her fingers opened; the knife clattered on the floor. Siamang picked it up.

Dartagnan swore under his breath. "But, Boss, I'm not qualified to pilot anything like this—"

"A ship's a ship." Siamang frowned. "You'll manage."

"Chaim"—she turned to him desperately—"help me. He won't kill us both, he'd never get back to the Demarchy if he did! Together we can stop him; don't let him get away with this—"

"I'll kill you both if I have to, and pilot the ship myself." Siamang's eyes turned deadly; Dartagnan saw the dilated pupils clearly now—and believed him.

"He's bluffing," Mythili said.

Chaim caught her eyes, pleading. "Mythili, for God's sake, change your mind. Tell him you'll keep your mouth shut. Go along with him. It isn't worth it, it's not worth your life."

She looked away from him, deaf and blind.

"Save your breath, Red. I wouldn't trust her anyway . . . she's got too much integrity. And besides, she hates me too much; she'd never change her mind. She's just been waiting for a chance like this, look at her." Anger strained his voice. "No, I think we'll just drop her off somewhere between here and the Demarchy, and let her walk home. And in the meantime"—he moved toward her suddenly—"we might as well have a little fun." He blocked her as she tried to escape, threw her back against the instrument board, ripping open the seal of her jumpsuit.

"No!"

Siamang turned, held her, struggling, against the panel. Dartagnan glimpsed her face beyond him, the loathing and the fresh, sudden terror; her shining, golden skin. Siamang pulled her away from the board, twisting her arm behind her. "Okay, Red, if you want her first. She's sweet on you any-way...." He pushed her at Dartagnan.

Chaim caught hold of her, dropped his crutch, fighting to keep his balance. "Mythili ..."

She spat in his face, pulling her jumpsuit closed. Siamang laughed.

Chaim let anger show, "Forget it; I'm not interested."

"Don't do me any favors, mediaman." She was flint-on-steel against him; her outrage burned him like a flame.

He let her go, wiped his face, said roughly, "Believe me, I'm not doing you any favor. . . ." *But, God help me, maybe I'm saving your life—and mine.* He looked back at Siamang, leaned down to pick up his crutch, covering sudden inspiration. "I've got a better idea. Instead of spacing her later, put her out here, now, in a suit with the valve jammed. The sun's going down . . . she'll suffocate or freeze . . . and we can watch, to make sure she's dead. A tragic accident." He felt her anguish, her helpless rage; felt a hot, stabbing pain in his stomach.

Siamang smiled as the possibilities registered. "Yes, I like it. . . . All right, Red; we'll do it your way. But there's no reason why I still can't have some fun with little Fukinuki, first. . . ." He reached up, began to unbutton his jacket.

"Yes, there is."

Siamang looked at him. "Oh?"

"It's getting late; the ship's batteries are running down. And besides, the wind's rising. If you expect me to get us up out of here safely, I don't want to wait any longer. . . . Won't you get enough pleasure watching her die out there?" Dartagnan's voice rose too much.

Siamang smiled again, slowly. "Okay, Red, you win. . . . Get into a suit, Mythili, before I change my mind."

She walked wordlessly past Dartagnan, clinging to the shreds of her dignity; he watched her put on a suit. She fumbled, awkward, made clumsy by gravity and nervousness. Wanting to help her, Chaim stood motionless, turned to stone.

She turned back to them at last, waiting, the helmet under her arm. "All right," barely audible, "I'm ready. . . ."

Siamang crossed the cabin to her side, reached behind her

head to the airflow valve at her neck. She shuddered as he touched her. Dartagnan watched him tighten the knob that shut off the oxygen flow, watched his body tighten with the effort.

"Put on your helmet."

She took a deep breath, put it on. Siamang latched it in place, motioned her toward the lock. She went to it, stepped inside, jerkily, like a broken doll.

"Red." Siamang gestured. "You do the honors."

Dartagnan hobbled to the control plate, counting seconds in his mind. He could barely see her face, staring back at him, saw her mouth move silently, *Damn you, damn you, damn you . . . !* He thought there were tears in her eyes, wasn't sure.

He nodded, whispering. "Goodbye, Goody Two-Shoes. Good luck!" His hand shook; he pushed a button, the door closed.

He turned back with Siamang to the control board, watched the viewscreen, waited. The seconds passed, the lock cycled. She appeared suddenly on the screen, stumbled as the wind gusted . . . fell, got up, fell again as she tried to run, tried to reach the sheltering dome, too far away. The shifting, slate-blue dust slipped under her feet, she fell again, tried to get up, couldn't. At last he saw her try to free the frozen valve one final time . . . and then unlatch her helmet. She raised her head, too far away for him to see her face; he dragged a breath into his own tortured lungs. Her hands rose to her neck, her face, she reached for her helmet again, frantically . . . crumpled forward into the dust, lay coiled like a fetus, lay still.

Dartagnan made himself look at Siamang; looked away again, sick. He sagged down into the pilot's seat, reached for the restraining straps. Siamang turned back from the screen, the obscenity of his pleasure fading to stunned disgust. "Get us out of this graveyard." He moved past Chaim, toward his own padded couch; stopped, turned back. "By the way, this time it was premeditated murder. And you did it, Red. Keep that in mind."

Dartagnan didn't answer, staring at the screen, looking down at the empty seat beside him.

He took the ship safely up through the atmosphere, learning that getting up off of a planet's surface was much simpler than getting safely down. He rendezvoused, docked the shrunken landing module at last within the stretched, arachnoid fingers of the parent ship; he heard his father's voice directing, guiding, encouraging . . . knowing with a kind of certainty that after what he had seen and done below, he couldn't make a mistake now.

On board the main ship again, he moved through the levels to the control room, found their flight coordinates already in the computer. Mechanically, he took the ship out of orbit, barely conscious of what he did; as he turned away from the panel Siamang congratulated him, with apparent sincerity. Dartagnan pushed on past, wordless, ducked into the aluminum-ringed well. He reached Mythili Fukinuki's cabin door, stopped himself, and with a sudden masochistic urge, opened it and went inside. He slid the door shut, drifted to the bed, pulling off his jacket, his shirt, one boot. He forced his aching body into the sleeping bag, settled softly, mumbling, "Good luck, Goody Two-Shoes . . . good luck . . ." And finally, thankfully, he slept.

When he woke again his face burned under his touch, his ankle was hot and swollen inside his boot. He went down into the commons, forced himself to eat, found a bottle of antibiotics and swallowed a handful of pills heedlessly. Then he went back to the cabin, locked the door, and slept again.

He repeated the cycle four more times, avoiding Siamang, before his fever broke and he remembered to check the ship's progress. He made minor alterations in their course, lingered at the screen for long seconds, searching the darkness for something he would never find. Then he tried to use the radio, and was deafened by a rush of static. He realized that Siamang had done something to the long-range antenna while he slept; there would be no more radio contact until they were back within Demarchy space. He checked the chronometer: less than half a megasecond of flight time had elapsed. Even without the added mass of the propellant tanks they had carried on the way out, more than three megaseconds still remained.

"How's our progress?"

He turned and found Siamang behind him. "Fine, as far as I can tell." His own voice startled him, unexpectedly.

"And how's your conscience?"

Dartagnan laughed sharply, nervously. "What conscience?"

Siamang smiled. Dartagnan risked a look straight into his eyes. They were clear, the pupils undilated; he wondered whether that was good or bad. "I wondered whether you might be suffering the pangs of remorse. You're not looking too well." Faint mockery, faint disapproval . . . faint suspicion.

Chaim scratched an unshaven cheek, cautiously expressionless. "Only the pangs of a fall down stairs." He glanced down at his unbuttoned jacket, the cheap, bedraggled lace on his half-tucked-in shirt. He looked back at Siamang, flawlessly in control, as always. He raised his hands. "I was just going to go clean myself up," and retreated.

Seconds sifted down through the hourglass of time, the ship moved through the darkness, slowly gaining speed. The casual persecution Siamang had inflicted on the trip out grew more calculated now, and more pervasive; until Dartagnan began to feel that Siamang only lived for his personal torment, a private demon sprung from his own private hell. He lived on soy milk, as the chronic tension exacerbated his ulcer; he began to lose sleep, as Siamang's probing found the hidden wounds of his guilt. He felt the armor of his hardwon, studied indifference wearing thin, wondered how much more he could stand. And he wondered what pathology drove Siamang to methodically destroy the loyalty of the only "witness" in his own defense. . . .

Until suddenly Dartagnan saw that it was no pathology at all, but a coldly rational test. In spite of what he was, in spite of everything, Siamang didn't trust him . . . and unless Siamang was completely convinced of his cowed submission and his totally amoral self-interest, there might be a third Tragic Accident before the end of this Odyssey of Lies and Death. They were safely on a homeward course; he was entirely expendable again. Three deaths might be hard to explain, but Siamang had the means to sway public opinion at any trial—as long as there was no one to testify against him.

His sudden comprehension of his danger steadied Dartagnan on the tightwire he walked above the abyss of his desperation. He would endure anything, do anything he had to do; there were only two things that mattered now—his own survival, and the reward that he would have earned a thousand times . . . not a ship, not his freedom, but the knowledge that Siamang and Sons would pay. They would pay to bring Mythili Fukinuki back to the Demarchy; they would pay for Sekka-Olefin's death . . . they could never even begin to pay enough, for what they had done to Heaven's future.

And so he endured, ingratiating, obedient, and smiling—always smiling. He lived for the future, the present was a darkness behind his eyes; he was a man on a wire, above the starry void between the past and their destination. And in the refuge of his cabin, he found the private world of Mythili Fukinuki, in a chest filled with books and papers. Ashamed at first, he rummaged through them, finding the precise impersonalities of astrogation manuals . . . and books on poetry and philosophy, not only recent but translations into the Anglo from all the varied cultures of her heritage on Earth. Passages were marked with parenthesis, question marks, exclamations; her own thoughts held communion in the margins of the shining plastic pages or spilled over, filling notebooks.

He began to read, as she had read, to fill the empty stretch of time. He felt her presence in everything he read, in each small discovery; beyond anger or bitter grief, she gave him comfort, brought him strength . . . and he understood at last that he had hated prospecting because he hated loneliness; that because of his resentment, being with his father had been the same as being alone. But he saw himself on his own ship, imagined Mythili Fukinuki as his partner—and knew he would need nothing more, need no one else, to be content. . . . A much-opened book of poems fell open again in his hands, and he saw her plain, backslanted writing in a margin: *It will be lonely to be dead; but it cannot be much more lonely than it is to be alive. . . .*

He found a grease pencil in the sack of his belongings, and slowly, as though there was no strength left in his hand, wrote *Yes, yes, yes* . . . The vision of her coiled form, the swirling dust of Planet Two, choked his memory; he snapped the book shut. *No, I wasn't wrong!* He put the book carefully into his sack, and after that he stopped reading.

But he realized then that if he was wrong, if he was as guilty as Siamang himself . . . if Mythili Fukinuki had died because of him, then even if he survived to give testimony, it would only be his own word against Siamang's and that might not be enough. Siamang had influence; he had nothing—he had no proof, without Mythili. And if she was dead, he had to be certain that Siamang would never get away with it. Somehow he had to find a way to make Siamang incriminate himself. But his camera was ruined, the radio was out; he didn't even have a tape recorder on him . . . or did he?

He got up silently, and slipped out of the room.

They were well within Demarchy space; one hundred kiloseconds remained before they would dock at Mecca. Dartagnan made radio contact at last, as Siamang looked on, and set up a media conference for their arrival. One hundred kiloseconds ... and still he had no proof.

"Come on, Red, let's celebrate our impending return to civilization." Siamang gestured, smiling openly, without sarcasm. "God, it'll be a relief to get back to the real world! This whole damned thing is an experience I only want to forget."

"The same here, Boss. The sooner the better." Dartagnan followed him below, humoring his apparent good humor. Chaim drank soy milk cut with water, trying to lull the chronic spasms of his stomach; Siamang drank something that he assumed was considerably stronger. But Siamang's mood stayed easy and congenial, his conversation rambled, innocuous, clever, only slightly condescending.

"Join me in one drink at least, Red." Siamang slid one of the magnetized drink bulbs across the metal surface of the table. "How much can it hurt?"

"It hurts plenty, believe me, Boss. I'd like to, I would; but I just can't take liquor."

"It's not vodka." Siamang's tone turned conspiratorial, and sharpened slightly. "I want you to have a drink with me, Red. I won't take no for an answer."

"No, I'm sorry . . ."

"Come on, drink it." Siamang laughed; Chaim felt his stomach tighten. "Do it—as a favor to me."

Dartagnan hesitated, toying absently with the wide metal band that circled his throat beneath the high collar of his jacket. "All right, Boss; just one . . . if you'll do me a favor in return?"

Siamang started. "What did you have in mind?"

"I want my payoff now. I want you to give me a corporate credit voucher for the value of my scoutship."

Siamang frowned. "I'm willing to transfer the credit to your account directly—"

He shook his head. "Sometimes direct credit transfers don't—get registered. I want it in writing before I do my bit to keep you clear of that murder."

Siamang's frown deepened, lifted slowly. "All right, Red . . . I'll humor you. I don't expect you'll let me down if I do; since you're in this as deep as I am, and you'll go right down with me." He went out of the room.

Dartagnan sat staring uneasily at the cup. *What the hell; it hasn't done anything to Siamang. . . .* He turned the metal collar slowly around his neck. *Dammit, it's worth a belly-ache; it's worth anything, to be sure I get what I need.*

Siamang returned, passed the voucher across the table to him. "Is that satisfactory?"

Dartagnan took it in his hands, like a starving man holding food. For a second the realization of what that money could mean to his own future rose into his mind, and made him dizzy. "Yeah," he said hoarsely, "that's just perfect." He folded it and stuck it into his boot. He lifted the drink bulb from the table, "I'll drink to that." He pulled up on the straw, and drank.

He tasted nothing, only the bland sweetness of pear juice; he went on drinking, surprised, finished it.

Siamang drank with him, smiled. "What are you going to do with a ship, Red? You mean you really don't enjoy being a garbage man to humanity?"

"I've recycled just about all the garbage I ever want to face, Boss. Just about all I can stand . . ." He squinted; the light glancing up from the tabletop hurt his eyes: *Come on, that's impossible* . . . suddenly afraid that it wasn't.

"Going to be a prospector, like Sekka-Olefin?"

He looked back at Siamang. "Not like Sekka-Olefin. He—made a mistake." Siamang's voice set his teeth on edge; his skin prickled, he began to feel as though his body was strung together on live wires. "Just like my old man . . . I'm not going to make that mistake." *Shut up!* He shook his head, the light broke up into prisms.

"What mistake was that, Red? What mistake could there be that a man who'd go into your profession hasn't made already?"

Chaim almost shouted it, shaking with uncontrollable rage. He choked back the words, gagged on sudden self-loathing. *Why isn't Siamang feeling it?* And then he realized that Siamang hadn't been drinking anything at all, except fruit juice. Siamang was entirely sober: and he had been given one last test. . . .

Mecca city opened around him, vibrant, brilliant, beautiful, an alien flower . . . his mind sang, a choir of voices, the voice of the city, eternal life. He cupped life in his hands and drank . . . life streaming through the prism of his fingers in rainstars of light. He was eternal, he laughed, inhaling the city fragrance of sound, chords of cinnamon and cloves, leitmotiv of gardenia . . . of corruption . . . a fragrance growing, that deafened him, shattering his ears, shattering his soul like crystal, shattering the crystal city . . . A cloying stench of decay clogged his nose, his mouth, his lungs, like slaty dust; the fragile towers withered, fading, shriveling around him: like bodies decaying, betrayed . . . death was eternal, only death: and her face, all their faces turned to him, turned to ruin, worm-eaten, rotting, decayed . . . *I know you . . . Mythili, I know you . . .* he had no voice *. . . I know you aren't! . . . I know you . . .* He heard her sobbing, like flowers, crystal acid-drops eating away his viscera like decay. *I don't want to! I don't want to die . . . I want to live . . . I have to . . . want to live. . . .* Cradled in the arms of death, worm-riddled, he saw his flesh rotting, falling from his bones . . . and it was the end, the end of the world. . . .

Dartagnan woke, moved feebly on the floor in the bathroom of his private cabin, trying to remember how he had gotten there, why he had eaten hot coals . . . why he was crying. He lay still, too weary to move, listened to the grating whine of a fan . . . the exhaust fan. He remembered, then, being sick to his stomach. He touched his face, filmed with wetness, sweat and tears—and vomit: God, he hadn't done a very clean job of it. He pushed himself up, drifted to the wash basin to shut off the fan. He saw himself in the mirror, shut his eyes instead, swore in a fury of humiliation—

Siamang. He reached down, dragged his boot off, swearing again as he wrenched his still-swollen ankle. But he laughed in satisfaction as his hand closed over the crumpled, drifting prize, the credit voucher. *Still there . . .* He tried again futilely to remember what else had happened; knowing that Siamang had drugged him for a reason, and that he could have said anything, *would* have said anything, and anything could have been the wrong thing. But he had the voucher; and he was still alive. A flicker of nightmare, a discontinuity, shook him; he ran his hands down his body in sudden fear. He was still alive. The metal collar was still around his neck; he had what he needed. Maybe, just this once, something was going to come out right. . . .

He stripped, went to the shower, sealed himself in along with his ruined clothes, and turned on the water. He let it run, heedless of the waste, through three full shower cycles, an entire kilosecond, until he finally began to feel clean. Life, and—almost—self-respect, stirred sluggishly in him again as the heat lamp dried the sheen of water from his skin, baked the shame and the last of the stiffness out of his mind and body. He shaved, did what he could with his clammy clothes, put on the one fresh shirt he had saved for their return to Mecca. Appearance was everything; he had to present a good appearance, when he faced himself in the eyes of the media cameras. . . . He investigated his ankle; the brown skin was still splotched with ugly bruises, but it was healing, slowly, with the passing of time. He forced it back into his boot, polished both boots with his dirty shirt. He thought about other wounds, and wondered how much time he would need before those were healed as well.

"Dartagnan—?"

He heard Siamang rap on his door, quietly, and then more loudly. He went to it, opened it, his face set. Siamang stared; Chaim wondered whether he was staring at the neatness of his clothes, or the haggardness of his face. "What do you want?"

Almost diffidently, Siamang held out a drink bulb; Dartagnan grimaced. "It's just milk; you can believe it. Look, I'm sorry about what happened to you, Red. I shouldn't have given you that big a dose, I didn't think about your not being used to it."

The hell you didn't, Dartagnan thought.

"I want you to know I'm sorry. How do you feel?"

"Like I'll be glad when I can forget it. How much time's left before we reach Mecca?"

"That's why I knocked—only five thousand seconds. Are you going to be able to bring us in all right?"

Dartagnan almost smiled, realizing the reason for Siamang's sudden solicitude. "I think so. I hope so." He moved out into the hall, hesitated, trying to make it sound casual. "I hope I didn't—say anything I shouldn't have, Boss. I . . . don't remember much about it."

"You told me you hated my stinking guts, Red."

He froze. "I'm sorry, Boss, I didn't mean it, I didn't know what I was—"

Siamang grinned forgiveness. "It's all right, Red. I don't blame you at all. In fact it's just what I wanted to hear . . . I wanted to hear you say what you really thought, just once. Because you also said that I'd given you what you wanted, and that was all that mattered. I know I can trust you now, Red; because I'm sure we understand each other. Isn't that right?" Mockery traced the words. His hand struck Chaim's shoulder lightly.

Dartagnan smiled. "Sure, Boss. Anything you say."

Dartagnan watched the elongated crescent of the asteroid Mecca grow large on the viewscreen, and gradually eclipse as he maneuvered them into its shadow. Siamang hung behind him, watching; oblivious. Chaim watched only the intricate, expanding pattern of strangely familiar ground lights below them. He began to pick out ships—the tankers like gigantic ticks, bloated or empty; the small, red-blossoming tows. He listened to the disjointed, disembodied radio communications, almost thought he could see the ships making way for him. He spoke calmly to the ground controller, explaining who he was, and boosted the response for Siamang to hear; the encouragements, the welcomings—interspersed with the terse, anxious coordinates to guide an inexperienced pilot down to the bright, scarred surface of the docking field. Their ship closed with the real world, Dartagnan felt the slight, jarring impact of a perfect landing rise through its structure. In his mind he compared the slow ceremony of docking to the terrifying urgency of their descent to the surface of Planet Two . . . remembered sharing the pride of a job well done. For half a second, he smiled.

The field was curiously empty, the helmet speakers strangely silent, as they disembarked at last and made their way along a mooring cable toward the exit from the field. One guard met them, greeting Siamang with deference, cleared them to pass downward through the airlock into the asteroid's heart.

"Where the hell is everybody, Red? My father should be here. Where's our media coverage?" Siamang's voice frowned. "I thought you radioed ahead about our arrival."

"I did, Boss; you heard me. They must be waiting for us inside." *They've got to be. . . .*

They were: Dartagnan followed Siamang along the corridor that dropped them inward from the surface, his broken camera floating at his shoulder, and saw his fellow mediamen clustered in wait on the platform at the city's edge. A surprisingly sparse crowd of curious onlookers, surprisingly quiet, bumped and drifted among them. *Awed . . . ?* he thought. He wondered if Siamang's rivals among the distilleries had kept their workers away. The irony pleased him, but not, he noticed, Siamang.

He watched the crowd flow forward to meet them, let it surround him, letting the mediamen get it out of their systems, "Demarch Siamang . . . Demarch Siamang . . . Hey, Red—?" He glimpsed the city, past and through them . . . a kilometer in diameter, towers trembling faintly, glittering in the shifting currents of air. Colored plastic stretched over fragile frames filled every square meter of ceiling, wall, floor, here where gravity was barely more than an abstraction: A man-made tribute to the magnificent generosity of nature, and the splendor of the Heaven Belt. The splendor made sterile because nature had turned its back on man; man the betrayer, who had betrayed himself. Chaim saw Sekka-Olefin's future, in a sudden, strobing nightmare of horror overlying every crystal-facet wall, every stranger's face that closed in on his own. . . . *My God . . . my God . . . and I'm the only one who knows!* He steadied himself, inhaling the spices of the scented air, summoning strength and resolution.

And then he raised his hands, raised his voice into the familiar singsong of a media hype. "Ladies and gentlemen . . . my fellow Demarchs . . ." Silence began to gather. "I'm sure you all know and recognize Demarch Siamang. But there's a side of him that none of you really knows. . . ." He stretched his silence until the silence around him was absolute; every eye, every pitiless camera lens was trained on him where he stood, Siamang complacently at his side. He took a deep breath. "This man—is a murderer. He went four hundred million kilometers to Planet Two, to save Kwaime Sekka-Olefin, and wound up killing him instead, over that box of—stolen—computer software you see there in his hand." He turned, bracing, saw Siamang's face, the perfect image of incredulous amazement.

Siamang's eyes were blank with a fury that only he could read. "This man is a psychotic. I don't have any idea what he's talking about. I obtained this salvage from Sekka-Olefin in a legitimate business transaction; and he was perfectly alive when we left him—"

A stranger pushed forward, touched Dartagnan's arm; golden eyes demanded his attention, assured, analytical. "Are you Chaim Dartagnan?"

Chaim nodded, distracted; Siamang broke off speaking abruptly. "Who the hell are you?"

"My name's Abdhiamal; I'm a government negotiator. . . . Demarch Dartagnan, what evidence do you have to support your charge?"

"Now, listen, Abdhiamal," Siamang interrupted, indignant. "No one needs any government interference here, this is simply a—"

"Demarch Dartagnan has the floor," Abdhiamal said evenly, his eyes never leaving Chaim's face. "You'll be permitted to speak in turn. Dartagnan?"

Dartagnan almost laughed; triumph filled him, overwhelming gratitude made him giddy. He kept his own eyes on the media cameras—his damnation, his salvation, his weapon. . . . "He got hold of my camera, I don't have the recording of the murder. But he bribed me, to cover the whole thing up . . . this's the corporate credit voucher, made out to me." He spread it between his hands, held it out to the thousands of hungry eyes behind every camera lens.

"That's a forgery."

"And this"—Dartagnan pulled open the collar of his jacket—"is a recording of the transaction." He twisted the jury-rigged playback knob on the note recorder he had ripped out of his spacesuit; he heard his own voice: ". . . I want it in writing, before I do my bit to keep you clear of that murder." And Siamang's, "All right, Red."

"That was an accident!" Siamang's voice slipped out of control. "I didn't mean to kill Olefin, it was an accident—but ask him about Mythili Fukinuki, ask him about our pilot: that was no accident. He murdered her in cold blood; there was nothing I could do to stop him. He's a madman, a homicidal maniac—"

"Mythili Fukinuki's not dead." Dartagnan turned to watch for the second it took to register on Siamang's face. He smiled; he turned back again to Abdhiamal, was surprised at the surprise he found in the golden eyes. "At least . . . I don't think she is. When I was alone with Sekka-Olefin, he claimed a human could survive in Planet Two's atmosphere; he said he'd breathed it himself. Siamang wanted to space her, because she overheard Olefin's murder. . . . I told him to put her out on the surface instead. He was on drugs, I couldn't stop it or he would've killed us all. It was the only thing I could think of. . . ." Ashamed, he looked down, away from the memory of her face, *Damn you, damn you.* . . . "If I was wrong, if she died, then I'm just as guilty as he is; the Demarchy can do anything they choose to me, I deserve it. All that matters to me now is that somebody made it back, to tell the truth. And to see that Siamang and Sons pays to get her home—because I don't believe that she is . . . dead. . . ." A sudden reaction took away his voice. "Has there . . . have you heard of any radio messages being received? Is there any word?"

"Better than that, as far as you're concerned." Abdhiamal smiled, without amusement. "Mythili Fukinuki returned to the Demarchy before you did, in that prospector's ship. She reported everything that happened . . . except the fact that you weren't actually trying to kill her, Dartagnan."

Dartagnan laughed incredulously. "My God, she would . . . she would!"

Abdhiamal smiled again, at something on Dartagnan's face. "As far as the Demarchy's concerned, your testimony leaves it up to her whether she wants to press her charges of attempted murder against you. But with a confession, and both your evidence and hers, I'd say the case against Demarch Siamang is a little more clear-cut. . . . You see, Demarch Siamang"—he looked back—"this isn't a news conference; consider it more of a preliminary hearing. The Demarchy had already been informed of Demarch Fukinuki's testimony and evidence before you arrived; your father is being considered as an accomplice, pending further questioning. All we needed was your version; and we have that, now."

Never underestimate the power of a woman. Dartagnan grinned, weak in the knees. He noticed that Siamang was ringed in now by "spectators"; vigilantes, volunteer police requested for the occasion. Siamang's eyes raked them with disdain. "This is an outrage. This is entrapment." He looked back at the cameras. "People of the Demarchy, are you going to stand by while a fellow Demarch is persecuted by the government?"

"The people asked me to come here, Siamang. Save your rhetoric for your trial. In the meantime, consider yourself confined to your home. . . . And I'll take charge of the software." Abdhiamal held out his hand: Chaim recognized a kind of gratification on the government man's face; realized that Abdhiamal was hardly older than himself, behind the mask of his self-assurance. In the Demarchy, a government agent earned less respect than a mediaman, and had considerably less influence.

Siamang passed the container to him, entirely in control once more. He faced Dartagnan again, at last; Dartagnan tried to read the expression behind his eyes, couldn't. Siamang reached out abruptly, caught Dartagnan's arm, jerked the voucher out of his hand. Chaim watched him tear it up, watched the pieces drift as they sought the lines of gravitational force. "You'll never have a ship now, Red." A final mockery showed in his eyes, traced his voice. "But I hope you never stop wanting one, so you'll never stop hating yourself for this."

Dartagnan smiled, filled with a terrible pride; smiled with a sincerity he didn't know he still had in him. He shook his head, met the aggressor's eyes at last. "Believe me, Boss, I never wanted a ship, or anything, half as much as I wanted to see this happen . . . to see truth win out in this lousy business, just once, because of me." He turned the smile on the cameras, and on the men behind them.

Siamang's escort led him away, to the rim of the ledge where an airbus waited. The handful of mediamen swarmed after them, onto the bus, into air taxis; Dartagnan stared at the bobbing mass of striped canopies, whirring propellers. The remaining crowd of strangers around him began to disperse, drifting over the ledge into the city, leaving him alone with Abdhiamal. "What about me?"

Abdhiamal shrugged. "You're not going anywhere, are you? Your further testimony will be needed when they call a trial; somehow I expect you'll want to be there. I'd hate to see Siamang promo his way out of a guilty verdict now."

Dartagnan frowned. "He won't, will he?"

"I doubt it. Public opinion's had too much time to build against him. His father couldn't do much to help him, because he didn't know enough about it. . . . You know, your fellow mediamen seem to be a lot more interested in the murderer than in your having exposed him." Abdhiamal looked at him.

Dartagnan grinned weakly. "It figures . . . I just paid 'em the biggest insult I could think of. Besides, a mediaman follows the smell of power . . . it smells like money, in case you're interested." He leaned down, picked up a corner of the ruined credit voucher. The full impact of what he had given up caught him like a blow. "Easy come, easy go." He laughed, painfully, embarrassing himself. "That reminds me—what about the software, the salvage? What happens to Sekka-Olefin's money, now?"

"The artifacts will be sold at a public auction; Siamang and Sons being disqualified from bidding, of course. Sekka-

Olefin's relatives have put in claims against it; the money will be distributed among them, since he didn't leave any will stating what he wanted done with it."

"But he did! He told me what he wanted done with it. He didn't want it to go to his relatives; he wants it used to establish a colony on Planet Two, against the time when the Demarchy's not habitable anymore—" Chaim broke off, realizing how it sounded.

Abdhiamal looked at him, tactfully noncommittal. "Do you have any proof of that?"

"Yeah. Every word of it, on film . . . at the bottom of a well. A gravity well." He swore. "His goddam relatives'll never listen. He was right! And it all went for nothing, because of Siamang." He saw the crystal city through a haze of death, knew he would have to see it that way for the rest of his life: the towers decaying, the fragile thread of life coming apart. "That stinking bastard . . . I hope they vote to space him. Because that's what he's done to their future, and they'll never even know . . ." His voice shook, with bitterness and exasperation.

"At least you've done something to try to make it up to him." The voice wasn't Abdhiamal's.

He turned back, incredulous. "Mythili?" She stood beside him, materializing out of the diminished crowd; Abdhiamal had moved away, discreetly. "Mythili." He started toward her; she pushed away, out of his reach. He stopped, pulled in his hands. "Sorry . . . I'm just . . . I'm glad. Just glad to see you." He noticed the patches of pink, healing skin on her cheeks and nose. "Are you all right?"

She nodded. "Some frostbite. Some burns, from the cold. I was a mess for a while. But I'm fine."

He nodded too, unthinking. "I'm glad. The old man was right, then—Sekka-Olefin. He told me that it was possible to live—"

"I know." She looked down abruptly, rubbed her eyes with the back of her hand. "I heard you."

"Do you believe it?"

She still looked down. "Yes . . . yes, I believe you, now, Chaim. But why did you do it? We could have stopped him; you could have—"

"—gotten us both killed?" Shame kindled anger, "Why did't you just keep your mouth shut, like I did; everything would've been okay."

Her eyes flashed up. "Because I'm not like you! . . . I

know, it was stupid, I know that now . . . But I couldn't have hidden it anyway; he would have known. I'm not good at hiding what I feel." She bit her lip. "I'm not like you, Dartagnan."

He let his breath out slowly, said stupidly, again, "I'm just glad you're all right. . . . I saw you, on the viewscreen, saw you take off your helmet. And then I thought I'd been wrong, that you—"

"I thought so, too." She laughed, tremulously, at the ghost of memory. "The air was so thin, so cold, I thought I couldn't breathe. I panicked, and I blacked out. The noise and heat when you lifted off saved me, it woke me, or I would have frozen to death instead. I almost didn't get up again . . . I thought I'd already died."

"You repaired Olefin's ship?"

"Yes . . . It's a good ship, a fantastic ship; he must have spent a fortune—"

"He did. Literally. On a dream."

"I brought his body back: a pleasant companion, for a trip of three-plus megaseconds." She shuddered. "Three and a quarter megaseconds, with a dead man, and frost-burned lungs, and memory . . . God, how I hated you, Chaim! How I hated you . . . and yet—" She wouldn't look at him.

"I know," he said, "I know. Three and a half megaseconds with Siamang, and memory; wanting to kill him, and afraid he'd kill me. But you were there, I could feel you, helping me get through. Helping me survive to make it right. I always planned to tell the truth, Mythili, I never meant to do anything else."

"So the end justifies the means, then?" Her voice teetered on the edge of control.

He didn't answer, couldn't.

"I won't press charges against you." She turned away.

"Mythili. Don't go yet." She looked back at him; he groped for words. "What . . . what will you be doing now? Are you still working for Siamang and Sons?"

"No. Siamang, senior, fired me, after I made my accusations." She almost smiled, not meaning it. "I'm hoping one of his competitors will offer me a job"—hopelessly. "So you won't have a ship of your own, now, either?"

"No." He looked down, at the torn corner of the voucher still wadded in his hand. "Not now . . . but someday, I will. And when I get it, I want you to be my partner. I want you to—to—" *To stay with me*. His mind, his eyes, finished it, uselessly.

" 'Good-bye, Goody Two-Shoes,' " she whispered. She shook her head. Her own eyes were mirrors of memory, for the face of a man who had tried to kill her; a man who had lied too well. "I might forgive you . . . but how could I ever forget?" An anguished brightness silvered the mirror of her eyes, she turned away again.

"Mythili, wait!" He fumbled in the sack of his belongings, pulled out the book of poetry. "Wait; this belongs to you." He held it out.

She came back, took it from his hand without touching him. Confused anger startled her face as she recognized the title. "What are you doing with this?" Pain and grief. "Shiva, isn't there anything that you wouldn't pry into? You'll never have a ship! You'll be a mediaman all your life, because that's all you were ever meant to be." She might have said "whore."

"I will get a ship. If it takes me the rest of my goddam life, I will . . . and when I do, I'll find you! Mythili—"

She didn't turn back, this time. He saw her hail a taxi, get in; watched it fall out and down into the vastness of the city air. Pain knotted his stomach; he clenched his teeth.

"Dartagnan—" Abdhiamal came up beside him, eyes questioning, sympathetic. "No?"

"No." Chaim produced a smile, pasted it hastily over his mouth. "But that's life. The only reward of virtue is virtue . . . the hell with that." He picked up his sack, readjusted his camera strap. "You can't afford it, in my business. . . . Good thing my camera's already broken; one of my good buddies will probably smash it over my head when I get back to work. Nobody likes an honest mediaman; you can't trust 'em."

Abdhiamal smiled, "I disagree."

Dartagnan laughed, still looking out into the city. "Everybody knows you've got to be crazy to work for the government." His eyes stung, from too much staring.

"You look like you could use a drink. On me?" Abdhiamal gestured toward the city.

"Why not?" Dartagnan nodded, hand pressing his stomach. "Yeah . . . that's just what I need."

Afterword

"Media Man" was one of the rare stories whose plot actually came into my mind full-blown. Usually I have to begin with bits and pieces; a beginning, an end, an incident here and there in the middle. In this case, I sat down to write out a summary of the basic idea and found that by the time I'd finished I had virtually the whole story plotted. It also fell very naturally into the "future history" of a novel I was working on, *The Outcasts of Heaven Belt*, which gave it a background already laid out. (One of the most difficult things about writing science fiction—unless you concentrate on a particular future history worked out beforehand, as some writers do—is having to create an entire new universe for each story. So far I've experimented with a variety of possible futures—although once I've created one, I always reserve the right to set other stories in it if I come up with an idea, like this one, that seems to fit.)

The original inspiration for "Media Man" came from a TV movie—one of those in which the naive, virtuous hero sees the villain commit murder in the middle of nowhere, and says staunchly, "I'm going to tell the police!" Of course the villain immediately tried to kill him too, and he spent the rest of the show trying not to become the next victim. It has always seemed to me that any reasonable person would attempt to placate the villain—to convince him that he was on the villain's side—in order to survive until he could reach help. (And then turn him in.) That was the hook that started me writing my version; although I found, as Dartagnan did, that even with the best/worst of motives, it's not a simple thing to convince the enemy that honor always has a price.

One of the interesting aspects of this story is people's reaction to its ending: I've found that in general women felt that the two main characters would eventually get back together again after the end of the story, while men felt that they would not. I don't know whether this is because the woman

138

was the one who rejected the man in the story, whether women simply tend to be more optimistic about relationships, or whether some other totally unrelated sociological factor is at work. No one quite seems to know why he or she came to such conclusions. (I had always assumed, myself, that the characters would be reunited. An upcoming project is writing the story of how it happened.)

The Crystal Ship

The Crystal Ship fell endlessly through orbit, tethered above the pinwheel-clouded world. Within its walls, among the many rooms, the dreamers sought oblivion in beauty. There were barely fifty of them now, none who remembered why their ancestors had come here, or even cared. But still they came, after five hundred years, as though it were a ritual.

Within the high-ceilinged torus hall, the dreamers gazed out over the bright crescent of their world or lay entranced in the liquid folds of lounge or chair. Ruby chitta syrup congealed along the clear rims of fallen cups, like dribbles of blood.

Chitta reddened Tarawassie's lips, while the stars danced on her fingertips, and she cast aside the false barriers of being and perception to become one with the limitless universe, formless, timeless, mindless. . . . Tarawassie dreamed, as she had always dreamed—as she always would have, if not for Andar's madness:

Colors fading from the sunset sky, petals crumbling to pastel, fragrance lost to all but memory. Soft barriers enclosed her; bonds of flesh, bars of bone, settled around her as Tarawassie fell back again, with sorrow, into the holding state.

"It is true! It's true—!" Sudden sound battered her, bursting inside her head in murky incandescence.

Her hands rose, not knowing what to cover; ears, eyes—a pale, burning face swelled into her sight, she was dragged up, shaking, shaken, through a tunnel of reverberating sound, "Look at youyouyou . . . you don't care . . . animals; rotting, rotting . . . !" She cried out feebly, coming alive to struggle as the pain released her and thrust her back into the undulating couch.

The face, moving away from her, took on reality and form; she recognized Andar, his bright robe billowing like wind through a field of grasses as he shouted: "I know the truth! But *you* can't *see* it!" His hands caught, accosted, rejected others as he stumbled through the rooms. Instinctively she rose and followed his progress through the transparent halls; watched him fall over other inert forms as he made his way to the thing at the heart of all beauty—to the Star Well. "I love you, I hate you—" He was laughing, or sobbing. "Your living death! I'm the only one—the only one *alive*—and I can't stand you any more." He had reached the rim of the Well, knelt down, hanging over the cool, pulsing depths. "I know your secret"—to his own shadow-face—"and I'm ready, I'm ready . . . to pass the dragon, and enter the dark abyss. Accept me! There is a heaven, and it is death. . . ." Sobbing now, clearly, he toppled forward into the Well, embracing its shadowy ambiguity. Ripples of phosphorescence spread in the unwater, vibrant with aquamarine; he lay still. Tarawassie stared, struggling with reality.

And he lay still; he lay so still. The others who had seen and could comprehend came to gather around her, moving slowly, silently, wonderingly up through the rooms to stand at last at the Well's rim.

Andar's body lay below them, not quite drifting, not quite supported, somehow suspended. Shadow waves of blue-green lapped him gently, shifting his patterned robe, his long, fair hair, cupping his curled fingers. Tarawassie knew that her own hand would find nothing, capture nothing and yet be cooled, reaching down through that blue-greenness. The mystery of it had never disturbed her; she had never thought to wonder why. The stars seemed very large, very near, as though they lay sleeping in the silken depths.

"Andar . . . Andar?" Someone reached out instead of her, caught a motionless hand, tugged. No response. She watched Sabowyn draw Andar's body to the rim, turn him softly, still suspended.

"What's wrong?"

"What did he do?"

Hushed voices murmured questions, Sabowyn shook his head. "I don't know. I think—I think he—died." His hand touched Andar's lips. Andar's mouth curved, fixed forever in a smile of joyous release. His eyes were open; unblinking, he gazed up through the dome crystal at the stars, and beyond them, lost in wonder. Tarawassie looked away from his face, avoiding the surge of unwanted emotion that it stirred in her. She looked down at her own face, mirrored dimly in the

Well's illusive surface: eyes blue-green, melting into the un-water; black hair falling forward to merge with its phantom reflection.

"He *is* dead," Mirro said, lying her hand on his chest.

"How could he be dead? How could he die?"

"He said he wanted to die."

"He was insane."

"But how could he—?"

The voices wove a net of incredulity around her. Tarawassie leaned away from her image. "The Well . . . the Star Well. It granted his wish."

"Is it a Wishing Well?" Someone laughed, tentatively, behind her. "Is that what it is?"

"Poor Andar. He was crazy . . . he was always crazy. He wasn't happy."

"He must be happy now." Sabowyn stretched, gesturing. "Look. Look—his face seems so peaceful." He sighed, pushing his own hair away from his face, and sat back.

"But it never does anything to us. The Well, I mean."

"I don't know." Sabowyn shook his head. "It doesn't matter. Poor Andar, he's happy now. It doesn't matter, now."

"What'll we do with the body?"

"Send it down to the city. Somebody'll take care of it."

"Poor Andar."

"Poor Andar . . . poor Andar . . ." Their voices gave a benediction. "But he's happy now."

Tarawassie shut her eyes, still crouching, her head moving from side to side as they pulled him up and bore him away. *Is he?*

"Tarawassie." Mirro's hands fell lightly on her shoulders. "I'm going to dream, now. Will you weave at the Loom?"

Tarawassie stood, aware of a painful stiffness in her joints. She shook her head; consciously, this time. "No. I can't. I have to go down to the city now."

"Why?"

"My mother is sick." She repeated it for the thousandth time. No one seemed to remember; but she was not surprised, or angry. "I have to see my mother."

"Oh." Mirro turned away, absently, moved down the spiraling ramp. "I'll find someone else."

Tarawassie followed the bearers of Andar's body down, to the lowest level of the Crystal Ship. The soft leather of her formless shoes moved silently on the transparent surfaces. She came to where they stood, waiting wordlessly for the arrival of the ferry-raft. She stood with them, gazing down through the transparency, serenely indifferent to the appalling void below her feet. The world was a mottled bird's egg, blue and rust clouded with white, the colors half hidden now by night's eclipse. She could encompass it in the circle of her arms—she spent a moment lost in the sensations of the possibility.

"It's coming," someone said. She shifted her gaze, saw the brittle glance of sunlight from the far-tinier ovum of the closing ferry. She watched it rising to meet them, felt the faint tremor pass into her as its droplet-form was absorbed into the greater continuity of the Ship itself, into the docking slip.

A soft chime sounded; she turned with the rest as a lock opened in the wall behind them, pulsing green. She waited as they settled Andar into a seat in the ferry's close cabin, fastened straps across him. She moved forward finally, as they finished, to step inside.

"Are you going too?" Sabowyn asked.

She glanced back through the short passageway from the cabin, sat down in another seat, fixed her own restraining straps. "Yes. My mother is sick. I have to see my mother."

"Oh. Well, when you get there—you know—if you see anyone, tell them to take care of him?" Sabowyn looked down, his dark hair half obscuring his face.

"All right." She nodded.

Sabowyn brushed the silver plate set in the wall, and when the airlock had closed between them, the ferry became a separate entity, complete in itself once more. Like a drop of rain it fell free from the tube of the docking slip, away from the Ship, beginning the long fall to earth. Tarawassie rose against the web of straps, her weight falling away too as they left the Ship behind. She looked up, pressing her head against the grayed, padded seat back; watched the Crystal Ship retreat, become a whole for her at last, a many-faceted berry seeded with light.

She closed her eyes, drained by her chitta dream, feeling the Crystal Ship grow insignificant now above, as the world grew wide and important below her. She tried to concentrate on her duty there, while her mind struggled to escape from the unaccustomed burden of reality, and grief. Her mother was dying, and there was nothing that she could do. Only see to her needs, try to ease a suffering for which there was no comfort anyone could give—and then flee, back up to the Crystal Ship, back into the dream world where all griefs were forgotten.

She opened her eyes, blinking at the sudden unutterable vastness of the world's blue-misted rim, crowding the sky now before them. A heaviness that was more than the gradual return of weight settled her once more against the seat; humming vibration transmitted to her skin, a mockery of anticipation. She turned her head slightly: beside her Andar gaped, unseeing, at the vision of a world in majesty—transcending it, and all worlds. He smiled fixedly, serenely.

"Andar." Awareness was stirring in her now; she turned in her seat to stare at him. "Oh . . ." She rubbed at her face in sudden confusion; felt her hair, the golden circlet that kept it back from her eyes, felt her fingers . . . and his own hanging hand, coldly translucent, like marble, as she reached out. She did not know him well; she did not know anyone well, any more than any of them knew her. But she knew them all, the handful of people of the city and the Crystal Ship, and loved them all as a family, for their gentle ways and shared dreams. But Andar had never been at peace, and his dreams had as often been weeping nightmares as things of beauty.

Andar's placid gaze looked through her at the sky below. "You are happy, now." It was not a question, because it had already been answered. "But why?"—knowing that she would never have that answer, wondering if perhaps the answer was only in having an end to all questions.

But the Star Well . . . She remembered her own voice: "It granted his wish." It had never done anything to anyone, for anyone, in all the time that she had known of it. And yet he had gone to it in his madness, tired of living, tired of his pain. He had asked it to accept him, to give him death—and it had answered him, she was certain. She was certain. He had died painlessly, joyfully, and he would suffer no more . . . no more. . . .

The clouds swept up to meet them, taking form; enfolded them and parted once more, showing her the concentricities of the city. The vibration grew against her as the city grew below, and at last they dropped through the slotted dome of the ferry shed to bump in semidarkness. The hatch slid open in the ferry's windowing side. She unstrapped and slipped out into the echoing gloom of the shed. It was empty, as usual; there was no one to tell about Andar's body. Other ferries, large and small, sat patiently in line, their transparency marred by films of dust. She did not notice the dust; she had never seen any of them in use.

Tight autumn gusts whipped the gaudy swirls of her robe,

as she moved through the long shadows of the deserted streets to her mother's apartment. She walked quickly, slowly, quickly again, oblivious to the chill wind that plucked her shivering flesh. She would tell her mother about Andar. . . . No, no, how could she? She watched image ripples glide along the darkly mirroring building walls, stumbled on the tree-levered, uneven pavement hidden by brown wind eddies of spade-shaped leaves. She reached the corner of her mother's street, skirted a small pile of rubble. Her steps slowed once more. The wind pushed at her back, insistent, until she stumbled into the dark building hallway and began to climb the stairs. Her mother had refused to move to a lower floor, or to a building where the others stayed now. Illness and age had made her stubborn; she had clung to the patterns of long familiarity, against the uncertain shape of the future. Now, she could no longer leave her bed. Old, doddering Zepher looked in on her occasionally when Tarawassie was gone. He was too old to bother with the journey up to the Crystal Ship, and he was the only other inhabitant, now, in all the six levels of the abandoned building.

"Tarawassie—is that you?" Her mother's voice came to her faintly; her mother had little to do now except lie and listen.

"Yes, Mother." Tarawassie followed the dark polished path her steps had worn through the dust to her mother's door, and went inside.

The air was always close and unpleasant here, even to her own dim sense of smell. Her mother had complained about it; but she could not make the windows open. "Mother, how are you?" She took one long breath and held it, against the constriction in her chest.

"Happy, now. Happy to see my daughter." There was no reproach in her mother's voice; but a strange sorrow lay in her faded eyes as they touched on Tarawassie, and beneath it, understanding for the helpless anguish that kept her daughter away from her.

Tarawassie moved across the bare expanse of floor to the bedside; kneeling, she pressed her mother's burning hand to her cheek, feeling the roughness of the loose skin, feeling her mother smile. "Oh, Mother . . ." When tears would have started, to wet the fragile hand within her own, she pushed herself up and hid them in a fury of pillow settling. Her mother sighed, a thin, rasping sound, as Tarawassie smoothed her dust-gray hair.

"I'll heat some dinner." Tarawassie forced optimism into

the words as she went to the cooler, pulled out the one half-filled dish of arbat stew she found inside. She frowned in fleeting concern. Tomorrow she must remember to go to the offering place for more food; she must—she *must* remember, this time.

She set the bowl in the small tabletop heater; the hood snapped shut, she saw the light go on. Light . . . She realized the room was growing dark, moved to rub a light globe, filling the space with soft silver, soft grays, that clothed the sharp nakedness of the room.

Tarawassie fed her mother one spoonful of heated stew, saw her choke convulsively, shaking her head. "No . . . no more, Tara. I can't eat." She lay unresisting as Tarawassie wiped off her face; tears spilled down into the hollows of her cheeks. She had eaten nothing for two days.

"Mother, let me bring you some chitta so that—so that—you can dream, again." Her voice trembled; she looked down. "Please try."

"No." Her mother turned away as if it were suddenly painful to look at her, gazing out the window at the twilight city. "It burns, inside me—it hurts too much. I'm past dreaming." Tears glittered as a tremor shook her, crystals in the globe light.

"Mother . . ." Tarawassie felt the words force their way out past the barrier of her denial, drawn to a greater need. "Mother, a strange thing happened today. Andar died. He—he went to the Star Well, and he asked for death. And he died. There was no pain. He smiled. . . ."

Her mother's eyes moved back to her face, searching, demanding, "How did it happen?"

"I don't know. But I—but he looked so peaceful. When he'd never been at peace." She buried her face in her hands. "He said, 'There is a heaven, and it is—death.' "

Her mother touched her arm, trembling with the effort. "Yes, Tara. I would like to go to the Ship, and try. I'm so tired . . . so tired."

Tarawassie left the room, searched out old Zepher. With his help she carried her mother's wasted form, bundled in blankets, back through the darkening streets to the ferry shed. She saw, thankfully, that someone had found Andar's body and taken it away. She settled her mother across three seats, making her as comfortable as she could; her mother lay very quietly, the muscles twitching in her face. Tarawassie tapped a signal, and the ferry sealed and rose, drawn up on a cord of silent vibration, retracing her journey from the Crystal Ship. Her mother did not speak to her, gazing outward as Andar had, at something beyond vision.

Sabowyn, at her asking, carried her mother up through the rooms of the Crystal Ship to the lip of the waiting Well. Tarawassie followed him, their progress woven into the strands of stimulation that Mirro coaxed from the Loom. The Loom's catch-spell of light/music clogged her senses; she struggled to clear her mind of the fragments of past dreams that called her away from reality. She clung to the sight of her mother's pallid face, given lurid life by the warp of unreal colors. A spark of strange emotion broke from within to fill her mother's eyes as she looked down for the last time over the crescent world. Dimly Tarawassie became aware that others were being drawn to them, out of their own dreams, following them up through the flaming pavane of a funeral procession.

Tarawassie stood once more at the Star Well's rim, gazing down through phantom depths darkened at last by the endless depths of night, afraid to find her own reflection. Sabowyn knelt beside her, his own face expressionless, to settle her mother on the ledge.

Her mother stirred slightly, lifting her head. Tarawassie found her eyes, sank down to hold her close, crying suddenly, "Mama, I don't want you to go!" A weak hand reached to stroke the night-blackness of her hair.

"I must . . . I must, Tarawassie. Because you love me, you must help me. Tell me again, what did Andar say—"

"He said he was ready. He said, 'There is a heaven, and it is death.'"

"Yes," her mother whispered. "Yes! Let me go, Tarawassie. . . ." Her mother stiffened within her circling arms, casting her off, casting off life. Slowly Tarawassie released her, and let her slip down into the starlit dreamwater.

Her mother sighed, closing her eyes as though a great weariness had risen from her, and smiled. Blue-green seeped between her fingers. She lay still.

Tarawassie leaned forward, her hand closing over her mother's hand for the last time. Her tears dripped into the Well, fell soundlessly. She drew back again, into the world of color and noise, into the dream that she could share. She heard the murmured astonishment of the others who had surrounded her, grew aware of them again, as she grew aware that they were already beginning to separate and drift apart. Someone lifted her mother's body from the Well and carried it away. Tarawassie sat back on her heels, barely aware that she was weeping—for the loss of a touch, the comfort of an embrace, that she would never have again.

"She's happy; her wish was granted." Sabowyn still stood beside her. He put his hand on her shoulder. From somewhere he offered a silver cup filled with chitta. "Be happy, too, for an end to suffering."

Tarawassie took the cup gratefully, swallowed the ruby syrup, concentrating on the sensation of cold fire in her throat. He led her down the spiraling ramp to the dreaming place. Lying back on the yielding viscosity of a lounge, she fell desperately through the fragile membrane that separated reality from rapture.

Tarawassie woke, tears streaming over her face, not knowing whether she had just begun, or whether she had wept for hours. She raised her head. Room, stars, rainbow symphony, and figures slowly separated as she blinked away tears and confusion. . . . There was no beauty! Her mind closed on the terror of disappointment, of disillusion, of colors mired in corruption, mindless noise . . . no comfort, no vision, only ugliness! She had never dreamed like this! How could she endure—?

Sabowyn lay on the couch across from her, his eyes vacant. She tipped toward him across the low crescent of table, shaking him uselessly, as Andar had shaken her. Andar . . . had all his dreams been like this? Dazed, she rose and followed his path to the Star Well's rim, to stand teetering, searching for his face, or her mother's face; but only finding her own, distorted by nothingness. She stepped onto the Well, breath held; coolness lapped her ankles. A sudden dizziness swept her; she swayed, like a reed in the water, in an unseen wind. And nothing happened.

She stood waiting, until she realized gradually that nothing would happen—realized with growing awareness what it was she had tried to do. Suddenly afraid of the taut, yielding surface that pressed her feet, afraid of falling through into the depth of stars, she stepped back onto the Well's rim.

She made her way back down the spiraling ramp, found Mirro alone, playing at the Loom. Tarawassie stepped into the room, forcing her way through the glaring web of Mirro's weaving. The closer she came to the Loom, the more profoundly its stimulation worked on her—the sensations of light and sound that were merely superficial, the truer harmonies that struck deeper resonances in the fiber of her nerves. She broke through into the cone of silence that surrounded the Loom itself.

"Mirro," Tarawassie whispered above the faint shadings of sound. "How can the Star Well give death? What is it? Why is it here? And why—why couldn't I die too?"

"Do you want to die?" Mirro looked at her curiously; her face settled back into deep lines of habit. Her finger slid over the surface of the Loom below the shining threads. Colors glimmered in the transparent bar, flared up the strands, wove a filigree cloth of light.

Tarawassie shut her eyes against the hypnotic flow, against the memory of a failed dream. "I don't know. But . . . I couldn't dream."

Mirro turned back to the Loom, her flame-dyed robe shimmering with the movement. "You were sad. But it passes. It always passes. You're young; you'll see."

"But the Star Well. You understand the Loom—can't you tell me about the Star Well?"

"I don't know about it." Mirro shrugged. "Nobody knows. It doesn't affect us; it doesn't matter. Don't worry."

"But I want to know. How can I learn—"

"You can't. No one here knows."

"What about in the city? What about the natives? Andar went out past the offering places, and he knew the answer." Tarawassie pulled at the sleeve of her own robe, fraying it.

Mirro shook her head; her hair rippled, silver and black. "Andar was mad. He shouldn't have gone. You shouldn't go; there's no point to it."

Tarawassie turned back through the barrier of sensation, went down to the lowest level where the ferry waited. She took up a cloak and a light globe from the scattering of cast-offs on the floor. She looked back once, as she touched the ferry entrance, but there was no one to see her go.

Tarawassie set out through the brightening canyons of the city, going first to the offering place, where the natives left them food and bright cloth and trinkets—and chitta, in clay pots or sometimes plastic pitchers. The natives and other wild creatures had come to share the city with her own people, who had no use for, and no interest in, the miles of glass and stone. Her people kept now to their few dwelling places near the ferry shed, and were content.

A raised platform, that might once have held something else, was thinly littered with the dressed carcasses of small animals, bowls of dried autumn fruits, baskets of coarse grain. Something rose, flapping and ungainly, and flew away at the sight of her, uttering sullen cries. Vaguely disappointed to find nothing else, no creature she could question, she sat on the edge of the platform, shivering in the chill dawn air.

Hunger stirred in her at the sight of food, almost a nausea. She could not remember how long it had been since she had eaten last. The raw meat repulsed her; she ate the tasteless fruit. A pitcher of chitta waited too, drawing tiny gnats to destruction on the surface of its sticky syrup. Her hands quivered, her gaze drawn to it as the gnats were. She turned her face away. *Later.* She would come back later, when there was a need. . . .

The edge of the city was very close, here: between the stubby towers she could see the plain; the golden-gray sweep of ripened grass flowing beneath the wind, the umbrella trees flaming and heavy with fruit. The cloud-banked sky brightened, pink and yellow and subtle green merged to stain the dome of violet-blue and stir her sluggish emotions.

Gazing into the morning, she almost missed the small flicker of movement at the perimeter of the square. A figure hesitated, bolted back into the deeper shadows as she stood and called out, "Wait!" She ran across the square, calling again, but finding only a street half blocked by shrubbery, empty of life. She heard a noise, far off, of something dislodged clattering down; the settling quiet oppressed her as the echoes died away. For a moment she stood, breathless with the abruptness of her movements, and uncertain about everything else. But someone had been here, and someone could give her an answer. How else could Andar have learned the Star Well's secret, out in the city's heart? Still uncertain, she entered the street.

Through the long day she probed the quiet, twisting city streets. Sometimes sounds reached her, distant and distorted; sometimes her mind filled with the awareness of a watcher— or only her own imagination? She never knew. She called, and echoes answered, or the scuttling of tiny scaled things, a flurry of wings in the trees above her head. A lattice of heavy beams and finer filaments cast shadow-netting down across her path, to end abruptly in vine-draped fangs above a mound of dust and twisted metal. Falls of stone masonry treacherous with burnished windowpane blocked her way.

Strangely reluctant, she did not try to enter one of the empty buildings until after midday. At last, her heart beating wildly, she passed through an arching, empty doorway into the darkness of the interior. Her light globe blossomed feebly, showing her a wall patterned with mosaic tiles, portrayals of human life—and twin embers gleaming. A snuffling growl, and the high yelping of a cub, sent her fleeing again into the sunlight. Tantalized and terrified, she did not try to enter another building.

As the shadows lengthened once more, irritability grew in her. She realized at last that she could not remember why she had come here, and what she had wanted to find. Her body ached with unaccustomed exertion, her stomach ached with hunger . . . hunger . . . craving hunger. . . .

She knew that the craving was for chitta. It had been too long, the residue of euphoria that filled the waking hours between her dreams was dissipating, leaving her to face the emotions she had never wanted to know. She needed chitta, she *needed* it—

She started back along the street, hurrying now, her new goal clear in her mind, until she began to see that she could never retrace her wandering journey out from the square. Struggling with her rising fear, she saw that she would have to climb, to reach a height that would let her find a familiar landmark to guide her home.

She chose a spiraling ramp that circled upward to support the airy lattice hung with vines that arched above the street. She wondered fleetingly at its purpose—whether it had ever been intended for human feet, whether it had ever had any purpose at all. But that didn't matter; only chitta mattered . . . only chitta. She put one foot carefully onto the ramp, clung with her hands. The incline was sharp, but her moccasins held to the time-marred surface. She did not look down. The path narrowed, and faint cracklings reached her ears as every step settled.

There was a tearing sound. Her foot came down on open air. She tumbled forward, and heard her own voice screaming into blackness.

Tarawassie opened her eyes, blinking away dust, wiped crusted dirt from her lips, her nose. She licked her lips, tasting salt, not recognizing the taste of blood. Around her, un-

der her, lay a pile of dust and something sharp which dug
into her side as she lay. She drew her hands in close, cautiously, to push herself up; one wrist flashed sharp warning
up her arm. Collapsing abruptly, she raised her face instead,
blinked her eyes clear again.

The watcher shifted, squatting beyond her reach, and met
her eyes apprehensively. The watcher was not human. His
eyes were gray, with pupils long and set obliquely in an iris
without white. His face was sharp to the point of being a
muzzle. . . . *His* face? She classified the sex instinctively, by
standards that were not entirely apt. A native? Her astonishment drove all else from her mind—her discomfort, the in-
congruity of her own presence here. She sat up frantically,
before she lost her nerve to pain. Startled, the watcher leaped
up, bounding backward, in one lithe movement.

"No, wait!" She flung out her hand, her voice breaking.

The native stopped, indecisive; silvery fur ridged his scalp,
along his shoulders. He lifted one foot, rubbed it nervously
against the ankle of the other leg; his feet were covered by
softly wadded leather shoes like her own.

She let her arm drop and sagged forward, aching, drained.
She held his eyes, wanting to speak again, not knowing what
to say, remembering that the natives were very shy—and very
stupid.

The native moved slowly back toward her, something in
his eyes that perhaps was concern. He crouched down again,
still out of reach, cocking his head and snapping his whiplike
tail across his shins. The tail was half-naked at the tip, and
gray, like the palms of his hands folded in his lap; the rest of
his body was silvered with clinging fur. He wore a kind of
loincloth wrapped around his hips, a formless, sleeveless
jerkin of faded red cloth, strings of beads. A leather bag was
belted at his waist, along with a steel knife. Her eyes caught
on the knife; she looked away at his hands. His hands were
abnormally slender; she realized that he had only three fingers on each, instead of four.

Abruptly he lifted one of the hands, pointing at her; the tip
of a retractable claw showed ivory. He made a series of
sounds, somewhere between a chirp and a bark, and sat back
again, watching her expectantly. She made no response. He
repeated the string of sounds, more slowly, waited again.

She shook her head, not understanding what he wanted.
Her eyes left him, searched the darkened walls. Only the tips
of the towers, like gilded nails, were dipped in sunlight, but

the fingertips of light were reversed. Had she lain there all night? She shuddered. But there was a more subtle wrongness about these brightening canyons. . . . Why were they empty? Bones . . . there were bones in the street. Dark eyes of shattered pane gazing down at her, piles of rubble raising new walls from old, arches that crumbled to dust. . . . This wasn't her city, not the city she remembered. *It wasn't like this yesterday!*

She covered her mouth with her hands, holding back the cries of madness.

"What . . . wrong?" the native asked.

He leaned toward her, stretching his neck, as though he were trying to touch her through a cage. The words were halting, misshapen, slurred—but she understood them. His eyes were too-human with tension and concern. "Are you bad?"

" 'Bad'?" She lowered her hands; laughed—unexpectedly, shakily. " 'Bad'?"

His face brightened at her response. "Bad . . . here?" The tip of his tail swept down his crouching form. "Or bad . . . here?" The tail tapped his head; he drooped into a perfect image of despair.

Tarawassie sank back down in the dust. "Bad . . . both, I think." Her voice trembled. "How . . . how did you learn to speak?" It did not occur to her to ask how he had learned to speak her language; it did not occur to her that there could be another one.

"Not learn." His silvery head moved from side to side. "Know. Always know." The silver rippled as his forehead wrinkled, as though forming the words—or the very act of speech itself—was a difficult task for him. "I human; all humans know."

"You're not a human!" She shrieked it at him. She pushed herself up, her muscles wrenching with stiffness and her skin raw with scratches. She made her way to the closest window's dark reflection. She stood very still for a long while, gazing at the scarecrow figure swaddled in dusty, ancient cloth, the gaunt misery of the bloody face—the incomprehension in the hollowed eyes of blue-green, all that remained of the dream-Tarawassie she had always known.

And then, gracelessly, she collapsed against the pane and slid down, to lie still in the dust.

Tarawassie opened her eyes again in semidarkness, lying on her side on a pile of rags. But dusty sunlight came through the break in the crumbled wall, and light flickered strangely at her back, warming her like the sun. She looked around her. The native crouched beside a small fire, his silver concentration highlighted by gold; he rubbed her light globe methodically with his hands. His tail looped out independently and caught up a stick to push into the fire. A coppery pot hung from a makeshift hook above the flames. She became aware of fragrance—the smell of food cooking, infinitely more appealing and appetizing than anything she could remember. . . . "I'm hungry!"

The native looked up, startled. He set down the globe, dropping forward onto his knees. "I hear you!" His head bobbed, his eyes shining with more than reflected light.

He produced a cup of fine ceramic ware, dipped it into the pot and held it out to her, full. She studied the delicate vining of fantasy flowers on its polyhedral surface as she swallowed mouthfuls of thick, steaming soup. She savored the sweet tang of herbs, the richness of the meat. Feeding herself had become a tedious duty long ago, and food a tasteless, textureless, unappealing thing choked down to stop weakness. She had never known hunger like this, never known the satisfaction of fulfilling it. The sickness, the weariness, the discomfort lifted; her mind cleared. . . . She remembered the sight of her own starved body, the reflection of a terrible truth. Because it was true, she was certain of it now. The self and the reality that she had always known had been a dream, a dream. But not a fantasy. She remembered her mother's death, the Star Well. Were this ruined world and her own wretchedness what her mother had seen without chitta? And was this what Andar had seen?

A bark of elation came from the native. Looking up again she saw the light globe brightening in his hands at last. He glanced up at her, making a peculiar chittering noise. "You want more?"

"Yes." She held out the cup. "It's good." He dipped it into the pot, passed it back. He picked up the globe again, stroking it now, almost worshipful. She realized how long it had taken him to bring light from it. She sipped her stew. "Does it always take you that long?"

He looked up again, the smile fading, and nodded. "Always hard, for me. But sunball last long time, better than torch."

"Did you bring me here?"

He nodded again. "I bring. I wait for humans come out into city, to show them. . . ." He stood up, tensing at some memory. Stringy muscles slid under his silver skin as he shifted his weight. He might be stronger than he looked. "You see more—natives, when you come?"

"No." She wondered why it mattered. "Only one, yesterday, who ran away. I—I came out into the city to . . . find someone to talk to, to learn about my people," knowing suddenly that she would have to have answers to more than the secret of the Star Well, before she could return again to the Crystal Ship. Her hands knotted together in her lap.

"Yes . . . ?" The native squatted down again, his eagerness breaking through his unease. She thought of the two children she knew; his impulsive openness struck her as childish. "Me, too—I know about Star People! One with yellow fur, he come here too. He throw things, hurt me. Not let me come in." His tail lashed, remembering fear and frustration.

"Come in where?" Andar—had he seen Andar?

"Building, over there." His tail jerked vaguely at the doorway. "Star People leave much good stuff. But door not let me in. Door let Yellow Fur in; *he* not let me in." His face turned hopeful. "You let me in?"

"Yes, if you'll take me there!"

He sat down suddenly, chittering. She realized all at once that he was laughing. "My friend, my friend! . . . I show you all I know!" He hugged his knees; his eyes came back to her, the dilated pupils making them almost black in the half-light. "Other Star People never come here now; no one come but me."

"Why do you call us 'Star People'?"

"Because you come here from Fixed Star, up in sky." He looked as though it were the most obvious thing in the world; she supposed that maybe it was, after all. She had seen the Crystal Ship in the night sky, been hypnotized by the beauty of it—a constant jewel that only the moon outshone, midway up the sky among the wheeling constellations. She wondered how it would look to her now, if she found it among the stars tonight.

"Real People"—the native's tail tapped his chest, as though his body were something separate from his mind—"they always live here, on world, from Real Time long ago. They say, when Star People come, Real Time end, forever. I say, Real Time come *with* Star People"—his hands reached out to caress the light globe—"but nobody hear me. Nobody let me *show* them. . . ." He slumped forward, his bitterness rattling the beads against his chest.

"I'll let you show me." He straightened up as she spoke; she felt her own shoulders lift, with a sudden insight. "I think—somehow we lost our Real Time, too." She raised a hand coated with grit. "That, maybe, we found a dream—and lost ourselves."

The native looked at her strangely, and scratched his back with his tail.

"What's your name? What do they—call you?"

"Moon Shadow." His open hand struck his chest; his face took on a perverse look of pride. "Moon Shadow Starman."

"Starman?" She frowned. "You mean—you said before that you were a human. But you don't—you don't *look* human. . . ." It sounded stupid, but he didn't seem to be offended.

"Not here"—he gestured down at his body—"here"—he tapped his head. "I last of Starman kith. Long, long time past, we show with Star People; they part of us, part of me. I last one be both Real and Starman."

"Oh." She smiled hesitantly. "I'm Tarawassie," she said.

"Human names not have reason. What it"—he grimaced, concentrating—"what it—mean?"

"It doesn't mean anything. It's my name." She smiled again. "Does it have to mean something?"

"All Real People have kith name. And birth name, tell of signs when they born. . . . When I come from pouch, Night Beast swallowing moon. People make much noise, Night Beast spit it out; but I come out while moon gone. They say"—he plucked at his beads, broke a string, so that they tumbled over his bony knees—"they say, I be strange—Moon-Shadow child. I be last of Starman kith, bad kith, born with evil spirit. Always, when show me things, they think I be strange . . . and so it come true." He picked up the scattered beads, dropped them into the bag at his waist. Tarawassie recognized strange bits of wire and glass, shiny flecks of etched metal.

"How are you—strange?"

"Starman ancestor-spirits guide me. But Real People say Star People have evil spirits, not Real spirits. They say only Real People show real way do things, no good learn anything else. They try make me stop, not learn about this, my city. But they live in Star-People city too! They give food and chitta, so Star People let us stay. They crazy ones, not me!"

Tarawassie thought of the offering place in the square, remembered that she had always known the natives brought the food that kept humans alive . . . and that she had never wondered why they should. She remembered the native who had run away. "Why are your people afraid of us? Aren't we 'real,' too?" *But we aren't even real to ourselves.*

Moon Shadow pondered, his fur settling. "But we only Real People. Star People like—like spirits. Much in sky—have much magic. Star People make Real Time change. My people not remember all of why—too long ago—but remember to fear spirit-people, give them much chitta. . . ."

"Chitta," she burst out. "You give us chitta! Of course . . . of course!" She made a small noise that was not really a laugh, that hurt her throat. "But where everyone is blind—who misses the day, who notices the darkness?"

"I call you Star Woman," Moon Shadow said, out of his own thoughts. "It be true calling—like Moon Shadow."

Tarawassie nodded absently.

He smiled, showing white, sharp teeth. "Moon Shadow, Star Woman—we be friends. I show you my secrets. Now?" He leaned forward, strangely intent. "I show you something now?"

"Yes. Can we go to where you saw Andar . . . Yellow Fur?" She sat up on her knees, hoping that it wasn't far.

He drew back, looking down, as though she had refused him.

"But I want you to show me—?" She frowned, puzzled. "Can't you show me the place?"

His tail flicked impotently. "Can only show what I learn already; not know secrets of new place yet! I show you others, then we go there; then you understand stuff good, like me."

Tarawassie shook her head, patience lost in the rush of her newly freed emotions. "What are you talking about? You mean you want to tell me what you've already learned, first? Is that it?"

"Not tell!" His own eagerness butted against the wall of incomprehension between them. "Show—I *show* you. Here . . ." He reached out at last to catch her hand, pulling her forward.

She started to get to her feet, but he pulled her down again, his hands locked around her wrist. "Aren't we going—? Let go of me!" She jerked back with all her strength, breaking his hold, as he forced her hand against the silver fur of his stomach. "What are you doing?"

Moon Shadow winced. "Not hurt you! Just *show* you—just show you. . . . Please, Star Woman." He rocked slowly on his knees, his hands clenched, his gray eyes yearning. "Nobody let me show them, nobody be my friend. . . ."

"Show me *what?*" Her face burned with unfamiliar indignation. "Why do I have to touch you?"

He stopped rocking. "You not have pouch. You not know!"

"How would I know? I don't know anything!" She brought her hands down hard on the dusty floor. The pain of her injured wrist shocked her free from the hold of feelings she couldn't handle. "I'm sorry."

Moon Shadow nodded. "It passes . . . I see. I try—tell you." He sighed. "With Real People, little one grow in pouch of mother, not come out long time, till strong. In pouch, mother show little one many things. After little one born, father show, kith-friends show. Man have pouch too"—he patted his stomach, searching her face for understanding—"can't carry, but can *show* little ones, *show* friends." His fingers twisted, claws protruding, as if he could wring clarity out of the air. "Put hand in pouch—and what friend know, you know, right now. Not tell—see, with friend's eyes. Friend *show*. . . ." As if he hoped by repeating it often enough, loudly enough, he could make her feel the meaning. He spread his hands, waiting.

Tarawassie sat back, sifting the words in her mind. "I see that it's more than just telling. But—but it's not like anything I know. We can't touch someone and read minds. How could I read yours, anyway? I'm not even a native. Can't you just—tell me?"

"Can't tell, Star Woman." He grinned forlornly. "No have enough words, no have way." His shoulders rose in something like a shrug. "Talk too hard. But *can* show you. I Starman because that be so." He held out his hand.

She half raised her own. But she drew back again, afraid, unsure. "Not yet. I'm not—ready, yet. Will you show—take me to the place we talked about, now? Then . . . I'll see."

His hand dropped; he nodded dispiritedly. "I take you. I keep my promise." A slight emphasis on *my.* "Anyway"—he straightened—"I get inside place! We go now, yes." His tail swept up the light globe, tossed it into his hands. He stood, kicking dirt into the fire, smothering it.

Tarawassie got up, bent like an old woman, another kind of fire burning her pulled muscles.

"Not far." He smiled encouragingly—not wanting her to

refuse him again, she supposed. His tail twitched toward the bright entrance. "Walk do you good."

She pressed her uninjured hand against her spine. "Several kinds of good, I hope."

"Here. Yellow Fur press here." Moon Shadow pressed his own palms flat against two incised ivory panels set at chest height in the high dark doors. Nothing happened. "Hurry, Star Woman. My people angry if see us here."

Tarawassie limped forward under the portico, shuffling through dry leaves. She stood staring up at the height of the entrance for a long moment, made dizzy by it. "Were they giants?" she whispered, frightened, shivering with the cold and anticipation.

"No," Moon Shadow said impatiently, rubbing his arms, rumpling the fur. "They like you—just like you. We go in now?" He looked back down the street.

"They weren't like us." She looked down. "No, never like us. . . ." Slowly, as though in a ritual, she raised her hands and placed them on the seals. The heavy doors parted, like water flowing, with a faintly metallic groan. The long afternoon light threw their distorted shadows ahead of them into the interior. Tarawassie stood swaying, indecisive. Moon Shadow stopped beside her, abruptly subdued. She took the light globe from his hands, holding it before her like a talisman. In the rectangle of double light, their tall shadows paled, were transformed.

"Spirit-people," Moon Shadow murmured.

"Our spirits." Tarawassie breathed in, held it, without realizing. "Maybe we are giants, after all. . . . ."

They crossed the threshold together, and as though in welcome, incandescence flickered around them, filling the vast darkness with artificial light. They froze, dumbfounded, gazing up and up, their eyes climbing the walls of the vault in which they stood. Somewhere, among the hidden secrets of this place, Andar had found the truth that had made him crazy and set him free. And set her mother free. And now she had to know for herself. . . .

"No good!" Moon Shadow's bitten-off voice leaped from surface to surface, raining echoes down on their heads. "No good stuff here, no real things!"

. . . *things . . . things . . . things . . .*

Tarawassie covered her ears against the echoes. "What do you mean? This is where Andar came to learn, isn't it?"

"But all word stuff here. No good. Not understand words, only things." He pointed at the light globe. "Things work—I make them work. But words . . ." He mimed throwing something down viciously. "Words! I no good at words. . . ." It ended feebly; he turned his back on her, hiding his face. "Always, ancestors tell me this be good place, important place— now I know it only words." He spoke something that she didn't understand, that sounded ugly. "You not need me, Star Woman. I go now."

"Wait, Moon Shadow—" He stopped, facing away, as she called. "Don't leave me alone. . . . I mean, I don't understand this place. I need you to help me learn how—how this place works."

He shrugged, but his voice brightened. "I find you word boxes. I work them good." He turned. "But you never find right words here, in long time. Too many—too many words." He gazed up past floor upon floor.

"Andar found something, somehow. He didn't have forever."

"Maybe he leave it; maybe not. We look, though. . . ." Moon Shadow moved away, peering down at the floor. "Here! I see—Yellow Fur walk much in here . . . go many times . . . this way . . . to lift box. We go up." His tail gestured to her to follow.

She followed, looking down, barely able to detect a pattern of ivory-on-ivory smudging in the floor's pale film of dust. She entered the lift with Moon Shadow, standing back to watch him touch the symbols on the wall with a flourish, one after another.

They rose, wrapped in a quiet vibration, to the second level. Moon Shadow peered out at the floor, shook his head. They rose past two more levels before he nodded, slipping out onto the ivory tiles of the mezzanine. He led, tracking, along half its circumference. Tarawassie looked out, and up, and down past the low, latticed fence, trying to imagine what ancient mysteries lay captive in this place.

She heard a barked exclamation, saw Moon Shadow disappear down one of the side corridors. She went after him, found a double width of floor between the ceiling-high banks of tiny compartments. The opening was crowded with tables and smooth seats. The tables were cluttered with mechanisms she didn't recognize, and strewn with oval disks no longer than a thumb. Some of the countless compartments along the walls gaped crookedly open, as though they had been forced.

"This where Yellow Fur come. Maybe this be what you want. Many words here." His hand swept the table.

"Where? How——?" Tarawassie felt the blind resentment rise up in her again, at her helplessness, at the fact that a dim-witted native should know more about her people's secrets than she did.

"In show boxes." Moon Shadow picked up a disk, tossed it to her. "Put in show box, egg talk, or make vision . . . or make only words. Egg have— Not work if you pull it open!"

Tarawassie stopped prying, irritated.

"Magic get out, only dust inside. . . . Green egg talk, black one show picture, red one only make words." Most of the disks on the table were red. "Show box not show like Real People—not remember good after, forget too much."

Her hand closed over the red disk. "What's the difference between 'making words' and talking? It's the same thing, isn't it?" She opened her hand again, looking down.

Moon Shadow shook his head. "This show box only show words. . . ." He reached out, did something to one of the odd constructs on the table. A dark square plate suddenly filled with light, patterning over with fine green symbols.

"That isn't 'words.'"

He nodded, facing her with pride and exasperation. "Draw word pictures, tell eyes story. I see"—his finger stretched, the claw tracking—"'and it . . . death.'" He paused, scratching his ear.

Tarawassie flung the red disk away. "No, it's not fair!" She clung to the table. "I want an *answer*."

Moon Shadow came back to her side. She felt his cool gray palms close over her shoulders, forcing her rigid body down into a seat. "Peace, Star Woman. It still bad with you. We go now. Tomorrow, next day——"

"I don't want to wait! I want an answer *now!* I've wasted my whole life already." She leaned forward on her elbows on the hard tabletop, her hands clutching at the limp tangle of her hair.

"Then day more not matter." Moon Shadow sat down on the next seat, awkwardly, as though he seldom bothered. "What Yellow Fur know that so important? Why you come here? What make you come?"

"He knew about the Star Well." She raised her head. "It's in the Crystal Ship. It made him die, or let him die. And it— let my mother die. She was sick and suffering and she just— died. I let her die. I let her go. But it wouldn't take me. I want to know how it passes judgment—and I want to know why nobody knows that!"

"And you want know if spirit of mother find home."

She met the gray eyes, startled. "Yes."

"You have chitta ceremony, after?"

"After she—died?" Tarawassie nodded. "I drank chitta. . . ."

"And you not dream good."

"H-how did you know that?"

"I know. I see why you come. . . ." Moon Shadow shifted on the chair, uncomfortable. "Happen sometimes with Real People, too. One die; kith have chitta ceremony, open selves to spirit—spirit of dead friend come among them, come into all who show with him when alive, become part of them forever. But sometimes kith-friend grieve much, and shut spirit out. Friend have no peace, spirit have no home. Grieving one must go out alone, search—search heart. When understand all, and—accept all, then spirit enter him. Spirit find rest, he find peace, all kith be glad, whole, again."

"How do you accept losing the one person that mattered to you—that you loved? How can you ever be glad again, knowing all the things you didn't do and couldn't do and should have done for her? I only let her die. And I never told her—I never even told h-her—" Her voice failed, as she sank into the waters of grief. *I love you, mother.*

"Only body die; spirit part of us—part of us." The clumsy voice reached out to touch her, like a comforting hand. "Ancestors live forever, become part of friends, of kith. With chitta, feel this; feel beauty of spirit when friend come into us."

There is a heaven, and it is death. Tarawassie rubbed her eyes, making her hands wet, making the scratches burn. *But that's not what Andar meant.* "We don't believe that—that chitta shows you the spirits of the dead."

"Not believe?" Barely aubible.

"No. They're only dreams, they don't mean anything."

"Maybe death not same for Star People, Real People . . . ?" Moon Shadow searched his own reflection on the tabletop. "But all people die. And my ancestors, they be human spirits. . . . But I be last Starman, and nobody show with me." Moon Shadow glanced up, glanced down again; she heard him sigh. "We go now, Star Woman, before somebody come. You rest. Tomorrow we find answers."

Tarawassie stood, accepting the support of his sturdy, fragile arm, and wondered whether there was any question that led to an answer, instead of to another question.

As they returned to Moon Shadow's camp, Tarawassie had searched the wedge of sky for the Crystal Ship's bright starpoint, but darkening clouds had closed down like a lid above the city. The wind was bitter; it drove her into her cloak, buffeted and oppressed by her isolation from everything she knew.

Now pale winking flurries of snow materialized in the shelter's entrance, as the wind gusted through the blackness beyond. The snow puddled, gleaming, as it found the floor, but Tarawassie huddled close to the fire, warming her hands on a cup of thick, hot soup. Moon Shadow's tail flipped sticks into the flames as he swallowed his own meal; his fur stood out from his body, insulating him against the cold.

"How—how did you learn to understand the word pictures we saw, Moon Shadow? How could"—she guarded the tone carefully—"you ever imagine what they meant?"

She heard his soft chitter of satisfaction through the crackling of the fire. "Always know, because I Starman."

"You mean, you didn't learn it somehow, somewhere? There isn't a place where I can learn it?"

He shook his head stupidly.

"Why didn't you tell me that? How am I ever going to—?"

"I show you." He looked up, his pupils dilated, disconcerting her. His hand quivered on his knee. "I show you, Star Woman, if you want?"

She nodded, desperate with frustration and fatigue. "Yes, then! Show me." Wearily she put out her hand. He took it hesitantly, drew it toward him locked in his own. "It won't hurt?"

He shook his head. "Not hurt you. Not hurt my friend."

Resolutely she did not pull back, felt her fingers brush the rough cloth of his faded jerkin, the gray-silver fur of his stomach; his fur was the consistency of clouds, the sleekness of water. Startled, vaguely embarrassed, she shut her eyes as her firmly guided hand entered the close, warm pouch in his flesh, where—some part of her tried perversely to laugh—where his navel should have been.

For a long moment she felt nothing more than clinging, formless warmth. And then, gradually, as though her fingers rested against a charged surface, a tingling grew, intensifying. Like numbness, it ate its way along the nerve paths of her arm. She tried to withdraw her hand, but Moon Shadow's grip pinned her arm. "Wait"—a plea, his face, his eyes, closed in concentration—"I see . . . you see."

The electric tingling grew more intense, verging on pain, as it spread through her shoulder, up her face. But sensation burst through into her mind, her fear and her anticipation were lost together in a storm of radiance brightening to blackness. . . . And beyond it, her eyes patterned from within with a blazing static of incoherent imagery. Paralyzed, she crouched stone-still, caught in a timeless dream of some- one else's making, fed from the spring of an alien perception.

Tarawassie sat blinking, blinking—slowly realizing that she had clear vision once more. The fire-bright center, the rim of shadowed darkness, took form before her, and Moon Shadow, silver and gold, sprawled on an elbow, staring.

"Moon Shadow?" She made her voice reach out to him, with no strength left in her to raise a hand.

He glanced up, his eyes vacant, shook his head to clear them. "You"—he shook his head again—"you see words, now? I show you. . . ."

Images crackled and spat behind her own eyes, making them water. "I don't know—what I see. Everything is going around and around . . . things that don't belong in my mind." She pressed her hands flat along the sides of her head, forced her concentration to fix on her own reality. "It didn't work!"

He nodded woodenly, pushing himself up. "It fight me. I feel—you come into me, not wanted. Is bad thing." He ges- tured at his head. "Wrong to feel that, never feel it with Real People . . . never." He grimaced, teeth flashing. "But ances- tors—ancestors say it *right!*" He stared into the fire, his pu- pils shrinking to oblique slits.

Tarawassie massaged her arm. It felt hot and swollen; tiny points of redness, like pinpricks, marked her hand. "How can it be right if it didn't work?" She lay down abruptly on the pile of rags, breathing in the smell of dust and smoke, and wrapped her cloak around her. She saw the golden-edged crest of fur rise with his irritation, settle again. With a grunt of weariness, or disgust, he curled into a knot at the fire's edge, shutting her out.

Shivering with the chill, her mind and body aching with bruises and defeat, she welcomed sleep, which was a kind of death.

There were many dreams, but unlike any she had known before. In vivid detail, they sorted and aligned a disorder beyond her comprehension—not disturbing her sleep, but instead guiding her unconscious through to a deeper peace.

She woke at a sudden noise, filled with a feeling of wholeness and well-being. Searching for the sound, she saw Moon Shadow duck his head as he entered the building, silhouetted against a leaden glare—and farther along the wall, a sealed doorway, marked by a sign, "EXIT."

Moon Shadow came on toward her, toward the fire, his hands clutching two small kirvat carcasses, and a peculiar snarl of three thongs and three round stones looped in the hook of his tail. She saw his breath frosting as he neared; saw, as the firelight illuminated his face, the disillusionment that thinned his lipless mouth. He dropped the two small animal carcasses by the fire and crouched down, pulling the knife from his belt.

"Moon Shadow." She sat up, remembering everything, suddenly—new to her—ashamed. "Moon Shadow, look at that word! *Exit!* I know what it means. I can—read!" Hoping that would mean more to him than any apology. "You did show me!"

His head came around, his eyes searching her face, anger forgotten. "Yes? Yes? Is true, Star Woman? I show you good?"

"Yes!" She nodded, laughter rose to her lips from deep inside her. "It's all come into place, I can understand everything. . . ." She felt fragments of stranger new memories eddying at the perimeter of her consciousness.

"Maybe"—Moon Shadow hesitated, struggling with some emotion she didn't understand—"maybe now I share what you see. I not understand words good. But your mind come into mine, like Star People long ago. Maybe you show me what you—read. And I show you all they know."

"Together we can find all the answers! And then . . ." She stopped, frowning. "And then . . ."

"We go soon to word place." Moon Shadow nodded eagerly. He turned back to dressing the carcasses, and she did not watch him with the dead.

Tarawassie went first to the reader that already held a tape, in the cramped alcove of the deserted library, where Andar had hoarded his truths. Moon Shadow hung at her shoulder, guiding her hands at the reader's row of buttons, reciting instructions as though he had learned them by rote from some unknown teacher. She rejoiced in her new-found cleverness, as she began to identify sounds with symbols, one after another; and then whole words, an entire sentence. The ultimate cleverness of the one who had first created symbols shaped like sounds, to preserve a thought across miles of distance or millennia of time, filled her with courage and hope.

And yet a small part of her mind rebelled against the clumsy, insufficient tedium of words and symbols. So pointless, so wasteful, so unnecessary, when a person could simply *show*— And startled by the obviousness of that truth, she recognized it as not her own, but a pocket of stubborn, mind-closing resistance that belonged to Moon Shadow, to whom too many words were only a confusion of the essential. For Moon Shadow, for the natives, only the barest, most obvious patterns of daily life needed words. For them any thought or feeling or piece of knowledge more intimate or complex would be shown and shared directly, mind to mind. And the very attitude of the donor was transmitted as well, fixing an entire matrix of attitude-idea firmly into the mind of the receiver.

Her own mind had a matrix of alien experience, to let her separate her own beliefs from his—and yet, even so, she almost hadn't known. To grow up in a group where absorbing pieces of another's mind was something that began even before birth—how would you ever know yourself from the attitudes that formed you? From your parents, your neighbors? From your ancestors?

Moon Shadow looked down at her, as if he felt her eyes on him; smiled questioningly, not needing words.

And taking one sentence at a time, each time a little more easily, she began to read

Who can worship death, and live? A credo, and an epitaph. *There is a heaven, and it is death. . . .*

Tarawassie pushed herself away from the reader plate, away from the table's edge, with the stiff motion of one transfixed by a terrible vision. Death's awful beauty had seeped through her eyes, hidden in the plain geometries of the printed words. . . . The reek of death had filled her being in that afternoon, and she had been answered. . . .

Moon Shadow had spent the first part of the day in nervous trips to the building's entrance—keeping watch, he had said, in case his people sent someone to search for him. But now he lay stretched on the floor, napping, having lost patience with, and finally interest in, her tortuous study. She did not wake him, wondering how she would—how she could—show him this truth: that her people had committed suicide—as individuals, as a group, as a world. They had worshiped death, not as a means to an end, but as an end in itself. They had died—died by means she could not even comprehend—died by their own hands, in an ecstasy of necrophilia. And their world had died with them, leaving its bones scattered over the earth to weather and decay and be eaten by time, leaving the handful of living to linger here, like the final flesh on the crumbling skeleton of the city. And she was alive . . . alone . . . among the living dead. *But why*—?

A hand brushed her shoulder; she started.

"What wrong, Star Woman?" The first words Moon Shadow had spoken to her he repeated now, and this time she could read the expression on his face. And reading the incomprehension on her own, he said softly, "I—hear you."

She turned her face away. "Everything is wrong. The more I search, the more I find answers—the more I wish I'd never started. And yet, the more I want to *know*. Why did this happen to me? I was happy!"

"What you find in words? It be bad thing? You try show me, and . . . I share bad with you." He stood expectantly, rubbing one foot against the other, as though it were a gift, an offer he was not used to making.

"I can't. I can't show you something so ugly about—about us."

"About Star People?"

She nodded. "You don't have to know—nobody should!"

He fumbled for words: "You show me, hurt go out of you . . . hurt shared. I know. I need, but nobody show with me. . . ." He toyed with a tape disk. "Need—*need* show, with somebody!" His fingers tightened; the disk shot away across the polished surface.

Startled, she was caught by a sudden memory of her childhood—as bright, as unreachable now as the starry depths of a Well in the sky. Her mother's arms, the muted rainbow of her mother's robe, the dreamy murmur of her mother's voice hushing the tears of a lost sorrow: "Don't cry, don't cry. Shared hands, shared hearts, will make a burden light, little Tara. . . ." Tarawassie nodded silently, and put out her hand.

This time, because she was not afraid of pain, pain was almost nonexistent in the tingling intrusion that rose through her nerves. And this time, it was as though the dinning static in her brain sucked a part of her back across the bridge of living electricity that bound them, sucked away the fragmented images. Struggling against the dazzling mental noise, she recalled the malignant death ecstasy that had reached out of the past to destroy her future, her people's world. And carrying her crippled memory picture, her confusion and isolation passed through into Moon Shadow's awareness . . . were shared . . . were eased by his acceptance.

But then, as though the images had tripped some switch deep inside his mind, Moon Shadow's memory began to fill her own mind with a responding image. And suddenly she *was* Moon Shadow, in a swift, disorienting transition. Saw herself through alien eyes, saw herself as an alien, felt silver fur ridging on her scalp in startled disbelief. . . . But as she drowned in alien sensation, she found that memory was not Moon Shadow's alone, and she was sucked down, as he lost control, into another mind—a human mind, preserved within the matrix of Moon Shadow's memory and rising to the present from the depths of generations past:

Her name (not Tarawassie, who was Tarawassie?) was Shemadans. *Shemadans*. She repeated it again, to stabilize herself, her heart beating too fast. She felt the cord from the sack of medical supplies cutting into her shoulder (Tarawassie grimaced), painfully real. She had come into the city only for supplies, but now she was returning to the camp with an infinitely heavier burden—the realization of their worst fears: the sabotage of the transporter. She forced herself to slow down, keeping to the shadowy edges of the crowded street. (Tarawassie stared wildly, her panic feeding on the impossible mass of humanity.) A fine powder of snow dusted the ground beneath her boots. Tarawassie/Shemadans glanced up at the airy, vine-hung snow screens, realized with a shock that they no longer functioned, that the vine leaves were graying with frost. . . .

Someone's hands closed over her arms; she almost cried out. But the rough face gazed through her, vacant; the stranger steadied himself and moved on. Tarawassie/Shemadans drew a shuddering breath. So hard, so hard to keep believing that she was a cultural historian, and not a frightened outcast. . . .

She realized gratefully that no one near her had noticed her sudden panic; all of them were strangers, now—strangers to reality. They drifted past her, oblivious to her, oblivious to the cold, the day, the world—Death Cultists, wrapped in a blanket of chitta dreams, thinking they dreamed of death. A sweetly repulsive stench reached her, as she passed the narrow space between two buildings; desperately she did not look to the side. . . . Because dreaming became an obsession with them, and if they were stopped from dreaming—*who could worship death, and live?* They had all gone insane! No part of her mind denied that, now. And it had happened so quickly. . . . How much longer could this city, or this colony, go on, before their autumn madness became the final winter for which there would never be a spring? *What will we do, if our world dies? We can't leave our kith-friends! Oh, Basilione, Basilione. . . .* She hurried on, the sack of supplies banging clumsily against her leg. She rounded the last corner, saw the snowtrack still sitting where she had left it. *What will become of us all, now that they destroyed the transporter?*

Sprawled across the orange hood of the snowtrack, a bright, unidentifiable thing, a pile of crimson-spattered rags. . . . *A suicide? Oh, no. No!* Shemadans stopped, screaming it within the sheltering walls of her mind, witnessing in microcosm the death of a world. . . .

"No . . . no . . . *no* . . ." Tarawassie came back into herself again, with the cries of someone else's horror still constricting her throat. "Moon Shadow!" She pressed her aching hand to her mouth, swallowed the bitter aftertaste of fear. "What—what happened? Who was it? It wasn't you!"

Moon Shadow shook his head. She saw the aftereffects of shared terror fading from his face as her eyes came into focus. "You call—call ancestor spirit, call Shemadans"—he struggled with the word—"when you show. Memory come to memory."

"She was a *human*. . . ." Tarawassie began to see at last how literally true his claim of a Starman—a human—kith must be. She had asked without knowing, and her question had been answered—by a vision from her own past (the memory of the living streets took her breath away once more), which had somehow become a part of his. How had it happened? How long ago? And what had happened to Shemadans? Suddenly she wanted desperately to know, to find

out more about this new part of herself, this new world opening up to her.

Because she knew now that all Shemadans had feared had
come to pass; knew that the people, their world, had died—
because of chitta. Tarawassie saw it so clearly now, in the anguished parallax of Shemadans' perspective and her own.
And she wondered numbly how this last handful of her
people had managed to survive for so long, in this imitation
of death—this imitation of life.

Moon Shadow touched her arm, breaking her out of her
reverie. "We go soon? Stay here too long, dark come. My
people see light, come, punish me. . . ." He hesitated, looking down. "I show with you, share bad thing. I make it less. I
be your kith-friend—?"

"Yes." She nodded, still unsure of whether the answer she
found in the showing had made her anguish less or only increased it, but knowing somehow that it was very important
for her to thank him for the sharing. "Yes, thank you . . .
my friend." She found a smile. And now that one question
had been answered, she knew that she had found the spring
of real knowledge, and that she could never leave it until she
had drunk her fill. "Moon Shadow"—she put out her hand
again, forgetting his warning—"show me what happened to
your ancestors, what happened to Shemadans?"

He took her hand. This time she felt no surprise, as her
mind and Moon Shadow's focused her question, her need to
know, and let it sink into the deeper levels of her/his
awareness, into images fragmented by transmission error and
incompletion through the years, but which still rose to let him
see through ancestral eyes whenever some need, or some sight
of this ancient city, called them up to guide him. . . .

For a fleeting instant she was changed again. Still pos-
sessing thin gray hands, a shining silver belly, but not Moon
Shadow's, Tarawassie looked down into a human face, a
man's face contorted with pain. She crouched below the
charred flap of a burned-out tent, needing all her strength to
absorb that terrible pain, as she tried to bring him comfort. . . .

And again. She became a human man—a *man*, this time,
her name/his name Basilione (Shemadans—where was Shemadans? Where was she, Tarawassie?) . . . .

Basilione turned slightly, lowering his hand, looking away from the procession of snow vehicles still working its way toward their camp along the river valley. *Shemadans.* . . . He reassured himself that she stood beside him, a shapeless bulk in her heavy clothing, only her chill-reddened face showing below her hood. She looked back from the river to him as he turned, as if their movements were one. Her face gentled as she met his smile. She reached out as he reached out; they drew each other close, the motion drawing their kith-friends closer around them, all of them together, as it should be.

But not all of them. . . . He had sent a part of the kith away—the vulnerable part, the *native* part (her/his mind protested against the need for a distinction, now). Because that was not simply a group of men approaching below, he was certain; it was a mob. He turned further, looking back through the dozen tense and anxious faces of their friends. The high whine of the approaching snow vehicles reached him constantly now. Across the snowdrifted tundra, past their own ordered, deserted camp, he could see the squalid, inadequate shelters of the main native village, where this group of wretched survivors of the human encroachment existed on lichens and grubs. All of the natives had fled at the first sign of trouble.

Tarawassie/Basilione's gaze moved mechanically across the too-familiar landscape left by retreating glaciation—a gouged cliff face, the rubble of a moraine, the powder-fine, sterile dust that lay beneath the snow, which one day would sweep south to settle into rich farmlands. . . . But here below the rim of the glacial lake this land was as barren as a moon, and the Real People huddled on the edge of extinction, and hated his own.

God, was it nine years since he had come through the transporter from the Homeworld? Only nine years, since he had come here to verify that the natives were subhuman, and believed, himself, that they were an evolutionary dead end, no better than animals? Shame flickered in him. But no, no need to feel ashamed now. That had been someone else, a different man. . . .

A sharp thrust of memory showed him his home, Homeworld, the man he had once been. Spring—and he had crossed the ancient quad of the university campus, with the scent of the flowering silth trees heavy in the air, to enter a lecture hall where the students had standing room only, because their world had standing room only. A world where he and his wife had been afraid of closeness, even between themselves, because then closeness had meant a crowd and nothing more.

He held his wife closer now, feeling the deeper closeness of spirit and mind that they shared with each other and with their friends—because of showing. Nothing could separate them now, not the ostracism of the Real People, not the anger of the human men below. If they could only make someone *see*—make both sides realize what kept their kith together in the face of hardship and persecution, what had made them glad to stay, the things they had come to know together—things neither people could achieve apart. . . .

Shemadans stiffened against him; he heard someone mutter uneasily and a child sneeze in the cold wind. The four snowtracks had stopped, fifty meters below them. He kept count as the vigilantes climbed down . . . fifteen . . . eighteen . . . twenty-four of them; watched them point, and begin to move upslope toward the camp on foot. He squinted into the wind, beginning to make out details—the set, vengeful faces, the glint of light on weapons, the parkas, patterned with the ebony fur stripped from a butchered native elder, the silvery-white of a murdered child. He set his teeth against a cry of grief that rose out of memories not wholly his own. Shemadans moaned softly, setting one foot against the other ankle, as though she would flee if she could. Behind her Pamello bit off a curse: "Butchers. . . ."

"No!" at himself, most of all. "We can handle this, if we don't lose control of ourselves! We knew they might come. They've got a good reason to be angry, this time—and afraid." *Good reason.* He remembered the kith meeting, three weeks before, when Shemadans had returned with the news of the transporter and the further deterioration of the city.

And these humans had come the four hundred kilometers from the city in snowtracks, not the flyers of the Colony Police, who had harassed the camp in the past. Things were falling apart faster now, goaded by fear. These men were not even quasi-official any more; this time they were out for blood.

"What do you want here?" he demanded.

The colonists stopped five meters below him on the slope. He saw the ugly projectile weapons clearly now, trained on his people, on him. "Stand where you are. You know what we want. We want your 'friends' "—their leader made on obscenity of that deepest honor—"kangaroo-lover! Where are they?"

He had seen that man before, or maybe only too many others like him, too many faces made faceless by blind bigotry. . . . "They've gone where you won't find them." His eyes swept the faceless mob.

"We'll find 'em." The leader signaled, sending a party to search their tents and the native camp beyond. "And when we do, you can watch what we do to them for destroying our world."

"We know what the Cultists did to the transporter." Basilione spoke quietly, evenly, with an effort. "We know they've cut off contact, that nobody else can come through to us now. But these natives aren't to blame for that!"

"Then who the hell is to blame? It's their chitta that's destroyin' our people, drivin' us all crazy! They planned it that way, to take our world!"

"*We* took *their* world." He had to include himself consciously in humanity. "Do you really think a bunch of—of 'kangaroos' could plan a revenge like that? It was our own fault, for letting the drug get out of hand!"

And yet, he remembered that Shemadans had said it was a kind of revenge, a kind of ironic justice. How many countless times throughout human history had "primitive" groups like the Real People been decimated and demoralized by the vices of a superior technology? And this time, this *once*, it had gone the other way. . . . "Can't you see that everything we've done here was wrong? We've got to change if we want to salvage something, our lives, from this disaster. We've got to work together, we've got to work with the natives. . . ."

His voice ran on, stumbling, fumbling over clumsy words, words that could never capture the essence of what it meant to see through the eyes of another being, to let them absorb a part of yourself in return, and to know that part of you would live forever. . . . If he could only *show* them how his own ingrained human selfishness had been altered by the presence of other viewpoints, other minds; how much all the humans in Camp Crackpot had grown less preoccupied with self, more tolerant of themselves and others—more concerned with the stability that had always seemed to elude humanity.

And the Real People had been changed by showing, as well. For their species, the stability of the showing ritual had evolved into an overspecialization that perpetuated mediocrity, that rejected change or innovation. Showing with humans had infected the Starman (he took a perverse pride in the native epithet) kith-friends with the humans' attitude that change was right. And any human could imprint the secrets of technology on a Real One's mind, directly, permanently, giving him instinctive knowledge of things that evolution's trap would have denied them forever.

And all that they learned could be taught, instantly, almost painlessly, to another human. "What could uniting our peoples bring to either one of us except good? There's never been a complementary union of alien cultures before, but we could have one now! Together we can—"

"Shut up!" the leader of the mob bellowed, raising his gun. "You're as bad as those goddam chitta zombies—worse! We don't have to listen to this kind of filth from you. We don't have to take it from a bunch of animal-loving queers! Take apart the camp, bust it up, burn it! Smash everything! The main camp too—don't leave anything! This's how they want it—let 'em all freeze here together." He raised his arm, sweeping the mob outward.

As though time had suddenly turned inside out, Tarawassie/Basilione saw the mob begin to spread like water, saw Pamello's little girl pick up a smooth round stone, lift it, hurl it—saw it strike a man full in the face. Blood spurted red against the leaden sky, as he heard Shemadans scream, "No!" But it was too late, too late. Living a nightmare, he saw the guns turning, training, but he could not move, and it was too late, too late even to run. . . .

Tarawassie came to herself, sitting hunched over her knees, sobbing with pain. Slowly she straightened, drawing her hands away from her breast. She stared at them for a long moment, stared at her faded robe. But there was no blood, no pain, no need to cough out her life, here in this abandoned library. . . .

A soft, heartbroken ululation filtered through to her as her dry sobbing eased. Moon Shadow sat back in his chair, eyes shut, hands against his own chest.

"Moon Shadow," barely a whisper, "what happened to us? What happened? Did we—did *they*—all die? All of them?"

His head moved listlessly in negation. "They me. They me. I all that still is them. . . ." He took a deep breath, opening his eyes.

"But they were murdered. They *died!*" And somehow it was so real, happening inside *her*, that she had believed—She sat forward, her hands twined before her on the tabletop, as the fog of images and loss began to lift, giving her a clearer objective view of all that she had seen. And she saw, suddenly, the true significance of the word *native*. "Moon Shadow, do you—hate me? The mob, they must have been my ancestors. And all the humans—what they did to your people . . ." The memories-within-memories of atrocity rose, as freshly vivid as though she had seen them done, after—after five hundred *years*. She could not comprehend the span of time. "Am I like them?" She remembered her own feelings about the natives, her mouth tightening.

Moon Shadow shook his head, not meeting her eyes. "You not like them, Star Woman. You like my ancestors. You like—you like me."

Basilione had not been ashamed, because the bigot had been another man. . . . "Yes," she nodded, "and—I think *you* are more like *me* than anyone I know." She laughed, very softly, as the full implication of it struck her. "Now. . . . But I still don't know what I am."

"You my friend." Moon Shadow's hand touched his chest. He smiled, "My kith-friend."

A clear, rising pleasure filled her like a light, as she grasped at the deeper meaning of the word. "And anyway"—shadows formed again behind her eyes—"what was done, was done long ago—to your people, to mine. Your chitta brought the humans to ruin, in the end. Your people are their inheritors. All that was theirs has been left to you, to let you prove how wrong they were in passing judgment on you."

"Maybe," Moon Shadow twitched his shoulders; his beads rattled. "Or maybe they prove right, prove we never change. We live here long time, inside human city, but nobody want magic, nobody use! Still say already know best way, not need new way. . . ."

"But if the Real People really were as—as primitive as the ones Basilione knew of, haven't they changed . . . ?"

"Little things! Stupid things. Not big things. Not enough."

Tarawassie shook her head, rubbing her hands together, rubbing her arms. "But—but the memories that you have, Moon Shadow. Couldn't they still change your people, through you?"

"My people not *let* me change them!" He shook his own head, in denial. He stood up, his foot rubbing his ankle in a strangely familiar gesture. "We go now, before they come."

"Moon Shadow, wait." She caught at his wrist as he rose. "Show me one more thing; please? I still need to find the answer to the first question I—I ever asked myself." She reached out, her mind shaping an image of the Star Well. "Somehow, someone in your mind must have known about the Crystal Ship, about the Star Well. . . ."

Reluctantly Moon Shadow dropped into his seat again, surrendering, like a sinner torn between dread and ecstasy. She saw him close his eyes as her numbed hand slipped again into the warm folds of his pouch, felt gratification fill him and become her own as the current joined them once more.

Shemadans sank wearily, cross-legged, into her place in the circle of expectant friends. (Tarawassie looked out through her eyes in disbelief, at the dark, worried face of Basilione, the faces of a dozen other humans interspersed with native faces—all alive, still alive?) Shemadans looked out across the double ring of faces, watched the gray tent wall heave in the frigid gusts of the night wind beyond. She ordered the thoughts that had been hers alone for the four long days of her return from the city. She began to speak, even as she showed to Hunter's Luck on her left; thinking that in a group this large, there was still a place and a time for the use of words. . . .

"The news is very bad, this time. The snow screens have failed, the city is falling apart, there aren't enough people left who care to do anything about it. Sixty percent must be using the drug now, I saw them everywhere. They drift like zombies, they barely look to their own needs, and they ignore everything else. . . . And if they're deprived of chitta, they—they kill themselves! It's true, I saw it myself. The others have become obsessed with the deaths. It fascinates them. . . . And there isn't enough chitta for them all any more." The awareness that she was not alone with the memory flowed back into her from Hunter's Luck, bringing her comfort. . . .

(And Tarawassie understood, finally, that all this had happened before the ultimate confrontation. Shemadans, Basilione, all the rest had never died, would never die; they continued to experience life—through the bodies of their descendants. They *were* Moon Shadow. And they would be a part of her now, for as long as she lived.)

Shemadans pushed back the hood of her jacket, refocusing bleakly on the present. "But that isn't the worst." Tarawassie/Shemadans watched their faces, the colors of flesh, the colors of fur blending into one continuity for her. "The Cultists have sabotaged the transporter." She braced against the rush of cries and questions, the striken faces. "But wait! Wait—they dismantled only the receiver, not the transmitter. We can still leave—if we want to." *The humans can.* She looked down.

"But no one can come to us? No one from the Home-world?" Basilione asked.

She nodded. "The damage was irreparable. The Cultists wanted to make sure no one could come through to stop them. If people want to leave, they don't care. They're glad—glad to see them go. . . ." She pictured them in her mind, clustering like flies in the transporter station, drawn by their morbid fancies to gaze at the corpse of one who had passed through, adrift in azure lines of force among the stars (The transporter? Tarawassie grasped frantically at the shred of image—the Star Well, *the Star Well?*—but Shemadans' mind shifted like dunes of snow). . . . "They aren't violent toward anyone but themselves. But the undrugged ones are panicking now, and between the two of them—"

"This colony is doomed, between the zombies and the mobs." Basilione nodded. "It's not as if we didn't see this coming. . . ."

"Help come," someone said. "Come from Homeworld, when afraid-humans pass through, tell all. Humans come again, in starship."

"But that takes forty years, at least," someone else said.

"If anybody ever comes at all. . . . What's going to happen to the Homeworld now? They'll fall apart, if they can't bleed off colonists to this world."

"What happen *here*, now?" Tarawassie/Shemadans turned her head to look at Beautiful Sky, whose life Basilione had saved, who had been the first Real One ever to show with a human. "Angry ones, they maybe blame Real People. This—blame us too. Where we go, what we do, then?"

"We may not have to worry," Shemadans said softly. "The humans may all kill themselves, kill each other. And all the Real People will have to do is wait a little longer, and this will be their world again." And the tragedy of it sickened her, but she couldn't deny its justice.

She pictured the transporter and the fragile threads that had tied this world so tenuously to reality, to sanity; pictured one of them already broken— *and the dark abyss* (Andar, what had Andar said? *Please*, Tarawassie cried silently, reciting in her mind: *'To pass the dragon, and enter the dark*

abyss.' . . . *Please, show me, show me now!)* . . . . And
obediently, Shemadans' mind slipped deeper into memory,
found the poem:

> Who will dissolve? Who coagulate?
> Who to pass the dragon and enter
> the   dark
> abyss?
> Silently   without   motion
> he enters   the ocean.

The poem by Grattan, the painter-poet who had captured, for
Shemadans, the mystical experience of a rite of passage, to
animate the cold substance of her knowledge about the
transporter's function. . . .

And Tarawassie absorbed all that Shemadans knew about
the Star Well: a transporter station (the Ship, the Crystal
Ship!) had been sent to this world from another, which was
one of many worlds already bound together by Star Wells.
For forty years a ship had journeyed across distances unimag-
inable to her, to deposit crucial materials to found a colony
and to establish a gateway here at journey's end. The gateway
was the Star Well, fixed in the transparent heart of the dismantled starship still circling endlessly above their world, a
gateway that let humanity cross the chasm between the stars
in scarcely more time than it took to cross a threshold.

But those who chose to cross paid the supreme price, for
the threshold between the worlds was Death's. The body must
be cast off, before the spirit—the essence?—of each traveler
could pass through the darkness and be reborn in the light of
another sun. By some process Shemandans/Tarawassie could
not even imagine, the Star Well's mechanism captured the
pattern, the precious thing that made each man or woman a
unique being, and transmitted it, leaving the husk of flesh behind, recreating the identical being, in an identical body, at
its destination.

But who would dissolve, who coagulate? Each person who
chose to journey must comprehend, and accept, the fact of
their own self-destruction. And that was the reason, Tarawassie realized, that the Well had never accepted any human she
knew, before her mother and Andar. Only Andar had known
the truth. Only her mother and Andar had been fully ready to
pass the dragon and enter the dark abyss—as all humans must
once have been, accepting death without qualm, thoughtlessly,

as a transition, never seeing their bodies drift lifeless behind them, only aware of their arrival, their renewal. . . .

"But that means," Pamello was saying (Shemandans' mind returned to the present, Tarawassie's to the past), "that through the rest of our lives, at least, things are probably going to go on getting harder and harder for us. Even if the colonists leave us alone, we won't have access to the equipment, the supplies. The question is, can *we* survive this now?"

Shemadans shook her head. "The question is, can we bear to leave our kith-friends now? No one is being forced to stay here. But no one who leaves this world can ever return. I know that, for my own part, this is my home now. My place—our place"—she glanced at Basilione—"is here in the kith, whatever comes." He smiled; his fingers squeezed hers on the hide mat between them.

"No one ever said any of us wanted to leave," Pamello said, a little gruffly. Lines of worry eased between his pale eyes. The other humans, one by one, shook their heads around the circle. "Only that now Camp Crackpot is not going to be such a luxury resort . . ."

Laughter spread around the circle, and Tarawassie/Shemadans understood the differing ironies and sorrows of human and Real One that lay beneath it. She looked down at her hand and Basilione's, both of them cracked and callused, aged by unaccustomed hardship. *Unaccustomed?* She smiled again, wistfully. *Surely not, after nine long years.* She looked up again, to see in her mind's eye Hunter's Luck repairing an infrared heater, Basilione bringing down an arctic springer buck with only three round stones knotted together by thongs. *We have changed, all of us. We can learn to live with the future, if we have to.*

In the corner of this tent—where they had shared so many sparse meals, sitting down cross-legged or crouching on the insulated floor—she saw the children now, sitting together in a showing/sharing session of their own. They would live to see a better future, when this time of hardship had passed—and through them her own spirit, and those of all the kith, would continue, would multiply, would see their hopes realized, and have their belief remembered. In time the fear and suspicion of the Real People would fade, the Starman kith would be able to reach them at last. And if help came from the Homeworld, they might already have begun to build a new colony, the *right* way. . . .

"But it didn't happen that way. . . ." Tarawassie clung to the fading glow of hope and pride, fighting the sense of desolation that filled her return to the present. "The humans were killed, and—and the Real People must never have listened to your ancestors. What happened, where is your kith now?"

"They all here," he said softly, not looking at her; it took her a moment to realize that he was speaking directly to her. "I last—last Starman. . . ." Seeing her incomprehension, he leaned forward, knocked a tape disk clattering. "I show you rest."

She offered her red-pricked hand; she barely noticed the discomfort now, locked into a deeper sense of realization, a different awareness. And this time, as she slid again into a silver body, a shared mind, she felt what it was to be the last of a kith.

A mosaic of minds, of images, of years, patterned within her/Moon Shadow's mind this time, as he relived his past again. . . . In the long, grueling winter after the village and their camp had been burned, their friends slaughtered, their Star People possessions destroyed, the thirty-odd members of the shattered Starman kith had tried to rejoin the main band of the Real People. They had tried to help them rebuild, recover, adapt—only to find themselves all the more unwelcome for it. And without the idea stimulus they had received from the humans of the kith, they found themselves unable to create new tools, new innovations, to replace all they had lost. Where once they had been feared for the magic they controlled, now, when they were powerless and friendless, they were scorned and mocked instead, held on the fringes of society.

As time passed and the Star People disappeared from the land, the Real People had dared to migrate back again into better lands and finally to enter the very cities of the decimated humans. But even in the city—especially in the city—the Starman kith was kept at bay, and few Real Ones would willingly show with them, or mate with them. Attrition grew as discontented descendants of the kith abandoned their outlaw beliefs, by choice or otherwise; as they left to join other roving bands, or were sucked away into the mass of the whole. And as the numbers of the parent kith shrank, inbreeding made their ancestral memories more and more aberrant. There were not enough friends to show with, to share with; there was not enough diffusion of memory to produce the integrated whole acceptable to their people, who came to regard the Starman kith more and more as fey, possessed by evil spirits, creatures to be shunned.

Until at last he, Moon Shadow, was born, the only child of the last Starman kith-woman. Haunted by the voices of the past, driven by the strange whims of ancestral spirits too strong for him to control, he had been hounded into this solitary, half-fugitive existence by the censure of his father's unyielding kith. His mother was gone; her spirit lived only in him now. But he had refused to submit to or join his father's kith. And so he was spied upon and abused for his searching of the ruins, by the ones who still feared the Star People, their memory, and particularly their power. There would be no kith-friend to hold the chitta calling for him, when his body died; no one to absorb his spirit and all of the ancestors who survived now in his mind alone.

He would be lost, abandoned, bringing evil dreams in the night to the unwilling souls that refused him shelter. All of his kith would end with him. He would die as no one in his memory had ever died; he would be forgotten forever, accursed, a part of no one's soul. . . .

Tarawassie clung to his sleek and callused hand, understanding now why he had pressed so desperately to be her friend. *A kind of immortality.* . . . She sat back. But even knowing that they were valued by one another, she knew that they would both always feel isolated, alienated, lost, because they had no purpose here, no reason for existing in an alien world. "There's only death, here!" Her voice caught; she saw in her mind Shemadans' memory of the Star Well, trying this world of madness to one which had been sane. . . . "What if my mother is still alive? The Star Well worked; it accepted her. Maybe she was—recreated, on our Homeworld, without her sickness, alive and well. Or maybe the people who could make a Star Well could cure her, and she's waiting for me, on a beautiful world, but she can't tell me how to come to her, she can't *reach* me." She remembered her mother's body and Andar's, drifting lifeless in the Well. "And I know, but I can't go. Because I'm afraid to die!"

"Maybe Star Well not work, maybe she die. . . . Nobody come here, long time. Maybe Star People all gone now; all gone everywhere. . . ." As though he didn't know whether it was a good thing or a bad one. A kind of possessiveness came into his voice. "You stay. . . ."

"They can't be. They can't be." She shook her head, not

hearing him, knowing too well what Shemadans and the rest had known—that the sabotaging of the Star Well might have meant the Homeworld's collapse. "They just gave up; they didn't want to send anyone more to this world, to go crazy."

"Maybe they come back now, if Mother go to them."

"Are you afraid of that? Afraid that it will happen again? The mob, the persecution . . ."

He nodded; his tail traced obscure patterns in the pale dust on the floor behind him.

"But Moon Shadow—the way we can show together, it's something the humans can't do at all, something they'd value if someone could only make them understand. Shemadans, Basilione, all your ancestors, believed that—that it could protect you and defend you; it could make you as important to the humans as—as they are to themselves. You could become transmitters of all knowledge. . . ." Shemadans' belief in the future, Basilione's vision, filled her, became her. "I can go to the Homeworld! I *can*. I want to go through the Well, I want to find my mother, and see—everything. I want to see a real human world. And if I go, I can make them want to come back here and find your people. I'll show them how special you are. They'll come, I know they will. And I'll come back on the ship—the Starman kith will live, we won't be forgotten. . . ."

"I not die?" Moon Shadow stood up, his sharp face twitching with emotion. "Yes, yes, you go—you come back!" He caught her hand, dragging her up from her seat. "Our peoples be one. My people learn all Star People know. . . . And I not die forever! Come, come, Star Woman, we go now to Crystal Ship"—chittering laughter—"while *I* believe!"

But I'm Tarawassie! Her own doubts, her unanswered fears, stirred again, denying the stranger in her mind. But Moon Shadow pulled her toward the lift, and back into the rush of his own bright emotion.

They went out through the high, heavy doors of the library entrance, into the chill autumn twilight.

And stepping out of the shadows into the glow of Tarawassie's light globe, five natives met them there. Tarawassie froze as the cold light glanced from spearpoints leveling toward her. She heard Moon Shadow's barked curse.

"So, evil one. Still you disobey your people!" The tallest of the natives, silvery-gray like Moon Shadow, confronted him; his eyes gleamed with triumph. Tarawassie realized that she understood him, even though he used the native speech. "This time we make you sorry enough. Drop spear!"

But she realized that the others were holding back, hesitant behind the shield of their spears, their eyes on her, fearful. As though he sensed it too, Moon Shadow kept his grip on his own sharpened metal tube, shaking his head. "Not so, brother! I be under protection of Star People. You not touch me, or you be sorry ones." He stood at her side, glancing from face to face, as though he dared them to approach. Surreptitiously he touched Tarawassie's hand, reassuring, seeking reassurance. Her fingers closed for a moment over his, giving what answer she could. "Leave us!" He dropped his own spearpoint, returning the challenge.

Two of the others backed up slightly, but Moon Shadow's—brother?—stood his ground. "Not let you go, evil one. Swift Springer judge you, and this spirit-woman, this time."

And Moon Shadow nodded, suddenly smiling; his teeth glistened. "Yes, then! This time, he not deny me. . . . I go to village with you."

His brother met his smile, his fur ridging slightly. "You not have choice."

They went ringed by spears through the windy, crumbling, blue-shadowed streets. Tarawassie gazed upward, her breath frosting the deepening blue-violet of the sky's dome, where one star shone, canted down from the zenith before her. The star that was not a star, but held the thread that spanned the darkness to all the stars. . . . She lifted her hand to it, in a promise, and an appeal; her hand dropped away again, tightened into a fist at her side. She looked down past her feet, picking a path through the half-seen rubble. "Moon Shadow," she murmured, keeping her voice steady. "What are they going to do to us? Who are they? You said, 'brother.'"

He spoke in a human, keeping his own voice low. "Is half-brother—father's son. Others be kith-friends." His voice roughened: "They take us Swift Springer. They not hurt you, Star Woman. See how they not touch you—fear you."

"Who is Swift Springer?"

"Shaman—show with all kiths, show very clear. Swift Springer know all; all people show with him, many many seasons past. He say, 'This thing Real, that thing not belong.' He say I full evil spirits. . . . But even he give you honor. You command him, and he not punish me this time. Instead, he lis-

ten to me, make them all see what we do, see future!" He
looked up at her, a kind of desperate determination burning in
him. "Maybe this be good thing, not bad . . . kith-friend."

"Kith-friend," she nodded, uncertain. "I hope so. . . ."

The final undulation of the street turned them out onto a
wide open space, like the square where the natives left their
offerings. This one lay at the hub of six streets, fronted on six
sides by reflection—building walls, a sheen of blue-black
now, with deeper, purer pupils of blackness, framed in fractures of snowflake symmetry.

In the center of the open space a fire leaped and fell back,
held in a palm of stone. Life's darting pulse mocked her, reflecting in the dark, abandoned eyes of this valley of mirrors.
Her senses vibrated with glare, with heat, with the tart, acrid
smoke smell of burning sapwood. And as though she had always known, she knew now that a spirit fire had burned there
once, had been a sign to the Real People that they should
settle here forever. When the spirit fire had died, they had
created their own eternal flame, for it was a holy sign.

Tarawassie brushed the rim of stone as they passed, black-
ening her fingers with soot. Beneath the charcoal patina she
could make out a faint tracery of color on the polished surface. And within the stained-glass golds and blues of the
flames, silhouetted in soot, she saw a form of obscure grace.
As she wondered what purpose it could have served, for a
startled second she glimpsed a second vision, of the stranger
beauty that human eyes had seen, when they had gazed upon
"spirit fire," and she knew that its only purpose had been
beauty.

Caught between the future and the past, she went on with
Moon Shadow and the guards through the gathering
darkness, to the base of a building that faced along the perimeter. And she saw at last that this place was not deserted,
abandoned to the ritual fire. Two natives watched them from
a doorway—two women, in sagging knee-length kilts suspend-
ered by chains of glittering metal and beads.

The women stood shifting, indecisive, looking from her to
Moon Shadow with silent awe. Behind them more fires
burned, subdued, small family cooking fires within a great
hall. She could see other figures inside, now, slender shadow-
forms, and wondered how many of these buildings had been
reclaimed by the world's new order. A child appeared
abruptly between the women in the doorway; its downy fur
showed silvery-white. Like a drop of liquid starlight, it

climbed its mother's leg; drawn up by her hands, it disappeared, impossibly, into her pouch. Tarawassie's mind filled with a sense image of soft warmth, security, pleasure—the tender communication of a mother's thoughts. Her hands against her distended stomach, the woman turned and slipped back through the doorway.

The other woman stayed where she was beneath the sheltering overhang, her iron-gray fur brightening, ridging on her scalp as Moon Shadow's brother approached her.

"Swift Springer." He pointed at the ground between them.

She nodded, slipped quickly, wordlessly, through into the warm interior. Moon Shadow's tail twitched, his light spear rapped out a soft challenge at his side. Tarawassie pulled her cloak closer around her.

The long moments passed; her face began to ache with the cold. "What are we—" She broke off as a new body filled the doorway; more natives clustered in the background, blotting out the light. A man in a knee-length sleeveless robe, stooped and shuffling, emerged into the cool light of Tarawassie's alien globe. He leaned on a staff; his unruffled fur stayed midnight black, even here. Moon Shadow's crest rose.

Swift Springer stopped, faintly smiling, "What now, Shadowman?" His glance shifted slightly to focus on Tarawassie. His pupils widened, narrowed; he shook his head as though he thought his eyes betrayed him.

"I am real." Tarawassie spoke in her own language, knowing instinctively that she could not manage the clipped sounds of the native speech. She moved forward into stronger light, brushing back her hair; stood straighter, aware of the creature the old native saw, which was not herself—trying to become the mystery that even she did not quite comprehend. She reached out to brush Moon Shadow's pouch with her hand, pointed at Swift Springer.

This time the old native's crest did rise. His ageless face rumpled with emotion. She knew the desire to refuse, to deny, to castigate Moon Shadow that burned in his eyes as they touched on him. But Swift Springer could not refuse or deny his fear, his awe, of the half-remembered ancestors she represented.

"You honor Star Woman." It was almost a command. Moon Shadow met Swift Springer's gaze with stubborn pride. "Call old ones, I show you all, this time. I show all; my right!"

Swift Springer shook his head. "You show me, I choose.

You think bad thoughts; no one here want twisted mind. I choose, if they see."

Tarawassie took a deep breath. "Call them all. They have a right to choose for themselves whether they want to know this. I want him to show them all!" She brought her palm up against her chest, as she had seen Moon Shadow do, trusting in the tone to make her meaning clear.

Swift Springer bristled, straightening, his fur ridged. She withdrew into her cloak, unsure of asserting herself, expecting failure.

"Coward, Swift Springer!" Moon Shadow brought the spearbutt down with a *clack* on the pavement, his voice reaching out past Swift Springer to the dark cluster of watchers at the door. "Springer's-dung, you fear your power come to me. Not fear I show them evil!"

Swift Springer shook his head again, violently, jarring his brittle frame. "We see, Shadowman, who give his kith most honor tonight!" Mockery edged the words; he turned abruptly to push through the cluster of onlookers. Tarawassie heard his speech—sharp, chattering, unintelligible barks echoing in the great hall. A gangly silver child squeezed out through the crowd at the door, and darted past them away into the night.

"It happens . . . it happens!" Moon Shadow murmured, almost disbelieving. "Old ones, young ones, all come; I show them all. This time I show them change—I show them change be right." His gray eyes found her, he smiled. "What we do tonight be shown forever!"

"A kind of immortality," Tarawassie whispered, glancing up into the moonless sky, at one star brighter than all others. "A kind you can be sure of."

Moon Shadow nodded, his elation shining; she realized his brother and the guards had retreated. He motioned her back across the plaza toward the fire.

Tarawassie waited, holding the light globe and spear clutched against her, warming her back at the blaze. The minutes passed, and a crowd of natives gathered, watching her watch them. From the crowd a handful of men and women came forward, led by Swift Springer, to stand between her and Moon Shadow. They chittered sharply, privately, among themselves. Most of them, she saw, had body fur grayed to black—elders. And also, ones who saw most clearly, Moon Shadow's memory told her—ones who could pick the most details from another's showing, and could pass the image they absorbed to others, intact, for the spreading of important news.

Moon Shadow did not look at her, trusting in her presence, lost in the attention of his own people and the obsession of his need to show. She felt the eyes of the others brush her from time to time, heard their halting inquiries. At last she saw the chosen group begin to form a chain, each one carefully placing a hand into the pouch of the next, until Swift Springer reached out, as though he approached something unclean, to make contact with Moon Shadow.

A muttering passed through the crowd. Moon Shadow closed his eyes, his face enraptured.

The crowd fell silent. Tarawassie hugged the light globe to her, feeling the barest trace of warmth, feeling the heat of the fire at her back and the cold air burning inside her head—imagining the heated tingling that passed along their arms. The flames snapped and spat beside her, like the electric dissonance of an alien presence in her mind, like the charge of hostility that flowed between old hatreds. She tried to picture what might fill the minds of Swift Springer and the other receivers now—a bright, tantalizing scatter of human magics, the secret power of the Star Well, herself swept away like a spirit to another world, bearing the secret of the Real People, the possibility of a future when Real People would prove the value of their gifts and share equality with the Star People and have for the showing all the secret magic. . . .

"Evil—!" Swift Springer broke away from Moon Shadow, the weakest link in a chain of hope. "Evil spirits come into me, from evil mind!" The others, who had been linked through him, stood dumbly, as though they had been stunned, watching as he struck at Moon Shadow with his staff. "Evil!"

Moon Shadow staggered but did not cry out, a strange, shattered expression growing on his face.

"This evil one *show* to Star People, give them power over him. He show us lies, hide truth, much evil! I show, all see, this evil. . . ."

Tarawassie leaned forward anxiously, not understanding. Her hands tightened around the spear as Moon Shadow began to back up, step by step, prodded by Swift Springer's staff.

"You not force me!" Half denial, half plea. Moon Shadow moved his head from side to side impotently.

Swift Springer gestured with his tail. Two men broke from

the crowd to seize Moon Shadow, pinning him between their arms, their tails wrapping his legs, holding him immobile.

"Moon Shadow!" Tarawassie called out, but he did not hear or see her now, his teeth showing bright with a snarl of fear, his hackles rising. His eyes were only for Swift Springer, moving forward again. One man seized Moon Shadow's hand, forced it into Swift Springer's pouch; Swift Springer placed his own hand in Moon Shadow's. The elders re-formed their chain, the nearest slipped his hand also into Moon Shadow's pouch.

Moon Shadow stiffened, with an anguish she could not comprehend. A high, thin wail, born of no physical pain, broke from him, continued, starting a susurration among the crowd. Why did he let them do this? What was happening? Should she—? "Stop it! Stop it!" Her voice beat ineffectually at Swift Springer. She forced herself forward, bracing the spear.

But even as she did, the chain separated again. Moon Shadow wavered, his cry fading away as his eyes came open. The two men who held him released him then; he sank down to hands and knees, as if all strength, all resistance, all pride had been drained out of him in one swift incomprehensible assault. Swift Springer looked away from him to her, the virulent satisfaction still plain as his eyes met hers. He pointed with his staff. "Stop!"

She stopped, but letting the spear's tip droop toward him. "What have you done?" She spoke as evenly as she could. They stood like fencers. The elders ringed them in; she felt the eyes that had touched on her with a kind of reverence branding her now with fear and suspicion, cold like the wind.

Swift Springer raised his voice to the crowd. "I give you truth! This one"—his staff whacked Moon Shadow—"and this one"—he brandished it threateningly at her, still not daring to strike her—"want us be swallowed by Star People again, like beforetime! We show you truth!" The elders moved past them at his sign, into the crowd. "Chitta save us, give chitta Star People, they die, forever! Give chitta this one now—watch her die. . . ." His staff struck the spear like lightning, jarred it clattering from her deadened hands.

She caught the light globe to her, feeling herself as they saw her now, shorn of her ancestral spirits—a wild-haired, ragged scarecrow-woman, powerless against the avenging they would claim for their ancestors'—their own—suffering. She saw Moon Shadow rise up on his knees, her own fear and despair magnified in the mirror of his face. "Go!" She could barely understand the words, "Star Woman, run!"

She was already turning, to break past the edge of the crowd. She fled blindly back across the plaza, plunged into the dark mouth of a street entrance and kept running.

Followed at last only by the memory of fear, she struggled on through the narrow canyons of night, stumbling, falling, half-mad with the jagged overlay of one world on another, memories of a city of life and noise that illuminated the broken silences of the dark and empty ruins. But finally no need, no vision, was strong enough to goad her frozen feet beyond a walk. She halted, pain twisting beneath her ribs, and raised her eyes to the battered symmetry of the skyline. The climbing moon, like a tiny silver face, peered down at her past the shadow towers, filling the dark windows with ghost lights like her own, as her mind filled them with the specters of the past. Something slithered through a puddle of liquid moonglow by her foot, disturbing a clutch of bones. Her half-cry of fright beat back at her, layering echoes, draining away into stifled silence. As though she alone were left living . . .

But as the realization grew in her that she was lost, in body, in spirit, moonlight touched the unmistakable form of the broken building where Moon Shadow kept his camp, a silver hand pointing the way to shelter. She moved on, pushing her aching legs, pushing all thought, all fear, all sorrow down, gratefully reaching out for the one concreteness left in this world of night.

She found the broken wall in the pooled shadows and slipped through into the empty interior. But no one tended the burned-out fire; no one sat waiting or lay stretched on the heap of rags—he had not come. Tarawassie dropped to her knees on his bedding; sank back, her mouth trembling. Would he ever come? Had he died, too? Had they seen his secrets, good and evil, and then killed him—as another mob had killed—as they would have killed her too, for both the good and the evil, for showing them the truth?

But the reason didn't matter, had no meaning. . . . He was gone! And she had no power to call home his soul. She had no power of immortality, no power over anyone's soul, not even her own. Only a terrible emptiness left within her. Moon Shadow, her mother, both were beyond tears, regret, loss and pain—and she was left behind with all those things. And there were so many things done or left undone—and no way she could change them now. All her opportunities to do or undo were lost . . . lost. . . .

Grief caught her by the throat and shook her with the fruitlessness of her waking dreams, which had been no more true or clearly seen than the dreams that chitta showed her. Why had she believed that the Star Well held the answer to everything—to anything? How could she have expected it to accept her, with her mind so full of unknown quantities, doubts, and fear? How could she have pretended to believe that they wouldn't matter? She was just learning what it meant to be alive—did she want to die so soon?

Because how could she *know* that there was a whole civilization waiting beyond the passage for her? Whether it was one she would want to spend her new life in, whether it would accept her—whether it had gone to dust like her own? Her mother was dead, had been dying, and it was only grief that made her believe, or need to believe, that some miracle, somewhere, had let her live. No one had come here in five hundred years to seek her people out—no one would ever come now. If her mother's spirit had found a home, it was nowhere the living could follow. . . . Or had she only been dissipated in darkness, lost among the spectral silences of frozen gas and dust? And did she care—did she even know?

"I don't *want* that! I don't want that!" Tarawassie jerked upright, sitting back on her knees, in the rebounding echoes of her own tormented cry. "I don't want her to be gone!" she threw the echoes back. "I don't want to know the truth about it, and I don't want to waste my *life*." She pressed her fists together in the lap of her ragged robe. "And I don't have to. There's no reason to go, no reason to try. I don't have to!"

A shuffling reached her, the clink of dislodged rubble, as the echoes fled. She twisted like a startled animal, pulled back into the present, squinting through the fingers of light that probed like a betrayer's hand into the dark haven of her lair.

She bit off another cry, knowing too well that her voice had played betrayer already.

Abruptly a figure blocked the light—a native. A voice called, a hoarse bark of sound, not demanding, but strangely familiar.

Tarawassie climbed stiffly to her feet, not quite breathing. "Moon Shadow? Moon Shadow?"

He came forward into the dim interior, moving awkwardly, like a cripple. She struggled to fix her vision on his silver-haloed face. He reached her where she stood beside the fire ring, hesitated a moment, gazing through her. His face quivered; confusion and something darker clouded his eyes. But then they came back to her; he lifted his hands and settled them on her shoulders, squeezing gently, in a gesture of reunion. She raised her own hands, pressed them down over his. A rueful smile split his face; the weight of his hands drew her down with him as he sank wearily onto the pad of rags. She lowered her own protesting body slowly, carefully, to keep him from falling. Splotches of darkness matted his rumpled fur.

"Moon Shadow . . ." She drew one of his hands down in her own, seeing the congealed blood trapped between fingers where a claw had been torn away. She opened her own battered hands. "Were they mad? Or were we . . . ? How could they hurt you?" Her hands folded close again over the thin three-fingered one. "How? Why?"

He shrugged slightly, as though it hurt. A low, mournful singsong came from him, like a dirge.

She glanced up, filled with a premonition. "What is it? What's wrong? What did they do?"

Moon Shadow shook his head, avoiding her eyes; he spread his hands in a gesture of emptiness, of incomprehension.

"You can't understand me?" Her voice rose. "What happened, what did they do to you?" She stopped. "Then, how can we—" Remembering, she put out her hand. As it slipped into his pouch, he jerked loose, his body rebelling against her touch. Her hand tightened on itself, empty. She pulled back in turn, wounded by surprise and dismay.

Moon Shadow reached out to catch her fist, smoothing the fingers, drawing it back toward him, his eyes filled with apology, his face set in frustration. He slid her hand into his pouch; she felt his own hands twitch with some emotion she couldn't read. And then, as though in explanation, he let the memory pass into her of what had been done to him at Swift Springer's will:

She/he endured again his humiliation, held helplessly, like a criminal, while Swift Springer extracted his guilty secret and inflicted punishment together. She lived the indignity of an intrusion—the forced revelation of a memory not given freely, that was also a kind of perversion, committed in full view of all his people, permitted by them, as though he were less than nothing.

The singsong dirge filled his throat again. Tears brimmed in her own eyes, slipped out and down, unheeded this time as someone else grieved within her. She watched through his eyes as Swift Springer turned against her, and she/Moon Shadow could do no more to help her/Star Woman than tell her to run away. . . .

And then she/he crouched, without the strength to rise, watching the fresh, evil truths of the humans' brutality that had been torn from him spreading like ripples over water through the crowd, knowing that the promise, the hopes, all the possibilities of a new life that had been in him too would not be carried with them, but would sink like a stone into the depths of oblivion, lost . . . lost . . . he began to moan.

Swift Springer began to speak again, with all the halting eloquence he could muster. He heard himself, Moon Shadow, called a committer of perversions with the Star People, a madman who preferred the madness of his bastard ancestors to the proven truths of the Real People. One who would have them all lose their Reality, be destroyed again by the evil of the Star People, as they had almost been swallowed by the Star People before, as this one, Moon Shadow, had been swallowed by the Night Beast. . . .

Moon Shadow struggled to his feet again, found his voice, denouncing Swift Springer in one final half-formed defiance, crying that here, in the place made holy by the eternal fire, he had not been heard fully, or judged fairly. . . .

Swift Springer's staff came down across her/his shoulders to knock him sprawling, and the Real People, infected and inflamed by the transfer of his own memories of human atrocity, had closed around him then, and passed judgment.

"*No!*" Tarawassie broke contact, screaming her horror, his horror, as she felt the hatred of a hundred strange minds forced into his own, exploding him, shattering him; an overload of image burning out the circuits of his brain, stripping him of his identity, his ancestors, his Reality. . . .

Moon Shadow swayed and collapsed against her. She slipped her arm free, supporting his narrow back, stroked the warm, matted fur with fierce tenderness. She whimpered helplessly, with the knowledge of why he had been afraid of her touch, any touch. . . . But how could it have happened? He had been in *control* of the showing, in control of Swift Springer, with her presence—until Swift Springer had broken the showing bond and turned on him. And then he had surrendered, losing control, losing his confidence, forgetting even his goal. How could it happen, what had made it happen to him? Why? Why?

Moon Shadow stirred, raised his head from her shoulder, keening softly. Tarawassie drew a ragged breath at what she found in his eyes, and another as it began to fade. He nodded at last, sighing, and met her eyes again. Gently she reached out to place her hand in his pouch, picturing in her mind the crucial instant, trying to convey her own failure to understand *why.* . . .

Moon Shadow made a small exclamation—at what, she wasn't sure. Her mind began to fill with memories of Swift Springer—Swift Springer the shaman, the clear-seer, the eldest among the old ones who absorbed all knowledge, who passed judgment on the validity and the fitness of what was shown. Swift Springer, who embodied the absolute in attitude and behavior in the mind of every Real One—even in Moon Shadow's own mind. Even knowing that his ancestral belief was right, still he believed in the omniscient judgment of Swift Springer. She saw again Swift Springer's denunciation of him, felt his own belief turning against him, to make him falter. And Swift Springer had known that he would have to falter, and that had been enough. The static system that he had hoped to transform had defeated him instead, because he himself had always been a part of it. . . .

Tarawassie broke contact again, lurching with the sudden giddiness of fatigue. Leaning to catch Moon Shadow's supply sack, she dragged it close so that they could reach the store of dried meat and fruit. They ate silently, despondently, not wasting strength on useless words. Words might be useless forever now.

But Moon Shadow took her hand again—the other hand this time, not stiff and tingling—letting her touch him now with no hesitation. Her head echoed with the plans for her passage through the Star Well, and a sense of urgency, demanding. . . . Demanding to know, she realized, whether she would still try, and urgent with the need for her to agree.

She shook her head, clearing it, denying. She could not, she would not—she let all of the unanswerable questions, all of her doubts and fears, flow patternless back into his mind in response. There was no reason, and no need. . . .

A burst of anger-sounds startled her ears; she opened her eyes to the anger on his face. Insistently, he pictured her plan again, her longing, her curiosity, her mother's face. And his mind groped, fumbled, forced out a disoriented, fragmentary vision of the Starman kith together, sharing their secrets and their unique talents. He was the last, the last Starman, and his people had destroyed his ancestors. If she never brought her people back—never returned to realize their hope—then he had suffered for nothing! Only she could save his ancestors or make him real again. If she never brought her people back, never returned to him, he would die too, he would die forever. She was his kith-friend, his only friend, and she had promised . . . promised. . . .

Again she let her doubts make an answer, picturing her people gone, as his ancestors had feared. Nothing would be gained. . . .

The image of her passing through battered again at the back of her eyes, clouded with starbursts of brightness by his vehemence; she was his only hope, the only hope of his kith, the only hope of all. . . .

"But I'm afraid!" She broke away from him. "I'm afraid, for me. No one else has to do this—not you, not them, not anyone but me. Damn you! Damn our people—there's never going to be anything between them, they're too afraid, too selfish! I'm selfish too. I have to be certain, I have to be sure, or I won't be able to pass through—I have to be sure that it's all there is, the best thing for *me*. . . ." She plucked at a rag beside her ankle, not looking up at his face, watching his hands rub distractedly across the fur of his stomach. She lifted her eyes finally to the desolate incomprehension on his face, that could only answer her unspoken question with another.

Moon Shadow sank back on one elbow, and then down onto his side with a sound like a grunt. His eyes held her for a moment longer, the oblique pupils wide and black; and then, as though he had kept them open for as long as he could, the lids fell shut. He sighed, without comfort.

Slowly she stretched out beside him, easing her own stiffened limbs down onto the narrow pad of rags. The faint radiance of his body heat joined with her own in the space between them, soothing her, soothing them both, with no fire to warm them. She breathed in the subtle, dusty, alien scent of his body, letting the tension of enduring release her, letting go.

Moon Shadow's breathing fell away into the unobtrusive rhythms of sleep. Yet her own mind resisted her body's demand, searching the depths of her being, weighing, measuring, assessing. . . . If she did not try to enter the Star Well, or if she failed to pass through, what was left to her? To live here in the ruins with Moon Shadow forever, picking through the secrets of the past, forever reminded of death and loss. And they could not communicate forever about the past. They had proved the bond that showing could have been between their peoples—but how could they communicate the future, or even the present now? Would his crippled mind even be able to re-create her speech again?

But she could not go back to life as she had always known it, lost in dreams among the dying—to a living death in a crystal coffin. Was it better? Was it worse? Was it better to hoard this meaningless, futureless, living death, only because if was a thing she could be sure of? Or better to gather her life in her hands and fling it into the unknown, where all happiness and fulfillment might reward her—or nothing might, nothing at all . . . ?

She opened her eyes abruptly, to stare at Moon Shadow's sleeping face. His fears, his own awareness of death made bright static against her denial, telling her that she *must* try, for his sake/her own sake—in order to live, to live forever. But she was only Tarawassie! Tarawassie, not Moon Shadow, not Shemadans, or Basilione or the savior of anyone's aspirations—Tarawassie. And it was her body that would drift lifeless in the blue-green limbo of the Star Well, her soul that might never be reclaimed. It would be so easy, so much easier, if she could have shared enough to truly believe as he did, or to trust, as Shemadans had, in the Star Well. If she could *know* that someone waited to recapture her disembodied soul, as she gazed down through the transparent mysteries of the Well . . . *To pass the dragon, and enter the dark abyss* . . . So easy, if she could be certain. But was anyone ever certain, really certain, of anything? Was it possible ever to know the future?

She had experienced so little, and she wanted to experience so much—and no amount of measuring or assessing would answer the question of whether she was willing to accept the terms of the gamble, willing to gamble her very life, in order to live. Only her heart could tell her, only her heart—and the Star Well would hear the answer. . . .

A thin drift of snow lay in the entrance of the building with the coming of a new dawn; the flakes sifted down like the pale dust of ages. Moon Shadow moved haltingly, as though he sometimes forgot his purpose; he struck a stone against his knife blade, finally sparking a fire to warm their aching bones.

He glanced at her often, his eyes searching her expression as they ate, huddled before the flames. But she kept her thoughts hidden, assembling images, putting her house in order. At last she reached out to him, showing him an image of the Crystal Ship, promising nothing, except that she would go that far.

He nodded, but the sudden joy in his eyes dimmed, was transformed into a deeper emotion which had more of sharing and an understanding of her fear. She felt again how great a part of him, within her, would share in her success or her failure.

They went out, then, and through the twisting maze of streets, on a final journey to an uncertain end. The snow wrapped them in a purity of whiteness, clinging to her lashes and hair, to her ragged cloak, to Moon Shadow's stained fur, anesthetizing, disguising. For a moment Tarawassie recoiled from the sight she would present, the wretched, wasted thing that would greet new life if she passed through the Well. . . . But she remembered that this body was no more than a vessel for the pattern, the code, the essence that would be transmitted, poured forth into the universe—a vessel that would be re-created in perfection, surely, without the superficial scars and wounds of life's careless handling. She saw her mother waiting for her, well and strong—clung to that vision, to keep from seeing the endless, dark abyss.

They reached the snow-capped dome of the ferry shed at last. She entered slowly, feeling like a stranger, Moon Shadow trailing behind. She heard the irregular pattern of his new hesitation as he walked, saw around her the signs of decay, the unnatural gapings in the domed vault of the shed. No one else was waiting. But a ferry was down. She was glad, not wanting to be given time to hesitate, to vacillate.

She stopped by the opening in the ferry's transparent hull. Moon Shadow stopped beside her, his eyes fixed on it with total incomprehension. She pointed up through the dome at the opaque sky above, getting no more response; reached out then and showed him a memory of this tiny jewel-facet rising, to rejoin the Crystal Ship where the Star Well waited. He stepped back, his crest rising at the vision of flight, fearful incredulity in his eyes and no human words to express his awe. For half a second delight began to brighten where fear had been, but abruptly his gaze blanked, wandered.

Pain wrenched her. No, she couldn't—she couldn't leave him behind like this, not like this. . . . Somehow there must be a way for them to go on together, for him to explore this final secret with her. She gestured at him to come with her into the ferry.

He shook his head, the fear not fading, but underlain now by a kind of defiant resolution. He touched his chest. "I not forget. I wait till you come. I never forget!" He squatted down, told her with gestures that he would wait for her—whatever happened, he would wait for her return.

She nodded, accepting, remembering that Shemadans had known that the Star Well had never been intended to serve the Real People. Realizing that this was meant to be her journey alone, depending on her decision, her courage, her strength, that this separation was to be a partial payment she must make, a test of resolution.

Moon Shadow rose again and placed his hands on her shoulders, squeezing gently, glancing away and down, as her eyes would have touched him. He spoke very softly, a short, chirping phrase: "My friend . . . my friend . . ."

She lifted her own hands again to cover his, drew him to her, and for a long moment held him close in her arms. "Yes, my friend . . . my friend . . . my friend! Goodbye . . ." She broke away, before her resolution failed, and entered the ferry. She watched his strange silver face through the glass, with its rainbow play of emotions, watched its astonishment as the ferry began to rise, watched it abruptly blotted out as she left the ferry shed, and the world, behind. And she felt a part of herself being torn away, and remaining, the part of him within her alive in her mind forever. And she knew that she had been wrong to think that they would lose one another forever, even in this parting. . . . The clouds closed around her in a shroud of gray.

Tarawassie stepped through the passageway from the ferry, her feet on crystal, her head among the stars. Somewhere there was music, of a kind, playing—loud and toneless, out of tune. Wall surfaces filmed with murky bleeding color. She stood still in the heedless clutter of the waiting area, covering her ears, blinking back her disbelief. It wasn't, not—the Loom? Not Mirro, at the Loom? This bleating, bleeding stridency was not the gossamer cloth with warp of light and woof of music? But what else could it be? She shut her eyes then, too, but could not close out the deeper violations in the fibers of her nerves. *You knew what it would be like, you knew, you knew—from the moment you saw your own reflection. Go on! Go on. Face reality. . . .*

She went on through the corridors, almost running now, to the room where Mirro had always played: Where she wove still, snared inside the web of distorted sensation that she could not tell from beauty. Tarawassie stood shuddering in the doorway, wanting to scream at her, wanting to tear her loose from the abused console that had never been meant for music, and make her stop, stop. . . . But she knew she would achieve nothing, against chitta, and nothing would ever be gained. . . .

She went on, trailed by the wraiths of her reflection, through the hallways to the main dreaming place. The dreamers lay as she had lain so often, or wandered aimlessly, wondering at the stars. A few looked up as she entered, without interest or surprise. Faded robes hung like sackcloth on their emaciated bodies. Faces she had known for years were the masks stripped from the faces of strangers, empty-eyed and gaping. The smell of chitta, and of human stagnation and filth, choked her, nauseated her. . . . Someone stumbled against her. She turned to find Sabowyn, recognized only after long, agonizing seconds. He caught her to him, steadying himself, smiling at her inanely. "You were gone. . . ."

"Sabowyn . . ." She worked her hands loose to seize him, shake him. "Listen to me. You can't drink chitta any more, you've got to stop! You're dying, dying, because of chitta! Please, *please*, listen to me!" Suddenly, too vividly, she remembered Andar's madness.

"Let me kiss you, Tarawassie . . . I'm going to dream now, but I want to kiss you. . . ." His hand stroked her hair awkwardly, as though he couldn't remember why he did it, his beard scraped her cheek. She pushed him away, her face twisting with despair, saw him fall onto a couch, still smiling through his confusion.

She found the spiraling ramp beyond the room and did not stop until she reached the Star Well's rim. She knelt beside it, gazing down at the endless pattern of stars that moved imperceptibly below the azure lines of force. She passed her hand through the cool, reassuring blue-green mist, searching her own eyes of deeper blue and green, reflecting. And behind them, below them, she found the face of her mother, and Andar's face—smiling, at peace. And locked into the essence of her being was a part of one other, to be carried with her always, whatever came to pass. One who carried within him a part of her own essence, wherever she herself might be. A kind of immortality, an eternal flame. . . . Slowly she rose and stepped onto the rim.

Silently, without motion, she entered the ocean.

Epilog

And Moon Shadow received the body of Tarawassie, which came down in a crystal tear from the Crystal Ship, where the Star Well lay. He bore the body away, and where it lies no one knows, for that was the custom of the kiths, to keep a body safe from evil spirits. He held the chitta ceremony, to call the spirit of his kith-friend back to him from the far silences, in case it had found no truer home. But whether he dreamed, or what he dreamed, was never shown.

Then, as he had promised, he waited for her return. He waited for thirty years, scorned and shunned among the Real People of the ruined city. But in that time she never came. And after thirty years he died, and there was no one among his own people who would hold the chitta calling or give his spirit rest, for he was the last Starman.

So is shown the legend of Tarawassie and Moon Shadow. May their souls show our peoples the way to true understanding.

Afterword

"The Crystal Ship" is a story that grew out of a song, in this case the haunting Doors song of the same name. I'd first had the idea of writing a story based on the song about ten years ago, before I was actually writing seriously. The story plot I'd created then had certain seeds of this story in it, but it was an entirely different kind of story, basically an adventure. When I seriously set out to write the story some years later, I decided that I wanted to do something more substantial—something that had to do with the basic questions of life and death, reality and illusion, that the song itself evoked.

This story was another in which a character began to take charge unexpectedly—in this case the alien, Moon Shadow. "The Crystal Ship" was the hardest to write of any of the stories in this collection, largely because his character took it off in directions I hadn't anticipated, and tangled his own life up inextricably with the heroine's. His problems became equally important with hers, and forced me to give him equal attention.

"The Crystal Ship" also painted, almost inadvertently, one of my most pessimistic images of human nature—perhaps simply because of the themes it was handling. But someone asked me once whether I was particularly depressed when I wrote it; at the time I said no, but looking back, I realize that I was in a particularly negative period of my life, which may have been why I chose that time to write it.

The poem which appears in the story, by artist Russell Grattan, was one that I had found years before on a reproduction of one of his paintings. Even then the poem seemed to fulfill perfectly the essence of the Star Well; that I couldn't imagine being able to create anything myself that would work better. I wrote to Grattan, asking his permission to use the poem, and he agreed, in return for a copy of the story. Actually making contact with him, and exchanging words and works, was a unique pleasure of writing this particular novella.

Along with being the most difficult story I've written, "The Crystal Ship" had an additional problem after it appeared in print—its ending. I had intended that the last line of the story would subtly let the reader know that Tarawassie did return to her world, and that her dreams and Moon Shadow's were eventually realized; but unfortunately, I made it too subtle—only about one reader in ten realized that the story had not simply been left open-ended. I hope that the version that appears here has lowered the odds, and brightened an otherwise dark canvas of words.

Tin Soldier

The ship drifted down the ragged light-robe of the Pleiades, dropped like a perfect pearl into the midnight water of the bay. And reemerged, to bob gently in a chain of gleaming pearls stretched across the harbor toward the port. The port's unsleeping Eye blinked once, the ship replied. New Piraeus, pooled among the hills, sent tributaries of light streaming down to the bay to welcome all comers, full of sound and brilliance and rash promise. The crew grinned, expectant, faces peering through the transparent hull; someone giggled nervously.

The sign at the heavy door flashed a red one-legged toy; TIN SOLDIER flashed blue below it. EAT. DRINK. COME BACK AGAIN. In green. And they always did, because they knew they could.

"Soldier, another round, please!" came over canned music.

The owner of the Tin Soldier, also known as Tin Soldier, glanced up from his polishing to nod and smile, reached down to set bottles out on the bar. He mixed the drinks himself. His face was ordinary, with eyes that were dark and patient, and his hair was coppery barbed wire bound with a knotted cloth. Under the curling copper, under the skin, the back of his skull was a plastic plate. The quick fingers of the hand on the goose-necked bottle were plastic, the smooth arm was prosthetic. Sometimes he imagined he heard clicking as it moved. More than half his body was artificial. He looked to be about twenty-five; he had looked the same fifty years ago.

He set the glasses on the tray and pushed, watching as it drifted across the room, and returned to his polishing. The agate surface of the bar showed cloudy permutations of color, grain-streak and whorl and chalcedony depths of mist. He had discovered it in the desert to the east—a shattered imitation tree, like a fellow traveler trapped in stasis through time. They shared the private joke with their clientele.

"—come see our living legend!"

He looked up, saw her coming in with the crew of the *Who Got Her—709*, realized he didn't know her. She hung back as they crowded around, her short ashen hair like beaten metal in the blue-glass lantern light. *New*, he thought. Maybe eighteen, with eyes of quicksilver very wide open. He smiled at her as he welcomed them, and the other women pulled her up to the agate bar. "Come on, little sister," he heard Harkané say, "you're one of us too." She smiled back at him.

"I don't know you . . . but your name should be Diana, like the silver Lady of the Moon." His voice caught him by surprise.

Quicksilver shifted. "It's not."

Very new. And realizing what he'd almost done again, suddenly wanted it more than anything. Filled with bitter joy he said, "What is your name?"

Her face flickered, but then she met his eyes and said, smiling, "My name is Brandy."

"Brandy . . ."

A knowing voice said, "Send us the usual, Soldier. Later, yes—?"

He nodded vaguely, groping for bottles under the counter ledge. Wood screeked over stone as she pulled a stool near and slipped onto it, watching him pour. "You're very neat." She picked nuts from a bowl.

"*Long* practice."

She smiled, missing the joke.

He said, "Brandy's a nice name. And I think somewhere I've heard it—"

"The whole thing is Branduin. My mother said it was very old."

He was staring at her. He wondered if she could see one side of his face blushing. "What will you drink?"

"Oh . . . do you have any—brandy? It's a wine, I think; nobody's ever had any. But because it's my name, I always ask."

He frowned. "I don't . . . hell, I do! Stay there."

He returned with the impossible bottle, carefully wiped away its gray coat of years and laid it gleaming on the bar. Glintings of maroon speared their eyes. "All these years, it must have been waiting. That's where I heard it . . . genuine vintage brandy, from Home."

"From Terra—really? Oh, thank you!" She touched the bottle, touched his hand. "I'm going to be lucky."

Curving glasses blossomed with wine; he placed one in her palm. "*Ad astra*." She lifted the glass.

"*Ad astra*; to the stars." He raised his own, adding silently, *Tonight . . .*

They were alone. Her breath came hard as they climbed up the newly cobbled streets to his home, up from the lower city where the fluorescent lamps were snuffing out one by one.

He stopped against a low stone wall. "Do you want to catch your breath?" Behind him in the empty lot a weedy garden patch wavered with the popping street lamp.

"Thank you." She leaned downhill against him, against the wall. "I got lazy on my training ride. There's not much to do on a ship; you're supposed to exercise, but . . ." Her shoulder twitched under the quilted blue-silver. He absorbed her warmth.

Her hand pressed his lightly on the wall. "What's your name? You haven't told me, you know."

"Everyone calls me Soldier."

"But that's not your name." Her eyes searched his own, smiling.

He ducked his head, his hand caught and tightened around hers. "Oh . . . no, it's not. It's Maris." He looked up. That's an old name, too. It *means* 'soldier,' consecrated to the god of war. I never liked it much."

"From 'Mars'? Sol's fourth planet, the god of war." She bent back her head and peered up into the darkness. Fog hid the stars.

"Yes."

"Were you a soldier?"

"Yes. Everyone was a soldier—every man—where I came from. War was a way of life."

"An attempt to reconcile the blow to the masculine ego?"

He looked at her.

She frowned in concentration. " 'After it was determined that men were physically unsuited to spacing, and women came to a new position of dominance as they monopolized this critical area, the Terran cultural foundation underwent severe strain. As a result, many new and not always satisfactory cultural systems are evolving in the galaxy. . . . One of these is what might be termed a backlash of exaggerated *machismo*—' "

" '—and the rebirth of the warrior/chattel tradition.' "

"You've read that book too." She looked crestfallen.

"I read a lot. *New Ways for Old*, by Ebert Ntaka?"

"Sorry . . . I guess I got carried away. But, I just read it—"

"No." He grinned. "And I agree with old Ntaka, too. Glatte—what a sour name—was an unhealthy planet. But that's why I'm here, not there."

"Ow—!" She jerked loose from his hand. "Ohh, oh . . . God, you're strong!" She put her fingers in her mouth.

He fell over apologies; but she shook her head, and shook her hand. "No, it's all right . . . really, it just surprised me. Bad memories?"

He nodded, mouth tight.

She touched his shoulder, raised her fingers to his lips. "Kiss it, and make it well?" Gently he caught her hand, kissed it; she pressed against him. "It's very late. We should finish climbing the hill . . . ?"

"No." Hating himself, he set her back against the wall.

"No? But I thought—"

"I know you did. Your first space, I asked your name, you wanted me to; tradition says you lay the guy. But I'm a cyborg, Brandy. . . . It's always good for a laugh on the poor greenie, they've pulled it a hundred times."

"A cyborg?" The flickering gray eyes raked his body.

"It doesn't show with my clothes on."

"Oh . . ." Pale lashes were beating very hard across the eyes now. She took a breath, held it. "Do—you always let it get this far? I mean—"

"No. Hell, I don't know why I . . . I owe you another apology. Usually I never ask the name. If I slip, I tell them right away; nobody's ever held to it. I don't count." He smiled weakly.

"Well, why? You mean you can't—"

"I'm not all plastic." He frowned, numb fingers rapping stone. "God, I'm not. Sometimes I wish I was, but I'm not."

"No one? They never want to?"

"Branduin"—he faced the questioning eyes—"you'd better go back down. Get some sleep. Tomorrow laugh it off, and pick up some flashy Tail in the bar and have a good time. Come see me again in twenty-five years, when you're back from space, and tell me what you saw." Hesitating, he brushed her cheek with his true hand; instinctively she bent her head to the caress. "Goodbye." He started up the hill.

"Maris—"

He stopped, trembling.

"Thank you for the brandy. . . ." She came up beside him and caught his belt. "You'll probably have to tow me up the hill."

He pulled her to him and began to kiss her, hands touching her body incredulously.

"It's getting—very, very late. Let's hurry."

Maris woke, confused, to the sound of banging shutters. Raising his head, he was struck by the colors of dawn, and the shadow of Brandy standing bright-edged at the window. He left the rumpled bed and crossed cold tiles to join her. "What are you doing?" He yawned.

"I wanted to watch the sun rise, I haven't seen anything but night for months. Look, the fog's lifting already: the sun burns it up, it's on fire, over the mountains—"

He smoothed her hair, pale gold under a corona of light. "And embers in the canyon."

She looked down, across ends of gray mist slowly reddening, and back. "Good morning." She began to laugh. "I'm glad you don't have any neighbors down there!" They were both naked.

He grinned. "That's what I like about the place." He put his arms around her. She moved close in the circle of coolness and warmth.

They watched the sunrise from the bed.

In the evening she came into the bar with the crew of the *Kiss and Tell*—736. They waved to him, nodded to her and drifted into blue shadows; she perched smiling before him. It struck him suddenly that nine hours was a long time.

"That's the crew of my training ship. They want some white wine, please, any kind, in a bottle."

He reached under the bar. "And one brandy, on the house?" He sent the tray off.

"Hi, Maris . . ."

"Hi, Brandy."

"To misty mornings." They drank together.

"By the way"—she glanced at him slyly—"I passed it around that people have been missing something. You."

"Thank you," meaning it. "But I doubt if it'll change any minds."

"Why not?"

"You read Ntaka—xenophobia; to most people in most cultures cyborgs are unnatural, the next thing up from a corpse. You'd have to be a necrophile—"

She frowned.

"—or extraordinary. You're the first extraordinary person I've met in a hundred years."

The smile formed, faded. "Maris—you're not exactly twenty-five, are you? How old are you?"

"More like a hundred and fifteen." He waited for the reaction.

She stared. "But, you look like twenty-five! You're real—don't you age?"

"I age. About five years for every hundred." He shrugged. "The prosthetics slow the body's aging. Perhaps it's because only half my body needs constant regeneration; or it may be an effect of the anti-rejection treatment. Nobody really understands it. It just happens sometimes."

"Oh." She looked embarrassed. "That's what you meant by 'come back and see me' . . . and they meant— Will you really live a thousand years?"

"Probably not. Something vital will break down in another three or four centuries, I guess. Even plastic doesn't last forever."

"Oh . . ."

"Live longer and enjoy it less. Except for today. What did you do today? Get any sleep?"

"No—" She shook away disconcertion. "A bunch of us went out and gorged. We stay on wake-ups when we're in port, so we don't miss a minute; you don't need to sleep. Really they're for emergencies, but everybody does it."

Quick laughter almost escaped him; he hoped she'd missed it. Serious, he said, "You want to be careful with those things. They can get to you."

"Oh, they're all right." She twiddled her glass, annoyed and suddenly awkward again, confronted by the Old Man.

Hell, it can't matter. . . . He glanced toward the door.

"Brandy! There you are." And the crew came in. "Soldier, you must come sit with us later; but right now we're going to steal Brandy away from you."

He looked up with Brandy to the brown face, brown eyes, and salt-white hair of Harkané, Best Friend of the Mactav on the *Who Got Her—709*. Time had woven deep nets of understanding around her eyes; she was one of his oldest cus-

tomers. Even the shape of her words sounded strange to him
now: "Ah, Soldier, you make me feel young, always. . . .
Come, little sister, and join your family; share her, Soldier."

Brandy gulped brandy; her boots clattered as she dropped
off the stool. "Thank you for the drink," and for half a second the smile was real. "Guess I'll be seeing you—Soldier."
And she was leaving, ungracefully, gratefully.

Soldier polished the agate bar, ignoring the disappointed
face it showed him. And later watched her leave, with a
smug, black-eyed Tail in velvet knee pants.

Beyond the doorway yellow-green twilight seeped into the
bay, the early crowds began to come together with the night.
"H'lo, Maris . . . ?" Silver dulled to lead met him in a face
gone hollow; thin hands trembled, clenched, trembled in the
air.

"Brandy—"

"What've you got for an upset stomach?" She was expecting laughter.

"Got the shakes, huh?" He didn't laugh.

She nodded. "You were right about the pills, Maris. They
make me sick. I got tired, I kept taking them. . . ." Her
hands rattled on the counter.

"And that was pretty dumb, wasn't it?" He poured her a
glass of water, watched her trying to drink, pushed a button
under the counter. "Listen, I just called you a ride—when it
comes, I want you to go to my place and go to bed."

"But—"

"I won't be home for hours. Catch some sleep and then
you'll be all right, right? This is my door lock." He printed
large numbers on a napkin. "Don't lose this."

She nodded, drank, stuffed the napkin up her sleeve. Drank
some more, spilling it. "My mouth is numb." An abrupt chirp
of laughter escaped; she put up a shaky hand. "I—won't lose
it."

Deep gold leaped beyond the doorway, sunlight on metal.
"Your ride's here."

"Thank you, Maris." The smile was crooked but very fond.
She tacked toward the doorway.

She was still there when he came home, snoring gently in
the bedroom in a knot of unmade blankets. He went silently
out of the room, afraid to touch her, and sank into a leather-
slung chair. Filled with rare and uneasy peace, he dozed,

while the starlit mist of the Pleiades' nebulosity passed across the darkened sky toward morning.

"Maris, why didn't you wake me up? You didn't have to sleep in a *chair* all night." Brandy stood before him wrestling with a towel, eyes puffy with sleep and hair flopping in sodden plumb-bobs from the shower. Her feet made small puddles on the braided rug.

"I didn't mind. I don't need much sleep."

"That's what I told *you*."

"But I meant it. I never sleep more than three hours. You needed the rest, anyway."

"I know . . . damn—" She gave up and wrapped the towel around her head. "You're a fine guy, Maris."

"You're not so bad yourself."

She blushed. "Glad you approve. Ugh, your rug—I got it all wet." She disappeared into the bedroom.

Maris stretched unwillingly, stared up into ceiling beams bronzed with early sunlight. He sighed faintly. "You want some breakfast?"

"Sure, I'm starving! Oh, wait—" A wet head reappeared. "Let me make you breakfast? Wait for me."

He sat watching as the apparition in silver-blue flightsuit ransacked his cupboards. "You're kind of low on raw materials."

"I know." He brushed crumbs off the table. "I eat instant breakfasts and frozen dinners; I hate to cook."

She made a face.

"Yeah, it gets pretty old after half a century . . . they've only had them on Oro for half a century. They don't get any better, either."

She stuck something into the oven. "I'm sorry I was so stupid about it."

"About what?"

"About . . . a hundred years. I guess it scared me. I acted like a bitch."

"No, you didn't."

"Yes, I did! I know I did." She frowned.

"Okay, you did. . . . I forgive you. When do we eat?"

They ate, sitting side by side.

"Cooking seems like an odd spacer's hobby." Maris scraped his plate appreciatively. "When can you cook on a ship?"

"Never. It's all prepared and processed. So we can't overeat. That's why we love to eat and drink when we're in port. But I can't cook now either—no place. So it's not really a hobby, I guess, any more. I learned how from my father—he loved to cook. . . ." She inhaled, eyes closed.

"Is your mother dead?"

"No—" She looked startled. "She just doesn't like to cook."

"She wouldn't have liked Glatte, either." He scratched his crooked nose.

"Calicho—that's my home, it's seven light years up the cube from this corner of the Quadrangle. It's . . . a pretty nice place. I guess Ntaka would call it 'healthy,' even . . . there's lots of room, like space; that helps. Cold and not very rich, but they get along. My mother and father always shared their work . . . they have a farm." She broke off more bread.

"What did they think about you becoming a spacer?"

"They never tried to stop me, but I don't think they wanted me to. I guess when you're so tied to the land it's hard to imagine wanting to be so free. . . . It made them sad to lose me—it made me sad to lose them; but, I had to go. . . ."

Her mouth began to quiver suddenly. "You know, I'll never get to see them again, I'll never have time, our trips take so long, they'll grow old and die. . . ." Tears dripped onto her plate. "And I miss my h-home—" Words dissolved into sobs, she clung to him in terror.

He rubbed her back helplessly, wordlessly, left unequipped to deal with loneliness by a hundred years alone.

"M-Maris, can I come and see you always, will you always, always be here when I need you, and be my friend?"

"Always." He rocked her gently. "Come when you want, stay as long as you want, cook dinner if you want, I'll always be here. . . ."

∞

. . . Until the night, twenty-five years later, when they were suddenly clustered around him at the bar, hugging, badgering, laughing, the crew of the *Who Got Her—709.*

"Hi, Soldier!"

"Soldier, have we—"

"Look at this, Soldier—"

"What happened to—"

"Brandy?" he said stupidly. "Where's Brandy?"

"Honestly, Soldier, you really never *do* forget a face, do you?"

"Ah-ha, I bet it's not her *face* he remembers!"

"She was right with us." Harkané peered easily over the heads around her. "Maybe she stopped off somewhere."

"Maybe she's caught a Tail *already?*" Nilgiri was impressed.

"She could if anybody could, the little rascal." Wynmet rolled her eyes.

"Oh, just send us the usual, Soldier. She'll be along eventually. Come sit with us when she does." Harkané waved a rainbow-tipped hand. "Come, sisters, gossip is not tasteful before we've had a drink."

"That little rascal."

Soldier began to pour drinks with single-minded precision, until he noticed that he had the wrong bottle. Cursing, he drank them himself, one by one.

"Hi, Maris."

He pushed the tray away.

"*Hi*, Maris." Fingers appeared in front of his face; he started. "Hey."

"Brandy!"

Patrons along the bar turned to stare, turned away again.

"Brandy—"

"Well sure; weren't you expecting me? Everybody else is already here."

"I know. I thought—I mean, they said . . . maybe you were out with somebody already," trying to keep it light, "and—"

"Well, really, Maris, what do you take me for?" She was insulted. "I just wanted to wait till everybody else got settled, so I could have you to myself. Did you think I'd forget you? Unkind." She hefted a bright mottled sack onto the bar. "Look, I brought you a present!" Pulling it open, she dumped heaping confusion onto the counter. "Books, tapes, buttons, all kinds of things to look at. You said you'd read out the library five times; so I collected everywhere, some of them should be new. . . . Don't you like them?"

"I . . ." He coughed. "I'm crazy about them! I'm—overwhelmed. Nobody ever brought me anything before. Thank you. Thanks very much. And welcome back to New Piraeus!"

"Glad to be back!" She stretched across the bar, hugged

him, kissed his nose. She wore a new belt of metal inlaid with stones. "You're just like I remembered."

"You're more beautiful."

"Flatterer." She beamed. Ashen hair fell to her breasts; angles had deepened on her face. The quicksilver eyes took all things in now without amazement. "I'm twenty-one today, you know."

"No kidding? That calls for a celebration. Will you have brandy?"

"Do you still have some?" The eyes widened slightly. "Oh, yes! We should make it a tradition, as long as it lasts."

He smiled contentedly. They drank to birthdays, and to stars.

"Not very crowded tonight, is it?" Brandy glanced into the room, tying small knots in her hair. "Not like last time."

"It comes and it goes. I've always got some fisherfolk, they're heavy on tradition. . . . I gave up keeping track of ship schedules."

"We don't even believe our own; they never quite fit. We're a month late here."

"I know—happened to notice it. . . ." He closed a bent cover, laid the book flat. "So anyway, how did you like your first Quadrangle?"

"Beautiful—oh, Maris, if I start I'll never finish, the City in the Clouds on Patris, the Freeport on Sanalareta . . . and the Pleiades . . . and the depths of night, ice and fire." Her eyes burned through him toward infinity. "You can't imagine—"

"So they tell me."

She searched his face for bitterness, found none. He shook his head. "I'm a man and a cyborg; that's two League rules against me that I can't change—so why resent it? I enjoy the stories." His mouth twitched up.

"Do you like poetry?"

"Sometimes."

"Then—may I show you mine? I'm writing a cycle of poems about space; maybe someday I'll have a book. I haven't shown them to anybody else, but if you'd like—"

"I'd like it."

"I'll find them, then. Guess I should be joining the party, really, they'll think I'm antisocial"—she winced—"and they'll talk about me! It's like a small town, we're as bad as lubbers."

He laughed. "Don't—you'll disillusion me. See you later.

Uh . . . listen, do you want arrangements like before? For sleeping."

"Use your place? Could I? I don't want to put you out."

"Hell, no. You're welcome to it."

"I'll cook for you—"

"I bought some eggs."

"It's a deal! Enjoy your books." She wove a path between the tables, nodded to sailor and spacer; he watched her laughing face merge and blur, caught occasional flashes of silver. Stuffing books into the sack, he set it against his shin behind the bar. And some time later, watched her go out with a Tail.

The morning of the thirteenth day he woke to find Brandy sleeping soundly in the pile of hairy cushions by the door. Curious, he glanced out into a water-gray field of fog. It was the first time she had come home before dawn. *Home?* Carefully he lifted her from the pillows; she sighed, arms found him, in her sleep she began to kiss his neck. He carried her to the bed and put her down softly, bent to . . . *No.* He turned away, left the room. He had slept with her only once. Twenty-five or three years ago, without words, she had told him they would not be lovers again. She kept the customs; a spacer never had the same man more than once.

In the kitchen he heated a frozen dinner, and ate alone.

"What's that?" Brandy appeared beside him, mummified in a blanket. She dropped down on the cushions where he sat barefoot, drinking wine and ignoring the TD.

"Three-dimensional propaganda: the Oro Morning Mine Report. You're up pretty early—it's hardly noon."

"I'm not sleepy." She took a sip of his wine.

"Got in pretty early, too. Anything wrong?"

"No . . . just—nothing happening, you know. Ran out of parties, everybody's pooped but me." She cocked her head. "What is this, anyway . . . an inquisition? 'Home awfully *early*, aren't you—?'" She glared at him and burst into laughter.

"You're crazy." He grinned.

"Whatever happened to your couch?" She prodded cushions.

"It fell apart. It's been twenty-five years, you know."

"Oh. That's too bad. . . . Maris, may I read you my poems?" Suddenly serious, she produced a small, battered notebook from the folds of her blanket.

"Sure." He leaned back, watching subtle transformations

occur in her face. And felt them begin to occur in himself, growing pride and a tender possessiveness.

> ... Until, lost in darkness, we
> dance the silken star-song.

It was the final poem. "That's 'Genesis.' It's about the beginning of a flight . . . and a life." Her eyes found the world again, found dark eyes quietly regarding her.

" 'Attired with stars we shall forever sit, triumphing over Death, and Chance, and thee, O Time.' " He glanced away, pulling the tassel of a cushion. "No . . . Milton, not Maris—I could never do that." He looked back, in wonder. "They're beautiful, you are beautiful. Make a book. Gifts are meant for giving, and you are gifted."

Pleasure glowed in her cheeks. "You really think someone would want to read them?"

"Yes." He nodded, searching for the words to tell her. "Nobody's ever made me—see that way . . . as though I . . . go with you. Others would go, if they could. Home to the sky."

She turned with him to the window; they were silent. After a time she moved closer, smiling. "Do you know what I'd like to do?"

"What?" He let out a long breath.

"See your home." She set her notebook aside. "Let's go for a walk in New Piraeus. I've never really seen it by day—the real part of it. I want to see its beauty up close, before it's all gone. Can we go?"

He hesitated. "You sure you want to—?"

"Sure. Come on, lazy." She gestured him up.

And he wondered again why she had come home early.

So on the last afternoon he took her out through the stone-paved winding streets, where small whitewashed houses pressed for footholds. They climbed narrow steps, panting, tasted the sea wind, bought fruit from a leathery smiling woman with a basket.

"Mmm—" Brandy licked juice from the crimson pith. "Who was that woman? She called you 'Sojer,' but I couldn't understand the rest . . . I couldn't even understand you! Is the dialect that slurred?"

He wiped his chin. "It's getting worse all the time, with all the newcomers. But you get used to everything in the lower city. . . . An old acquaintance, I met her during the epi-demic, she was sick."

"Epidemic? What epidemic?"

"Oro Mines was importing workers—they started before your last visit, because of the bigger raw-material demands. One of the new workers had some disease we didn't; it killed about a third of New Piraeus."

"Oh, my God—"

"That was about fifteen years ago. . . . Oro's labs synthe-sized a vaccine, eventually, and they repopulated the city. But they still don't know what the disease was."

"It's like a trap, to live on a single world."

"Most of us have to. . . . It has its compensations."

She finished her fruit, and changed the subject. "You helped take care of them, during the epidemic?"

He nodded. "I seemed to be immune, so—"

She patted his arm. "You are very good."

He laughed; glanced away. "Very plastic would be more like it."

"Don't you ever get sick?"

"Almost never. I can't even get very drunk. Someday I'll probably wake up entirely plastic."

"You'd still be very good." They began to walk again. "What did she say?"

"She said, 'Ah, Soldier, you've got a lady friend.' She seemed pleased."

"What did you say?"

"I said, 'That's right.'" Smiling, he didn't put his arm around her; his fingers kneaded emptiness.

"Well, I'm glad she was pleased. . . . I don't think most people have been."

"Don't look at them. Look out there." He showed her the sea, muted greens and blues below the ivory jumble of the flat-roofed town. To the north and south mountains like rumpled cloth reached down to the shore.

"Oh, the sea—I've always loved the sea; at home we were surrounded by it, on an island. Space is like the sea, bound-less, constant, constantly changing . . ."

"—spacer!" Two giggling girls made a wide circle past them in the street, dark skirts brushing their calves.

Brandy blushed, frowned, sought the sea again. "I—think I'm getting tired. I guess I've seen enough."

"Not much on up there but the new, anyway." He took her hand and they started back down. "It's just that we're a rarity up this far." A heavy man in a heavy caftan pushed past them; in his cold eyes Maris saw an alien wanton and her overaged Tail.

"They either leer, or they censure." He felt her nails mark his flesh. "What's their problem?"

"Jealousy . . . mortality. You threaten them, you spacers. Don't you ever think about it? Free and beautiful immortals—"

"They know we aren't immortal; we hardly live longer than anybody else."

"They also know you come here from a voyage of twenty-five years looking hardly older than when you left. Maybe they don't recognize you, but they *know*. And they're twenty-five years older. . . . Why do you think they go around in sacks?"

"To look ugly. They must be dreadfully repressed." She tossed her head sullenly.

"They are; but that's not why. It's because they want to hide the changes. And in their way to mimic you, who always look the same. They've done it since I can remember; you're all they have to envy."

She sighed. "I've heard on Elder they paint patterns on their skin, to hide the change. Ntaka called them 'youth-fixing,' didn't he?" Anger faded, her eyes grew cool like the sea, gray-green. "Yes, I think about it . . . especially when we're laughing at the lubbers, and their narrow lives. And all the poor panting awestruck Tails, sometimes they think they're using us, but we're always using them. . . . Sometimes I think we're very cruel."

"Very like a god—Silver Lady of the Moon."

"You haven't called me that since—that night . . . all night." Her hand tightened painfully; he said nothing. "I guess they envy a cyborg for the same things. . . ."

"At least it's easier to rationalize—and harder to imitate." He shrugged. "We leave each other alone, for the most part."

"And so we must wait for each other, we immortals. It's still a beautiful town; I don't care what they think."

He sat, fingers catching in the twisted metal of his thick bracelet, listening to her voice weave patterns through the hiss of running water. Washing away the dirty looks. . . . Absently he reread the third paragraph on the page for the eighth time; and the singing stopped.

"Maris, do you have any—"

He looked up at her thin, shining body, naked in the doorway. "Brandy, goddamm it! You're not between planets—you want to show it all to the whole damn street?"

"But I always—" Made awkward by sudden awareness, she fled.

He sat and stared at the sun-hazed windows, entirely aware that there was no one to see in. Slowly the fire died, his breathing eased.

She returned shyly, closing herself into quilted blue-silver, and sank onto the edge of a chair. "I just never think about it." Her voice was very small.

"It's all right." Ashamed, he looked past her. "Sorry I yelled at you. . . . What did you want to ask me?"

"It doesn't matter." She pulled violently at her snarled hair. "Ow! Dammit!" Feeling him look at her, she forced a smile. "Uh, you know, I'm glad we picked up Mima on Treone; I'm not the little sister anymore. I was really getting pretty tired of being the greenie for so long. She's—"

"Brandy—"

"Hm?"

"Why don't they allow cyborgs on crews?"

Surprise caught her. "It's a regulation."

He shook his head. "Don't tell me 'It's a regulation,' tell me why."

"Well . . ." She smoothed wet hair-strands with her fingers. "They tried it, and it didn't work out. Like with men—they couldn't endure space, they broke down, their hormonal balance was wrong. With cyborgs, stresses between the real and the artificial in the body were too severe, they broke down too. . . . At the beginning they tried cyborganics, as a way to let men keep space, like they tried altering the hormone balance. Neither worked. Physically or psychologically, there was too much strain. So finally they just made it a regulation, no men on space crews."

"But that was over a thousand years ago—cyborganics has improved. I'm healthier and live longer than any normal person. And stronger." He leaned forward, tight with agitation.

"And slower. We don't need strength, we have artificial means. And anyway, a man would still have to face more stress, it would be dangerous."

"Are there any female cyborgs on crews?"

"No."

"Have they ever even tried it again?"

"No—"

"You see? The League has a lock on space, they keep it with archaic laws. They don't want anyone else out there!" Sudden resentment shook his voice.

"Maybe . . . we don't." Her fingers closed, opened, closed over the soft heavy arms of the chair; her eyes were the color of twisting smoke. "Do you really blame us? Spacing is our life, it's our strength. We have to close the others out, everything changes and changes around us, there's no continuity—we only have each other. That's why we have our regulations, that's why we dress alike, look alike, act alike; there's nothing else we *can* do, and stay sane. We have to live apart, always." She pulled her hair forward, tying nervous knots. "And—that's why we never take the same lover twice, too. We have needs we have to satisfy; but we can't afford to . . . form relationships, get involved, tied. It's a danger, it's an instability. . . . You do understand that, don't you, Maris; that it's why I don't—" She broke off, eyes burning him with sorrow and, below it, fear.

He managed a smile. "Have you heard me complain?"

"Weren't you just . . . ?" She lifted her head.

Slowly he nodded, felt pain start. "I suppose I was." *But I don't change.* He shut his eyes suddenly, before she read them. *But that's not the point, is it?*

"Maris, do you want me to stop staying here?"

"No— No . . . I understand, it's all right. I like the company." He stretched, shook his head. "Only, wear a towel, all right? I'm only human."

"I promise . . . that I will keep my eyes open, in the future."

He considered the future that would begin with dawn when her ship went up, and said nothing.

∞

He stumbled cursing from the bedroom to the door, to find her waiting there, radiant and wholly unexpected. "Surprise!" She laughed and hugged him, dislodging his half-tied robe.

"My God—hey!" He dragged her inside and slammed the door. "You want to get me arrested for indecent exposure?" He turned his back, making adjustments, while she stood and giggled behind him.

He faced her again, fogged with sleep, struggling to believe. "You're early—almost two weeks?"

"I know. I couldn't wait till tonight to surprise you. And I did, didn't I?" She rolled her eyes. "I heard you coming to the door!"

She sat curled on his aging striped couch, squinting out the window as he fastened his sandals. "You used to have so much room. Houses haven't filled up your canyon, have they?" Her voice grew wistful.

"Not yet. If they ever do, I won't stay to see it. . . . How was your trip this time?"

"Beautiful, again . . . I can't imagine it ever being anything else. You could see it all a hundred times over, and never see it all—

> Through your crystal eye,
> Mactav, I watch the midnight's
> star turn inside out. . . .

Oh, guess what! My poems—I finished the cycle during the voyage . . . and it's going to be published, on Treone. They said very nice things about it."

He nodded smugly. "They have good taste. They must have changed, too."

"'A renaissance in progress'—meaning they've put on some *ver*-ry artsy airs, last decade; their Tails are really something else. . . ." Remembering, she shook her head. "It was one of them that told me about the publisher."

"You showed him your poems?" Trying not to—

"Good grief, no; he was telling me about *his*. So I thought, What have I got to lose?"

"When do I get a copy?"

"I don't know." Disappointment pulled at her mouth. "Maybe I'll never even get one; after twenty-five years they'll be out of print. 'Art is long, and Time is fleeting' . . . Longfellow had it backward. But I made you some copies of the poems. And brought you some more books, too. There's one you should read; it replaced Ntaka years ago on the Inside. I thought it was inferior, but who are we . . . What are you laughing about?"

"What happened to that freckle-faced kid in pigtails?"

"*What*?" Her nose wrinkled.

"How old are you now?"

"Twenty-four. Oh—" She looked pleased.

"Madame Poet, do you want to go to dinner with me?"

"Oh, *food*, oh yes!" She bounced, caught him grinning, froze. "I would love to. Can we go to Good Eats?"

"It closed right after you left."

"Oh . . . the music was wild. Well, how about that seafood place, with the fish name—?"

He shook his head. "The owner died. It's been twenty-five years."

"Damn, we can never keep anything." She sighed. "Why don't I just make us a dinner—*I'm* still here. And I'd like that."

That night, and every other night, he stood at the bar and watched her go out, with a Tail or a laughing knot of partiers. Once she waved to him; the stem of a shatterproof glass snapped in his hand; he kicked it under the counter, confused and angry.

But three nights in the two weeks she came home early. This time, pointedly, he asked her no questions. Gratefully, she told him no lies, sleeping on his couch and sharing the afternoon. . . .

They returned to the flyer, moving in step along the cool jade sand of the beach. Maris looked toward the sea's edge, where frothy fingers reached, withdrew, and reached again. "You leave tomorrow, huh?"

Brandy nodded. "Uh-huh."

He sighed.

"Maris, if—"

"What?"

"Oh—nothing." She brushed sand from her boot.

He watched the sea reach, and withdraw, and reach—

"Have you ever wanted to see a ship? Inside, I mean." She pulled open the flyer door, her body strangely intent.

He followed her. "Yes."

"Would you like to see mine—the *Who Got Her?*"

"I thought that was illegal?"

" 'No waking man shall set foot on a ship of the spaceways.' It is a League regulation . . . but it's based on a superstition that's at least a thousand years old—'Men on ships is bad luck.' Which is silly here. Your presence on board in port isn't going to bring us disaster."

He looked incredulous.

"I'd like you to see our life, Maris, as I see yours. There's nothing wrong with that. And besides"—she shrugged—"no one will know; because nobody's there right now."

He faced a wicked grin, and did his best to match it. "I will if you will."

They got in, the flyer drifted silently from the cove. New Piraeus rose to meet them from beyond the ridge; the late sun struck gold from hidden windows.

"I wish it wouldn't change—oh . . . there's another new one. It's a skyscraper!"

He glanced across the bay. "Just finished; maybe New Piraeus is growing up—thanks to Oro Mines. It hardly changed over a century; after all those years, it's a little scary."

"Even after three . . . or twenty-five?" She pointed. "Right down there, Maris—there's our airlock."

The flyer settled on the water below the looming semitransparent hull of the *WGH—709*.

Maris gazed up and back. "It's a lot bigger than I ever realized."

"It masses twenty thousand tons, empty." Brandy caught hold of the hanging ladder. "I guess we'll have to go up this . . . okay?" She looked over at him.

"Sure. Slow, maybe, but sure."

They slipped in through the lock, moved soft-footed down hallways past dim cavernous storerooms.

"Is the whole ship transparent?" He touched a wall, plastic met plastic. "How do you get any privacy?"

"Why are you whispering?"

"I'm no—*I'm not*. Why are you?"

"*Shhh!* Because it's so *quiet*." She stopped, pride beginning to show on her face. "The whole ship can be almost transparent, like now; but usually it's not. All the walls and the hull are polarized; you can opaque them. These are just holds, anyway, they're most of the ship. The passenger stasis cubicles are up there. Here's the lift. We'll go up to the control room."

"Brandy!" A girl in red with a clipboard turned on them outraged, as they stepped from the lift. "Brandy, what the hell do you mean by— Oh. Is that you, Soldier? God, I thought she'd brought a man on board."

Maris flinched. "Hi, Nilgiri."

Brandy was very pale beside him. "We just came out to —uh, look in on Mactav, she's been kind of moody lately, you know. I thought we could read to her. . . . What are *you* doing here?" And a whispered, "Bitch."

"Just that—checking up on Mactav. Harkané sent me out." Nilgiri glanced at the panels behind her, back at Maris, suddenly awkward. "Uh—look, since I'm already here don't worry about it, okay? I'll go down and play some music for her. Why don't you—uh, show Soldier around the ship, or something. . . ." Her round face was reddening like an apple. "Bye?" She slipped past them and into the lift, and disappeared.

"*Damn*, sometimes she's such an ass."

"She didn't mean it."

"Oh, I should have—"

"—done just what you did; she *was* sorry. And at least we're not trespassing."

"God, Maris, how do you stand it? They must do it to you all the time. Don't you resent it?"

"Hell, yes, I resent it. Who wouldn't? I just got tired of getting mad. . . . And besides"—he glanced at the closed doors—"besides, nobody needs a mean bartender. Come on, show me around the ship."

Her knotted fingers uncurled, took his hand. "This way, please; straight ahead of you is our control room." She pulled him forward beneath the daybright dome. He saw a handprinted sign above the central panel, NO-MAN'S LAND. "From here we program our computer; this area here is for the AAFAL drive, first devised by Ursula, an early spacer who—"

"What's awful about it?"

"What?"

"Every spacer I know calls the ship's drive 'awful.' "

"Oh— Not 'awful,' AAFAL: Almost As Fast As Light. Which it is. That's what we call it; there's a technical name too."

"Um." He looked vaguely disappointed. "Guess I'm used to—" He made it into curiosity again, as he watched her smiling with delight. "I—suppose it's different from antigravity?" Seventy years before she was born, he had taught himself the principles of starship technology.

"Very." She giggled suddenly. "The 'awfuls' and the 'aghs,' *hmm* . . . We do use an AG unit to leave and enter solar systems; it operates like the ones in flyers, it throws us away from the planet, and finally the entire system, until we reach AAFAL ignition speeds. With the AG you can only get fractions of the speed of light, but it's enough to concentrate interstellar gases and dust. Our force nets feed them through the drive unit, where they're converted to energy, which increases our speed, which makes the unit more efficient . . . until we're moving almost as fast as light.

"We use the AG to protect us from acceleration forces, and after deceleration to guide us into port. The start and finish can take up most of our trip times; the farther out in space you are, the less AG feedback you get from the system's mass, and the less your velocity changes. It's a beautiful time, though—you can see the AG forces through the polarized hull, wrapping you in shifting rainbow. . . .

"And you are isolate"—she leaned against a silent panel and punched buttons; the room began to grow dark—"in absolute night . . . and stars." And stars appeared, in the darkness of a planetarium show; fire-gnats lighting her face and shoulders and his own. "How do you like our stars?"

"Are we in here?"

Four streaks of blue joined lights in the air. "Here . . . in space by this corner of the Quadrangle. This is our navigation chart for the Quadrangle run; see the bowed leg and brightness, that's the Pleiades. Patris . . . Sanalareta . . . Treone . . . back to Oro. The other lines zigzag too, but it doesn't show. Now come with me. . . . With a flare of energy, we open our AAFAL nets in space—"

He followed her voice into the night, where flickering tracery seined motes of interstellar gas, and impossible nothingness burned with infinite energy, potential transformed and transforming. With the wisdom of a thousand years a ship of the League fell through limitless seas, navigating the shifting currents of the void, beating into the sterile winds of space. Stars glittered like snow on the curving hull, spitting icy daggers of light that moved imperceptibly into spectral blues before him, reddened as he looked behind: imperceptibly time expanded, velocity increased and with it power. He saw the haze of silver on his right rise into their path, a wall of liquid shadow . . . the Pleiades, an endless bank of burning fog, kindled from within by shrouded islands of fire. Tendrils of shimmering mists curved outward across hundreds of billions of kilometers, the nets found bountiful harvest, drew close, hurled the ship into the edge of cloud.

Nebulosity wrapped him in clinging haloes of colored light, ringed him in brilliance, as the nets fell inward toward the ship, burgeoning with energy, shielding its fragile nucleus from the soundless fury of its passage. Acceleration increased by hundredfolds, around him the Doppler shifts deepened toward cerulean and crimson; slowly the clinging brightness wove into parabolas of shining smoke, whipping past until the entire flaming mass of cloud and stars seemed to sweep ahead, shriveling toward blue-whiteness, trailing embers.

And suddenly the ship burst once more into a void, a universe warped into a rubber bowl of brilliance stretching past him, drawing away and away before him toward a gleaming point in darkness. The shrunken nets seined near-vacuum and were filled; their speed approached $0.999c$ . . . held constant, as the conversion of matter to energy ceased within the ship . . . and in time, with a flicker of silver force, began once more to fall away. Slowly time unbowed, the universe cast off its alienness. One star grew steadily before them: the sun of Patris.

A sun rose in ruddy splendor above the City in the Clouds on Patris, nine months and seven light-years from Oro. . . . And again, Patris fell away; and the brash gleaming Freeport of Sanalareta; they crept toward Treone through gasless waste, groping for current and mote across the barren ship-wakes of half a millennium. . . . And again—

Maris found himself among fire-gnat stars, on a ship in the bay of New Piraeus. And realized she had stopped speaking. His hand rubbed the copper snarl of his hair, his eyes bright as a child's. "You didn't tell me you were a witch in your spare time."

He heard her smile, "Thank you. Mactav makes the real magic, though; her special effects are fantastic. She can show you the whole inhabited section of the galaxy, with all the trade polyhedra, like a dew-flecked cobweb hanging in the air." Daylight returned to the panel. "Mactav—that's her bank, there—handles most of the navigation, life support, all that, too. Sometimes it seems like we're almost along for the ride! But of course we're along for Mactav."

"Who or what is Mactav?" Maris peered into a darkened screen, saw something amber glimmer in its depths, drew back.

"You've never met her, neither have we—but you were staring her right in the eye." Brandy stood beside him. "She must be listening to Giri down below. . . . Okay, okay!—a Mactavia unit is the brain, the nervous system of a ship, she monitors its vital signs, calculates, adjusts. We only have to ask—sometimes we don't even have to do that. The memory is a real spacer woman's, fed into the circuits . . . someone who died irrevocably, or had reached retirement, but wanted to stay on. A human system is wiser, more versatile—and lots cheaper—than anything all-machine that's ever been done."

"Then your Mactav is a kind of cyborg."

She smiled. "Well, I guess so; in a way—"

"But the Spacing League's regulations still won't allow cyborgs in crews."

She looked annoyed.

He shrugged. "Sorry. Dumb thing to say. . . . What's that red down there?"

"Oh, that's our 'stomach': the AAFAL unit, where"—she grinned—"we digest stardust into energy. It's the only thing that's never transparent; the red is the shield."

"How does it work?"

"I don't really know. I can make it go, but I don't understand why—I'm only a five-and-a-half technician now. If I was a six I could tell you." She glanced at him sidelong. "Aha! I finally impressed you!"

He laughed. "Not so dumb as you look." He had qualified as a six half a century before, out of boredom.

"You'd better be kidding!"

"I am." He followed her back across the palely opalescing floor, looking down, and down. "Like walking on water . . . why transparent?"

She smiled through him at the sky. "Because it's so beautiful outside."

They dropped down through floors, to come out in a new hall. Music came faintly to him.

"This is where my cabin—"

Abruptly the music became an impossible agony of sound torn with screaming.

"God!" And Brandy was gone from beside him, down the hallway and through a flickering wall.

He found her inside the door, rigid with awe. Across the room the wall vomited blinding waves of color, above a screeching growth of crystal organ pipes. Nilgiri crouched on the floor, hands pressed against her stomach, shrieking hysterically. "Stop it, Mactav! Stop it! Stop it! Stop it!"

He touched Brandy's shoulder; she looked up and caught his arm; together they pulled Nilgiri, wailing, back from bedlam to the door.

"Nilgiri! Nilgiri, what happened!" Brandy screamed against her ear.

"Mactav, Mactav!"

"*Why?*"

"She put a . . . charge through it, she's crazy-mad . . . sh-she thinks . . . Oh, *stop* it, Mactav!" Nilgiri clung, sobbing.

Maris started into the room, hands over his ears. "How do you turn it off?"

"Maris, wait!"

"*How*, Brandy?"

"It's electrified, don't touch it!"

"*How?*"

"On the left, on the left, three switches—Maris, *don't*— Stop it, Mactav, stop—"

He heard her screaming as he lowered his left hand, hesitated, battered with glaring sound; sparks crackled as he flicked switches on the organ panel, once, twice, again.

"—it-it-it-it!" Her voice echoed through silent halls. Nilgiri slid down the doorjamb and sat sobbing on the floor.

"Maris, are you all right?"

He heard her dimly through cotton. Dazed with relief, he backed away from the gleaming console, nodding, and started across the room.

"*Man*," the soft hollow voice echoed echoed echoed. "What are you doing in here?"

"Mactav?" Brandy was gazing uneasily to his left.

He turned; across the room was another artificial eye, burning amber.

"Branduin, you brought him onto the ship; how could you do this thing? It is forbidden!"

"Oh, God." Nilgiri began to wail again in horror. Brandy knelt and caught Nilgiri's blistered hands; he saw anger hardened over her face. "Mactav, how could you!"

"Brandy." He shook his head; took a breath, frightened. "Mactav—I'm not a man. You're mistaken."

"Maris, no . . ."

He frowned. "I'm one hundred and forty-one years old . . . half my body is synthetic. I'm hardly human, any more than you are. Scan and see." He held up his hands.

"The part of you that matters is still a man."

A smile caught at his mouth. "Thanks."

"Men are evil, men destroyed . . ."

"Her, Maris," Brandy whispered. "They destroyed her."

The smile wavered. "Something more we have in common." His false arm pressed his side.

The golden eye regarded him. "Cyborg."

He sighed, went to the door. Brandy stood to meet him, Nilgiri huddled silently at her feet, staring up.

"Nilgiri." The voice was full of pain; they looked back. "How can I forgive myself for what I've done? I will never,

never do such a thing again . . . never. Please, go to the infirmary; let me help you."

Slowly, with Brandy's help, Nilgiri got to her feet. "All right. It's all right, Mactav. I'll go on down now."

"Giri, do you want us——?"

Nilgiri shook her head, hands curled in front of her. "No, Brandy, it's okay. She's all right now. Me too—I think." Her smile quivered. "Ouch . . ." She started down the corridor toward the lift.

"Branduin, Maris, I apologize also to you. I'm—not usually like this, you know. . . ." Amber faded from her eye.

"Is she gone?"

Brandy nodded.

"That's the first bigoted computer I ever met."

And she remembered. "Your *hand?*"

Smiling, he held it out to her. "No harm; see? It's a nonconductor."

She shivered. Hands cradled the hand that ached to feel. "Mactav really isn't like that, you know. But something's been wrong lately, she gets into moods; we'll have to have her looked at when we get to Sanalareta."

"Isn't it dangerous?"

"I don't think so—not really. It's just that she has special problems; she's in there because she didn't have any choice, a strife-based culture killed her ship. She was very young, but that was all that was left of her."

"A high technology." A grimace; memory moved in his eyes.

"They were terribly apologetic, they did their best."

"What happened to them?"

"We cut contact—that's regulation number one. We have to protect ourselves."

He nodded, looking away. "Will they ever go back?"

"I don't know. Maybe, someday." She leaned against the doorway. "But that's why Mactav hates men; men, and war—and combined with the old taboo . . . I guess her memory suppressors weren't enough."

Nilgiri reappeared beside them. "All better." Her hands were bright pink. "Ready for anything!"

"How's Mactav acting?"

"Super-solicitous. She's still pretty upset about it, I guess."

Light flickered at the curving junctures of the walls, ceiling, floor. Maris glanced up. "Hell, it's getting dark outside. I expect I'd better be leaving; nearly time to open up. One last

night on the town?" Nilgiri grinned and nodded; he saw
Brandy hesitate.

"Maybe I'd better stay with Mactav tonight, if she's still
upset. She's got to be ready to go up tomorrow." Almost-guilt
firmed resolution on her face.

"Well . . . I could stay, if you think . . ." Nilgiri looked
unhappy.

"No. It's my fault she's like this; I'll do it. Besides, I've
been out having a fantastic day, I'd be too tired to do it right
tonight. You go on in. Thank you, Maris! I wish it wasn't
over so soon." She turned back to him, beginning to put her
hair into braids; quicksilver shone.

"The pleasure was all mine." The tight sense of loss dissolved in warmth. "I can't remember a better one either . . .
or more exciting. . . ." He grimaced.

She smiled and took his hands; Nilgiri glanced back and
forth between them. "I'll see you to the lock."

Nilgiri climbed down through the glow to the waiting
flyer. Maris braced back from the top rung to watch
Brandy's face, bearing a strange expression, look down
through whipping strands of loose hair. "Goodbye, Maris."

"Goodbye, Brandy."

"It was a short two weeks, you know?"

"I know."

"I like New Piraeus better than anywhere; I don't know
why."

"I hope it won't be too different when you get back."

"Me too. . . . See you in three years?"

"Twenty-five."

"Oh, yeah. Time passes so quickly when you're having
fun—" Almost true, almost not. A smile flowered.

"Write while you're away. Poems, that is." He began to
climb down, slowly.

"I will. . . . Hey, my stuff is at—"

"I'll send it back with Nilgiri." He settled behind the con-
trols; the flyer grew bright and began to rise. He waved; so
did Nilgiri. He watched her wave back, watched her in his
mirror until she became the vast and gleaming pearl that was
the *Whot Got Her—709.* And felt the gap that widened between their lives, more than distance, more than time.

∞

"Well, now that you've seen it, what do you think?"

Late afternoon, first day, fourth visit, seventy-fifth year . . . mentally he tallied. Brandy stood looking into the kitchen. "It's—different."

"I know. It's still too new; I miss the old wood beams. They were rotting, but I miss them. Sometimes I wake up in the morning and don't know where I am. But I was losing my canyon."

She looked back at him, surprising him with her misery. "Oh . . . At least they won't reach you for a long time, out here."

"We can't walk home any more, though."

"No." She turned away again. "All—all your furniture is built in?"

"*Um.* It's supposed to last as long as the house."

"What if you get tired of it?"

He laughed. "As long as it holds me up, I don't care what it looks like. One thing I like, though." He pressed a plate on the wall, looking up. "The roof is polarized. Like your ship. At night you can watch the stars."

"Oh!" She looked up and back, he watched her mind pierce the high cloud-fog, pierce the day, to find stars. "How wonderful! I've never seen it anywhere else."

It had been his idea, thinking of her. He smiled.

"They must really be growing out here, to be doing things like this now." She tried the cushions of a molded chair. "Hmm . . ."

"They're up to two and a half already, they actually do a few things besides mining now. The Inside is catching up, if they can bring us this without a loss. I may even live to see the day when we'll be importing raw materials, instead of filling everyone else's mined-out guts. If there's anything left of Oro by then. . . ."

"Would you stay to see that?"

"I don't know." He looked at her. "It depends. Anyway, tell me about this trip." He stretched out on the chain-hung wall seat. "You know everything that's new with me already: one house." And waited for far glory to rise up in her eyes.

They flickered down, stayed the color of fog. "Well—some good news, and some bad news, I guess."

"Like how?" Feeling suddenly cold.

"Good news"—her smile warmed him—"I'll be staying nearly a month this time. We'll have more time to—do things, if you want to."

"How did you manage that?" He sat up.

"That's more good news. I have a chance to crew on a different ship, to get out of the Quadrangle and see things I've only dreamed of, new worlds—"

"And the bad news is how long you'll be gone."

"Yes."

"How many years?"

"It's an extended voyage, following up trade contacts; if we're lucky, we might be back in the stellar neighborhood in thirty-five years . . . thirty-five years tau—more than two hundred, here. If we're not so lucky, maybe we won't be back this way at all."

"I see." He stared unblinking at the floor, hands knotted between his knees. "It's—an incredible opportunity, all right . . . especially for your poetry. I envy you. But I'll miss you."

"I know." He saw her teeth catch her lip. "But we can spend time together, we'll have a lot of time before I go. And—well, I've brought you something, to remember me." She crossed the room to him.

It was a star, suspended burning coldly in scrolled silver by an artist who knew fire. Inside she showed him her face, laughing, full of joy.

"I found it on Treone . . . they really are in renaissance. And I liked that holo, I thought you might—"

Leaning across silver he found the silver of her hair, kissed her once on the mouth, felt her quiver as he pulled away. He lifted the woven chain, fixed it at his throat. "I have something for you, too."

He got up, returned with a slim book the color of red wine, put it in her hands.

"My poems!"

He nodded, his fingers feeling the star at his throat. "I managed to get hold of two copies—it wasn't easy. Because they're too well known now; the spacers carry them, they show them but they won't give them up. You must be known on more worlds than you could ever see."

"Oh, I hadn't even heard. . . ." She laughed suddenly. "My fame preceded me. But next trip—" She looked away. "No. I won't be going that way anymore."

"But you'll be seeing new things, to make into new poems." He stood, trying to loosen the tightness in his voice.

"Yes . . . Oh, yes, I know. . . ."

"A month is a long time."

A sudden sputter of noise made them look up. Fat dapples

of rain were beginning to slide, smearing dust over the flat roof.

"Rain! not fog; the season's started." They stood and watched the sky fade overhead, darken, crack and shudder with electric light. The rain fell harder, the ceiling rippled and blurred; he led her to the window. Out across the smooth folded land a liquid curtain billowed, slaking the dust-dry throat of the canyons, renewing the earth and the spiny tight-leaf scrub. "I always wonder if it's ever going to happen. It always does." He looked at her, expecting quicksilver, and found slow tears. She wept silently, watching the rain.

For the next two weeks they shared the rain, and the chill bright air that followed. In the evenings she went out, while he stood behind the bar, because it was the last time she would have leave with the crew of the *Who Got Her*. But every morning he found her sleeping, and every afternoon she spent with him. Together they traced the serpentine alleyways of the shabby, metamorphosing lower city, or roamed the docks with the windburned fisherfolk. He took her to meet Makerrah, whom he had seen as a boy mending nets by hand, as a fishnet-clad Tail courting spacers at the Tin Soldier, as a sailor and fisherman, for almost forty years. Makerrah, now growing heavy and slow as his wood-hulled boat, showed it with pride to the sailor from the sky; they discussed nets, eating fish.

"This world is getting old. . . ." Brandy had come with him to the bar as the evening started.

Maris smiled. "But the night is young." And felt pleasure stir with envy.

"True, true . . ." Pale hair cascaded as her head bobbed. "But, you know, when . . . if I was gone another twenty-five years, I probably wouldn't recognize this *street*. The Tin Soldier really is the only thing that doesn't change." She sat at the agate counter, face propped in her hands, musing.

He stirred drinks. "It's good to have something constant in your life."

"I know. We appreciate that too, more than anybody." She glanced away, into the dark-raftered room. "They really always do come back here first, and spend more time in here . . . and knowing that they *can* means so much: that you'll be here, young and real and remembering them." A sudden hunger blurred her sight.

"It goes both ways." He looked up.

"I know that, too. . . . You know, I always meant to ask: why did you call it the 'Tin Soldier'? I mean, I think I see . . . but why 'tin'?"

"Sort of a private joke, I guess. It was in a book of folk tales I read, *Andersen's Fairy Tales*"—he looked embarrassed—"I'd *read* everything else. It was a story about a toy shop, about a tin soldier with one leg, who was left on the shelf for years. . . . He fell in love with a toy ballerina who only loved dancing, never him. In the end, she fell into the fire, and he went after her—she burned to dust, heartless; he melted into a heart-shaped lump. . . ." He laughed carefully, seeing her face. "A footnote said sometimes the story had a happy ending; I like to believe that."

She nodded, hopeful. "Me too. . . . Where did your stone bar come from? It's beautiful; like the edge of the Pleiades, depths of mist."

"Why all the questions?"

"I'm appreciating. I've loved it all for years, and never said anything. Sometimes you love things without knowing it, you take them for granted. It's wrong to let that happen . . . so I wanted you to know." She smoothed the polished stone with her hand.

He joined her tracing opalescences. "It's petrified wood—some kind of plant life that was preserved in stone, minerals replaced its structure. I found it in the desert."

"Desert?"

"East of the mountains. I found a whole canyon full of them. It's an incredible place, the desert."

"I've never seen one. Only heard about them, barren and deadly; it frightened me."

"While you cross the most terrible desert of them all?—between the stars."

"But it's not barren."

"Neither is this one. It's winter here now, I can take you to see the trees, if you'd like it." He grinned. "If you dare."

Her eyebrows rose. "I dare! We could go tomorrow, I'll make us a lunch."

"We'd have to leave early, though. If you were wanting to do the town again tonight . . ."

"Oh, that's all right; I'll take a pill."

"Hey—"

She winced. "Oh, well . . . I found a kind I could take. I used them all the time at the other ports, like the rest."

"Then why—"

"Because I liked staying with you. I deceived you, now you know, true confession. Are you mad?"

His face filled with astonished pleasure. "Hardly . . . I have to admit, I used to wonder what—"

"*Sol*-dier!" He looked away, someone gestured at him across the room. "More wine, please!" He raised a hand.

"Brandy, come on, there's a party—"

She waved. "Tomorrow morning, early?" Her eyes kept his face.

"Uh-huh. See you—"

"—later." She slipped down and was gone.

The flyer rose silently, pointing into the early sun. Brandy sat beside him, squinting down and back through the glare as New Piraeus grew narrow beside the glass-green bay. "Look, how it falls behind the hills, until all you can see are the land and the sea, and no sign of change. It's like that when the ship goes up, but it happens so fast you don't have time to savor it." She turned back to him, bright-eyed. "We go from world to world but we never see them; we're always looking up. It's good to look down, today."

They drifted higher, rising with the climbing hills, until the rumpled olive-red suede of the seacoast grew jagged, blotched green-black and gray and blinding white.

"Is that really snow?" She pulled at his arm, pointing.

He nodded. "We manage a little."

"I've only seen snow once since I left Calicho, once it was winter on Treone. We wrapped up in furs and capes even though we didn't have to, and threw snowballs with the Tails. . . . But it was cold most of the year on our island, on Calicho—we were pretty far north, we grew special kinds of crops . . . and us kids had hairy hornbeats to plod around on. . . ." Lost in memories, she rested against his shoulder; while he tried to remember a freehold on Glatte, and snowy walls became jumbled whiteness climbing a hill by the sea.

They had crossed the divide; the protruding batholith of the peaks degenerated into parched, crumbling slopes of gigantic rubble. Ahead of them the scarred yellow desolation stretched away like an infinite canvas, into mauve haze. "How far does it go?"

"It goes on forever. . . . Maybe not this desert, but this merges into others that merge into others—the whole planet is a desert, hot or cold. It's been desiccating for eons; the sun's been rising off the main sequence. The sea by New Piraeus is the only large body of free water left now, and that's dropped half an inch since I've been here. The coast is the only habitable area, and there aren't many towns there even now."

"Then Oro will never be able to change too much."

"Only enough to hurt. See the dust? Open-pit mining, for seventy kilometers north. And that's a little one."

He took them south, sliding over the eroded face of the land to twist through canyons of folded stone, sediments contorted by the palsied hands of tectonic force; or flashing across pitted flatlands lipping on pocket seas of ridged and shadowed blow-sand.

They settled at last under a steep outcurving wall of frescoed rock layered in red and green. The wide, rough bed of the sandy wash was pale in the chill glare of noon, scrunching underfoot as they began to walk. Pulling on his leather jacket, Maris showed her the kaleidoscope of ages left tumbled in stones over the hills they climbed, shouting against the lusty wind of the ridges. She cupped them in marveling hands, hair streaming like silken banners past her face; obligingly he put her chosen few into his pockets. "Aren't you cold?" He caught her hand.

"No, my suit takes care of me. How did you ever learn to know all these, Maris?"

Shaking his head, he began to lead her back down. "There's more here than I'll ever know. I just got a mining tape on geology at the library. But it made it mean more to come out here . . . where you can see eons of the planet laid open, one cycle settling on another. To know the time it took, the life history of an entire world: it helps my perspective, it makes me feel—young."

"We think we know worlds, but we don't, we only see people: change and pettiness. We forget the greater constancy, tied to the universe. It would humble our perspective, too. . . ." Pebbles boiled and clattered; her hand held his strongly as his foot slipped. He looked back, chagrined, and she laughed. "You don't really have to lead me here, Maris. I was a mountain goat on Calicho, and I haven't forgotten it all."

Indignant, he dropped her hand. "You lead."

Still laughing, she led him to the bottom of the hill.

And he took her to see the trees. Working their way over rocks up the windless branch wash, they rounded a bend and found them, tumbled in static glory. He heard her indrawn breath. "Oh, Maris—" Radiant with color and light she walked among them, while he wondered again at the passionless artistry of the earth. Amethyst and agate, crystal and mimicked wood-grain, hexagonal trunks split open to bare subtleties of mergence and secret nebulosities. She knelt among the broken bits of limb, choosing colors to hold up to the sun.

He sat on a trunk, picking agate pebbles. "They're sort of special friends of mine; we go down in time together, in strangely familiar bodies. . . ." He studied them with fond pride. "But they go with more grace."

She put her colored chunks on the ground. "No . . . I don't think so. They had no choice."

He looked down, tossing pebbles.

"Let's have our picnic here."

They cleared a space and spread a blanket, and picnicked with the trees. The sun warmed them in the windless hollow, and he made a pillow of his jacket; satiated, they lay back head by head, watching the cloudless green-blue sky.

"You pack a good lunch."

"Thank you. It was the least I could do"—her hand brushed his arm; quietly his fingers tightened on themselves—"to share your secrets; to learn that the desert isn't barren, that it's immense, timeless, full of—mysteries. But no life?"

"No—not anymore. There's no water, nothing can live. The only things left are in or by the sea, or they're things we've brought. Across our own lifeless desert-sea."

" 'Though inland far we be, our souls have sight of that immortal sea which brought us hither.' " Her hand stretched above him, to catch the sky.

"Wordsworth. That's the only thing by him I ever liked much."

They lay together in the warm silence. A piece of agate came loose, dropped to the ground with a clink; they started.

"Maris—"

"*Hmm?*"

"Do you realize we've known each other for three-quarters of a century?"

"Yes. . . ."

"I've almost caught up with you, I think. I'm twenty-seven. Soon I'm going to start passing you. But at least—now you'll never have to see it show." Her fingers touched the rusty curls of his hair.

"It would never show. You couldn't help but be beautiful."

"Maris . . . sweet Maris."

He felt her hand clench in the soft wave of his shirt, move in caresses down his body. Angrily he pulled away, sat up, half his face flushed. "Damn—!"

Stricken, she caught at his sleeve. "No, no—" Her eyes found his face, gray filled with grief. "No . . . Maris . . . I—want you." She unsealed her suit, drew blue-silver from her shoulders, knelt before him. "I want you."

Her hair fell to her waist, the color of warm honey. She reached out and lifted his hand with tenderness; slowly he leaned forward, to bare her breasts and her beating heart, felt the softness set fire to his nerves. Pulling her close, he found her lips, kissed them long and longingly; held her against his own heart beating, lost in her silken hair. "Oh, God, Brandy . . ."

"I love you, Maris . . . I think I've always loved you." She clung to him, cold and shivering in the sunlit air. "And it's wrong to leave you and never let you know."

And he realized that fear made her tremble, fear bound to her love in ways he could not fully understand. Blind to the future, he drew her down beside him and stopped her trembling with his joy.

In the evening she sat across from him at the bar, blue-haloed with light, sipping brandy. Their faces were bright with wine and melancholy bliss.

"I finally got some more brandy, Brandy . . . a couple of years ago. So we wouldn't run out. If we don't get to it, you can take it with you." He set the dusty red-splintered bottle carefully on the bar.

"You could save it, in case I do come back, as old as your grandmaw, and in need of some warmth. . . ." Slowly she rotated her glass, watching red leap up the sides. "Do you suppose by then my poems will have reached Home? And maybe somewhere Inside, Ntaka will be reading *me*."

"The Outside will be the Inside by then. . . . Besides, Ntaka's probably already dead. Been dead for years."

"Oh. I guess." She pouted, her eyes growing dim and moist. "Damn, I wish . . . I wish."

"Branduin, you haven't joined us yet tonight. It is our last together." Harkané appeared beside her, lean dark face smiling in a cloud-mass of blued white hair. She sat down with her drink.

"I'll come soon." Clouded eyes glanced up, away.

"Ah, the sadness of parting keeps you apart? I know." Harkané nodded. "We've been together so long; it's hard, to lose another family." She regarded Maris. "And a good bartender must share everyone's sorrows, yes, Soldier—? But bury his own. Oh—they would like some more drinks—"

Sensing dismissal, he moved aside; with long-practiced skill he became blind and deaf, pouring wine.

"Brandy, you are so unhappy—don't you want to go on this other voyage?"

"Yes, I do—! But . . ."

"But you don't. It is always so when there is choice. Sometimes we make the right choice, and though we're afraid we go on with it anyway. And sometimes we make the wrong choice, and go on with it anyway because we're afraid not to. Have you changed your mind?"

"But I can't change—,"

"Why not? We will leave them a message. They will go on and pick up their second compatible."

"Is it really that easy?"

"No . . . not quite. But we can do it, if you want to stay."

Silence stretched; Maris sent a tray away, began to wipe glasses, fumbled.

"But I *should*."

"Brandy. If you go only out of obligation, I will tell you something. I want to retire. I was going to resign this trip, at Sanalareta; but if I do that, Mactav will need a new Best Friend. She's getting old and cantankerous, just like me; these past few years her behavior has begun to show the strain she is under. She must have someone who can feel her needs. I was going to ask you, I think you understand her best; but I thought you wanted this other thing more. If not, I ask you now to become the new Best Friend of the *Who Got Her*."

"But Harkané, you're not old—"

"I am eighty-six. I'm too old for the sporting life anymore; I will become a Mactav; I've been lucky, I have an opportunity."

"Then . . . yes—I do want to stay! I accept the position."

In spite of himself Maris looked up, saw her face shining with joy and release. "Brandy—?"

"Maris, I'm not going!"

"I know!" He laughed, joined them.

"Soldier." He looked up, dark met dark, Harkané's eyes that saw more than surfaces. "This will be the last time that I see you; I am retiring, you know. You have been very good to me all these years, helping me be young; you are very kind to us all. . . . Now, to say goodbye, I do something in return." She took his hand, placed it firmly over Brandy's, shining with rings on the counter. "I give her back to you. Brandy—join us soon, we'll celebrate." She rose mildly and moved away to the crowded room.

Their hands twisted, clasped tight on the counter.

Brandy closed her eyes. "God, I'm so glad!"

"So am I."

"Only the poems . . ."

"Remember once you told me, 'you can see it all a hundred times, and never see it all'?"

A quicksilver smile. "And it's true. . . . Oh, Maris, now this is my last night! And I have to spend it with them, to celebrate."

"I know. There's—no way I can have you forever, I suppose. But it's all right." He grinned. "Everything's all right. What's twenty-five years, compared to two hundred?"

"It'll seem like three."

"It'll seem like twenty-five. But I can stand it. . . ."

∞

He stood it, for twenty-four more years, looking up from the bar with sudden eagerness every time new voices and the sound of laughter spilled into the dim blue room.

"Soldier! Soldier, you're still—"

"We missed you like—"

"—two whole weeks of—"

"—want to buy a whole *sack* for my own—"

The crew of the *DOM—428* pressed around him, their fingers proving he was real; their lips brushed a cheek that couldn't feel and one that could, long loose hair rippling over the agate bar. He hugged four at a time. "Aralea! Vlasa! Elsah, what the hell have you done to your hair now—and Ling-shan! My God, you're pretty, like always. Cathe—" The memory bank never forgot a shining fresh-scrubbed face, even after thirty-seven years. Their eyes were very bright as he welcomed them, and their hands left loving prints along the agate bar.

"—still have your stone bar; I'm so glad, don't ever sell it—"

"And what's new with *you?*" Elsah gasped, and ecstatic laughter burst over him.

He shook his head, hands up, laughing too. "—go prematurely *deaf?* First round on the house; only one at a time, huh?"

Elsah brushed strands of green-tinged waist-length hair back from her very green eyes. "Sorry, Soldier. We've just said it *all* to each other, over and over. And gee, we haven't seen you for four years!" Her belt tossed blue-green sparks against her green quilted flight-suit.

"Four years? Seems more like thirty-seven." And they laughed again, appreciating, because it was true. "Welcome back to the Tin Soldier. What's your pleasure?"

"Why you of course, me darlin'," said black-haired Brigit, and she winked.

His smile barely caught on a sharp edge; he winked back. "Just the drinks are on the house, lass." The smile widened and came unstuck.

More giggles.

"Ach, a pity!" Brigit pouted. She wore a filigree necklace, like the galaxy strung over her dark-suited breast. "Well, then, I guess a little olive beer, for old time's sake."

"Make it two."

"Anybody want a pitcher?"

"Sure, why not?"

"Come sit with us in a while, Soldier. Have we got things to tell you!"

He jammed the clumsy pitcher under the spigot and pulled down as they drifted away, watching the amber splatter up its frosty sides.

"Alta, hi! Good timing! How are things on the *Extra Sexy Old—115?*"

"Oh, good enough; how's Chrysalis—has it changed much?"

The froth spilled out over his hand; he let the lever jerk up, licked his fingers and wiped them on his apron.

"It's gone wild this time, you should see what they're wearing for clothes. My God, you would not believe—"

He hoisted the slimy pitcher onto the bar and set octagonal mugs on a tray.

"Aralea, did you hear what happened to the—"

He lifted the pitcher again, up to the tray's edge.

"—*Who Got her—709?*"

The pitcher teetered.

"Their Mactav had a nervous breakdown on landing at Sanalareta. Branduin died, the poet, the one who wrote—"

Splinters and froth exploded on the agate bar and slobbered over the edge, *tinkle, crash.*

Stunned blank faces turned to see Soldier, hands moving ineffectually in a puddle of red-flecked foam. He began to brush it off onto the floor, looking like a stricken adolescent. "Sorry . . . sorry about that."

"Ach, Soldier, you really blew it!"

"Got a mop? Here, we'll help you clean it up . . . hey, you're bleeding—?" Brigit and Ling-shan were piling chunks of pitcher onto the bar.

Soldier shook his head, fumbling a towel around the one wrist that bled. "No . . . no, thanks, leave it, huh? I'll get you another pitcher . . . it doesn't matter. Go on!" They looked at him. "I'll send you a pitcher; thanks." He smiled.

They left, the smile stopped. *Fill the pitcher.* He filled a pitcher, his hand smarting. *Clean up, damn it.* He cleaned up, wiping off disaster while the floor absorbed and fangs of glass disappeared under the bar. As the agate bartop dried he saw the white-edged shatter flower, tendrils of hairline crack shooting out a hand-breadth on every side. He began to track them with a rigid finger, counting softly. . . . *She loved me, she loved me not, she loved me—*

"Two cepheids and a wine, Soldier!"

"Soldier, come hear what we saw on Chrysalis if you're through!"

He nodded and poured, blinking hard. *Goddamn sweet-smoke in here . . . goddamn everything!* Elsah was going out the door with a boy in tight green pants and a starmap-tattooed body. He stared them into fluorescent blur. And remembered Brandy going out the door too many times. . . .

"Hey, *Sol*-dier, what are you doing?"

He blinked himself back.

"Come sit with us?"

He crossed the room to the nearest bulky table and the remaining crew of the *Dirty Old Man—428.*

"How's your hand?" Vlasa soothed it with a dark, ringed finger.

"It only hurts when I laugh."

"*You* really are screwed up!" Ling-shan's smile wrinkled. "Oh, Soldier, why look so glum?"

"I chipped my bar."

"Ohhh . . . nothing but bad news tonight. Make him laugh, somebody, we can't go on like this!"

"Tell him the joke you heard on Chrysalis—"

"—from the boy with a cat's-eye in his navel? Oh. Well, it seems there was . . ."

His fingers moved reluctantly up the laces of his patchwork shirt and began to untangle the thumb-sized star trapped near his throat. He set it free; his hand tightened across the stubby spines, feeling only dull pressure. Pain registered from somewhere else.

"—'Oh, they fired the pickle slicer too!' "

He looked up into laughter.

"It's a tech-one joke, Soldier," Ling-Shan said helpfully.

"Oh . . . I see." He laughed, blindly.

"Soldier, we took pictures of our black hole!" Vlasa pulled at his arm. "From a respectable distance, but it was bizarre—"

"Holograms—" somebody interrupted.

"And you should see the effects!" Brigit said. "When you look into them you feel like your eyes are being—"

"Soldier, another round, please?"

"Excuse me." He pushed back his chair. "Later?" Thinking, *God won't this night ever end?*

His hand closed the lock on the pitted tavern door at last; his woven sandal skidded as he stepped into the street. Two slim figures, one all in sea-blue, passed him and red hair flamed; he recognized Marena, intent and content arm in arm with a gaudy, laughing Tail. Their hands were in each other's back pockets. They were going uphill; he turned down, treading carefully on the time- and fog-slicked cobbles. He limped slightly. Moist wraiths of sea fog twined the curving streets, turning the street lights into dark angels under fluorescing haloes. Bright droplets formed in his hair as he walked. His footsteps scratched to dim echoes; the laughter faded, leaving him alone with memory.

The presence of dawn took him by surprise, as a hand brushed his shoulder.

"Sojer, 'tis you?"

Soldier looked up fiercely into a gray-bristled face.

"Y'all right? What'ree doin' down here at dawn, lad?"

He recognized old Makerrah the fisherman, finally. Lately it amused the old man to call him "lad."

"Nothin' . . . nothin'." He pulled away from the brine-warped rail. The sun was rising beyond the mountains, the edge of fog caught the colors of fire and was burned away. It would be a hot day. "G'bye, ol' man." He began to walk.

"Y'sure y're all right?"

Alone again he sat with one foot hanging, feeling the suck and swell of water far below the pier. *All right . . . ?* When had he ever been all right? And tried to remember into the time before he had known her, and could find no answer.

There had never been an answer for him on his own world, on Glatte; never even a place for him. Glatte, with a four-point-five technology, and a neo-feudal society, where the competition for that technology was a cultural rationale for war. All his life he had seen his people butchered and butchering, blindly, trapped by senseless superstition. And hated it, but could not escape the bitter ties that led him to his destruction. Fragments of that former life were all that remained now, after two centuries, still clinging to the fact of his alienness. He remembered the taste of fresh-fallen snow . . . remembered the taste of blood. And the memory filled him of how it felt to be nineteen, and hating war, and blown to pieces . . . to find yourself suddenly half-prosthetic, with the pieces that were gone still hurting in your mind; and your stepfather's voice, with something that was not pride, saying you were finally a real man. . . . Soldier held his breath unaware. His name was Maris, consecrated to war; and when at last he understood why, he left Glatte forever.

He paid all he had to the notorious spacer women; was carried in stasis between the stars, like so much baggage. He wakened to Oro, tech one-point-five, no wars and almost no people. And found out that now to the rest of humanity he was no longer quite human. But he had stayed on Oro for ninety-six years, aging only five, alone. Ninety-six years; a jumble of whiteness climbing a hill, constant New Piraeus; a jumble of faces in dim blue lantern light, patterning a new life. A pattern endlessly repeated, his smile welcoming, welcoming with the patience of the damned, all the old/new faces that needed him but never wanted him, while he wanted and needed them all. And then she had come to Oro, and after ninety-six years the pattern was broken. Damned Tin Soldier fell in love, after too many years of knowing better, with a ballerina who danced between the stars.

He pressed his face abruptly against the rail, pain flickered. *God, still real; thought it all turned to plastic, damn,*

damn. . . . And shut out three times twenty-five more years of pattern, of everyone else's nights and cold, solitary mornings trying to find her face. Ninety-one hundred days to carry the ache of returned life, until she would come again, and—

"See? That's our ship. The third one in line."

Soldier listened, unwillingly. A spacer in lavender stood with her Tail where the dock angled to the right, pointing out across the bay.

"Can't we go see it?" Blue glass glittered in mesh across the boy's back as he draped himself over the rail.

"Certainly not. Men aren't allowed on ships; it's against regulations. And anyway—I'd rather stay here." She drew him into the corner; amethyst and opal wrapped her neck in light. They began to kiss, hands wandering.

Soldier got up slowly and left them, still entwined, to privacy. The sun was climbing toward noon; above him as he walked, the skyline of New Piraeus wavered in the hazed and heated air. His eyes moved up and back toward the forty-story skeleton of the Universal Bank under construction, dropped to the warehouses, the docks, his atrophying ancient lower city. Insistent through the cry of sea birds he could hear the hungry whining of heavy machinery, the belly of a changing world. *And still I triumph over Death, and Chance, and thee, O Time—*

"But I can't stand it." His hands tightened on wood. "I stood it for ninety-six years; on the shelf." Dolefully the sea birds mocked him, creaking in the gray-green twilight, *now,now—* Wind probed the openings of his shirt like the cold fingers of sorrow. *Was dead, for ninety-six years before she came.*

For hours along the rail he had watched the ships in the bay; while he watched, a new ship had come slipping down, like the sun's tear. Now they grew bright as the day ended, setting a bracelet on the black water. Stiffness made him lurch as he turned away, to artificial stars clustered on the wall of night.

Choking on the past, he climbed the worn streets, where the old patterns of a new night reached him only vaguely, and his eyes found nothing that he remembered anymore. Until he reached the time-eaten door, the thick, peeling mud-brick wall beneath the neon sign. His hand fondled the slippery lock, as it had for two hundred years. TIN SOLDIER . . .

loved a ballerina. His hand slammed against the lock. *No— this bar is closed tonight.*

The door slid open at his touch; Soldier entered his quiet house. And stopped, hearing the hollow mutter of the empty night, and found himself alone for the rest of his life.

He moved through the rooms by starlight, touching nothing, until he came to the bedroom door. Opened it, the cold latch burning his hand. And saw her there, lying asleep under the silver robe of the Pleiades. Slowly he closed the door, waited, opened it once more and filled the room with light.

She sat up, blinking, a fist against her eyes and hair falling ash-golden to her waist. She wore a long soft dress of muted flowers, blue and green and earth tones. "Maris? I didn't hear you, I guess I went to sleep."

He crossed the room, fell onto the bed beside her, caressing her, covering her face with kisses. "They said you were dead . . . all day I thought—"

"I am." Her voice was dull, her eyes dark-ringed with fatigue.

"No."

"I am. To them I am. I'm not a spacer anymore; space is closed to me forever. That's what it means to be 'dead.' To lose your life. . . . Mactav—went crazy. I never thought we'd even get to port. I was hurt badly, in the accident." Fingers twined loops in her hair, pulled—

"But you're all right."

She shook her head. "No." She held out her hand, upturned; he took it, curled its fingers into his own, flesh over flesh, warm and supple. "It's plastic, Maris."

He turned the hand over, stroked it, folded the long limber fingers. "It can't be—"

"It's numb. I barely feel you at all. They tell me I may live for hundreds of years." Her hand tightened into a fist. "And I *am* a whole woman, but they forbid me to go into space again! I can't be crew, I can't be a Mactav, I can only be baggage. And—I can't even say it's unfair. . . ." Hot tears burned her face. "I didn't know what to do, I didn't know—if I should come. If you'd want a . . . ballerina who'd been in fire."

"You even wondered?" He held her close again, rested her head on his shoulder, to hide his own face grown wet.

A noise of pain twisted in her throat, her arms tightened. "Oh, Maris. Help me . . . please, help me, help me. . . ."

He rocked her silently, gently, until her sobbing eased, as he had rocked a homesick teenager a hundred years before.

"How will I live . . . on one world for centuries, always remembering. How do you bear it?"

"By learning what really matters. . . . Worlds are not so small. We'll go to other worlds if you want—we could see Home. You'd be surprised how much credit you build up over two hundred years." He kissed her swollen eyes, her reddened cheeks, her lips. "And maybe in time the rules will change."

She shook her head, bruised with loss. "Oh, my Maris, my wise love—love me, tie me to the earth."

He took her prosthetic hand, kissed the soft palm and fingers. *And make it well* . . . And knowing that it would never be easy, reached to dim the lights.

Afterword

"Tin Soldier" was the first story I ever seriously sat down to write. Up until the beginning of 1973 I had only written bits and pieces of things, beginning stories and putting them aside, with no real idea of where they were going, or any intention of trying to publish them. But my husband Vernor (who is also a science fiction writer) encouraged me to take my writing seriously; and this was the result.

Although it was my first story, it seems to be the one a lot of readers like the best. (I may wind up someday feeling like Isaac Asimov, who complains that after all these years, people still like his first story best—everything has been downhill ever since.) But actually this story is one of my personal favorites as well. A writer has the opportunity to play God when working on a story; to be in complete charge of the world that's being created and the lives of the inhabitants—for better or worse. There is a kind of omniscient detachment from what's being written; because whatever happens, you are in complete control of your (imaginary) universe. Once a story is finished and in print, however, I find that it becomes very much like a story written by someone else, for me; I lose my detachment and feel a different kind of emotional response, as though I'd never seen it before. As a result, some of the stories I've written have turned out to be more downbeat than the kind I generally prefer to read; and I find that I don't have much of an urge to go back and reread them. This story is one that I have no regrets about when I see it with stranger's eyes. If I never write a story that people like better, I won't really be all that disappointed.

And this is one more story that had its roots in song—in this case a song called "Brandy," which was about a woman waiting for her man to return from the sea; always knowing, and accepting, that the sea would always come first for him. I had remarked to Vernor that a similar kind of story set in space would have terrific potential for descriptions of the beauty of deep space. He made the suggestion that it ought to be the woman who went into space, the man who stayed patiently behind. . . . The story grew from there, and somewhere in the planning stages I noticed the parallel between my story as it was developing, and the Andersen fairy tale "The Steadfast Tin Soldier." Having a background in anthropology, I've always been fascinated by mythology (and fairy tales, or folk tales, are frequently a degenerate form of mythology); so I decided to make use of the symbolic aspects of the Andersen story within the framework of my own.

Recently I became aware of another uncanny parallel to this story—George R. R. Martin has written a story which was also inspired by the song "Brandy," and also involves a woman who goes into space and a man who stays behind. Much to our mutual relief, the resemblances end there, and the basic stories are very different. Which perhaps goes to prove the three-thousand-year-old adage that there is nothing new under the sun. But there *are* always new ways of looking at it, and always other suns. . . . And that, I think, is what science fiction is really all about.

ABOUT THE AUTHOR

Hugo Award winner Joan D. Vinge is the author of a novel, *The Outcasts of Heaven Belt* (available in a Signet edition), and has had stories published in *Analog, Orbit, Isaac Asimov's SF Magazine,* and various anthologies, including *The Crystal Ship* (title novella) and *Millennial Women.* Two of her novellas have been published as a book entitled *Fireship.*

Joan has a degree in anthropology, which she feels is very similar to science fiction in many ways because both fields give you an opportunity to view human relationships from a fresh and revealing perspective. She's worked, among other things, as a salvage archaeologist, enjoys horseback riding and needlecrafts, and is married to Vernor Vinge, who also writes science fiction.

LEGENDS FROM
THE SPACESHIP LOUNGE

"Cassandra"—the Hugo Award-winning tale of a woman cursed with a unique, prophetic madness.

"Threads of Time"—an unforgettable reminder that when you play tricks in time, Time itself may play the greatest trick on you.

"The Last Tower"—in which an old man discovers how an "ally" may conquer defenses an enemy could never breach.

"The Brothers"—a brand-new story set in a land of castles, kings, and curses, where the Fair Folk presume to meddle in the affairs of men.

So check your boarding pass one more time, then settle back to while away a traveler's wait with these and the other interstellar tales gathered for you in—

VISIBLE LIGHT

C.J. CHERRYH has also written:

The Morgaine Trilogy
GATE OF IVREL
WELL OF SHIUAN
FIRES OF AZEROTH

The Chanur Series
THE PRIDE OF CHANUR
CHANUR'S VENTURE
THE KIF STRIKE BACK (CHANUR'S REVENGE)
CHANUR'S HOMECOMING
   (available from DAW Books January 1987)

The Faded Sun Trilogy
THE FADED SUN: KESRITH
THE FADED SUN: SHON'JIR
THE FADED SUN: KUTATH

other science fiction titles
BROTHERS OF EARTH
HUNTER OF WORLDS
HESTIA
THE GREEN GODS (with N.C. Henneberg)
SERPENT'S REACH
DOWNBELOW STATION
MERCHANTER'S LUCK
SUNFALL
WAVE WITHOUT A SHORE
PORT ETERNITY
VOYAGER IN NIGHT
FORTY THOUSAND IN GEHENNA
CUCKOO'S EGG
ANGEL WITH THE SWORD

fantasy
THE DREAMSTONE
THE TREE OF SWORDS AND JEWELS